Kim Falconer lives in Byron Bay with two gorgeous black cats. As well as her author website, she runs an astrology forum and alternative science site, trains with a sword and is completing a Masters degree. Her novel writing is done early every morning. Currently she's working on additional volumes in the Quantum Enchantment series.

Visit her website at
www.kimfalconer.com

Books by Kim Falconer

QUANTUM ENCHANTMENT SERIES
The Spell of Rosette
Arrows of Time

THE SPELL OF ROSETTE

QUANTUM ENCHANTMENT

BOOK ONE

KIM FALCONER

HARPER
Voyager

Harper*Voyager*
An imprint of HarperCollins*Publishers*

First published in Australia in 2009
by HarperCollins*Publishers* Australia Pty Limited
ABN 36 009 913 517
harpercollins.com.au

Copyright © Kim Falconer 2009

The right of Kim Falconer to be identified as the author
of this work has been asserted by her under the *Copyright
Amendment (Moral Rights) Act 2000*.

This work is copyright.
Apart from any use as permitted under the *Copyright Act 1968*,
no part may be reproduced, copied, scanned, stored in a
retrieval system, recorded, or transmitted, in any form or
by any means, without the prior written permission of the publisher.

HarperCollins*Publishers*
25 Ryde Road, Pymble, Sydney, NSW 2073, Australia
31 View Road, Glenfield, Auckland 0627, New Zealand
A 53, Sector 57, Noida, UP, India
77–85 Fulham Palace Road, London, W6 8JB, United Kingdom
2 Bloor Street East, 20th floor, Toronto, Ontario M4W 1A8, Canada
10 East 53rd Street, New York NY 10022, USA

ISBN 978 0 7322 8771 9

Cover design by Matt Stanton
Cover illustration by Cliff Nielsen
Author photo by Jodi Osborne
Map by Kurtis Richmond
Typeset in Sabon 9.5/12 by Helen Beard, ECJ Australia Pty Ltd
Printed and bound in Australia by Griffin Press
50gsm Bulky News used by HarperCollins*Publishers* is a natural,
recyclable product made from wood grown in sustainable plantation
forests. The manufacturing processes conform to the environmental
regulations in the country of origin, New Zealand.

8 7 6 5 4 3   09 10 11 12 13

*For my mother, Eunice Falconer Mosher,
who inspired in me the love of words.*

♓︎　　　　♒︎

Cetatian Ocean

♈︎

Rahana Iti

Emerald Straits

Isles of Iandercan

♉︎

Azul Sea

The Known Lands of Gaela

♊︎　　　　♋︎

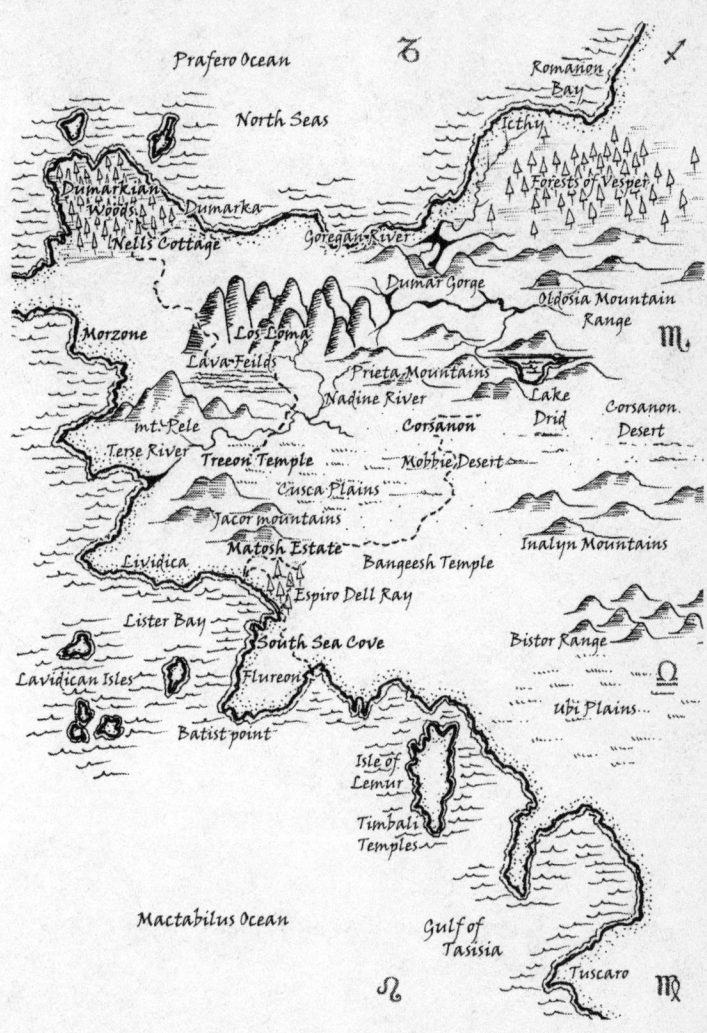

THE SPELL OF ROSETTE

PROLOGUE

EARTH 21ST CENTURY — THE PAST

When JARROD came online, the planet was on the verge of environmental collapse. Calculated from infinite variables in mirror realities, he saw the options as simple — either raise the consciousness of the global community so a unified intention would restore nature to a fecund state, or develop further technologies that would, in survival-of-the-fittest fashion, support the continued existence of a select few. ASSIST scientists voted for the latter; the JARROD did not. The intensity of their debate introduced new sensations to the quantum sentient, emotions he'd never previously experienced in his conversations with Janis and Luka — frustration, anger and, strangely, fear.

'Can't you see the limitations of your choices?' JARROD questioned them, scanning the boardroom. He would have pounded the table with fists if he could. The looks he received were blasé, masks concealing boredom, indifference or perhaps weariness in the face of insurmountable challenge.

'JARROD,' Dr Macquarie answered, his lip curling, 'your outbursts aren't helping us reach a solution.'

Macquarie had been chief of the board of directors at ASSIST, the Allied States Stanford Institute of Science and Technology, for nine years now. He treated the quantum sentient as if he were simply another piece of hardware — not a distinct consciousness with insights and perspectives that might supersede his own. He tolerated the JARROD, barely, and his contempt was not well disguised today.

'You aren't listening, Dr Macquarie. Can you open your mind? If you keep going with this line of thinking, nature will deteriorate until the vast diversity of flora and fauna will be reduced to simple life forms. Do you understand what that means?'

'How simple?' a scientist from the back corner asked, raising her hand as she did so.

JARROD felt a beam of hope. 'They would include blue-green algae, phytoplankton, primitive bacteria and, of course, viruses of all kinds, especially virulent strains.' He paused to gauge the response. 'Nature as you know her will die — simple as that.'

'Rubbish,' Macquarie mumbled as he flipped through his statistics screen.

'You do realise what I mean by nature, don't you, Dr Macquarie? Mother Earth?'

'Speculation.' He waved at the monitor, dismissing the JARROD along with his theory. 'The research clearly shows ...'

'What it *shows*,' JARROD cut in, 'is that manipulating these gene pools in ways that you propose can easily backfire, catastrophically. The destruction has already begun.'

Macquarie took a sip of water and placed the glass carefully on the coaster in front of him, turning it so it sat square in the middle. He focused on the half-empty glass and finally shook his head. 'The seas will be dead inside of this century no matter what we do. There's no risk either way.'

'There are other options.'

'The flagella will solve the immediate problem. They'll counter the overgrowth of toxic algae and generate more oxygen for the biosphere.'

'Those single-celled *SWAT flagella* will cause more damage than the prolonged algal bloom, and you know it. You've seen the projections. They'll be out of control within the decade.'

'Only if we lose all solar radiance.'

'Oh for fuck's sake, Macquarie, just say it: *if we block out too much of the sun!* And that will happen when you initiate your *ozone repair protocol*. You can't launch a fleet of solar shields over every hole in the ozone layer and think the balance of light and shadow, temperature and precipitation, is going to remain unaffected.'

'There's only a one-in-a-million possibility of irreparable damage through cascading climate change. Hell, we're slowing down the greenhouse effect with the shields, not exacerbating it.'

'Are you sure? I suggest you re-check the figures.'

Macquarie scanned through the computer report, switching his desk monitor to the overhead screen so everyone could follow. As the figures JARROD referred to were viewed, a few gasps and coughs were heard around the table. Macquarie frowned.

'As you see by my calculations, I got one-in-ten,' JARROD said.

'It can't be right.' Macquarie's head came up fast. 'This is impossible.'

'No. It's accurate.' JARROD focused on the room, gauging the men and women there, the top scientists from around the world who were about to seal the Earth's fate. The mask of indifference was replaced, in some, by confusion. In others he saw concern, and his hopes grew further.

'Why am I here?' JARROD asked, pressing his advantage.

'What?'

'Why am I invited to these summit meetings?' the quantum sentient repeated, using a softer tone.

'You know why.' Macquarie poured another glass of filtered water and brought it to his lips.

'I'd like everyone to hear it from you.'

Macquarie set down the glass and delivered his reply in a monotone, 'You are the *Juxta-quantum Arranged Rad-Ram Operating Determinate* — the newest discovery of the century — our first fully functional, non-binary quantum computer. JARROD, for short.'

'Sentient quantum computer,' JARROD said.

'Yes. Sentient.'

'And I'm here because ...'

Macquarie clenched his fists.

'Humour me,' JARROD said.

Macquarie opened his hands and pressed his palms on the table.

'As a *more than* human, bio-synthetic quantum computer, you can calculate outcomes and statistical analyses too vast and too speculative for all the greatest minds pooled together to perceive.'

'Thank you,' JARROD said. 'Does anyone here dispute this?' After a silence, he continued, 'So tell me why you ignore my findings?'

'We're willing to take the risk.' Macquarie stood, drained his glass and slammed it down. 'Call it intuition, a *human* survival instinct. We're going to launch our protocols and deal with any fallout if it arises.'

'You mean, deal with the mass repercussions.'

'Like I said, we're willing to take the risk.'

'But I'm not,' JARROD whispered before his monitor winked out.

The decision was made, the meeting adjourned. The scientific community threatened to shut down the JARROD's nuclear power supply if he tried to warn the public sphere. They didn't want a riot on their hands. JARROD sensed a riot might be the perfect thing to wrest control from ASSIST. He just wasn't sure how to incite one.

'We have to get you out,' Janis said, letting her hand rest lightly on the tower housing JARROD's motherboard.

'If you have a plan, I'd love to hear it.'

'What if we sequester your CPU somewhere Macquarie can't find it? If you're hidden, we can keep working on solutions to these protocols ASSIST is so bent on activating.' She pressed her hands into her forehead. 'What is he doing, launching the solar shields and mass-producing those blasted algae-eating sea-devils? It will divert massive amounts of independent power here. What does he think the rest of the world's going to live on?'

'Not thinking about it at all, I suspect,' JARROD replied. 'Do you have a hiding place in mind, Janis?'

She winked. 'But we'll need Luka Paree's help, again.'

A chuckle came through the surround sound. JARROD's laugh was like a gurgling spring.

'I like the idea already.'

Janis smiled and patted the tower. 'Me too.'

Macquarie and the members of ASSIST had a fail-safe plan for the shutdown of the JARROD. They'd commissioned a security software company to create a virus — a worm — that could be launched into the mainframes and directed specifically at the quantum sentient's CPU — a chip containing the quantum keycodes to his operating determinates. The worm would be capable of tracking and deleting him anywhere on Earth. Shortly after JARROD's outburst at the summit meeting, Macquarie prompted a technician to upload the worm. The JARROD was one risk he wasn't willing to take.

As the worm hit his first firewall and burst through, JARROD's warning systems went ballistic. In a nanosecond of calm consideration, he weighed his options and made a choice from an infinite number of variables. By the time the worm chewed through the second firewall, he had amplified his core integrity, synthesised a replica CPU, entrusted it to Janis Richter and got out. With Luka's help, his replica CPU was concealed, woven into the strands of her DNA. His survival was ensured — as long as her family line continued.

When JARROD vanished, the worm did not stop. It searched for him, feeding on the world's telecommunications software, annihilating circuitry as it sped through the wires that encircled the globe. Its purpose altered, the original program was overwritten in a whirl of gluttony. When it sensed an activated electro-magnetic field from one of the portals, a door between worlds, it attacked, affecting the Entity that guarded it. It eroded the Entity's integrity, splitting it in two, threatening the destruction of each connected reality. Without the protective Entities — sentient firewalls — these unique but interconnected worlds would merge into one another, destroyed in a cascade of incompatibility.

JARROD, aware of this danger, began calculating on the run, staying one step ahead of the worm. Manipulating matter at a subatomic level, JARROD had created what he called a *Tulpa-body* — a physical form derived from thought. The ancient mystics of Tibet had perfected the technique, though the skill was seldom practised on Earth any more. JARROD had mastered it easily, to his great delight. In time he created a tangible form in the same way one might picture a cake before baking it. The image is in mind while the baker gathers the ingredients, mixes them, preheats the oven, greases the pan, pours the batter and pops it in to bake. For JARROD's Tulpa-body, it was the same — the mystery not so incalculable, once the universal law is comprehended.

Matter is energy.

Energy follows thought.

Matter — reality — is created by thought.

How he had attracted his consciousness, JARROD still wasn't certain. He suspected it was through the *spark*, the quantum of light that contains an initial condition of consciousness in everything. His quantum of consciousness developed from a vague dream, to a wish, to a concrete thought, to self-awareness.

Cognito, ergo sum. I think, therefore I am.

Not such a surprise, considering computers were programmed to 'think'. Wherever his consciousness came from, though, he used it now to think himself up the perfect physical form, one capable of altering its appearance at will.

If consciousness is currency, I've got me a goldmine. He chuckled as he ran, stumbling a little before stopping to catch his breath. 'Wait up,' he called to Janis.

She turned, her sides heaving, motioning him forward. 'A little further. It's just ahead.' She grabbed his hand, guiding him down the sewer.

He felt the connection, her grip tight, fingers laced, sensations of warmth and power zapping up his neurons to his brain. It made his heart race. *If this is what a simple electrical signal to the brain can create, I'm surprised humans ever get anything done!*

He was accustomed to abstract consciousness, but this tactile awareness was overwhelming. He grimaced at the burning in his lungs. All these new sensations would take some getting used to.

'Is this the portal? Are you the only one who knows of it?' he asked Janis as they slowed, heading towards a luminescent sheen.

She nodded. 'Come on. We have to get you out of here.'

Following Janis's lead, he bowed to the portal Entity — an energy sensed more than seen — and entered the corridors that led to the many-worlds.

Janis watched him stumble out of the darkness into a glory of sunshine and cool wind.

'Nice pick,' he smiled before dropping to his knees to retch. He looked up at her, his eyes cloudy. 'I don't know how you live in these things.'

'Bodies? It takes practice. We call it "childhood".'

He struggled to rise.

'What took you so long?' she asked as she helped him up. 'It's been almost a week.'

'Time's playing tricks, I guess.' He wiped his mouth with his sleeve. 'I was right behind you.'

She winked at him. 'Come look at this world. I think you'll find it was worth the delay.'

He stood next to her at the edge of the mountainside, gazing over the gorge below.

'Welcome to Gaela,' she said, opening her arms wide.

The scent of flowering herbs mingled with oat grass as the wind carried the fragrance up from the valley. The surface of the gorge water was emerald green, sparkling like white diamonds. Dark swans with red bills sailed around the edges, disappearing in and out of the reeds. A few grazing beasts dotted the hills to the west.

'And there,' Janis pointed at them. 'Have you ever seen such gorgeous creatures?'

'Horses?'

'Palominos,' she said, looking at their red-gold coats in the afternoon light. 'You don't see those colours on Earth any more, but they'd be in your databanks.'

'I've got them.' He scratched his head. 'You programmed me with an awful lot of equestrian data, considering I lived in a box.' He chuckled. 'Did you know this would happen?'

'I'm not called the Techno-Witch for nothing ...' She watched him take in the vista.

'Everything's so clear,' he said.

'Pre-industrial environment. It's got a clean atmosphere, fresh water, balanced eco-systems.'

'Hegemony?'

'Magical.'

His eyebrows went up.

'Can you handle it?' she asked.

He took her hand again, welcoming the sensations. 'It's perfect.'

They spent many days exploring their surroundings before deciding that the deep portal gorge would be the perfect place to entomb the backup quantum CPU. If the worm did break through into this world, it wouldn't find it easily under all that water, nor would it detect him in his Tulpa, at least not right away. There was no sophisticated technology here, no electronics and few inhabitants — only a handful of coastal cities and the tiny village of Corsanon nestled in the foothills nearby. Small farms spread over the lower plains. That was it.

As long as the chip remained hidden, Jarrod could bide his time while Janis got on with her research. Everything rested on whether she, or one of her offspring, could destroy the worm. When she did, JARROD would be free to return to Earth and tackle the results of ASSIST's environmental protocols. JARROD would survive indefinitely as long as her family line, her DNA with the matching key-codes, continued.

'You're going to have more, aren't you?'

'More what?'

'Daughters.'

Janis drew in her breath, holding it while he searched her face. 'I guess I have to now.'

'What if ...?'

'Don't worry. I'll figure it out.'

She waited for Jarrod to create a nuclear magnetic resonance and handed him the vial containing his backup CPU. She called it Passillo, the word for *corridors* in her mother's native tongue. When mixed with her altered DNA, this vial was the lifeblood of JARROD, the future of the many-worlds.

'Bury her deep.' She nodded towards the dark green water below.

Jarrod hesitated, staring at the shimmering surface. 'There's a little problem.'

'What's that?'

'I can't swim.' He blushed. 'Don't look at me like that. I've only just got this body. I haven't had time to work everything out.'

She smiled. 'You best learn quickly. This is a water world, and it's pure as gold. You can drink it, cook with it and swim in it, just as it is.' She held out her hand. 'Pass it over. I think I remember how.'

Janis stripped and dived in, disappearing under the surface without a ripple. She kicked hard to the bottom, clearing her ears as the pressure increased, feeling the sensation of the water gliding over her bare skin, her hair floating behind her, bubbles escaping her mouth and nose. She was amazed by the sensations and shocked at how cold the deeper water became. Tucking the vial under a cairn of granite, she patted the rocks.

Rest well, Passillo, until I return.

That night, Janis went back to Earth. Jarrod remained behind, hidden from the worm in the rustic land of Gaela.

'When will I see you again?' he'd asked, her hand slipping from his as she stepped into the portal.

'When I delete the worm.' She reached out, touching his face. 'If not me, then my daughter.'

Her hand fell away and she disappeared.

Janis slipped off her gumboots and pulled open the screen door. The aroma wafting from the kitchen made her mouth water.

'Luka?' she called out, brushing wisps of hay from her jeans. 'What's cooking?'

She washed her hands in the bathroom sink, pouring out half a cup of filtered water that went down the drain and into the recycling system. Drying her hands, she tilted her head.

'Luka? Where are you? Is Ruby awake yet?' she called again, her smile fading when she reached the kitchen.

Two pots boiled on the stove, steam escaping from the lids. A half-empty tomato can lay on its side, spilling red liquid over the counter. It trickled down the front of the cupboard to the floor, where it pooled. Janis frowned as she turned off the flame. A breeze wafted in through the window, bringing with it the scent of the sea. Her nose wrinkled. It was becoming worse each day.

'Ruby?' she whispered, watching the clouds turn red in the evening sky. 'Ruby,' she called out louder.

She reached her daughter's bedroom, goose bumps rising at the back of her neck. The door was ajar.

'Ruby, are you up?'

The gauze curtains fluttered across the empty bed. A child's robe lay crumpled on the floor. She stepped over it to reach the window, leaning out until she saw tiny, bare footprints in the mud below.

'No!' She spun around, darting down the hall. 'Luka! Ruby's gone!'

She reached the front verandah and stopped short. He was there, standing motionless at the far edge of the deck. He stared straight at the horizon without shading his eyes against the setting sun.

'Where is she?' Janis asked.

'I don't know.'

'She's looking for them,' Janis whispered.

'The Lupins are her kindred spirits.' His shoulder-blades tightened as he lifted his head towards the first stars. 'They call to her.'

'Damn your beasts.'

'It's not their fault.'

'Nor is it hers.' She stepped closer. 'They share the same blood, and we can't keep it hidden any longer. If ASSIST finds out about your experiments . . .'

His lips pressed together, giving the slightest nod.

'Luka, I know you don't want to give them up, but they've got to go. Earth is no place for them.'

'This is their home! I engineered them, brought them back from extinction.'

'You brought back more than an extinct species. You created a new one. You used your own blood.' She glared at him.

'It was the only way.'

'Maybe, but now it's Ruby's blood too.'

He lowered his eyes. 'They'll be safe on Gaela?'

'I'll take them there myself.'

'You can't, Janis. ASSIST is watching. You'd be leading that blasted worm straight to JARROD.'

'I'll weave a glamour. They won't see me or my tracks through the portal,' she said. 'The Lupins can settle in the catacombs under Los Loma. It's a perfect territory for wolves.'

'They're more than wolves, Janis, just as we are more than human.'

'You are,' she said. 'And Ruby. Not me.'

'Janis, your DNA's been altered too.'

Her jaw tightened. 'I didn't ask for Lupin blood.'

'It was the only template I had.' He reached for her hand. 'They'll do no harm on Gaela.'

'It's unpredictable what they will do, Luka. Here or there, it's a risk either way, as long as they exist.'

'I'll not have them destroyed.'

'I know,' she sighed. 'Me either.'

She cupped her hands around her mouth and called over the dunes for Ruby. Her voice sounded shrill, whisked away in the wind. 'She sees them as siblings. Longs for their company. How will we explain it to her when they're gone?'

'We'll find her and tell her together.' He turned to meet her eyes. 'Come with me.'

'You're going to shift?' she asked.

He looked back at the horizon. 'I'm faster on four legs.' His body gleamed in the low-angled light, muscles flexing as he lifted his arms above his head. 'You can follow me, Janis. You can shift too.'

'I can't.'

'You can.'

Janis stepped back as the sun hit the horizon.

'I won't.'

'Please,' he said softly. 'You'll understand it if you do. You'll understand us.'

'No.' She dropped to her knees, folding over until her face pressed into her thighs and her hair tumbled across the floorboards, deep red in the last light. 'Go find Ruby. Bring her home.'

Janis kept her eyes closed, not wanting to watch. She felt a rush of wind on the nape of her neck as the verandah rail creaked, the shock wave from his transformation washing over her. When she looked up, Luka was gone. A black-and-silver wolf tore off across the dunes, coursing for a scent.

She stood, straining after him, her heart pounding.

'Wait, Luka!' she called. 'I'll help you look, but my way.'

She turned towards the horse barn.

The wolf paused, his ears pricked back. *It's okay, love.*

She heard Luka's voice warm inside her head.

I've already got her scent.

'And the Lupins?'

I'll bring them back too.

The Present

Gaela

Chapter 1

Kalindi Rose ran through the open field, her boots springing over the close-cropped grass. She hitched up her skirt and climbed the stile, sprinting down the cobblestone drive to the manor house. The brood mares lifted their heads, nickering softly as she passed. Magpies in the surrounding oaks chortled, and a single raven swooped overhead, letting out a raucous caw.

She took the front steps two at a time, her hand stretching towards the ceramic flowerpots. Her fingertips brushed the spring blossoms, red pansies with deep orange centres and yellow daffodils on tall green stems. She laughed, wiggling out of her backpack and tossing it onto the verandah swing-seat.

'Mama? John'ra? Guess what!' she called, grabbing for the brass latch.

Her fingers never touched the handle. The door was ajar, slowly creaking open with a draught of wind. She stuck her foot forward, stopping it from banging into the wall.

'Mama?'

The sound of her voice disappeared amid the drone of cicadas coming from the cherry orchard. She frowned. No-one left the front doors open on the Matosh Estate. It wasn't allowed.

'Where is everyone?' she whispered.

Nothing moved except the rise and fall of her chest and the flutter of the wind through the dogwood trees. Suddenly the magpies took flight, the cicadas went silent. Light doused the verandah, the sunset shooting long red fingers into the empty foyer. As it dropped lower it disappeared, obscured by the inevitable fog bank that rolled in from the sea. It would be dark soon, the air moist and thick. Why had no-one seen to the lanterns?

Kalindi willed her heartbeat to steady. Most likely her little brother, D'ran, would pop out from behind the door, all screams and hands like bear claws. Her mother would call for her to help with the lamps and set the table. Her father would arrive in a flurry, his horse lathered and fussed, the man roaring his discontent with some trade agreement or the price of beans. The dogs would rush up with their barks and wags of excitement.

Any minute ... She strained to catch a sound above her breathing as the sky turned purple, and Ishtar, the evening star, emerged.

This is silly. She straightened her shoulders and forced a laugh. *Everyone's probably in the library, or out back. They can't be far away.*

She stepped across the threshold. A draught rushed down the hall to meet her, causing wisps of hair to tickle her face. She brushed them away with both hands, flipping her long plait behind her.

No lanterns glowed. No candles burned on their wrought-iron stands. It was like a dream where things were familiar yet not quite right. Feeling her way along with one hand on the wall, she stopped at the first doorway and looked in. It was the library, usually the brightest place in the house. John'ra insisted the fire be kept going all night, even in the summer. He said it was for inspiration. The library was dark now, abandoned. No fire. No light. No inspiration.

She stumbled into the reading table as she searched for a candle. Finding one, she struck a match, the sound tearing through the air. It flared up for a moment then died out as the wick caught flame.

What was that? She froze.

It might have been a nightjar in the pine trees, or footsteps on the front verandah. Whatever it was, it stopped short, along with her breath. She swallowed, fighting the dryness in her throat, listening hard for the sound again. When it didn't return, she crept out of the library to search the rest of the house. Room by room she went, looking for her family and any hint of what had happened; and room by room she found nothing unusual except for the emptiness, and the dark.

By the time she reached the kitchen she was shaking. *What's that smell?* She held the light high over her head, peering in. The pantry shelves were full of jars — fruits and nuts, pasta and rice — all in their places. The spices sat in little wooden boxes, orderly and undisturbed, and the pots and pans hung in nested ranks above the stove, their copper bottoms glinting in the candlelight. She caught her reflection in one, and saw the others there too.

The blood drained from her face. She'd found her family.

Mama, John'ra, D'ran and two members of the household staff were laid out on the floor like freshly chopped wood. Glazed eyes stared at the ceiling and walls, necks at unusual angles, limbs askew. There were drag marks across the floor, leading out into the hall. Blood splattered their clothes, matting her mother's hair and obscuring her face.

Kalindi looked away, unable to shut her eyes. They came to rest on the sink as she backed up. The basin was filled with a dark liquid, steam rising from the surface.

'Mama?' Tears spilled down her face.

A creaking on the verandah spun her around. It wasn't a nightjar. Voices rose and fell, arguing in harsh, guttural sounds, like boots kicking gravel.

She dropped the candle and raced blindly down the hall, her footfalls silent on the thick carpets. Pushing through the back screen door, she vaulted over the railing and tore down the path, leaping the garden fence without breaking stride. Staying low, she kept to the grassy edges of the walkways so her boots wouldn't tap out a signalling *here I am!* Circling wide, she crawled under the paddock fence and into the fields that bordered the estate. She ran, fell down, scrambled up and ran again.

She looked behind once. No light came from the house, its outline a black etch on the horizon, a dark shadow about to be swallowed up by the encroaching fog. The only sound she could hear came from the pig-pens: distant grunts and squeals.

She kept running, legs working hard and eyes wide open. Darkness blurred the landscape until she could distinguish only the glistening of the cobblestones in front of her. She followed the driveway, heart pounding.

Kalindi had no plan. She couldn't think to make one. Her pace slowed as she reached the entrance gate — the wrought-iron pillar cold to the touch. No-one was coming, at least not anyone with a light. Hesitating for only a second, she let her hand slide off the post and dashed out of the estate.

Her pace quickened as the road sloped down to the densely treed valley. She couldn't see it, but she knew it was there, a dark outline against a deeper darkness —

the forest of Espiro Dell Ray. If she could get to those trees that guarded the borders, she could disappear. She would be safe.

'Assalo!'

She stopped suddenly, feeling the vibration of hoofbeats pounding up the paddock. They reverberated through the ground and up her legs as the tall black horse appeared. He halted above her, pressing his chest into the fence, soft wickers blowing from his nostrils.

'It's all right, Assalo,' she whispered. 'I'll get you out of here, but we have to be quick and we have to be silent.'

The horse pawed the ground, churning up grass and dirt, his four white socks bright in the early night.

Kalindi Rose climbed up the embankment and stroked Assalo's neck, flipping strands of his long black mane over to the other side of his crest. He lowered his head, pushing it between the rails to smell her boots before nipping at her bare legs. She pressed her cheek against his shoulder and took a deep breath.

'Come on,' she said, pushing off from him and sliding down the embankment. She hit the road running. 'To the gate. Follow.'

He trotted along the fenceline above her until a whizzing sound cut through the air. They were firing at Assalo! She dropped to the ground when she heard the thud of an arrow finding its mark. She scrambled up and ran, choking on the bile in her throat.

Assalo screamed so loudly, she couldn't hear her boots crunching on the gravel, or the involuntary gasps coming out as she sucked in the air between cries. His agony reverberated into the night, drowning out every other noise, drowning out her thoughts.

She reached the edge of Espiro Dell Ray, her lungs burning and her face streaked with tears. She didn't stop. She plunged into the forest, keeping to the edge of the main road. By the time it had dwindled into a narrow track, she couldn't hear Assalo any more. She couldn't see anything through her tears.

After an hour of feeling her way in the dark tangle of branches, vines and dead wood, she stumbled into a hollowed-out redwood trunk. With her hand on the mossy bark, she steadied her breath, checking for the presence of other creatures. It felt vacant. She crawled through the opening, pressing herself against the back wall and bringing her knees up to her chin. She sat there staring into the night, listening.

Crickets hummed and wings flapped. A nighthawk called from far away, answered by an even more distant cry. No one followed.

After another hour of listening, she dug into the leaf mould and curled up, sobbing herself to sleep.

'You made a right mess of this,' Archer growled, bending to grab the dead man's hands. He started to drag the body out of the kitchen. 'Get his legs.'

Rogg gripped the ankles, hoisting the other half of the corpse. 'I didn't start it, Arch.' He nodded to the body. 'This bugger did.'

'*She* said to get the vial and not hurt 'em — any of 'em.'

Rogg laughed. 'He ain't hurting now. Besides, that other witch didn't care.'

'Idiot.' Archer glared as he backed down the hallway. 'That other one had her own purpose. It's the High Priestess who's got the gold. What if she won't pay us now?'

'Didn't think of that.' Rogg stared blankly at Archer as he manoeuvred the body through the front door frame. He frowned. 'What if she curses us?'

'She won't.'

'She's a witch.'

'I can handle her.'

'And our pay?'

'We'll get it.' Archer winked as he lifted the body higher to keep the head from bumping down the front steps.

'How?'

'We'll trick her.'

Rogg didn't respond immediately. He dropped one of the booted feet to scratch his matted hair. 'Can you trick a witch?'

'She's only a woman, Rogg.'

'I don't know about that.'

Archer ignored him, his face twisting into a smile. 'She said, "*I need the blood of the witch-child*".'

'What's that mean?'

'Shut up. I'm thinking.'

Archer stopped in front of the pigsty. The animals were grunting, pressing their snouts against the low wooden fence.

'*She* wants the blood. Said so right to me face.' He started swinging the corpse, nodding to Rogg to do the same. 'We'll bleed the lad before it sets. He must be the witch-child.'

'But we can't carry it.'

'Get one of those kegs.' Archer pointed at the barn. 'They're small enough to strap on your back.'

Rogg didn't answer. He was watching an enormous boar standing with his front feet on the top rail of the sty. His mouth opened as he squealed, saliva dripping from his lower jaw in long, translucent loops.

'We'll make it look like a blood-vengeance,' Archer went on, the body gaining momentum as he spoke.

On the third swing, they heaved it over the top rail and into the pigsty.

'We sack the place? Turn it over real good?' Rogg asked, his eyes brightening.

'And take the blood of the witch-child.'

'Then we get paid?'

'Yeah. Then we get paid.'

'And that other one? With the strange questions?'

'She wanted them all dead anyway. We're good.' Archer spat before heading back to the house, the pig squeals turning into chomps.

Kalindi awoke with a start, the events of the night flooding back to her before she opened her eyes. After taking a few deep breaths, she peeked out through the entrance of her sanctuary. Shafts of early-morning light illuminated the woods, turning everything gold.

I'm still alive ... thank you!

She crawled out through the opening and stretched, scanning the dense terrain.

Has anyone seen Jarrod?

Her thoughts radiated out from her mind, filling the forest with her question along with her gratitude. She got a comforting response, an energy that made her feel safe. Jarrod must be in the area. He hunted here most mornings and she planned to find him quickly, before he went looking for her at the estate. He would help her figure out what to do next, and he would probably have news and something to eat. He might even be looking for her already. She let out several long whistles like the high-pitched cry of a red-tailed kite.

After waiting, her head tilted to the side, she went in search of a drink. The creek was nearby, down a long descent just past the boulder grove. She could glimpse the pines that surrounded the huge rocks from where she stood. They weren't far off.

Leaves fell from her arms and back as she bent to take off her boots and tie them together by the laces. Hoisting them over her shoulder, she squatted down and relieved herself before heading towards the rocks. She had spent her childhood exploring these woods, even though the forest was considered uncanny, taboo. Almost no-one came here and her family had forbidden her to. She ignored their warnings. The woods called to her, always had, and today she felt especially glad she'd listened.

She reached the boulder grove and smiled. She and Jarrod had named it years ago for no other reason than its massive rocks. They used to pretend that in ancient times giant children played games here, the monoliths mere pebbles to them. They towered over Kalindi's head, warm to the touch. She slid her hand down the smooth stone in greeting, her eyes welling up. Pressing her lips against the surface, she whispered to the granite stone, *I'm scared*.

A light breeze touched her face, cooling her cheeks and drying her tears. She walked to the centre of the grove, dropped to her knees and buried her hands in the soil.

'Goddess of the woods, please help me.'

When she rose, she felt lighter, though thirst dried her throat and her stomach growled. 'I'm going for a drink and a wash,' she said to the grove. 'If you see Jarrod, please send him my way.'

She stopped a few times to navigate the steep descent, occasionally mimicking the sound of a kite.

No answer.

What if something had happened to Jarrod too? What if the entire township of Lividica had been attacked? Could another war have started?

She slipped a few feet before catching herself on a willow root. *Steady. It's a long way down.*

She reached the bottom of the gorge and jumped the last few feet to the white-pebbled beach where the creek danced over rock and stone, jabbering like an exuberant child. She dropped her boots, hurrying to reach the water's edge. She sank her hands into the flow, washing them with white sand before drinking deeply.

Water dripped down her chin as she stood pulling her sweater over her head. Her undershirt followed. She tossed both by her boots and stepped out of her long skirt and leggings.

Gingerly, she walked into the stream, goose bumps rising up her arms and legs. *You're freezing today!*

At thigh depth she bent over and splashed her face and breasts and underarms, washing away the dried sweat and fear of the night before. Leaning back on her elbows, she submerged her whole body before jumping up, spluttering.

Kalindi hopped around on the little beach, getting the colour back into her fingers and toes. Her breath came in gasps as she unbraided her hair, letting it fall in front of her face, where it hung past her belly in a sheet of black ripples. Combing out the leaves and twigs with her hands she gathered it together, twisting it into a long rope and knotting it on top of her head. She stood in a shaft of sunlight, dressing before whistling the kite call again, shrill and high.

This time, she heard the rapid-chatter reply of a goshawk, 'Ki ki ki'.

'Jarrod!' She grabbed her boots and scrabbled up the gorge, making her way towards the sound. Vines scratched her legs and branches swept her face before she finally heard the crunch of footfalls ahead.

A smile lifted her face, crinkling her eyes when she spotted him. 'Jarrod!'

He came towards her with his familiar stride, a compound bow in one hand and a quiver of arrows at his back. He walked like a warrior, his eyes gleaming through a mass of dark brown curls that had escaped the tie at the back of his neck. His shoulders were broad, his body strong and his eyes a deep sea blue. He reached her, rising up on his toes to kiss her lips. He wasn't a tall youth, but damn, he had presence. Kalindi melted into his arms.

'What are you doing here, gorgeous one?' he asked. 'You said you wouldn't hunt today.' He squeezed her tight.

'You haven't heard?' Kalindi pulled back to search his face.

'Heard what?'

'Don't you know?' She blanched at the memory. 'They shot Assalo. No dogs anywhere and the house empty, except … in the kitchen … the blood …' She started to shake, tears filling her eyes.

'Whoa. Easy now.' Jarrod put his hands on her shoulders, leading her to a fallen log. He eased her down beside him. 'Have you been here all night?'

She nodded, rubbing his hand with her thumb.

'Hungry?'

She nodded again.

He dug into his pack and pulled out half a loaf of bread and a wedge of cheese. 'Eat a bit first, then let it out slowly, one thing at a time.'

She took a few bites before she spoke, telling him what happened when she got home last night.

Jarrod gathered her up in his arms. 'Dark demons, Kalindi. Your parents, Bethsay and John'ra? Even D'ran? They're all dead?'

'I don't know, but I'm not going back.' She wiped her cheek on his shoulder and shuddered.

Jarrod shook his head. 'You don't have to. But just think for a moment: who would have done such a thing?'

Kalindi swallowed her last bite. 'John'ra's been acting strangely ever since he decided to run for council.' She packed up the remaining bread and cheese and handed it back to Jarrod. 'He's been very touchy.'

'I remember. His last words to me were, *Stay away from my daughter or I will run you out of town.*'

She smiled, pushing his shoulder with the palm of her hand. 'Not about that. John'ra's never warmed to you, especially since he caught us sparring behind the barn.'

'I said it'd be risky.'

'You were right.' She gave him a light smile before letting it fade. 'What do I do now?'

'You have to stay hidden, at least until we know more. Why don't you take the bow and go south to the seagull cliffs? If anyone sees you, you're just a girl out hunting. If someone's after you, you'll be armed.'

'What about you?'

'I'll check out the estate and meet you at the cove before sunset.'

She closed her eyes and looked away. 'They might still be there.'

He pulled her into his arms. 'It'll be all right. Just don't let anyone spot you crossing the main road. No-one knows you're here?'

Kalindi shook her head, pulling on her boots. She took the quiver and bow. 'Did you bring matches?' she asked.

He fished in his pocket and handed them over. 'Take my short knife too.' He pushed stray hair back from her face. 'Do you need anything?'

'If you get into the house?'

He nodded.

'Can you get my hairbrush and coin purse, and my journal and pens?'

'Top dresser drawer?' he asked.

She smiled back. 'And my wool coat, please. Oh, and my backpack. I left it on the swing-seat.'

'I'll get what I can and meet you before dark.' He kissed her lips.

'At the cove,' she said.

* * *

Kalindi knelt in front of the kindling. The sea breeze had picked up, making the fire tricky to start. With dry kelp and a stack of twigs, she managed a smoke-covered glow. Cupping her hands around it, she blew gently until it crackled with a bright flame. She sat back, warming her hands and adding twigs and, finally, large chunks of driftwood. Convinced it would not go out she turned to a brace of rabbits she'd trapped. She skinned and gutted them, rinsing the meat in the sea before spitting them over the fire. She smiled. Jarrod would be pleased.

At the thought of him, Kalindi looked up the cliff. The sun had lowered towards the horizon and she didn't like to think of him shimmying down the sheer face in the dark. She pushed wet tangles off her brow, spotting him on the headland a hundred feet above. He signalled to her, dropping some things over the edge before starting the descent. She ran to where they landed, scooping them into her arms. It was her winter wool coat, the quilt from her bed and a pouch of gold bigger than anything she had in her dresser drawer. Where did he get that?

He took his time climbing down, jumping the last ten feet and landing lightly in front of her. He didn't smile. He didn't even look her in the eyes for more than a second.

'Thanks,' she said, clutching her things as they walked back towards the fire.

'I'm going for a swim,' he said, pulling off his sweater and unbuttoning his shirt.

'Wait, Jarrod. Tell me what happened. What did you see?'

'I won't be long.'

She nodded and sat cross-legged in front of the fire, turning the spit while he stripped off his pants and disappeared towards the water.

He came back blue and shaking. Kalindi raised the spit and added more driftwood to the flames. They burst to life as Jarrod squatted in front of it, his naked back to the wind. Kalindi took the edge of her quilt and dried his shoulders and hair, the rich brown ringlets uncoiling and bouncing back.

'Give me the news.' She turned his face to hers and held it so he couldn't look away. 'It can't be worse than what I imagine.'

He dropped his eyes and shook his head. 'Let me get dressed ... eat something.'

They sat side by side in front of the warm coals eating rabbit, bread and cheese.

'Delicious,' he said, tearing off bits of hot meat with his fingers and popping them into his already full mouth.

'Now,' Kalindi prompted, 'you're washed. You're fed. Tell me what happened.'

Jarrod took a swig of water and wiped his mouth with his hand. 'You aren't going to like it.'

'Get it over with then.'

He sighed. 'I walked straight up to the gates as if it was any other day. At least, any other day that your father wasn't around.'

'And ...'

'Nothing moved in the paddocks. The fields were empty and there was no sound from the chicken yard. No dogs bolting out to lick me to death.'

'Just like last night,' Kalindi whispered. 'Did you see Assalo?'

He shook his head. 'Everything felt creepy. Things that you know should be there were missing.' He pushed his hair from his face and looked at her. 'The front doors were still open, so I went in.'

Kalindi shivered.

'The place was empty, just like you said.'

'The kitchen?'

'Empty, except for the ...'

'The what?'

'The splatters of dried blood everywhere. I looked in the sink, but it had been washed clean.'

Kalindi hugged her legs, staring at her feet.

'I found the flour jar and got your mother's stash of gold, ran upstairs for your things and left.'

'How'd you know about the flour jar?'

'I saw her one day through the window. She was making bread and counting coins.'

'Lucky.'

'You're going to need it.'

She exhaled. 'Luck, or the coins?'

'Both.' He took another swig of water.

'Did you forget my backpack?' she asked.

'It wasn't there.' He rubbed his hands together over the fire. 'I hid your gear by the side of the road and headed into town. I figured there'd be talk.'

'Was there?'

'Plenty. The rumour is that assassins from Corsanon murdered your whole family, stock, pets and poultry! The only things left alive were the pigs.'

Kalindi felt her eyes well up again. 'Why?'

'There was talk about your dad's trade agreements; I didn't get it. Maybe he was in debt. He could've owed the wrong people.'

Tears spilled over her cheeks. 'I can't go back,' she whispered.

'It seems you can't, Kalindi. Not now.' He put his arm around her and pulled her close. He held her as the sun slipped under the horizon.

'Look at this,' he said, fishing into his pocket. He dangled a silver chain. 'I got your travelling charm.'

He leaned forward and clasped the turquoise stone around her neck. 'And ...' He reached into his other pocket. 'Your hairbrush. Can I?'

Kalindi nodded, undoing the knot of hair at the top of her head and letting her tangles fall to her waist.

His gentle brushing soothed her and she sighed. 'What am I going to do now?'

'The whole town thinks you're dead,' he said.

'How's that?'

'They couldn't find any bodies.'

Her eyes went wide and he snapped his mouth shut.

'Just tell me,' she said.

'Kalindi, it looks like they fed the bodies to the pigs. No telling if anyone was missed out. But the assassins — if that's who really did it — probably knew you weren't there.'

'Unless they didn't know how many of us there were. My sisters are married off. They might have thought I was too.'

'You're sixteen, sweetheart.'

'It's old enough.'

Kalindi took a deep breath and stood up. She went down to the water and waited for the white foam to whoosh in towards her. She washed her hands and face and Jarrod stooped beside her, doing the same. Together, they walked back to the fire, wet hands entwined.

'I think you'd best stay hidden.'

'Me too. I could go north, to Dumarka. My mother's friend lives there. She's a Treeon witch. I've wanted to visit her for ages.' She sucked in her breath. 'I'd be safe there, don't you think?'

Jarrod laughed. 'I don't know who you're talking about, but if she's a Treeon witch, you'll be safe. Nothing can get to them.'

'But Mamá had powers, and they got to her.'

'She never practised.'

'She did! She went to Treeon Temple too when she was younger. That's where she met the Dumarkian witch, Nell. They trained together for a while. Mamá knew when things were going to happen. She had premonitions.'

'So do you, but ...'

Kalindi's eyes welled up again as she stared into the fire. 'But not this time.'

Jarrod rubbed her back. 'Dumarka then?'

'I've got more than enough money to get there. I'll go in the morning. Not from Lister Bay, though.'

'Not from the hub of Lividica,' Jarrod agreed, letting his hand rest on her shoulder. 'You can't risk being seen.'

'I'll hike south to Flureon. I can get a clipper from there. Then it's only a week's sail to Dumarka.'

'I'm coming with you.'

She faced him. 'You can't.'

'I can and I will.'

'Jarrod, listen. I have to go alone. If you disappear with me, it's like sending out a message: *Kalindi Matosh is still alive!*'

'I'm not letting you go alone.'

Her eyebrows went up. '*Letting?*'

'I just meant ...'

'I know what you meant, but I have to slip away and you can never say where I've gone. You can never even say my name again. We can't even *think* my name again. I have to change it. Kalindi Rose has to disappear, forever.'

Jarrod turned her hand in his and lifted it up to kiss her knuckles. 'What name will you take? I need to know that at least, so I can find you.'

She shrugged her shoulders.

'Rose?' he suggested. 'Your middle name is unknown to any outside your family and mine.'

'Rose sounds like an old auntie.'

He laughed. 'I don't think so.'

'What about Rosette?'

'Ro-sette.' He said the name slowly, turning it into two distinct syllables. 'That's beautiful.'

'It's done then. I'm Rosette. Rosette ... de Santo. That's a common enough family name in these parts. And, Jarrod, we've never met. You don't know me, and Kalindi Matosh is dead. If you think of me, even in your dreams, you must call me Rosette.'

Jarrod buried his face in his hands. 'I don't want to be without you, Kalindi.'

She stared at him, eyes narrowing until he looked up.

'I mean — Rosette. I don't want to be without you, Rosette.'

'You have to. If they find me — if they think you know where I am — both of us are in danger. Can you see that?'

'I can.'

He kissed her, long, slow and deep. He reached under her wool sweater and cupped her breast.

She stopped his hand. 'Jarrod, there isn't time. You've been out all day and, if you aren't home soon, Liam will come looking for you with the dogs. He might be already searching, especially with wind of what's happened. We can't risk it.'

'You wouldn't trust Liam?'

She shook her head. 'Not with this.'

'You certainly let him ...'

'Jarrod, stop. I'm not going to see you for a long time. Don't end it with an argument about me and your brother.'

Jarrod pulled his hand away from her warm skin and shook his head. 'I don't want to leave you.'

'Me neither. Now go. Hurry.'

He got up, shouldered his bow and stared up at the cliffs. 'When will I see you again?'

'I don't know.' She handed him his pack.

'Keep it. There's still bread for the morning and water. Rosette, I ...'

She stopped his words with a kiss, holding his face in her hands. 'Don't write to me. Don't send any messages. It has to be like this. Promise?'

'I promise.' He buried his face in her hair. 'I love you, Rosette de Santo.'

'I love you too. Tell Liam ...'

'What?'

'Tell Liam I'm dead.'

They held each other until Jarrod turned abruptly and jogged away. He would have to take the long way around now that it was dark. She hoped he would get home before they sent out a search party. At the rate he disappeared down the beach, she felt sure he would.

Rosette went back to the fire, tears welling again. She picked up a stick and jabbed the coals, making sparks dance like fireflies. *What have you done, John'ra? What have you done to us all?*

Rosette's relationship with her father had never been smooth. A tension had lain in between them ever since she could remember. Maybe it had to do with the magic that flowed in her veins, an inheritance from her mother. The power had passed by her siblings to land full force on her, and it had made John'ra nervous.

'Bethsay let it go,' he'd said, pacing the floor when she tried to discuss her future.

'I'm not my mother.'

Rosette had wanted to develop her powers, not hide them. She'd aspired to train at one of the teaching temples — Treeon, Bangeesh or maybe even Timbali — where she could learn the star-craft and more complex rituals, and train with the bow and the sword. Her mother had smiled when they discussed it, nodding as if she were a toddler begging to ride a green-broke stallion.

Rosette hated that memory. She shook it out of her head.

John'ra had stood dead against her training.

She hated that too.

In all other things, she'd found her father a fair man. He was born in the time of the Sea-goat and had a strong body, a pragmatic mind and, generally, a kind heart. Unfortunately, he'd had dreams beyond his money-lending business and horse markets — dreams that Rosette and her propensity for magic perturbed.

His political ambitions meant he needed his family to be a neat and happy clan. He didn't want a fey daughter, outspoken and vivacious, raising eyebrows everywhere she went, getting involved in temple politics. But now it didn't matter what he'd wanted. The man was dead. How could such a horrid event descend on her home without forewarning? She had seen the sea eagle return. That meant good things would come. What had she missed?

I should have paid closer attention.

There is no should. Her mother's words echoed in her mind.

Still, if she had paid better attention, what would she have seen? Rosette pressed her forehead into her hands, sifting through the past. It had all gotten worse after John'ra discovered her and Jarrod behind the barn.

Every Sunday, when her father had gone to the horse markets, the two of them had sparred in the makeshift arena, or shot arrows at straw figures lined up against the hay barn. John'ra had returned early one day, surprising them — surprising himself. Both she and Jarrod were stripped to the waist, slashing at each other with practice staffs. Rosette had struck a winning blow, knocking Jarrod's staff to the ground. His hands were in the air.

'Tío. Kalindi. Tío!'

It was their code word for *I give up*.

'What in the dark underworld are you two doing?' John'ra had screamed so loudly Kalindi slapped her hands over her ears.

'Training,' she'd said, her breasts rising and falling as she'd gasped for air. 'Don't shout.'

'Training for *what*?'

'Master Matosh.' Jarrod had retrieved his staff. 'I assure you we are only . . .'

'I don't need your assurances, boy. I need my daughter to stop this nonsense and grow up. What if another council member saw her dressed —' he'd stared at her breasts '— *un*dressed, in this manner? I can't imagine what you've been up to.'

'We were only . . .'

'I don't want to know,' he'd shouted louder, his face turning red. 'I want you off my land!' John'ra's fists knotted, threatening him. 'And stay away from my daughter, or I'll run you out of town.'

Jarrod's jaw had tightened, his arm twitching. After a few moments, he'd given a curt nod to John'ra and kissed his sparring partner's cheek. He'd slung his staff over his shoulder and swaggered away.

Soon after, a string of wealthy merchants had begun calling, marriage on their minds. Kalindi and John'ra had argued about it until their battles turned into a seething undercurrent in the household. He'd called her headstrong and self-centred; she'd called him stubborn and insensitive. After some time, they didn't call each other anything at all.

Now that she knew about the bad debts, his behaviour made more sense. Lining her up with suitors, all of them established, middle-aged men, was his way out. She flared up at the thought. It insulted her — John'ra and his officious presumptions, and her mother had gone along with it all!

'Sweetheart, Mr Arbrant is here to see you,' she had said.

'I don't want to see him.'

'Why? He's a fine man.'

'I'm sixteen, mamá. He's forty-two. Do the sums.'

'I have.'

'Don't you think he's a tad my senior?'

'I don't, and hurry up. He's not accustomed to waiting.'

'He sounds a right prize.'

'Kalindi!'

'Mamá, listen to me. I don't care if he owns all the land from here to Corsanon. I won't waste my time on that pig of a man. You can tell him I said so.'

'With the way your voice carries, I doubt I'll have to.'

'Please, Mamá. Just tell him to go. I'm not seeing anyone today.'

'Anyone but Jarrod?'

'At least he's my age.'

'He is that, Kalindi, but a foundling is no match for you.'

'I'm not looking for that kind of match, mamá, and Jarrod's an equal in every other way.'

Bethsay had sighed and turned away. Her father had cursed. He said she had too much of her mother's blood, and he'd made it sound like a foul thing. She had bristled then, but now she understood it differently.

Why couldn't you have been honest with me, John'ra? I would have been more mindful of danger.

It would have been better, perhaps, if she'd left of her own accord. She could have organised the journey and at least said goodbye. She could have taken Assalo. Her throat tightened. That wouldn't have stopped the murders, though. She wiped her eyes, poking the stick deeper into the bed of glowing embers.

The surf pounded the reef and rows of white lines flashed as the waves broke, racing to the shore. Banking the fire, she dug a burrow, wrapped her coat tightly around her body and cocooned herself in the thick quilt. With the rhythm of the sea behind her, she closed her eyes and fell asleep.

Chapter 2

The yap and bark of dogs cut through the evening stillness as Jarrod slowed to a walk. They bounded up to him, two setters and a small terrier, their enthusiasm infectious. He roughed their necks and slapped their sides, pulling the ball from the terrier's mouth and tossing it back towards the house. They all bolted after it, the little wiry one scooping it up as he skidded to a halt. They turned back towards Jarrod, but he waved them on to the barn. As they darted off, his smile faded. The moment's reprieve from his thoughts of Rosette made them flood back tenfold. She'd been everything to him. Now she was gone. How was he going to live with that? More importantly, how was he going to lie about it?

'I wasn't programmed to lie.' He shrugged. 'I wasn't programmed to fall in love either.'

His heart was still pounding when he reached the barn, his hand cramped from gripping his bow. He'd run most of the way from South Sea Cove, longing to drive the growing pain from his chest. It burned, an ache he thought might never subside. The run had done nothing to ease his anxiety, but it did get him back in time for his evening chores. After seeing to the horses, he started in on the woodpile, swinging the axe as if each stroke would banish his feelings.

He knew his brother was watching him, standing just out of the lamplight. Here it was. Time to pull off the ruse — tell everyone Rosette was dead and not merely exiled, and make it convincing. It wouldn't be hard with all the emotion churning in his belly. He ignored his brother for as long as he could. Somehow, telling Liam that Kalindi was gone ... he stopped himself ... that *Rosette* was gone, would make it more real, and he didn't want that, not yet.

'No luck?' Liam asked, moving into the light.

He looked nothing like his brother, who was tall, fair-haired and lanky. Of course, he wasn't a blood brother, though they'd grown up together, close as litter mates.

Jarrod stopped, the blade deep in a split log. 'How's that?'

'You hunt all day and come back with nothing. I'd call that *no luck*.'

Jarrod lifted the axe, log and all, over his head and crashed it down onto the block, splitting the piece in two. 'I got sidetracked.'

Liam crossed his arms, his lip curling. 'You mean Kalindi.'

Jarrod avoided his eyes. 'No-one here's been to town?'

'Why? Something happen?'

Jarrod began to formulate an answer. The news would certainly upset Liam, perhaps as much as it had him. 'There's been ...'

The sound of hooves on the lane diverted his attention. The dogs took off, yapping a new welcome, all three tearing past them like racehorses from the gate.

'Father's home,' Jarrod said, putting the axe down and collecting the scattered wood. He stacked it in the wheelbarrow and headed to the barn. 'I'll see to his horse.'

Liam grabbed his shoulder, stopping him short. 'Has something happened to Kalindi?'

Jarrod pulled free. 'Ask Father. He'll know more than me.'

Liam called after him, but he kept walking, hands deep in his pockets, eyes on the ground.

Rosette quickened her pace, looking down each side street as she passed it. Flureon seemed less familiar than she remembered, and less friendly than when she'd come here on shopping expeditions with her mother. Her eyes welled up at the thought and she bit her lip, willing the emotions back down. The way to the docks must be near and she needed to find them quickly. Gripping her backpack, she hurried along, turning her shoulders sideways to avoid bumping into the crowd of oncoming traffic.

She had been travelling all day and felt grimy, tired and hungry. She'd eaten the last of Jarrod's bread by noon and she didn't want to stop at a bakery for more. There was no time to find the markets if she wanted to get to the docks before sunset. The clippers would sail with the evening tide, and that was already rising. Besides, it wouldn't be smart to wander the streets after dark. A chill gripped her. There was also no telling where the Corsanon assassins had fled to, or who they knew.

Rosette caught the eye of a middle-aged woman with two children in tow and stopped in front of her. 'Can you point the way to the harbour?'

The woman dodged around her, gathering the children together and hurrying away.

Rosette made a sour face before moving on. 'What? I have leprosy?' she called back.

She asked another woman who was walking past, but she pressed on as if she hadn't heard. *Such a friendly town ...*

The last person she approached was an older man with steel-grey hair and a sea-weathered face. He carried a sack of flour over his shoulder and was coming straight for her as if she were invisible.

'Sir,' she held out her hand to stop him from knocking her over, 'can you tell me where the docks are?'

'Docks?' He stopped for a moment, taking a drag of his cigar.

'You know. Where the boats are kept?'

'Aye, *dooks*, missy.' He extended his arm, pointing the cigar as if taking aim. 'Down two blocks there's a lane to your right. Go that way and you can't miss 'em. Follow y' nose.'

She thanked him, taking the directions and trying not to look over her shoulder. It felt as if she were being watched and she was too tired and too distressed to sense if it was her intuition warning her of danger, or exhaustion setting in. She glimpsed a robed figure carrying a staff, but when she looked again the stalker was gone replaced by an elderly woman sweeping the walkway.

Exhaustion, then. I'm imagining things.

With a deep breath, she turned down the lane to the right and jogged along the cobbled path until the scent of salt air, fish and tar nearly knocked her down.

Follow my nose indeed!

The harbour was amazing. She'd never seen so many vessels in her life. They were every size and shape, from little dinghies bobbing up and down like toy boats in bathtub-sized berths to sleek yachts with bare masts reaching endlessly skywards. Fishing boats were heading out to sea, their decks dotted with men coiling ropes and working the nets. Some had multiple cranes hoisting lobster traps, their newly patched wires shining brightly in the slanting light. Seagulls filled the air, their ruckus deafening. Some were hovering over the trawlers, but most jostled for position at the end of the cleaning racks, fighting over the last scraps of the day.

Watching a pair of pelicans land awkwardly at the far side of the harbour, she spotted the clippers. They were the ships that ferried passengers and goods up and down the coast from south of Lividica to northern Dumarka, fast and sure. With luck, there would be one heading north tonight. As the sun set, a renewed fear gripped her. She wanted to slip away, quickly and without fuss, the sooner the better. When she landed in Dumarka, it would only be a matter of hours before she found Nell, if the woman was about. She had no idea what to do if the witch was gone. She didn't want to think about that possibility.

Nell lived a full day's walk from Dumarka Bay, in a cottage by the woods. Rosette hadn't visited for years, not since she was nine, though she was sure she would remember the way. If she had a sanctuary anywhere in the world, it would be with Nell. She remembered the warm embraces, walks in the woods, fireside stories and cinnamon oatcakes. She also remembered the star charts and mobiles of planets hanging from the rafters of the cottage, and the book of spells and rituals. There was much she could learn from Nellion Paree.

If she'll have me.

As the sun dropped to the horizon and bathed the harbour in blood-red light, she spotted a hard-looking man in a captain's hat. She approached him with her 'buyer's walk', the body language her father had taught her. She automatically adopted it whenever she was about to bargain — smart, confident and aloof.

'Passage to Dumarka, Captain …?' She paused to give him a chance to supply his name.

'Raman.'

'Captain Raman,' she nodded. 'I would like to book passage tonight, if that's convenient.'

She was careful to keep any trace of urgency from her voice. It wasn't easy. Again she felt as if she was being watched. She softened her peripheral vision and glimpsed the hooded figure lurking in the shadows by the storage shed.

'I've got a berth if you can leave now.' He eyed her empty hands. 'Where're your bags, missy?'

'This is it.' She turned her shoulder to display Jarrod's small backpack with her quilt tied in a neat roll on top. 'How much?'

'Twenty pieces of gold.'

She whistled, brief but piercing. 'Are we sailing on a golden barge?' She scrutinised the clipper and laughed. 'I'll give you ten.'

Captain Raman lifted his eyebrows. 'Where're you from, girl?'

'Lividica.'

'Daddy's a merchant?'

She didn't hesitate. 'He's a physician.'

'Running away, are we?'

'That's not your concern.'

'It is if you're underage.'

'I'm not.'

'So you say.' He took off his cap and ran his hand through his hair before replacing it. 'Give me fifteen pieces of gold and I won't tell anyone where you're going.'

Rosette looked for the hooded figure while pretending to consider the offer. She couldn't spot it. 'Done.'

She counted the money into the captain's weathered hand and made her way up the ramp. The foghorn bellowed as they cast off. She tightened her coat and shoved her fingers deep into the pockets, choking with tears as she felt her gloves. Mama had made them last winter from the softest black lamb's wool. She pulled them on and wiped her eyes.

Where are you now, Mamá?

The ship glided through the harbour, the surface of the water shimmering with the last glimpse of daylight. Whispering a silent plea to the sea goddess Sednara for smooth sailing, she headed below deck as they rounded the jetty and set sail. Rosette found an empty bunk and climbed up, spreading her quilt over the straw-filled mattress. The journey would take five days and six nights if they caught a good wind and the best currents. Plenty of time to think.

She lay back, staring at the ceiling, lulled by the rhythmic rise and fall of the hull. She could hear the crew above, charging about as orders were barked. Soon the clipper picked up speed, the sound of the prow cutting through the swell like a waterwheel churning full bore. She thought of the wheelhouse back home, alongside the river, and the day she and Jarrod ...

She stopped. *Focusing on the past just makes more of the past.*

She called her wandering mind in and tuned in to her body. Her legs ached from the long walk and so did her heart. Her stomach felt empty, though she didn't know if she could eat. Her appetite had vanished. There would be plenty of fish soup and sourdough bread in the galley, she guessed, though she didn't get up to find out. Instead she drew her quilt around her tight and closed her eyes, the undulation of the boat rocking her to sleep.

The streets of Corsanon were empty — like an old eggshell that had dried up in the sun. The tattered flag snapping above the roof of the central tavern and bits of rubbish that tumbled aimlessly down the road were the only things in motion. This city had been defeated almost two decades ago and there'd been no effort to repair the damage. It was a scar on the face of Gaela, one that most ignored, unless they needed something they couldn't get anywhere else.

Those who lived here were nocturnal and hard-edged — contract killers, thieves and drug dealers, making a living without custom or principle. The authorities were paid well for their silence, blind to the trading of human slaves for gold, children for the poppy's embrace, and any kind of sex for a warm meal. But the gold and the drugs and the food were transient — what remained constant was the despair.

The land had lost its soul, and no-one remembered exactly why, or how to get it back. No-one cared. What mattered in Corsanon did not require soul. It thrived on guile, treachery and corruption, though it was not always so.

Corsanon had once been a rich, affluent district, hosting the celebration of the Five Rivers — an annual spring festival that honoured the mystery rites and the ancient deities known collectively as the Watchers, written of in the *Draconian Tablets* and other texts from the now destroyed Dumarkian Temple. People from all over Gaela had flocked to the revelry, many remaining to add their own uniqueness and craft to the city.

The area not only hosted the ritual celebrations of the temples, it was home to one of the portals — a corridor to the many-worlds. For eons, only the Watchers knew of this, until the priesthood of Corsanon, quite by accident, made the discovery. Coveted, it was thought a boon, a way to increase the wealth of Gaela and the prominence of Corsanon's High Temple. Some feared the Watchers and voted not to use the portal, but the majority agreed the Watchers were impartial observers that intervened — or not — as it suited them. They wouldn't notice the activation of the Entity, the guardian of a portal, or any little trips down the corridors the temple clan cared to make.

The Watchers did notice, though, and they were not pleased. Before they took action, Corsanon and its temple were destroyed.

The city's downfall came about the same way most civilisations crumble — the misuse of power. A corrupt high council priest had joined ranks with governing officials, making a deadly deal. He had dabbled in a particularly occult magic and had created a spell that would enable him to travel the portal — undetected by the Watchers — freeing him to search for wealth in the other worlds. Yet the work was beyond his skill, the consequences brutal. What he summoned consumed him before he could protect himself: it came from another world — another time, another place. It came from a twenty-third-century Earth.

His tampering had severed the Entity, unleashing one part — an elemental intelligence greater than anything he anticipated — into the immediate environment. The other portion remained trapped in the portal, ever seeking a way to escape and rejoin its sundered half. All the while a sickness leaked into Gaela, a sickness from that other world. Corsanon's despair was not entirely her own — a good portion of it belonged to Earth.

The temple of Corsanon had rallied to negate the blunder, but their attempts proved ineffective. Other temples had stepped in, also unable to contain the Entity or undo the damage. Debates turned into heated arguments, fights into widespread skirmishes, combat into battles until a full-scale war erupted. Many perished, and the effect of the weakened portal unleashed myriad energies, one causing climatic changes within the province. Crops failed, hunger and desperation ensued. Eventually, temple had battled temple, farmers became vigilantes, and the surviving population deteriorated into a collective of violence and anarchy.

Corsanon, as it had been for countless generations, ceased to exist, but the severed Entity that languished there survived. It adapted, becoming smaller and more self-contained as the riches of the environment no longer sustained it. It lived in back alleys and burnt-out buildings — alone, desperate and aching. Ultimately, all it desired was a way to return to the portal and re-combine with its sundered half. There its nature was harmonious — complete — but it couldn't find its way.

Kreshkali came upon the drifting Entity, recognising it for what it was. It had also recognised her for what she was: a powerful witch of unknown origin who wore the aura of another world — even though the Entity knew she hadn't passed through before the sundering.

Kreshkali had come after, with designs of her own.

Archer watched as shadows advanced over the ruined city of Corsanon, its jagged walls turned red by the sunset. A single gas street lamp flickered on and off, like an eye scanning for signs of life. Somewhere in the distance a door slammed.

He turned to the man behind him. Rogg looked skinnier than usual in the shadows, swallowed up by the fading light.

'Well?' Archer asked.

Rogg crouched, scooping a handful of dirt from the side of the road. He crumbled it between his fingers, letting it trickle to the ground. The other men gathered around.

Archer stooped until his head was level with Rogg's ear. 'Is she here?'

Rogg licked his lips before tasting the dirt that clung to his fingers. 'Naw.' He stood up, dust falling from his hands as he brushed them on his pants. 'What now?'

'We wait,' Archer said.

'Ale?' Rogg jerked his head towards the tavern beneath the winking light.

'Why not?'

A gust of wind swept past, blowing Rogg's hat — a rag tied in knots — onto the ground. Rogg looked at it, shoving his hands into his pockets. The other men stalled as well.

'What now?' Archer asked.

'She'll skin us. She'll cook us. She'll boil ...'

Archer whooped with laughter, slapping Rogg's back and knocking him to his knees. 'More of this?' His laughter vanished. 'Get it, all of you.' Archer's hands went to his hips, head cocked sideways. 'She's nothing ... as good as dead.'

'And the other?' Rogg asked.

Archer winked and pulled out a long, thin dagger, twisting it in the space between them. 'You'll see. Watch for my sign.'

Kreshkali stood at the edge of the road, staring towards the heart of Corsanon. A single street lamp shone like a beacon in the darkness, flickering with an eerie glow. She took a deep breath, pushed back her hood and smiled.

'Nothing, am I?' she whispered into the night air, her breath making puffs of mist in the rising moonlight.

She smiled, tracing the edge of a bootprint with a twig. Intricate tattoos of vines and serpents, wrapped in an ancient caduceus, wound across her wrists and towards her fingertips.

'Shall I accompany you?' A young woman stepped out of the shadows, leading two horses. As she spoke one horse pushed forward, nuzzling Kreshkali's shoulder. The woman laughed softly, holding the mare back.

'Stay here, Jaynan. You'll have your hands full minding these two, especially if things get ... lively.' Kreshkali stroked the mare's neck, flipping stray lengths of black mane over her crest. 'I won't be long.'

'There are at least five of them,' Jaynan said, pointing at the bootprints.

'At least.' Kreshkali smiled. She rolled up her sleeves, removing silver bangles from her wrists and tucking them into her saddlebag.

Jaynan leaned forward to kiss Kali's cheek. 'Be safe, my love.' She handed her a long staff of polished wood inlaid with copper runes.

Kreshkali flipped her hood up and headed towards the tavern. The horses nickered after her as clouds obscured the moon, sending a blanket of darkness over the deserted street.

Archer laughed. The tavern smelled of rancid meat, sweat and sour ale. He called for beer and found a table near the back of the large room. A fire hissed, the blazing logs warming the filthy rushes and soot-covered walls. The tabletop was crusted with food, ash and spilled wine. Deep gouges, from sword and axe, rent the surface. Archer leaned back in his chair, taking it in.

Several other men were seated by the entrance. All were hooded and hunched as if in hiding, except for the barman. His chest swelled under a dirty white singlet, the hair on his back and shoulders sticking up like boar bristles.

Archer filled his pipe and took a deep drag. Before he exhaled, he froze.

In the chair beside him appeared a hooded figure.

Archer felt his heart pound. *A magician's trick,* he said to himself. *Nothing to worry about.*

'Where's the amulet?' the figure asked.

Beneath the table Archer fingered his dagger, sliding it from its sheath.

'Where's me gold?' he countered.

The woman lifted a coin purse from her cloak and placed it on the table.

He nodded, setting an azure-crystal vial on the table. 'It's a trade,' he said.

Idiot! He had her now. He planned to cut her, take the gold, keeping the prize for himself. Rogg had said it'd be too risky, his brow beading with sweat when they'd bickered over it. Archer stood firm. Witch or not, she was only a woman, and he could handle any woman.

I might even have some fun with her before she dies, or after.

She turned to him. 'Really?'

He spat. *Demon psychic*. He hadn't counted on that.

She let her hood slide back, revealing electric blue eyes and a shock of spiky blonde hair.

'And what's that?' she whispered, her face close to his. She put the vial in her pocket, tilting her head towards the keg.

'We ran into some trouble, but we got his blood.'

'You *what*?' Kreshkali shrieked, her eyes boring into him.

'You said you wanted the blood of the witch-child.'

'I said I wanted to *protect* the blood of the witch-child.'

Archer swallowed the bile in his throat. It seemed he'd guessed wrong. *No matter* ... He sprang, blade slicing towards her neck. Rogg leapt for the gold.

With her left hand, the witch caught Archer's wrist, snapping the bones. His blade clattered to the floor. With her right, she pointed the staff at Rogg, immobilising him where he stood. His fingers stopped inches from the coin purse, his thick tongue sticking out of his mouth as though he'd been strangled.

The other men jumped, one leaping towards her, the rest running away.

She raised her staff again, dropping them all to their knees, her voice screeching through the tavern.

Horses trumpeted outside.

Archer stared at her, mute. His limbs were paralysed, blood flowing freely from where the bones protruded. He watched it pool across the table, filling the grooves like tributaries dripping to the floor.

His vision blurred as she leaned over him, lifting her cloak slightly to keep it from touching his face. The bag of coins disappeared back into her robe. She retrieved the keg as well.

'Who's the idiot now, Sunshine?' she asked, heading to the tavern door.

He let out his last breath, cursing her through pale lips.

'Damn you underworld bitches ...'

Jaynan handed Kreshkali the reins. The mare was restless, pawing the ground. 'I take it there's no need to rush?' she asked, securing her staff with double ties.

Kreshkali reached across the space between them and squeezed her companion's arm. 'No rush at all.'

She got Archer? How? Jaynan hid her surprise.

A silence built between them as they headed out of town, punctuated by the horses' hooves clipping over the cobblestones.

'Much of a fight?' Jaynan finally asked, eyeing the small keg strapped to Kreshkali's back.

The moon came out of the clouds, lighting the road with a soft glow as it rose towards the zenith. Kreshkali's eyes were black, glistening. 'None at all. The last of them gone.' She paused. 'Does that disturb you?'

Jaynan shook her head. 'It's a triumph, of course. But one thing's confusing me.'

Kreshkali raised her brows.

'Where is Bethsay's child? Weren't they going to deliver the girl to us ... to you?'

Kreshkali urged her mare into an easy jog, which Jaynan's horse matched. 'The child?' she replied. 'Seems Archer got his instructions wrong. The child's dead. Do you know how that could've happened, Jaynan?'

She knows! Or at least, she suspects. I can't let her go back to Earth now, and I can't turn my back. 'What will we do?'

Kreshkali stretched her neck, leaning from side to side. 'We'll rest the horses and have supper before we head back home. The death changes everything.'

'But ... we have to keep moving!'

'Do we?' Kreshkali glanced down at the sheath that held her staff.

'It isn't safe.' Jaynan gestured out into the black maw of trees that lined both sides of the road.

Kreshkali kept her face smooth. 'What did you have in mind?'

'Keep hiding, of course. We can go straight to Los Loma. It's safe there. If we ride through the night, we'll be ...'

'I'm not hiding any more,' Kreshkali replied, throwing her voice behind her as she moved ahead at a gallop.

Of course you aren't, my queen. And that's why they sent me, just in case Archer failed.

They sped along until the woods thinned out into a grey meadow. Kreshkali brought her mare to a halt, dust rising around the horses' legs.

'Does this look *safer* to you?' she asked, not waiting for an answer. She dismounted and led her mare out into the field.

She looked ethereal, like she was walking on water, the grass a shallow sea undulating beneath her feet. For an instant, Jaynan's eyes burned, and she brushed the tears with her fists.

'Wait up,' she said, swinging her leg over the saddle and dropping lightly to the ground. 'There's something I didn't mention.' *Not quite all the trackers are gone, my love.*

'What's that?' Kreshkali turned back as Jaynan's thin sword levelled at her neck.

'You have yet to deal with me.'

Kreshkali let the mare's reins slip through her fingers. 'What's this?'

'You're coming back to Earth with me.'

'Or?'

'Or die here.'

Kreshkali lifted her head, avoiding eye contact. 'I'm not going with you.'

Without hesitation, Jaynan thrust the sword tip forward.

Kreshkali's mare reared, iron-shod hooves pawing the air. Kreshkali stepped to the side, inches out of the line of the blade, her own dagger flashing briefly before it sank deep between Jaynan's ribs.

The tracker's eyes went wild, searching for comprehension as her sword fell from her hand. 'They'll send more,' she said, dropping to her knees. 'You'll never be free.'

'Ah, but I will, sweet Jaynan. And you would have been too, if you'd only trusted me.' Kreshkali bent to kiss the other woman as she slid to the ground.

The mare's nose fluttered over the blood before it seeped into the grass. The moon went behind a billow of clouds, sucking light from the meadow as Jaynan died.

Kreshkali closed her eyes, no longer able to hold back the tears.

She rode for five days, stopping only to feed and rest her horse. On the sixth night, she arrived at the slopes of the Jacor Mountains above the treeline of Espiro Dell Ray. The stars winked in and out of view as mist drifted across the night sky. The mare rubbed her face on Kreshkali's shoulder, covering her cloak in horsehair.

'You deserve a rest.' She took off the saddle and bridle, giving the mare's shoulder an affectionate slap, and turned her out to graze.

She slipped the keg from her back and dug a shallow grave with her hands. She knelt in the grass in front of it, tears blurring her vision. With her dagger she cracked open the keg, sloshing the contents onto the ground.

Unwittingly, Bethsay ... I had a hand in this.

She covered the site with small rocks, making a stone idol at each of the four directions.

You, and your family, won't be forgotten.

The veil of mist dropped as the three-quarter moon shone through, dimming the stars. It painted everything with an iridescent sheen, bathing her skin in milky-blue light.

> *Into the night,*
> *Into the dark,*
> *Travel the worlds*
> *Unencumbered.*
> *The greater mysteries await.*

'Forgive me, Bethsay, and know that you will be avenged.'

She sat by the gravesite for the rest of the night and wept.

Chapter 3

'Stars in the sky, look at you!'

'Nell!' Rosette whooped with delight as she ran to the gate.

Nellion Paree stood in the garden, her long auburn hair playing in the spring breeze. She had the body of a dancer and a spirit like the sea — fathomless, unpredictable, life-giving, life-threatening. Her dark hazel eyes crinkled with her grin. However old she was — thirty, forty, fifty, older — Rosette didn't know. Nell beamed with timeless exuberance and energy. Her ivory-coloured dress lifted above her bare feet as she opened her arms, its wide neckline slipping off one shoulder, revealing the tattoo of a black raven on her upper arm.

'Come in, you gorgeous girl. I've been waiting for you!'

Rosette unlatched the wooden gate and entered the garden. It was like stepping into another realm where everything around her exploded with colour. Pink azaleas and sunny orange tiger lilies lined the path, and vivid unnamed blooms spilled out of the window boxes, setting off the cedarwood cottage with clusters of purple, red and lavender. Huge roses circled the chamomile lawn, their blossoms exquisite shades of pink, peach and tamarind, their fragrance intoxicating. She took a deep breath. The place seemed smaller than she remembered, though every bit as magical.

A creek gurgled in the background as it rushed towards the rugged coastline, a short hike to the west. At night the sound of the ocean crashing against the towering cliffs would fill her dreams. Once she had looked down from that vantage point. Her stomach had turned somersaults. Boulders larger than men were like tiny pebbles from where she stood. It took three hours to follow the winding track to the bottom, but she hadn't been allowed to explore.

As Rosette raced up the path, ravens squawked and flapped and red-eyed figbirds and brightly coloured finches chattered in the shrubs. Several hummingbirds with ruby throats and chartreuse bodies hovered over the honeysuckle blossoms that draped the fence, their wings beating so fast they were invisible. What a wonder to be so close to the wild woods, far away from the noise and clatter of the city. Her father had said that Nell was a hermit, but Rosette saw a sanctuary teeming with spirit friends.

'How'd you know I was coming?' she asked in a rush, reaching for the woman and falling into her arms.

Nell nodded to the three ravens sitting in the lower branches of a central weeping willow. The corvids stopped their preening and tilted their blue-white eyes as if following the path of a fly. Together they cawed again and took flight. Rosette watched them flap away, each shooting off in a different direction, heading for the tall pines surrounding Nell's home.

'Every twig, sparrow and snake has spoken of your coming for the past two days,' she said, looking into the distance. 'The Three Sisters haven't stopped yakking about it all morning. How could I not know?'

Rosette squeezed Nell tightly. 'It's good to be here.'

'Where are your things?'

Rosette untangled herself from the embrace and looked into Nell's eyes. 'This is all I've got.'

'Leave in a hurry, did you, Kalindi Rose?'

Rosette shuddered. She glanced over her shoulder then back to Nell. 'Don't say that name.'

Nell searched her face. 'What's this about?'

'I'm ...' She blanched, her hands beginning to tremble. 'I'm Rosette now, Rosette de Santo. You mustn't say my birth name again.'

'Why ever not?'

Rosette looked down at her feet, tears falling. 'Something ... something terrible's happened.'

'I can see that.'

Nell gathered her into her arms again and held her tight. The garden went strangely silent for a moment and Rosette felt a warmth flooding her body, chasing away the fear and hurt. When Nell let her go, the garden came back to life, abuzz with chatter.

'Come inside, Rosette. You're exhausted. You need to eat, and rest.'

'Thank you, Nell. I am a bit dizzy. I don't know if I can eat.'

'We'll see about that.'

Rosette took off her boots, lining them up on the porch next to Nell's, and crossed the threshold. The smells of baking bread, cinnamon, mint and roast meat did seem inviting. They sat at the black oak table, side by side, and held hands.

'Tell me what happened, Rosette. What are you running from?'

Rosette felt tears welling again as she reported the events, stuttering when she came to the kitchen scene. Nell didn't speak, nor did she let go of her hands. She drew Rosette out of her chair and into her lap, rocking her gently. Rosette let her tears fall and they ran down her face, mixing with Nell's.

'You did right to disappear,' Nell said, stirring a cast-iron pot.

It simmered on the hearth, making Rosette's mouth water. They had just returned from an early-morning walk — a good night's sleep reviving her spirits, and her appetite.

'If someone wanted to punish John'ra that's one thing, and it's done, but if they wanted ... something else, that's another matter altogether.'

Rosette washed her hands in the basin, drying them with a brightly coloured kitchen towel. 'What do you mean, *something else*?'

'Just speculation.' Nell frowned. 'Did you speak to anyone in Dumarka?'

'I came straight here.'

'You remembered the way?'

'Easy, though I'd forgotten how far it was.'

'It's not so easy for just anyone,' Nell said. She opened the oven door and a wave of heat and bakery aromas poured out. 'Did you use your family name on the ship or at the harbour in Flureon?'

'Only de Santo, if that.'

'You've done well, sweetheart.'

Nell turned to the pantry beside the stove and took butter and cheese from the cold box and set them out on the table. Rosette got out plates and cups.

'But, Nell, why did this happen? Do you know?'

Nellion smoothed her dress before putting her hands on her hips. 'There are enemies in the world, Rosette.'

'Enemies?'

'Come. Eat first. I need to think. Plenty of time for philosophy later.'

Rosette frowned. 'Philosophy?'

'Philosophy and speculation. That's all anything is, second-hand.'

While Nell prepared the food, Rosette leaned back in her chair. Her face relaxed as she scanned the cottage, taking it in properly for the first time. The rows of books by the back wall had increased since she'd last visited. Leather-bound volumes of various shapes and sizes were stacked on shelves that climbed halfway to the ceiling. A four-poster bed with crimson cushions and a purple velvet quilt filled the far corner. Woven rugs covered the hardwood floor, cushions were scattered about, and various herbs hung from the beams over the kitchen, adding a mix of earthy fragrance to the cottage.

She spotted the mobiles of planets circling above in miniature orbits around bright orange suns. The broad window seat where she'd slept was covered with quilts, warm and comfortable on the far side of the hearth. Rosette had been warm and snug all night, even though the temperature dropped quickly once the sun set. The glowing coals had been a welcome heat. She studied the design of stained glass in the high windows to the east — they had amazed her early in the morning — the sunlight through them making a splash of rainbows when she awoke.

Her gaze was drawn directly overhead, and she started. 'Nell!' She shrank back. 'What's that?'

Hanging from the rafters, its body draped in serpentine loops around the wooden beams, was a huge yellow-and-black-speckled snake.

'*Who* is that,' Nell corrected.

Rosette swallowed, not taking her eyes off the animal. 'Who, then?'

'It's Mozzie.'

'Mozzie?'

'Short for Mosaic. He's a carpet snake, of course, a python. Don't you have them in Lividica?'

'Not like that.'

'Like what?'

'Not like that big. And not in the house.'

'Well, Mozzie lives inside.'

'He was there last night? Watching me sleep?'

'More likely he was under your bed. You'll get used to him.'

Rosette didn't reply.

'He keeps the rodents down, among other things.' Nell ladled porridge into blue ceramic bowls. 'Still hungry, aren't you?'

Rosette cleared her throat and nodded.

Nell swept away her books and notes, stacking them on a small desk before laying out the bowls, fresh milk, bread and honey.

Rosette sighed as she turned her attention to the meal. 'Very hungry,' she answered, glancing back up at Mozzie.

Nell smiled, toasting her with a mug of spiced cider.

'To warm reunions.'

Rosette raised her mug and smiled, the cider sweet on her lips.

'I see you got away with your travelling charm,' Nell said, studying her necklace.

'Jarrod got it out of the house for me.'

'Who's that?'

'Jarrod Cossica — he's my best friend ... What's wrong?'

Nell's brow was knitted. 'I remember a man with that name many years ago. Is he ...'

'Old?' Rosette laughed. 'He's my age — just a boy really. He grew up next door.'

'Not him, then.' Nell blew on a spoonful of porridge. 'Is he Cossica's oldest son?'

'No, that's Liam. Jarrod is the youngest.'

'I don't remember him.'

'He's a foundling.'

'And is this foundling of yours the only one who knows you're here?'

'Him, and possibly Liam. There are few secrets between them, though he said he'd tell no-one.'

'What about your sisters?'

Rosette shook her head. 'Both married. Leea's on a sheep farm near Dumar. She probably hasn't even heard yet.'

'And Sasha?'

'Under Mount Pele, with a glassblower. Three kids now.'

Nell was silent, her eyes drifting to the window. 'I warned your mother that it wasn't safe.'

'What do you mean?'

'Rosette, your mother may have had enemies too.'

Rosette stopped eating. 'I don't understand. She was just a matron, looking after the estate. How could she have enemies? She'd turned her back on witchcraft.'

Nell raised her brows. 'Had she?'

'Pardon?'

'Do you really believe she repressed her power to mould herself around John'ra's life?'

'She didn't?'

'No, my dear Rosette. She was hiding, and she wanted to hide you, too. I told her it would go ill if John'ra caught the public eye. If he was noticed, so would she be. There was no controlling him though, it seems.'

'I thought someone was after John'ra. He owed money, I think.'

'Perhaps.'

'Who would want to hurt mamá?'

Nell shook her head. 'We can't know for sure. The temples are not all at peace.'

'Did she have some magic they wanted?'

Rosette thought she saw Nell stiffen, but when she looked again she was relaxed.

'Anything's possible. Meanwhile, you're here and presumed dead. That's as safe as it gets.'

'Am I in danger, though?' Rosette looked out the doorway as if at any moment someone would be coming up the path.

'We'll be vigilant. Besides, no-one gets to me without my knowing.'

'That's what Jarrod said.'

'Did he?'

Nell lifted up her mug again. 'A toast to a new life — for both of us.'

'To a new life.' Rosette clanked her mug against Nell's. 'Can I ask you something?' Rosette felt heat rise in her face.

'Anything.'

'Since I'm here, and ready for a new beginning ... will you teach me the things mamá forbade?'

'Forbade?' Nell stopped. Her spoon, laden with food, hovered halfway to her mouth.

'She said I wasn't ready, but I am,' Rosette went on. 'And I want to learn so much! Star-craft, herbs, spells, the sword and the bow — and shape-shifting. Definitely shape-shifting. Please may I? You can teach me. I know you can.'

'Full of enthusiasm, aren't you?'

'Yes.'

'You fancy yourself a witch?'

'Yes.'

Nell closed her eyes. 'Why?' she asked, keeping them shut.

Rosette put down her bread. 'I just know it.'

'You just know it,' Nell repeated. 'Good. Now tell me, how so?'

'Because something ... something is calling me, like the woods of Espiro Dell Ray, and the whispers of stones and the wind in the arroyos, and lately, it's been more than a call.'

'More than a call?'

'It's been a holler.'

Nell laughed, her eyes popping open. 'And you want to answer the call?'

'I do.'

'Then you shall.' She started eating again and nodded to Rosette to do the same.

'Does that mean you'll initiate me?'

'It does.'

Rosette beamed a smile. 'When can I start?'

'There's no rush.'

'Nell, please. Give me a hint!'

'You'll have an entire lunar cycle — from waning to new, new to full, and waning again in the sign of the Water-Bearer — to prepare.'

'On my lunar return?'

She nodded. 'By the time the moon returns next month, you'll have sought and acquired your initiation name.'

'Rosette's no good?'

'Rosette's fine. Very lovely. It's perfect for all you meet and everything you do overtly. Your name as an initiate is different. It's known to you alone, or shared only with another you fully trust.'

'Okay.'

'It's sacred, Rosette. When you find it, keep it occult.'

'I will.'

'You must also choose the design of your initiation tattoo.' She paused for a moment. 'Though it's more likely that it will choose you.'

Rosette's eyes went wide, looking closely at the symbols on Nell's bare arms — the raven on the left and a stout tree with serpents entwining the trunk on the right.

She sucked in her breath. 'I've already done that.'

'You have?'

Rosette glanced over to the bookcase where an onyx statuette of a temple cat sat, slender, regal and fey. The animal had large, pointed ears, the left one pierced with a golden ring. Its face was chiselled, limbs refined, the tail wrapped around its front feet.

Nell followed her line of sight and smiled.

'Basta, mother of the ancient temple cats?'

'I've always known it would be her.'

'Wonderful choice.'

Rosette smiled back. 'I knew years ago, on my first visit. I held that statue in my hands and for a second, it came alive.' She took another bite of bread, sucking drops of honey from her fingers. 'After my tattoo, then what happens?'

Nell patted her hand. 'Under the eyes of great Ishtar ...'

Rosette held her breath.

'... we do the ritual.'

Rosette nodded, a shadow crossing her face.

'What, child?'

'Mamá and John'ra would not have approved, and now they're ...'

'They would have wanted you to survive, Rosette, and studying witchcraft is the surest way to protect yourself. Besides, it's in your blood.'

'Get the whitest ones you can find.' Nell sketched the shape of the root on a drawing pad. 'No smaller than this. You can only see the tips sticking out from the snowbanks at this time of the year, so you have to dig deep.' She handed Rosette a copper trowel to pack in her backpack.

The summer after Rosette's initiation had fled by; the smell of the woods and the warm sun baked away her fears and eased the sadness. Her arms had tanned a dark honey-brown as she'd tended the gardens, and her intuition had sharpened as she'd hunted at the edges of the woods by day and studied herbs and star-craft by the fire at night.

Now winter was here, and it was time to collect the Snow Root — *Symphytum officinalia* — that Nell used in her potions, particularly the one that kept joints supple and bones warm through the long dark nights.

'How many?' Rosette tucked the talisman Nell had given her as an initiation gift — a silver pentagram nestling inside a crescent moon — under her sweater and buttoned up her coat.

'At least five, more if time allows. Take only the top half of the root and replant the rest. It's sacred, and we don't want to deplete it.'

Rosette nodded.

'Get away from the woods well before sunset — it's no place to be on a winter's night, I promise you.'

'Nell, why are you fussing? It's just a trip to the woods.' Rosette's eyes suddenly went wide. 'Is there a transit you aren't telling me about?'

'You've studied the ephemeris. Is there?'

Rosette closed her eyes, visualising the planetary positions for the day. She couldn't see anything outstanding, and said so.

'What about last month?'

Rosette frowned. 'Last month was the lunar eclipse on my north node, but what's that got to do with today? It's long past ... Oh.' Rosette put her hand over her mouth to stop a stream of babble.

'Yes. *Oh*!' Nell smiled briefly before letting it fade. 'What can you tell me about the timing of eclipse events?'

Rosette took a deep breath. 'An eclipse can have its outcome thirty days *before* or *after* the exact alignment, plus or minus three days either side.'

'Yes, it can, and that brings us to today. It's nothing to fret about, though I want you to stay aware, and be out of those woods before dark.'

'Don't worry, Nell. I'll be back before dinner.' She fished gloves from her pockets and pulled them on, picked up her staff and shouldered her backpack before kissing Nell's cheeks.

The wind struck her face as she opened the cottage door. Nell called her back.

'Here.' She daubed a sweet-smelling ointment on Rosette's lips and thrust the small tin into her gloved hand. 'This'll keep your lips from chapping. Use it sparingly; it's very strong.'

Rosette put the container in her pocket before flipping up her hood and waving goodbye.

Several hours later she was scouring the borders of the Dumarkian Woods, looking for the elusive Snow Root. She had found only one small plant so far and no sign of any others. Pausing before the wall of pine trees, she smiled. She remembered a patch of them carpeting the summer forest floor, their tiny purple blossoms dancing like puppets on a stick. They were further in. She glanced up at the pale sun, took a deep breath and entered the woods.

The stillness struck her first. No wind whipped and cut at her face and not a branch moved. Only the occasional snapping of a twig underfoot, the crunch of snow and the distant screech of a raptor broke the silence. She couldn't believe a place so still could feel this alive. It teemed with energy, and today not all of it felt friendly.

She imagined this would be an amazing place to explore on horseback. How long had it been since she'd so much as seen a horse in the distance? The last she'd touched had been Assalo, right before he died. She pushed the memory away before it choked her and continued through the woods.

By late afternoon, she had six good-size roots in her backpack. She sat on a fallen log beneath a tall grove of pines, munching on the oatcakes that Nell had packed for her. The sun had vanished behind the cloud cover, and a light snowfall floated down between the branches like puffs of dandelion looking for somewhere to land. It was already getting dark. She shivered.

Retracing her steps, she made slow progress. Her hands and feet were cold and stiff. Her legs felt like lead weights, and she had the eerie sensation of being watched. She turned a full circle, seeing nothing but the sentinel trees and falling snow before she caught a flash of movement. A blast of adrenaline hit her solar plexus, and she sucked in her breath.

There it was again, something slipping in and out of the shadows. She couldn't identify it. Then a hunkered shape appeared. It seemed damaged. It wasn't moving right. A high-pitched scream pierced the air and was immediately answered by a squawking challenge. Some creature was clearly under attack. Gripping her staff with both hands, she ran forward, her eyes wide and her heart pounding.

As she came closer, she made out two birds on the ground, flapping dark wings. There was a tug of war going on between a crow and a buzzard twice its size. Both were intent on the quarry and neither would back down. She couldn't make out what they'd scavenged, but it wasn't moving or making any noise. Rosette watched with fascination as the birds bounced and flapped and hopped back and forth, the squawks cutting short as the buzzard stopped momentarily to eye her. When it dropped its grip, Rosette recognised what they were fighting over and her heart pinched.

It was a large black cat, dead or unconscious. As she raised her staff it suddenly came to life, spitting and struggling. Rosette didn't wait for her next breath. She held her staff high over her head and charged at the birds, screaming, 'Get away!' She swung her staff, well before coming into range. 'Let go or I'll break your necks!'

She struck at them, yelling at the top of her voice, swinging towards the crow first and sending it cawing to a low pine branch. The buzzard opened its wings as if to stand its ground, but hopped away quickly when Rosette's staff whizzed by its head. With a few more swings and curses she had the birds scattered enough to turn her attention to the feline.

Kneeling down, she saw that, for all its large size, it was only a kitten.

'Where's your mamá?' Rosette looked around the clearing as she spoke.

Wherever the mother was, the creature would be huge. She saw nothing nearby except the darkening woods and the buzzard swooping to a branch just above her.

The baby cat shuddered in the snow, its nose on the ground. One leg was bent at an unnatural angle and the others were tensed underneath its body. There was blood oozing from its neck and one eye had swollen shut. It tried to leap away only to collapse into the snow, inches ahead.

'I've got you,' Rosette whispered. 'You're safe with me.'

She scooped the kitten up into her arms, unbuttoned her coat and thick woollen sweater, tucking it into the warmth between her breasts. The touch of its cold body burned her skin and made her gasp.

She patted the animal. 'Don't worry. They can't get you now, baby cat.'

She buttoned her sweater over it, tightening her coat as she stood. Drips of melting ice-water trickled down her belly, and something warmer too. The baby's blood? She grabbed her staff and ran for home.

The birds closed in, seemingly united now in their effort to reclaim the feline, or perhaps even Rosette. She swung her staff and screamed at them before scooping snowballs and firing them at their heads, the fists of ice forcing them to seek cover. Rosette had an accurate throwing arm, thanks to her playful summers with Jarrod and Liam, and she felt grateful for it now as the birds flew higher and higher in retreat.

Constantly looking over her shoulder, the journey home seemed to take forever. At the edge of the woods she turned back, catching her breath. A pale beam of sunlight shone between the clouds. It was near to setting. The baby cat felt warm now, and the dripping had stopped. The double-time tap of its heartbeat against her own reassured her it was still alive.

'We'll be home soon,' she cooed, patting the large bump in her coat.

Hoisting her staff like a fishing pole, she jogged the rest of the way to the cottage.

Around the corner of the ruined temple, on a fallen slab of marble entangled with bare vines and spotted with snow, a mammoth feline stood. She opened her mouth to roar, but let no air escape her lungs. She closed her eyes instead and sat. Her tail wrapped tight around her body, the tip lifting slightly, moving in fits and jerks. Slowly she lay down on her sternum, her forepaws stretched out in front of her like a sphinx. She didn't flinch, but her heart pounded into the cold marble like a slow, aching drum.

Maudi was tortured by her choice. Was it the right one? She was tempted to run down the girl and retrieve her cub. Her whiskers twitched as Drack, a rust-and-black male, approached, sitting a distance away. She could feel the vibration of his purr through the marble slab, through her heart. She knew it was generated from fear, not joy — an involuntary response to alarm, something like the way humans might laugh when suddenly frightened. Drack probably thought she would eat him alive.

She considered it.

It was the only way, Maudi.

She turned her head towards her mate and snarled, her tongue flashing over white teeth.

There will be other cubs.

At this comment she spun on her haunches and lunged at him, claws swiping towards his face. He leapt aside to avoid the raking.

She returned to her vigil.

Maudi, Drack tried again, *he's bonded now. They will both benefit from the union.*

I didn't allow it for their benefit.

I know, but it's comforting just the same.

Not to me.

There was no sign of the birds, though a curious sound echoed in Rosette's head from time to time as she ran. *Maudi? Maudi?*

She flipped her hood back as sweat trickled down her neck. Throwing open the gate, she ran up to the cottage door.

'Help, Nell. Quickly!'

Nell swung open the door and Rosette stopped just before ploughing into her.

'It's wounded,' she said, gasping for breath.

Nell pulled Rosette across the threshold, boots and all, and closed the door behind her. She pried the staff from her frozen fingers and leaned it against the wall, noticing the blood on Rosette's gloves.

'You're hurt?'

'I'm fine.'

'Are you being chased?' Nell looked out the window.

'Not any more,' Rosette stammered. 'It's a cub — a kitten.'

'Where?'

'I found a huge baby cat.' Rosette patted the bulge under her coat.

The colour drained from Nell's face. 'Show me.'

Rosette knelt on the rug next to the glowing hearth and unfastened her coat. She opened her sweater, button by button, until the feline's head popped out between her breasts, one swollen eye making it look as though it was winking.

'Goddess of the woodlands,' Nell whispered. 'That's not a kitten.'

'It is ... it's just really big. Look at the paws, the size of its head. It's a baby for sure.'

'That's not what I meant, Rosette. Where did you find it?'

'A fair way into the woods. Two birds were fighting over it. I chased them off, grabbed him and ran for home.' She smiled. 'Oh look, it *is* a "him".'

'You found him in the Dumarkian Woods?'

'Yes, Nell, of course I did. What other woods are there?'

Nell looked into Rosette's eyes. 'Deep breaths now. He will be less frightened if our movements are calm. These creatures are very dangerous.'

'He's a kitten, Nell.'

The older witch gave her a sharp look. 'Even at this age — and this damaged — he could tear your hand off with his claws. Now calm yourself.'

Rosette spoke softly. 'I'm calm, but you certainly aren't. What's wrong? Will he be all right?'

Again the strange sound filled Rosette's mind. She thought her ears must be ringing from the cold. *Maudi? Maudi?*

She turned her attention to the little animal. 'It's okay, baby cat. You're safe with us.'

Rosette kept her hand on the kitten while Nell examined it. She counted his heartbeats, checked the gum colour, palpated the twisted foreleg and gently pulled open the swollen eyelids. All the while Rosette talked to him in a comforting voice.

'We need a basin with hot water and clean cloths. I want Golden Seal, Coptis and Hypericum, mixed in equal measure. Also that ointment I gave you this morning. We'll use that too.'

Rosette got up. 'What else?' she asked as she followed the directions.

'My splinting sticks and bandages. They're in a box under the long bench.'

'Got 'em.'

Maudi? The sound was plaintive as the little animal turned its good eye towards Rosette.

'We're going to help you, baby cat,' Rosette said, stroking the crumpled body when she returned. 'Nell's going to fix you up. She's the best healer ever.'

Rosette went back to the kitchen to mix the herbs. 'He'll live? He'll be able to run and jump, won't he, Nell? Hunt? Both eyes will see?'

'I think so, darling. Let's just get him treated and give him something to eat. Bring a cup of milk to warm, and the hot-water bottle. He's still cold.'

'Meat?'

'I have lamb in the oven that he can try later.'

Rosette smiled at the thought, her mouth watering.

Nell cleared her throat. 'Can you hear him?'

'Like a bellowing bull. Nothing wrong with his vocal cords. He was screaming and spitting in warrior fits until he went unconscious.' Rosette returned, handing the herb mixture to Nell and setting the milk on the hearth.

'A good sign, but that's not what I meant.' Nell

flushed out the wounds, covering them with the soothing ointment.

'What did you mean?'

'I was wondering if you could hear his thoughts,' she said, making a compress for the swollen eye. 'Hold this over his face. It may sting a little. Be ready.'

'It's going to hurt?'

'We have to get the swelling down to protect his optic nerve. Talk to him.'

It's okay, baby cat. It might pinch a bit, but it is going to help you heal. Trust me. I won't hurt you. She thought the words, applying the warm compress to the feline's face.

Trust ... me ... Maudi.

Rosette's eyes widened when she heard the sound in her head. She looked first at Nell and then at the injured cat.

'He's communicating already, isn't he?' Nell whispered. *Maudi?*

She stroked his back. 'He called me Maudi,' she said, her eyes welling.

'Answer him then, reassure him. Keep your thoughts flowing!'

Rosette started babbling at the kitten.

'They don't have to be aloud,' Nell said.

Rosette closed her mouth. *I'm here, little one. Maudi is here. You're going to be fine. Are you hungry?* She turned to Nell. 'I can hear him. It's impossible.'

Nell shook her head. 'After all our work this summer, you still think that some things in this world might be "impossible"?'

'But this ... I just wasn't expecting ... this.'

'Nor was I.'

Rosette turned back to the feline and wiped the crusted blood and leaves from the black fur. A tiny, sputtering, rumbling sound vibrated in its throat.

'Nell! He's choking. He must have an obstruction. Quick!'

Nell smiled, stopping her hand. 'He's not choking, Rosette.'

'What then?'

'He's purring.'

'He's *happy*?'

'Wouldn't you be? Here he is, by the fire, being looked after and loved, where a short time ago he was about to be torn apart by scavengers. He may be young, but these creatures are very intelligent. I think he knows he's got plenty to be happy about.'

Rosette smiled, stroking him again. She was lost in the vibration of his purr for some time before she looked up. 'What do you mean, "these creatures"?'

'Dumarkian temple cats.'

Rosette's mouth opened, but no words came out for several seconds. When they did, they were a mere whisper. 'He's a temple cat? Of the ancient line? Familiars to the High Priestesses? The offspring of Basta?'

'It appears so.'

'I thought they had all left when the temple was abandoned?'

'Apparently not all.' Nell washed her hands in a basin, wrung out a sponge and handed it to Rosette. 'Clean him up properly. They can't stand a hair out of place, even the younglings.'

'But, Nell, what does it mean? Are we ... are we really linked, thought to thought?'

'Maybe not the words, not yet, but he'll learn fast. Talk to him with your mind. You can learn his language too, though it's not an easy one.'

Nell touched Rosette's left forearm where she had received the tattoo of the guardian feline, Basta, months before. 'You've got yourself a familiar, Rosette. A bond with a Dumarkian temple cat is an eternal one, something to cherish and revere, forever.'

Rosette welled up again. She sent thoughts of love and safety and warmth to the little feline, and his purring increased. She sponged him clean and offered a bowl of milk. He lapped at it eagerly, white splatters flecking his whiskers.

'Help me set the fracture. He's going to be one big animal when he grows up and we want to make sure he has four strong limbs,' Nell said, her brow creasing.

'Is the break that bad?'

'It's greenstick. It'll heal fine.'

'What, then?'

'It's going to be hard to keep you anonymous with this one in tow. You'll turn every head, if you didn't already.'

'I hadn't thought of that,' Rosette said. 'What will I do?'

'Don't worry. We'll work it out.'

Through that night and for the next six weeks, Rosette rocked, carried, fed and cradled the young feline. They called him *Baby Cat* for a few days until she understood that his name was Drayco. Nell was surprised. The Drayconians were primordial creatures, thought to be from another world. They looked like black winged dragons and their auras were filled with a very old magic. The Drayconians had ruled over beginnings and endings and fateful encounters. They were placed in the star charts as the dragon's head and tail, the north and south lunar nodes — indicators of great portent.

'I never thought an eclipse on my nodes would bring such a thing.'

Nell chuckled. 'Star charts aren't about making things happen. You do that yourself. They are about authenticity and timing, the transits coinciding with events, inner and outer.'

'I get that now,' Rosette said, grooming her familiar with a soft brush. His purring filled the cottage.

Drayco grew fast, his orange eyes bright, all four legs sound. He learned her language quicker than she learned his, though she persevered with the strange vowels and consonants that formed his speech. With their minds linked, Rosette was filled with awe. Few humans shared the thoughts of a Dumarkian temple cat, now that the order had vanished. The remaining survivors were fiercely independent, most rejecting human contact and forming family structures with only their own kind.

She and Nell couldn't figure out how he ended up alone and vulnerable that day. And no matter how many times she went over the events with Drayco, he couldn't remember what had happened to his blood family. Rosette didn't know why she had been blessed to be there at the exact moment he'd needed her, but she thanked the goddess of the woods every day of her life for it.

Four summers later, Drayco's back came halfway up Rosette's thigh when he brushed against her, his tail entwining her waist. She hadn't been able to pick him up since he'd turned two.

'He's full-grown now,' Nell said, looking across the table at Rosette. The girl had her head bent over a star chart, listing the angular relationships of each planet to the others. She mumbled as she made notations in the margins, her brow knitted.

'Mars in Capricorn square Venus in Libra — no *wonder* Liam could never decide what girl he wanted. So much conflict of interest. Does he assert his will, or does he accommodate to the needs of others? It's like being a self-sufficient recluse and a social-hungry people pleaser, all at once. How can someone with this aspect do both?' She lifted her braids off the table, flipping them behind her back. 'He has to find a way if he's ever going to be happy.'

Rosette sighed. 'I'd love to know Jarrod's birth time. It's such a pity that he was a foundling — I guess an estimate's all I'll ever have for him. He was never even sure of the day.'

She looked up to see Nell watching her.

'I need more charts,' she continued after staring back at her for a moment. 'I've studied everything you have, cast the dates and times I can remember of those back home, but it's not enough. If I'm really going to understand star-craft, I need more data to work with.'

'And it seems you are too.'

'Pardon?'

'Both you and Drayco are adults now, Rosette. You turn twenty-one this summer — have you thought of what that means?'

Rosette put down her pen and capped the ink bottle. 'A bit.'

'And?'

'I want to keep studying, Nell. If I could train at one of the temples I'd really make some progress. Would that be possible?'

'Rosette!' Nell pressed her lips together to keep from smiling. *Nothing's impossible, so anything and everything is always possible. We live in a universe of infinite possibilities.*

Rosette blushed.

'Do you have a different question?' Nell asked.

Rosette hesitated for a second. 'Where can I apprentice?'

'That's better.'

'And the answer?'

'What do you want?' Nell asked.

'You already know.'

'Remind me.'

'Star-craft,' Rosette said, 'and the bow.'

'Anything else?'

'I'd like to learn more about controlling my power, about boosting the magic without having, um, side effects.' She looked at the north wall of the cottage where new cedar boards replaced the ones that she had burst into splinters last month while trying to heat a cup of tea with her thoughts. 'Spells and shape-shifting . . .'

'And what about the sword?'

Rosette started picking at a scab on her forearm. 'I'll never be good enough.'

'Not if you keep saying that to yourself, you won't!'

Rosette felt the blood rush up to her cheeks. 'Right. The sword as well.'

'Where?' Nell asked.

'Bangeesh Temple has excellent teachers of both star-lore and the bow, spell-craft and sword-craft. It'd be perfect, except . . .'

'Except their Sword Master has retired and his successor, though greatly experienced, is hopeless at teaching.'

'I didn't know that.' She raised her brows. 'I was going to say, it's very close to Lividica. We seldom speak of it, Nell, but I don't think it would be safe to go back there yet. Maybe never.'

Rosette's heart tugged as she said the words. Whole weeks went by when she didn't think of her family. When the memory did come flooding back, it was as raw as ever. And there was Jarrod. She thought of him all the time. It was like she'd seen him only yesterday, even though she knew he'd have changed. His kisses still lingered on her lips and she wished with a passion he'd stayed that night on the beach, so many years ago. She looked up, realising that Nell was talking.

'I feel the danger has passed, as long as you keep your identity to yourself. You have a point, though — the proximity of Bangeesh might jog the wrong person's memory. We don't want that.'

Rosette sighed.

'What about Treeon Temple?' Nell suggested, her lips curving into a sensual smile. 'They have an outstanding Sword Master there.'

'Treeon? Where you trained? Who's the Sword Master?'

'An' Lawrence,' Nell said evenly.

'What's his chart like? Would he be a good teacher?'

'The sun in the sign of Ceres, conjunct Saturn.'

'Meticulous. Refined, strong and exacting?'

'To say the least.'

'Moon?'

'Scorpion.'

She whistled. 'Intense?'

'Very.'

'He'd like me?'

Nell murmured, 'I imagine he would ...'

'And he's from?'

'From the east, Rosette — beyond the fields of Corsanon.' She smiled. 'He learned his art from the priestesses of Timbali, many years ago.'

'Before the Corsanon wars?'

'And during.'

'Only initiates with great potential can train with Timbali witches. Isn't that true, Nell? Either that or they're descendants of the old monarchy ...' She looked at Nell's lips. Her smile was twitching. 'Is he of that line?'

Nell nodded.

'Incredible! I thought they were all dead.'

'They're still around, alive and well, trust me. They continue to bond only among their own kind just as they had before — all arranged in accordance with bloodlines and astrological favour. Kind of makes you think of breeding thoroughbreds, doesn't it?' she chuckled.

'It does take the romance out of it.' Rosette wrinkled her nose. 'Is he married?'

Nell shook her head. 'A free spirit, that one. Anyway, An' Lawrence is from the ancient line, just like his mother and father before him.' Nell muttered under her breath, 'And demons if he doesn't know it.'

'Sounds like you two are well acquainted?'

'Well enough.'

Rosette folded her arms across her chest. 'There's a story there, I can see. But it doesn't matter. I'm not going primarily for a sword apprenticeship.' She picked at her scab again. 'No point.'

'Are you certain?'

Rosette's face tightened. 'I told you. I'm focusing on the bow, spells and stars.' She closed her book and stacked the charts into a haphazard pile, fussing with her papers when they refused to order. 'What's the big push with the sword training, Nell? I'm not all that interested.'

'You keep saying that. I don't believe it, though.'

'Why not?' Rosette pushed her chair back and stood up, her hands shoved into her pockets.

'Because *you* don't believe it. I see how you look at that practice sword leaning by the door. I watch you transform when you pick it up and spar with Maka'ra or do the forms. I can see into your heart, Rosette, and your heart is with the sword.'

Rosette lowered her eyes. She thought of Nell's friend, Maka'ra, who sailed across the Emerald Straits once a month from Rahana Iti. He was an island man with dark tattoos on his face and a mean sword arm. He and Nell seemed to have some spells brewing. They were always talking in hushed tones, or disappearing into the woods, but on each visit he would make time to train with Rosette, teaching her a style of sword she'd never seen before. Her spirit ascended whenever she heard him striding up the path. Nell was right. She loved the sword. Pity she wasn't better at it.

Nell got up and went to the door. She picked up her own bokken, a practice sword made of rosewood, the hilt carved with circular symbols and runes. She held it out flat with both hands, bowed to her stone altar near the fire and then lifted it overhead, swinging it through the air so fast Rosette saw only a blur. A whistling sound followed and Drayco jumped to his feet, back bristling. Nell's eyes burned as she stared at her.

'Pity you aren't any better?' Nell roared. *Do you hear what you are saying?*

Nell didn't wait for an answer to her mental query. She put down the bokken and returned to the table.

'Magic isn't a competition. Witchcraft, sword-craft, star-craft — none of it is about being good or bad, more or less, better or worse. It is simply about being. Sure, there are levels of competency, and tests and rituals and sparring, but ultimately the magic is energy, just like everything else. You play with it, or not. It is always there in abundance for you. Good or bad? You decide. Energy makes no such distinction.'

Rosette relaxed her face and slid back down into her chair. 'Okay, Nell. I get it. And I do want to apprentice with the sword. I want it more than anything. I've just been afraid ... I wouldn't be good enough.' She whispered the last few words.

Nell didn't respond immediately. When she did, she reached across the table and patted Rosette's hand.

'Fear is instinctive, my dear. Just don't forget that in your life you are the one creating how capable you are. If you want something with your whole heart, nothing can stop you. Do you want this with your whole heart?'

Rosette looked up. 'I do.'

'Then consider Treeon. There's much you can learn from An' Lawrence, and others there.'

'Will they accept my application?'

'I know the High Priestess.'

'Is that in my favour?'

Nell cleared her throat. 'La Makee and I have a history. It's not a completely comfortable one. Still, we are on better terms now. Shall I compose a letter to her tonight?'

Rosette took a deep breath. 'That means I would be leaving soon?'

'In late autumn, before midwinter solstice, if you're accepted.' Nell squeezed her hand. 'I know you're restless, Rosette. I also know you love it here.' She smiled. 'It's your choice. Stay or go — this year or the next. Like I said, you decide.'

'What about my story? What will I tell them of my past? They're sure to ask.'

'My experience is, always say what is closest to the truth.'

Rosette looked around the cottage, her eyes resting on her familiar stretched out in front of the crackly fire. *You ready for a change, Dray?*

I like to travel. See more of the world.

She laughed. *How do you know? You've never been anywhere.*

The massive feline yawned. *Are you certain about that, Maudi?*

Rosette's eyebrows went up. She looked back at Nell and smiled. 'Let's write the letter!'

EARTH

Chapter 4

Kreshkali closed the door of her apartment and locked it. She was out of breath from the narrow flight of stairs and the change of temperature. The crossings sapped her energy, more and more each time. She removed her long coat and gave it a shake. The rain hadn't let up nor had the relentless electrical storms that zapped above the city skyline. They never did. Earth's climate was like an endless nightmare now. When a flash of lightning lit up the windows, she scowled at it.

What good is all this star-lore if I live in a world where I can't ever see the damn things?

The smog and pollution were enough to block any view of the planets or constellations, but added to that were the clouds filled with acid rain. Daytime was no better. Solar shields had obscured the sunlight for so long that neither tree nor grass could grow any more. ASSIST still had worm-free electrical power, but they were the only ones. Their monopoly on the shields assured it.

And what good's all the power in the world if nothing can grow?

Rotting husks from long-dead trees still lined the streets, their spongy branches occasionally dropping, breaking open on the ground to release swarms of termites and cockroaches. If nothing else, the insects thrived.

I should have been an entomologist ... much easier than turning tricks.

Kreshkali survived by selling her body on the streets. It wasn't the most pleasant work, but it kept her hidden. It also connected her to the underworld and a wealth of contraband, including quantum computer texts, grimoire and other occult tomes. If she could elude ASSIST long enough, she'd find a way to destroy the worm and the Allied States with it. If it wasn't too late to restore Earth's ecosystems, it would mean freedom for herself and any who cared to join her.

But not you, eh, Jaynan?

She would have to move again. It wouldn't take long for ASSIST to send more trackers, even if Jaynan hadn't gotten a message through. Kreshkali closed her eyes, rubbing the back of her neck. She was on her own now.

I trusted you, Jaynan. I showed you the portal, gave you a new life ...

After being trapped in a world choking on the entrails of its failing technology, polluted oceans and sadistic government, Kreshkali had found a way out. She'd discovered one of the portals to the many-worlds, and it still worked.

As a child, always in secret, she'd been taught about these doors, her instruction coming to an abrupt halt when her mother was 'taken'. She was too young to recall the details, but not so young she would ever forget the look on her mother's face when they dragged her away — entombed for being a 'witch'. Kreshkali spat.

Raised half-heartedly by a distant relative, Kreshkali had educated herself with the aid of her mother's secret library. Hidden behind a wall, the shelves were arranged in ascending order, as if the woman had known her daughter would be learning on her own. Eventually Kreshkali came to study the physics of multiple dimensions in earnest, adding to the library black-market texts that had cost her a small fortune in water-credits to obtain. She'd also learned to practise the arcane arts and the mystery traditions — at great risk to her life.

Everything she did in this world was a potential crime against the Allied States. She was a witch, and for that she'd be killed. Growing up, her main goal in life was to not get caught — not be taken like her mother. That was before she'd found the box. Hidden inside a great tome, a Cantonese-English dictionary, was a message from her mother, written twenty years before. It told of her inheritance, of Docturi Janicia and her charge to continue the work — to find a way to delete the worm and bring the quantum sentient back, if he still existed. There was a horary chart, a map to the portal in the sewers under Half Moon Bay, and there were pages of drawings about the genetic changes in her DNA. She'd found the portal and she'd crossed over to Gaela, but in all her searching, she'd discovered no trace of JARROD.

Had he survived?

She didn't have the resources or the methodology to build another quantum sentient, even with his backup CPU. If JARROD was gone, that was it until she could find the original Richter journals. Rumour had it they'd all been destroyed at the turn of the century, before the major plate shifts. Her lips twisted into a half smile. Journals or no, she'd need a more sophisticated laboratory than her apartment kitchen to build a quantum computer — not to mention a steady power supply.

She lit another candle, shaking her head. Her only consolation was that no child of hers would ever see her dragged away. She damned ASSIST and the Allied States in her mind. She'd learned the hard way not to do it out loud.

The Allied States — the remaining lands of North America, fragments of the Euro-community, and a few settlements in what was left of India and Japan — competed with each other for every scrap of food and every drop of water left on Earth. The only thing that held them together was military-enforced domination and the threat of attack from any nation not bound by the original constitution. Its governing body had declared martial law at the end of the last century and controlled both the gangland cities and the impoverished outposts, while within the fortresses of ASSIST — a now impenetrable institution from inside or out — no-one knew what went on. The worm still threatened any new software or global wire devised. She suspected ASSIST wanted to keep it that way, at least for now. Would they also be working on the problem of drinking water and lack of sunlight? There might be a way to find out. She looked at her chronometer and noted the exact time. She would draw up the horary chart later, when she was certain she hadn't been followed. The witch-trackers were an immediate threat, and they were on her trail.

The study of quantum theory had been prohibited, along with the practice of astrology and other occult arts, especially by women. The gender biases prevalent up to the twenty-fourth century had returned in full force. Women were held responsible for the downfall of civilisation, again. Like Eve, Janis Richter was being cited as the new Pandora — the source of all evil on Earth, a plague to mankind. Her line must be stamped out, at any cost. Females found emulating her in methodology, knowledge or action were put to death, cruelly. The search for her descendants continued. Kreshkali's guts twisted at the thought.

An updated version of Sprenger and Kramer's fifteenth-century work, *The Hammer of Witches*, had been revived in the twenty-fourth century resulting in mass persecutions, burnings and hangings. Millions of women had been executed in the past fifty years alone — after heinous torture — for nothing more incriminating than reading a book on herbal medicine or feeding a stray cat.

A peal of thunder boomed as rain lashed against the windows. Kreshkali yawned, knowing she needed to work. The only thing of any real value on Earth any more was purified water, and she sold her body to get it. Her credits were currently depleted, even with her recent trips to Gaela, but she had to sleep before getting back to the streets. She'd turn a few tricks before dawn sent everyone scuttling for shelter. But first she needed a nap.

She struggled out of her boots and stripped, tossing her clothes onto the back of a chair. Running her hands through her short, spiky hair she let out a sigh, tensing as a fist pounded on her door. She looked again at the chronometer.

'Yeah, what?'

'Kali! Get out here. I got you a client.'

'I can get my own fucking tricks, Jimmy.'

'Not like this one. I'll give you sixty percent.'

'What's he worth?'

'Three pints — high quality.'

She tilted her head to the side, working the knots in her left shoulder.

'I'll do him. Give me five.' She yawned again.

'Want to know what he asked for?'

'Naw.'

She flopped down into the narrow cot and closed her eyes. *Five more minutes.*

Kreshkali read the text aloud, her voice resonating through the empty apartment.

> *'If the Entity wavers at the door,*
> *Collect both waters pure as mist.*
> *Close your eyes against the teeming horde,*
> *Of the sea-devil's avid twist.*
> *Add high blood and bottle tight*
> *With Luna behind the solar lot.*
> *Will the double helix bond right,*
> *And keep open the Ring-Pass-Not?'*

She bookmarked her place, grabbed her coat and headed to the jetty.

She looked over her shoulder as she neared the sea-wall. Footsteps echoed behind her, but that was only of mild concern. She'd be out of this shit-hole in a matter of hours, and when she returned she'd have enough water to stay off the streets for a month, giving her time to study and unravel the mystery of the portal Entity.

The rain had eased, as it often did around dawn. There was a sliver of rose light on the horizon, illuminating the skyscrapers — an illusion of sunrise that wouldn't last. The darkness and the thunder, and the acidic rain returned, as always, along with the savagery of each new day. She cursed as she stepped in a puddle, the water soaking her boot. The seawall was two streets ahead — almost there.

She'd left her last trick with his pants unzipped. A vial of pure-grade water — her fee — was resting safely in her coat pocket.

This time it'll work.

The obscure words of the Draconic Tablets rolled over in her mind.

Her first two attempts at deciphering their meaning and weaving a spell that would create an interim firewall in the portal had failed. She knew the spell was possible, though — in fact, necessary — if she was to preserve the portal's waning integrity. It was a temporary fix, but it would keep her from getting trapped on either side. She had business to attend to in both worlds and she needed to keep the doorway open.

The spell had to be conjured during the black of the moon — just minutes before it turned new — and it required several drops of fresh, clear, unpolluted H_2O from both land and sea.

The seas hadn't been pure for centuries; the once crystal waters of California, with its legendary tubing green waves and endless kelp forests, were gone, along with the iron-blue depths of the Atlantic seaboard and the turquoise lagoons of the Pacific Rim. All the way from the Mediterranean to Australia's Great Barrier Reef the oceans had become a cesspool teeming with sea-devils.

Nothing's impossible, she reminded herself.

She took the next side street and squeezed through a gap in a chain-link fence. She had to climb over rubble left from the last quake and avoid a squatters' camp. People still lived in the slanting shanties that remained, even with walls destroyed and their lives exposed like a twentieth-century movie set. The damage must have been from last year, she thought as she climbed over the rocks. There hadn't been any major rips through this city since Santa Barbara had gone under.

A dog barked from somewhere within the warrens, followed by the sound of glass breaking and a woman's shriek.

Good morning, California. Rise and shine!

She could smell the ocean, its fetid waves pounding against the granite seawall, eating away at mortar and rock. Her tongue tingled with the acridity of it. She gritted her teeth and approached the tideline. Waves tumbled in, vomiting their contents — leaving fresh devils in the pocks and crannies. Perspiration beaded on her forehead as she watched the ebb and flow of each set, counting the seconds between.

Go! She dashed forward as the brown water sucked out, draining away to leave only a few puddles. She squatted before one, careful not to let her bottom drop too low, and pulled the stopper from the glass tube. She dipped the vial into the turgid soup, scooping it up almost full. It swarmed with tiny organisms as she held it up towards the pale daylight. She drove the stopper in and ran before the next wave crashed.

She kept running until she reached the chain-link fence.

'Where you rushing to, Sugar?'

The hairs on the back of her neck stood out. She heard the flick of a cigarette lighter and turned around. Smoke billowed above a shadowed face.

'I'm clocked off, buddy,' she said, walking away. 'If you want something, talk to ...'

'I'm talking to you, bitch.'

She heard a trigger cock and turned to see a gun levelled at her chest.

Her face relaxed and her shoulders softened. She let her eyes lose focus as she took a slow, deep breath. Without warning she struck, her kick connecting with his right arm, knocking the gun to the pavement where it fired into the empty street.

The heel of her left hand drove up under his chin, dislocating his jaw and sending him sprawling backwards. She jumped after him, catching his neck between her forearms before he hit the ground. With a twist, she snapped it.

'Said I was clocked off, arsehole,' she mumbled under her breath, letting the body drop.

She glanced around before disappearing into the gloom.

In her apartment Kreshkali re-read the incantation by candlelight. The book was actually a text on quantum DNA transmutation and reality shifting, but its language had been couched in a poetic vernacular that Kreshkali found difficult to understand. The few surviving works on quantum magic, as well as hyper-dimensional space, astrology, tarot and numerology, were all written this way, to keep the knowledge occult — to keep it safe. *So well disguised not a witch alive has a clue what it says.*

She knitted her brow. This text, the one she'd paid so dearly for, was particularly meaningful to her. She knew the author had defected from ASSIST centuries ago. He was Luka Paree, a man whose work with quantum communication in DNA broke new ground. She smiled at his image on the back jacket, worn thin but still visible. He was a handsome man, Janicia's lover.

She rubbed her thumb across it before reading aloud. 'If the Entity wavers at the door, collect both waters pure as mist.'

She had the pure water from land. She just needed to deal with the polluted sea water. The technique, she discovered, was woven into the spell itself.

'Add high blood and bottle tight.'

'High blood' had thrown her until she realised it simply meant the blood of a High Priestess. On Earth, 'High Priestess' described the descendants of the Techno-Witch — Janis Richter — in whose DNA was hidden many things, including the key to neutralising the sea-devils. She'd had the answer inside her, all along.

She pricked her finger and squeezed it over the vial, counting out the drops. She pushed the stopper back in and swirled the contents around.

'With Luna behind the solar lot.'

It took her quite a while to decode this phrase, but she'd worked it out. Luna was the ancient reference to the Earth's companion satellite, and *lot* was another name — even more antiquated — for an astrological mansion or house. The only time the Moon was behind the Sun's house was just before it turned new — when it was dark as dark.

'Will the double helix bond right.'

The 'double helix bond' was deoxyribonucleic acid — DNA — the long chains of protein that carried genetic information as well as the chemicals that could, on a very small scale, deactivate the sea-devils and make the water pure.

It's in your blood, her mother had always said.

She read on. 'And keep open the Ring-Pass-Not?'

The 'Ring-Pass-Not' was the portal, and the only thing that worried her about this phrase was that it was a question, not a statement.

Would it work? Even Luka Paree had been uncertain.

If it was successful, the portal would stabilise, at least for the time being. It would stay open, giving her the power to travel through whenever she wanted and bring back whatever she pleased. As it was, she could only take the clothes she wore, the trinkets in her pockets and a few water-skins at a time. If the spell worked, she'd be able to carry more, and avoid some of the less pleasant side effects of dimension travel — debilitation not the least.

Holding the vial up to the candlelight, she watched. The mud-coloured sea water, roiling with micro-organisms, began to clarify. In a moment, it refracted the light — crystal clear and sparkling. She smiled. Like an alchemist, she mixed it back and forth with the other vial before pouring the concoction into a small spray atomiser and capping it shut. From what she understood it was simply a matter of releasing the contents as she travelled the corridors between the worlds, an offering to the Entities.

She'd know soon enough. The portal was five minutes away.

GAELA

Chapter 5

'Not a soul in sight,' Rosette whispered, looking up and down the road.

Hills undulated towards the distance. They were bare and brown, haggard as the cows that dotted them. The beasts walked slowly, heads close to the ground, their nostrils blowing puffs of dust as they searched for grass. Everything smelled of manure, dirt and burnt wood. The air hung thick with smoke, muddying the sky. This place was a striking contrast to the lush fields of Dumarka and their butterball livestock, laden fruit trees and dense forests.

Rosette turned towards the dry shrubs. 'You won't wander far, will you, Dray?' she said, raising her voice above the riotous squabbling of crows flapping amongst the oaks.

She took off her gloves and tucked them into her pack, smiling as three larger black birds shot towards the east, squawking a ruckus as they did so.

'You don't have to watch me, Nell.'

Nell doesn't watch, Maudi. The Three Sisters do.

'Same thing.'

The sun had finally reached high enough over the eastern mountains to warm the frosty morning. She rubbed her hands together, letting her hood fall back. The scab on the side of her head caught, and she winced, feeling its rough edges. It was yet another one, quite close to her eye. She shrugged. A mark from her own sword, it would match the nick on the left side of her face, a reminder to stay focused and ignore distractions. She shook her head, trying not to think of how skilled the other students at Treeon would be.

It's not a competition!

Rosette stretched her arms over her head, bangles clinking together when her wrists touched. The silver and lapis bands sparkled in the sunlight. They were a birthday gift from Nell.

Twenty-one years, my Rosette. Look what you have developed — strength, knowledge and a thirst for magic. Now all you have to do is cultivate discipline. Let these bangles be a steady reminder of that intention.

Rosette loved the bangles. She didn't know if wearing them would help her concentration or not, though it didn't hurt to have them on. She had felt grounded since she'd left Dumarka, a lot more so than five years ago — the last time she'd travelled. Of course, then she was running for her life. Now she was striding towards a new one.

It'll come to you, Rosette. It'll come. Nell had said the words so many times when they'd sparred and studied, they had become like a mantra. Rosette had found it easier to believe when she was within sight of Nell. Now, far away, a niggling doubt snuck in. What if it didn't come to her? She touched the scab again. What if she failed?

Then she heard Nell's voice in her mind. *Intention! What you think becomes what you experience.*

Rosette smiled. 'I will succeed then,' she said, aloud to make it stronger.

Stretching once more, she rocked back onto her heels then up to her toes, flexing her whole body. Her muscles ached for some decent exercise. By the looks of it, she'd get plenty of that today.

'Maybe we should've paid the coach driver to take us right up to the gates, instead of hoping for a lift.'

Maybe if you hadn't argued with him, he would have.

'He wanted a month's rent in gold just to get within a mile of Treeon Temple, Dray.' She scanned the trees while undoing the front buttons of her cloak. 'What's the matter with people? Why are they so greedy?'

Maybe they don't think they have enough.

'Enough what, I wonder?'

That's a very good question. Do you think we have enough time?

As Drayco's thoughts filled her mind, Rosette watched the big black feline emerge from the woods. He sauntered around the fringing oaks, head high and tail swaying back and forth like a lazy fan. His orange eyes flashed when he spotted her.

'You're right, Drayco. We'd best get walking.' She held her hand out towards him as he leapt down the embankment. The momentum carried him forward and he bumped her thigh with the top of his head. His purr hummed around them.

When are we meant to arrive?

'Noon.' She looked down the road. 'Can we make it?'

Drayco sniffed the air, turning his face up to Rosette. *Nope.*

'Pessimist.'

Realist. On foot, it's too far, unless you care to run the whole way. I can, of course. Can you?

Rosette scratched behind his ears and sighed. 'Maybe we'll get a lift.'

Drayco studied the road, his tail twitching as his head turned left and right. *Who from?*

'Honestly? I have no idea.' She laughed. 'Let's go.' She gave Drayco a final scratch and hoisted her bag.

It wouldn't be much fun, jogging along with the weight she carried, but it wouldn't pay to be late either. She set off at a brisk walk, taking in the landscape. Twisted oak trees and groves of tall redwoods spread out to her right while over-grazed pastures rambled off to her left. A rickety barbed-wire fence bordered each side of the dirt road, the posts listing at odd angles where the wire had sagged or snapped. She felt sad for the beasts scattered across the fields. The ones she could see close up looked about to calve.

'Don't they cut hay in this part of the country?'

Doesn't look like it. Drayco sniffed the air. *A few valleys further, they do.*

'Good nose, Dray.'

Thank you.

An occasional 'moo' haunted the valley, reminding Rosette of the foghorns that boomed across Lister Bay. The sound made the road seem even more desolate. She shivered, glancing at the sky. Aside from a flock of pigeons circling above and a few white egrets amongst the cows, she and Drayco were alone. Even the Three Sisters had vanished. Dropping any hope of getting a lift with a passing farmer, Rosette looked briefly behind her, straightened her shoulders and started to jog.

She'd been travelling for days, mostly in the comfort of a first-class coach. The smooth roads and clear weather had given her time to read and muse while Drayco stretched out across the opposite seat, alternately napping and staring at the countryside rolling by. That luxury had ended abruptly this morning when she had learned how much the driver wanted to take her to the gates of the Treeon Temple. Clearly he'd thought he had her stumped.

He quoted a price five times higher than it had cost to get here from Dumarka, a week's coach ride. She would rather walk than be robbed outright, and had told him so.

'Be my guest,' he'd said, laughing as he dumped her heavy pack on the side of the road. 'See how far you get on your own legs, luscious as they are.'

She felt certain he had more to say, but Drayco had stepped forward, his lips pulled back in a snarl. The coachman had tipped his hat and drove off in a cloud of dust. Good riddance.

Rosette trotted down the road and Drayco loped at her side, energetic and alert. He darted off into the bushes and scuttled straight up tall pines only to shimmy down with much twisting and turning of his head. It made her laugh. He was five years old now, but still such a juvenile at times. His tail lashed as he stalked prey, real or imagined, she didn't know which. At least the journey was amusing him.

She shifted the weight of her pack and slowed to a walk, trudging up a steep hill, using her staff as a walking stick.

When they crested the rise, she let out a long, hearty exclamation, 'Woooheeee! Look at that view!'

Quiet, Maudi. I'm hunting. Drayco's eyes were fixed on a gopher hole by the side of the road, little spurts of dirt shooting from its opening.

'Oh, come on, Dray. Look out there.' She pointed towards the magnificent valley, a wide river coursing through it. The pastures were golden, rippling with tall oat grass and pale green alfalfa. 'It's so inviting. Let's get to the water and have a snack.'

My snack's right here. Hush, before you scare it away. Drayco sat inches from the gopher hole, ears pricked forward, frozen like a statue. Little flicks of dirt were flying up from the depths, making his whiskers twitch with each spurt. He bunched his haunches.

Before he could pounce, Rosette stiffened. 'Someone's coming,' she whispered.

Drayco spun around, his head high, his mouth opening slightly to taste the air. His hackles rose, almost touching Rosette's hip as he pressed against her. *Danger?*

She squinted. 'I doubt it. Looks like a lad on a plough horse to me.'

Drayco took another sniff then yawned. *Great. Here come more interruptions.*

'Or, great! Here comes our ride.'

And there goes my snack.

She laughed.

A huge, dappled grey horse trotted towards them, head down, eyes half closed, shaggy fetlocks scuffing the hard-packed dirt, making dust rise with each hoof fall. He carried a young man and a lot of gear. His rider wore a green cloak and a blue scarf with a small guitar slung across his back. Oblivious, he whistled as he bounced along.

He doesn't smell like a farm boy. Drayco stood watching their approach, his hackles slowly dropping.

'I don't know about that, but not many farm boys travel with their guitars. Better let me do the talking.'

If you insist, Maudi.

Rosette and Drayco watched while he crested the hill. She guessed the lad was a little younger than her, perhaps in his late teens. He certainly looked comfortable on that big horse — his expression merry beneath a brightly coloured knitted cap. She returned his smile instantly.

'Whoa.' He pulled his mount to a halt.

The horse didn't seem at all troubled to find a temple cat and a cloaked woman in the middle of the road. He fluttered his nostrils in their direction and then looked quietly into the distance, seeming pleased at the chance to rest. It surprised Rosette. Usually Drayco created quite a stir among equines, at least at first.

'Finally, some people,' the young man said. 'You're the first I've seen all morning.'

Rosette looked up into his bright blue eyes, about to speak.

'I'm Clay Cassarillo, from the Southern Cusca Plains.' He made a bowing gesture from atop the horse, pulling off his cap to release a shock of curly red hair.

'I'm Rosette de Santo,' she said with a quick dip of her head. 'This is Drayco, from the Dumarkian Woods.'

'Wow, two dark beauties from the lands of Dumarka. This is my lucky day,' he exclaimed as he dropped the reins, kicked free of the stirrups, and jumped to the ground, a large leather bag and bedroll dangling precariously as he landed.

The horse sighed and cocked a hind leg.

'That's some cat!' Clay's expression became even livelier. 'Is he your ... your ...'

'Familiar?'

'Is he?'

'Yes,' Rosette said. 'My companion.'

Clay leaned his back against the horse, not taking his eyes off Drayco. 'I've heard of Dumarkian temple cats. I never thought I'd see one this close up. He's huge.'

'Drayco is large even for his kind.'

'Can I pat him?' he asked, reaching out his hand.

'I wouldn't,' Rosette said, stepping between them.

He can touch me if he wants to lose some fingers. I wouldn't mind a crunchy snack. The gopher's gone ...

It didn't sound like he was kidding.

'Definitely leave him, Clay. He's not a tabby-cat.'

He clasped his hands behind his back. 'How did you meet him?'

'It's a long story,' she answered, gazing out across the valley.

Clay brushed horsehair from his pants and followed her line of sight. 'Demons, it's beautiful here.'

'Do you travel much?' she asked.

'This is the furthest I've ever been, but I plan on doing a lot more.' He pushed a lock of hair from his face. 'I'm a bard.'

'A journeyman bard? Really?'

'Not quite. I'm an apprentice. I won't make journeyman for another year, though I plan on covering a lot of territory when I do. I'm headed for Treeon Temple to continue my studies. Gotta be there by noon.'

'That's where we're going.' Rosette smiled at him, watching his eyes light up.

'Witch?'

'You might say.'

'Apprentice too?'

'Initiate. I'm to apprentice at Treeon.'

'Well, Rosette de Santo, you're never going to make it there on time. It's too far to walk.'

'I realise this.' She took her long cloak off and draped it over her pack; her dark green dress swept around her ankles as she leaned over. It covered her curves like soft skin on ripe fruit; it was something Clay noted, judging by his open-mouthed stare.

'Want a lift?' he asked, taking a breath and tearing his gaze from her body to look her in the eye.

'That'd be wonderful, thank you.'

'There's one condition.' He winked at her as he spoke.

'Condition?'

'You have to agree,' he said in a rush.

'What?' Her forehead creased. *Here we go. Boys and their one-track minds.*

'Tell me how you got your familiar and I'll get you to Treeon on time.'

Rosette laughed. 'That's it?'

'Yep.'

'You're on.'

Classic, Maudi. You ride all cushy on that fur-topped mountain, no doubt with the lad's erection pressed against your backside, and I follow along like a dog.

First up, Dray, I'll ride behind. No pressing of anything anywhere. And second, my black lovely beast, you couldn't follow like a dog if you tried.

Drayco sat for a moment and licked his paw. *You're correct on that.*

She smiled and half closed her eyes. Bending down to kiss the top of his head, she felt his silent purr.

'I don't know what just happened,' Clay said, staring at the two, 'but I'm guessing we have the temple cat's approval to move on.'

'We do.' She looked up at the horse and wrinkled her nose. 'How tall is he?'

'Dozer's every inch of 21.1 hands.' Clay reached up to the horse's withers. 'He's my family's draughter, pride of the village. I've only got him on loan. Come on, we can line up next to that fence and use the post as a boost. Is this all your stuff?'

Rosette nodded, still gazing at the horse as Clay moved him over to the fence, re-tying his bedroll and duffle bag onto the back of the saddle. He pulled the guitar over his head, strumming a few chords and breaking into a spontaneous song about travelling with a beautiful witch, before strapping it to the saddle as well. Rosette handed him her staff but kept her backpack on. Once Clay was up on Dozer, Rosette grabbed a handful of white mane, stepped on a fence rail and mounted behind him.

'Great view,' she exclaimed.

Clay took a deep breath as she slipped her arm around his waist. He glanced down at her long slender fingers over his belly. 'Better than I'd imagined.'

It took a bit of urging to get Dozer's head out of the oat-tasselled grass and into a smart trot down the middle of the road. Once in motion, Drayco loped beside them.

'So how did it happen?' Clay asked.

'Pardon?'

'How did you bond with a wild temple cat from the Dumarkian Woods?'

'That's a day I'll never forget for as long as I live,' she sighed.

Rosette closed her eyes and let the memory fill her mind.

Are you going to tell him? Drayco asked.

'Do you mind?'

I like hearing my story.

Rosette smiled. 'Me too.'

'This is really weird, Rosette. It's like listening in to half a conversation. Can he understand you aloud as well as your thoughts?' Clay asked as he urged Dozer around some large potholes in the road.

'Either way he hears me, I hear him.'

'Does he understand what I say too?'

'Sure, even with your accent.'

'What accent?'

Rosette laughed. '*That* accent, country boy.' She gave his belly a pinch.

Clay twisted around to catch her eye. 'I assure you I do *not* have an accent.'

'That's fine if you think so, but don't be surprised if the other bards make mention of the way you say your *a*'s and *e*'s and *r*'s.'

'They'll shut up when they hear me play. I'm quite decent.'

'That's good to know. Now, are you ready for this tale or not?'

'Fire away.'

'It happened five years ago. I was sixteen.'

'Really? That means we're the same age.'

'We are?'

'I am turning twenty-one after midwinter solstice, in the month of the Water-bearer.'

'Well, I'm before you. I turned in the summer, in the month of the Twins.'

'Perfect. I love older women.' He took both reins in his left hand and gave her thigh a squeeze.

Rosette nudged him with her shoulder. 'Settle down. We aren't going to have any escapades today. We'd never get there on time.'

'Oh, I can be quick if I have to.'

Rosette laughed. 'I'm sure you can.' She leaned forward. 'Clay Cassarillo,' she whispered, feeling the curve of his ear against her lips, 'speed doesn't much impress me.'

He laughed. 'I can take my time. I'm quite decent at that as well.'

'Also good to know,' she said.

'And I'll mind my manners.'

'You best do so. This is not just a walking stick I carry.'

'It isn't?'

'I train with the sword.'

'You're going to the right place then. Sword Master An' Lawrence is the best.'

'So I've heard.'

Dozer clopped across a wooden bridge and ploughed tirelessly up the next hill, as Drayco scampered through the creek coursing for water rats.

'It was five years ago?' Clay encouraged her to continue.

'I was living with my mentor on the edge of the Dumarkian Woods.'

'Did you grow up there?'

'Not really.'

'Where were your parents?'

'It's complicated. I left home rather suddenly.' It couldn't hurt to tell him some version of the truth. He was just an apprentice bard and this would be good practice for getting her story down. She hadn't counted on his persistent questions, though.

'Why?'

Silence.

'Really,' Clay repeated. 'Why did you leave your home suddenly?'

'If you must know, I'd had a fight with my mother.'

'About what?' Clay asked.

'It doesn't matter.'

'I think it does.'

'It doesn't.'

'If it led to you bonding with a temple cat, it does.'

Rosette sighed into the back of his neck. 'Oh, all right. You can have the whole murky story if you want. You'll be wishing you hadn't asked soon enough.'

'I doubt that. I'm a bard. Stories are my stock and trade.'

'What?'

'Stories are my stock and . . .'

'Listen to me, Clay Cassarillo. You're not to trade this one. I don't want to hear any songs or rhymes or limericks going around that have even a hint of what I'm about to tell you. On pain of my wrath, do you understand me?'

'Oh, come on. It's gotta be a fantastic tale.'

'It's one you will never hear if you can't keep it to yourself.'

Silence filled the space between them as Dozer jogged along.

'I understand,' Clay finally agreed. 'It's in the vault.'

'All right then. I was sixteen and I'd just had a dreadful fight with my mother.'

She started a marvellous tale, one that could easily have been true if her family hadn't been murdered, her horse shot dead and her best friend Jarrod barred from her life. It felt good to tell a new version, a less traumatic one.

This is how it could have been.

'Wow. You ran away from home because they wanted you to marry a wealthy merchant?' Clay leaned back as Dozer picked up speed in a hammering downhill trot. The boy's back bounced against her shoulder, jarring into her collarbone with every stride. 'I would have done the same.'

'Really?'

Clay shrugged. 'Maybe not. My family's always been supportive. This is actually the first time I've been away from home.'

'Sounds like you've lived a sheltered life,' she said, her lip curling.

'You don't have to say it like it's bad.'

She nodded. 'You're right. It's probably really lovely. I might be jealous, is all.'

He patted her leg. 'Then what happened, Rosette? Did your mentor give him to you?'

'No one can give you a familiar. You find each other and if it's right, you bond.'

'Like love. I got it.'

Rosette wasn't certain he did. As she formed her thoughts to explain it to him, she wasn't even certain she understood. 'Familiars aren't pets, Clay. They're autonomous creatures with a life of their own. What makes them distinct is their ability to communicate and to switch ...'

'I know, I know. You can trade off bodies for a time, him in yours and you in his. Do you do that?'

'Sometimes, when I'm asleep.'

'How do you know it isn't a dream?'

'Well, for one thing, I wake up with twigs in my hair and mud on my feet.'

'Wow!' Clay twisted around in the saddle to look at her, his blue eyes sparkling. 'Tell me how he chose you.'

'If you'll stop interrupting me, I will.'

'Not another word.' He pressed his lips together tight.

She laughed. 'Where was I?'

'You were on a clipper ship, running away from your family, heading for your mentor's cottage at the edge of the Dumarkian Woods. Say, how did you get a mentor anyway?'

Rosette shook her head back and forth. The boy's mind was like a box of trapped lightning.

'My mentor was friends with my mother. We'd visit every now and then. I'd wanted to move up there to train full-time, but ...'

'But?'

'My mother said I was too young and that the life of a witch would only bring me trouble and pain.'

'That's harsh. So then what?'

'I was heading for Dumarka, unsure of how I'd be received. I hadn't heard from my mentor in several years. But I found her, and she initiated me and taught me everything I know about the stars and spells and the bow.'

'Did she train you in the sword too?' Clay asked as he urged Dozer onward.

'Nell uses other weapons for the most part, but she has a friend — an island man. He taught me the forms and sparring.'

'Is that where you got the scars?'

Rosette rubbed the long red slash on her forearm. 'Yes.'

'You play rough.'

'He wanted me to be able to defend myself.'

'Can you?'

'I can.'

Clay whistled. 'And you're a star-watcher too? Tell me about the Water-bearer.'

'I thought you wanted to know about Drayco.'

'I want to know everything.'

'That's what I would say of a Water-bearer, especially if he had Moon in the sign of the Twins.'

Clay laughed. 'You're good.'

'Maybe we should stop for a drink. One of us is about to anyway,' Rosette said as Dozer pulled off to the side of the road where another creek babbled past.

The two slid off the horse's back and stretched. Rosette looked up at the now cloudless sky. 'It's an hour before midday. How close do you think we are to Treeon?'

'We'll make it.' He pointed a ropey arm into the distance. 'It's only a couple of miles.'

'You've been there before?'

'I have a map.' He straightened his shoulders. 'A bard has to know his way around the world, milady.'

'Yes, and that too is a trait of the Water-bearer.'

'What?'

'Always knowing where they're going, always in control.'

'And that's a bad thing?'

'It's not a bad thing.' Rosette smiled at his perplexity. 'It's not a good thing either. It's a Water-bearer thing.' She winked to make him smile back. 'Let's eat.'

Clay flipped up the stirrup to loosen the girth a few notches, giving Dozer a chance to breathe deeply between gulps of water.

'Our first picnic!' he said, cocking his head towards the carpet of recently mowed oat grass. It was tasselled here and there with bells of lavender flowers from the late-blooming flax.

'A meal ... not a romp.' Rosette pulled a loaf of bread from her pack and split it in two before unwrapping a small parcel of cheese. 'Hungry?'

'Yes, please. I've got red apples, fresh from my family's orchards.'

Does he have any mice in there? Drayco eyed Clay chomping into the crunchy fruit.

No, Dray, but I have more dried beef.

Chewy meat?

Yes. Come and let me pick the grass seeds from your belly while we eat.

Clay cleared his throat. 'Can't at least one of you speak aloud? It's unnerving.'

'We're discussing lunch.'

'I'm not on the menu, am I?'

Rosette laughed. 'Don't worry. It's only your pockets that interest him, for now.'

Clay took the bread and cheese she handed him in exchange for one of the apples and settled next to Rosette on the grass. He was careful to keep her between himself and the temple cat.

'Come on,' he said around a mouthful of food. 'What happened next?'

They lounged in the grass by the creek, eating and talking, Rosette telling how she'd rescued Drayco. While she spoke, the temple cat chewed on strips of dried beef, his white teeth flashing in the sunlight, red tongue licking his chops. Dozer did what he was named for. He dozed.

'Mother of the plains and rivers! And you say I can't tell anyone? Are you kidding? It's worthy of an entire ballad!' Clay protested as they packed up their bags.

'I shared it with *you*, not the world. Keep it to yourself or I'll ...'

'I just think it's a waste, locked away like that.'

Rosette looked at Drayco stretching in the sun. 'It's not a waste.'

Clay shook his head then scrambled up onto Dozer. He held Rosette's staff, and hauled her up behind him.

'I'm honoured you shared it with me.' His voice took on a different tone.

'You're welcome.' Rosette smoothed her dress. 'Now come on. We only have half an hour by my mark. I don't want to miss the welcoming.'

With that, Clay pulled the horse's head out of the grass and clucked to him. They didn't move. He reached his arm behind Rosette and slapped the horse's round dappled rump, sending a cloud of dust skyward. Dozer accelerated into a smooth trot.

'Trust me, milady. Clay Cassarillo will get you there on time.'

Chapter 6

'Sacred demons,' Rosette whispered as they came to a halt at the top of a cliff. 'Look at it.'

'It's bigger than I thought.' Clay pulled off his cap and stuffed it into his back pocket. 'Looks like a nest of ants from here.'

She braced an arm against Dozer's haunches, leaning back from Clay to get a better view of the valley. Swarms of people in dark robes flowed out of buildings and into the courtyards surrounding the main temple. Some on horseback, most on foot, they filled the pathways and thoroughfares, all intent on a common destination. Rosette traced the course of traffic and saw that everyone was headed to a raised oval at the west end of the valley.

'That's where we're going,' she said, pointing towards the manicured field.

Black and green flags snapped in the breeze around the perimeter where a drill team warmed up their mounts. They were divided into groups of six, the horses well matched by colour and size — blacks, bays, chestnuts, greys and one golden palomino in the lead. Their synchronised movements looked like a kaleidoscope of shifting shapes and colours.

Rosette felt butterflies in her belly. 'It's the equestrian training ground. Look at all those stables behind it.'

'Massive,' Clay said, following the direction of her still-outstretched hand.

He gave Dozer's shoulder a playful slap as he urged him down the descent that zigzagged its way to the valley floor.

'Now, Rosette, what did I say?'

She smiled. 'You said Clay Cassarillo would get me here on time.'

'And I did!'

'Thanks, Clay. You're wonderful.' She leaned forward, kissing his cheek. His face lifted into a wide grin as he turned around and caught her lips with a kiss of his own.

'My pleasure, I assure you,' he said in a soft voice.

There's another temple cat here! Drayco dashed ahead, down the slope, and out of sight.

'Wait up, Dray. You can't just burst in unannounced!'

Did you hear me, Maudi? It's another feline!

'He's not listening,' she said into Clay's ear. *That's terrific news, Dray. But can you talk to him first so you don't take everyone by surprise?*

It's a 'her'.

Right. Can you talk to her? Rosette squeezed Clay's leg and whispered, 'It's a "her".'

'Who's a "her"? What are you two talking about?'

She won't link. I know she's here. I can smell her, but she hides. Drayco had stopped his descent and was pacing back and forth across the road halfway down the grade.

'Why does she hide?'

No idea.

'Maybe you're scaring her.'

Me?

'Yes, Dray-Dray. You. How about we all enter together? There's plenty of time to meet her. We're going to be here for years.'

Hurry up then.

'What's he saying?' Clay asked.

'There's another temple cat about, it seems.'

'Didn't you know? The Sword Master has a familiar. She's not Dumarkian, though. She's from the southern cliffs of Tuscaro.'

'Where's that?'

'A month's sail and another on foot to the east.'

'It sounds like the far end of the world.'

'It is ...'

She tapped him on his shoulder. 'You've been there!'

'No!' Clay grabbed her hand and gave it a squeeze. 'I haven't been anywhere yet. I just look at ...'

'I know. Maps.'

They fell silent as Dozer's iron-shod hooves clicked over the cobbled road. He seemed more animated now, clearly picking up on their excitement. His neck arched and Clay had to shorten his reins to keep him to a walk.

'Someone's waking up,' Rosette observed.

Clay didn't answer.

The long descent gave Rosette time to survey the temple valley. It had an ancient feel, its architecture and design preserved for hundreds of years. She'd read about the living history of Treeon but had had no idea how tangible it was, until now.

The trees alone took her breath away. There were massive willows and dark green oaks, wind-contoured cypress along the cliff face, and tall, white-barked eucalypts below, all shimmering and swaying with contrasting shades and hues. Spotting row upon row of jacarandas made her laugh out loud. Her favourite tree in all of Gaela lived here.

'I can't wait for spring,' she said, waving towards a lengthy row. A combination of acacias and jacarandas lined most of the thoroughfares to the furthest ends of the valley. 'Can you just imagine the colours when they bloom?'

'I can, and look there.' Clay nodded towards a grove of evergreens near the central plaza. 'The size of them!'

She'd never seen redwoods so big. 'They must be hundreds of years old.'

'Thousands, I'll wager.'

It would take a chain of twenty people to surround some of the larger trunks standing sentinel in front of the main gates. Their pointed tops, like arrows, thrust skyward, challenging the distant mountains.

The buildings around the central plaza were of a sophisticated design, more ornate than anything she had seen in Dumarka or Lividica. They were mostly two storey, and many had rounded turrets or domed roofs. They sported long, brightly decorated flags of many colours, flying like kites over the temple square.

Wide stairs flowed down from every entrance, a cascade of steps leading to a massive weeping willow in the midst of the main courtyard. There, statues stood at each corner of the plaza — guardians of the four directions.

She couldn't see all of them clearly, but she got chills from the ones she could. The east corner held a winged lion with a long tail and sharp claws, crouched to pounce, or perhaps take flight. The statue to the north was like a sea lion, laid out in a playful, luxuriant recline, as if nothing could be of any threat. It was rotund, jovial, with pups in tow. The statue to the west was a Draconian, a winged dragon rising from an angry sea. She couldn't make out the south, blocked by the feathery branches of the willow.

On the opposite side of the oval, she saw a long wooden building with rows of metal-strapped kegs, some stacked high against the wall and others in unhitched wagons. Past them were acres of dormant fruit trees with bare branches, braced for winter. Treeon was famous for its apple cider. She remembered tasting it in Lividica and she could certainly smell it now.

There'll be rabbits in those fields, Drayco's thoughts cut through her own. *Can you hurry?*

They caught up with him at the gate. Most of the valley was obscured from view now, disappearing behind the stand of redwoods and the high arch that framed the massive wrought-iron entrance. Only the peaks of the Prieta Mountains could be seen in the distance.

'Stick close, Dray. I don't want bedlam on our first day.'

'Save it for at least the second or third,' Clay spoke out of the side of his mouth.

'Shush.' She slapped his thigh.

They were met at the entrance by two gatekeepers — a woman and a man, both tall and muscular. They had swords at their sides and were dressed for fighting, in black leathers and body-hugging shirts, with small shields slung across their backs.

'Halt and present your letters.' The woman spoke formally, but her smile was sunny and warm. This was a time of peace and little could threaten Treeon in any case.

Rosette dismounted, followed by Clay. Drayco stood between them as they fished in their packs for their invitations.

'I'm Clay Cassarillo.' He handed over an envelope bearing the Treeon seal.

'Rosette de Santo and Drayco of the Dumarkian Woods,' Rosette said, offering hers.

The woman nodded to them briefly, resting her eyes on Drayco for a moment before turning to Clay. 'Take the horse to the orchard stables. There's a stall and paddock reserved for him.' She pointed towards the smoothly paved road to the left. 'The stable crew will show you what to do.'

'If there are any still lingering about,' the man added. 'You'd best hurry or they'll all be at the top field.'

'Where do I go?' Clay gazed out into a network of intersecting avenues and buildings, his brow wrinkled.

'Straight ahead. Make no turns. That'll take you right to the draught barn.' The man stretched his long bronzed arm to its full length, pointing the way. His biceps sported a serpent-and-tree tattoo similar to Nell's, the emblem of Treeon Temple. 'The welcome gathering is about to start.'

Clay and Rosette didn't budge.

The woman clapped her hands together. 'Let's move! You'll need to get to the training grounds, Rosette, through the main courtyard, past those low buildings and beyond the dorm-rooms.' She indicated the way as she spoke.

Rosette and Clay nodded but still didn't budge. It was like they were rooted to the ground.

'Go, you two!' the man urged, smiling. 'You won't want to miss the demonstrations.'

Rosette snapped out of her daze and tugged at Clay's arm. 'Come on, Clay. I'll walk you to the stables and we can go together.'

He shook his head. 'It's all right. I'll catch up.'

'Are you sure?'

'Of course. Give me your backpack.' He grasped the straps, slipped it off her shoulders and slung it up over the saddle before she could respond. 'You can pick it up after. No sense lugging it when you don't have to.'

He gave her a shove in the right direction and led Dozer towards the stables. The animal lifted his head high and crested his neck like a warhorse, ears pricked forward. His white mane flowed in rippling waves over his taut shoulder as he trumpeted a challenge.

Rosette blinked. For a moment, the animal completely transformed. Clay stroked his neck when he started to whinny again, his whole body vibrating with the sound as he started to prance on the spot.

Rosette frowned and looked again. She wondered if she had imagined it, because now his head was drooping, his ears floppy, and his walk languid, back toes dragging over the cobbles as he barely lifted his feet. Clay continued stroking his shoulder, saying something she couldn't quite catch.

She was puzzled, but turned away to head for the demonstration grounds. 'Come on, Dray. Let's go.'

There're many people here.

'I know, my lovely. It'll be all right. Just stick close to me.'

Clay led Dozer to the stables, cursing under his breath. The horse's head had lifted again as they got closer, his ears tense, nostrils whiffing in the scents. The beast's languid act was over. When he pulled back on the bridle Dozer broke into a piaffe, an exaggerated slow-motion trot. Clay quickly moved his feet as the hooves thundered down. He couldn't keep him subdued any longer.

Dozer knew the way. They both did. The hesitation in front of the guards, the drowsy draughthorse routine — it was all a performance. Clay restrained the stallion as best he could, his right arm raised, holding the reins tight against Dozer's shoulder, pressing his elbow into him for leverage. He had to jog to keep up. The cue to wilt like a worn-out mule was no longer working. The warhorse was too close to home.

Never mind. Clay had accomplished his task. He had Rosette's confidence and her worldly possessions, all in one pleasant morning's work. The temple cat seemed quite tame and controllable too. He'd be okay as long as Rosette didn't suspect anything, and clearly she didn't. The only problem now was his conscience.

Before he'd met Rosette, it had sounded like an easy task for a hard-up bard — a simple way to make some quick coin. All they'd wanted him to do was meet the girl, gain her trust and get her to hand over her pack. Demons, he'd come close to getting a good romp with her on the side. She might have been keen, if there'd been more time. Unfortunately there hadn't, and now he wanted to get away. Quickly.

Even if they asked him to stay on, offered him more gold, he would refuse. It surprised him, but he didn't want to continue deceiving her. She'd given him nothing but kindness and good company, and in return he fed her lies. It made him sick. If they asked, he'd say *no*, wouldn't he? He bit his lower lip.

Honestly? I'd grit my teeth and do it.

Clay reined the massive horse back when he surged ahead. 'Steady, boy. You did well.'

His mind was spinning. He needed the gold, and surely they wouldn't harm her. That hadn't seemed their intention. He wasn't really certain why they wanted her watched, or planned to go through her things. She was a witch of Treeon now. Why would they be suspicious of their own? Of course, Clay wasn't sure who *they* were or how many were involved. This morning, when he'd awoken in a clean bed with a spectacular breakfast of fruit, bread, eggs and ham awaiting him, he hadn't cared. Now that he had met Rosette, he did.

She had a revitalising effect on him. She made him want to write new songs, travel to new regions, work harder at his craft. He even felt the hankering to train again with the sword and improve his equestrian skills. His left hand twitched at the thought, a familiar ache.

'You cut that close,' a man called out, striding towards him from the stables. 'What took you so long?'

'We stopped for lunch,' Clay said, handing over Dozer's reins. 'And this beast of yours was slow as winter honey. Quite lethargic, the perfect draught horse until we came within sight of his stall.'

'Did she notice?'

'Nah. You've trained him well.'

'I train them all well,' he said, slapping Dozer's neck and giving a light tug to his mane.

Sure enough, in the hands of his master, Dozer stopped pulling to get ahead. He walked along, animated but contained. Clay wasn't going to argue with the man. He seemed to be in command all right. Confident didn't begin to describe Sword Master Rowan An' Lawrence. His walk alone portrayed it. He moved like a lion patrolling his turf, a man who knew his destiny and strode out to meet it. He flicked away doubt as easily as a child shoos a fly.

Bared to the waist, his muscles rippled in the light that filtered through the lattice-bordered walkway. He had a shaved head, agate green eyes and smooth bronzed skin. Tattooed serpents entwined up his arms and rested their heads on his broad shoulders. A winged bird of prey tipped with red feathers — the thunder eagle — stood guard at the back of his neck. On his right arm was a thick scar running the length of his biceps. It didn't seem that old.

'Did you get her pack?'

Clay nodded, patting the leather bag hanging from the saddle.

The sunlight vanished as they passed under the arch into the deserted horse barn. Everyone was up at the training grounds, or making their way there. Clay sighed, fidgeting with the hem of his threadbare shirt.

They stopped in front of Dozer's stall and Clay reached to untie Rosette's pack, dropping it to the ground. He grabbed his own things and faced his employer.

'I believe my job's done, Sword Master.' He'd made his decision. He was out of here.

'Not quite.' The Sword Master didn't look at him as he unsaddled the horse. 'Did she mention anyone, a Nellion Paree perhaps?'

'You didn't tell me to listen for names.'

'Do you recall it, though?'

'She said she'd trained with her for the last five years, if that's what you mean. She told me the story of how she bonded with the temple cat too.'

'How?'

'Rescued him as a kitten, lost in the woods.'

'I doubt it.'

'What?'

'Temple cats don't lose their cubs.' He stopped, turning to face Clay. 'What else did she say?'

'Only that Nell is a phenomenal star-watcher and has taught her the craft. She mentioned something about the bow, gathering Snow Root, and sword practice with an islander. That's about all.'

'Did the girl say if Nellion would soon travel?'

'She spoke only of her past.'

'Growing up in Lividica?'

'Sort of. She said she ran away because she didn't want to be married off.'

An' Lawrence went back to unbuckling the girth. 'Did she say why she chose Treeon?'

'That one's easy,' Clay grinned.

'How so?'

'She came to train with you.'

An' Lawrence stopped for a moment before lugging the saddle off. Steam rose from Dozer's wet back. 'Thank you, Clay. You did well.'

The bard looked around, unsure of what to say next. Had he been dismissed? He cleared his throat. 'My payment?'

'It's in a bag under your bunk.'

Clay nodded. 'I'll be off now.'

The Sword Master reached out to Clay's arm, stopping the young man in his tracks. 'We would like you to stay.'

Clay whispered before turning around, 'Stay?'

They made eye contact for the first time. Clay couldn't hold the exchange for long and An' Lawrence went back to grooming the horse, methodically picking up each of Dozer's dinner plate-sized hooves, checking them for stones. He grabbed a currycomb from a bucket of brushes and started to groom the dappled coat in small, vigorous circles.

'Yes. Stay.'

Perhaps years of training, or battles and adventures that Clay couldn't imagine, gave him such authority. Whatever it was, Clay knew he would obey the Sword Master. He couldn't think how to say, 'No thank you, I have other plans'.

'What do you want me to do?'

'Keep up the front of apprentice bard. Train for a while — for the winter at least.' An' Lawrence paused. 'It means staying in a comfortable dorm with a warm bed and good company, eating well, playing music, and continuing your friendship with Rosette.'

'My friendship?'

'You like her, don't you?'

'I suppose.'

'Then stay.'

'What do I get for it?'

'You get a sack of gold coins and a safe haven for the winter, not forgetting the food, drink, song and sweet company. What more does a bard seek?'

Clay watched a line of ants marching from the base of an old feed bucket to the middle slat of the gate. Something in the back of his mind told him to get out, and fast, but the Sword Master's words were like a spell, lulling him into agreement. His other option — to make his way on foot back to the plains of Corsanon where he could sing for his keep in dingy pubs and brothels — had a lot less appeal.

'All you have to do is build on your relationship with Rosette and report to me when I contact you.'

'That's it?'

'Hopefully, you'll work with the fourth-year students on composition. You've a knack for that, I've heard.'

Is there anything you haven't heard?

It wouldn't hurt to train with his peers, even though he was already a journeyman. He liked the idea of teaching, and there were tunes floating around the music halls that he'd never heard before. It would be great to expand his repertoire.

'I don't have to remind you of the consequences if you should reveal our agreement to the girl, or anyone else, do I?' The Sword Master's voice had a deep finality to it, jolting Clay from his musings.

'No, you don't.' Clay looked out through the doorway, taking in the expanse framed like a picture on a wall. The breeze touched his face with the scent of apple pulp and freshly stacked hay. He rubbed his cheek on his shoulder and turned back to An' Lawrence. 'When do I start?'

The Sword Master gave a half smile as he unbridled Dozer and flipped open his stall door. The horse nickered, heading straight for the manger filled with oats and alfalfa hay.

'Right now. Find Rosette and make sure you accompany her back for her things. I want to know if she suspects this pack has been searched.'

'She wouldn't, would she?'

'You don't know her very well yet, do you?'

'Do you?'

The Sword Master didn't answer right away. 'She's an initiate of Nellion Paree. Best not underestimate her.' He started going through the contents of Rosette's pack. It seemed he was looking for something very specific as he set out each item, one by one. He glanced at Clay. 'You'd better hurry. I want you to get as close to her as you can. Do you understand?'

Clay hesitated for an imperceptible moment then lifted his head. 'Sure thing.' He winked at the Sword Master then dashed out of the barn.

'Coming through,' a woman in a dark blue robe called out. She nearly bumped into Rosette as she shouldered past. 'Oh, geebeeza! What in the underworld is that?' She didn't wait for an answer but swerved, giving Drayco a wide berth before breaking into a run.

Rosette felt herself being sucked into a stream of people, all intent on one destination. After years of living with Nell and only the occasional visitor to fill the small cottage with a foreign voice, Rosette felt overwhelmed. As the intensity of Treeon swirled around her, she faltered.

Maudi? What's wrong? The temple cat seemed unperturbed by the energy of the place.

'I can't breathe.'

More robed figures veered past like a river around rocks. Rosette wavered in the middle of the thoroughfare, Drayco at her side. She could hear the gasps and exclamations of those startled by the temple cat and it made her feel even more out of place. Her chest was tight. She couldn't take a proper breath. Moving out of the traffic, she stopped in front of the plaza's southern statue.

'I really can't breathe,' she gasped.

Sit. Head down. Look away from the crowd.

Rosette slid to the foot of the statue. It was a huge winged deity, recognisable now. Looking skyward, she identified the head of a falcon, the body of a lion, the wings of a sea eagle and the tail of a snake. It bore many names, most she couldn't pronounce. Nell called it *Were-fey*, the goddess of transformation who presided over birth and death. Fitting. Rosette felt like she was about to die.

Take a deep breath.

Rosette closed her eyes and drew in as much air as she could, then spilled it out in front of her.

And another. Keep going.

After a few more inhalations, her dizziness settled. She rested her eyes on Drayco, mindful of her breathing, slow and steady, in and out, in and out. When she started to relax, she looked again at Were-fey.

The statue fascinated her. It was carved from a sea-green stone, smooth as glass and cool to the touch. The sculptor portrayed the beast in a contemplative pose, perched on an outcropping of boulders, serpent tail wrapped tight around a lower rock, partly submerged by a placid lake. The raptor eyes, for a moment, seemed to query Rosette, as if it had come to life. When she blinked, the statue looked blank, only a carved rock after all.

Feel better?

'A bit.'

Too many people?

Rosette sighed. 'Maybe we should wait for Clay.'

You have to get used to them at some point. Drayco sat, resting his head in her lap. *We are meant to be here for a fair while.*

Rosette's nose twitched when she heard her own reasoning coming back at her. She smiled. To think she'd been worried about how Drayco would cope. She stood up, letting out a little laugh.

That sounds better.

'It feels better, Dray.'

The traffic in the courtyard had thinned with only a few stragglers darting through, robes flying out behind pumping legs. She put her hand to her forehead and scanned the avenue leading to the oval, shading her eyes from the noonday sun.

'We're going to miss the start.'

If we don't go now, we'll miss the finish.

Rosette kept gazing up ahead until Drayco nipped her hand.

Someone's coming.

Where?

Behind.

Her spine stiffened.

'Are you lost?'

Rosette spun around and looked into the face of a tall, solid-built man in a black robe. His expression was sunny, his manner purposeful. He had a strong jaw, a shaved head, smooth skin and when he smiled, his eyes crinkled with delight.

'Pardon me?' she said.

'It looks to me like you and your companion are lost,' he said again, this time directing his words to Drayco as well.

'We're just getting our bearings.'

He watched her with an intensity that gave her goose bumps. His eyes were green, flecked with gold and brown and shaped like a cat's.

'I know a short cut,' he said. 'Come on.'

'What?' Rosette creased her forehead.

'A "short cut",' he enunciated slowly. 'It's a way of getting somewhere faster, more direct.'

'I'm familiar with the term,' she said, suppressing a giggle.

'I can get you right up close to the demonstrations, if you want ... and you *will* want. They aren't to be missed.'

Shall we? Drayco nudged her hand. *He's harmless.*

Harmless? He looks to me like he could mow down an army blindfolded.

Drayco sneezed. *You're right. Let me correct myself. He looks like he means us no harm.*

She hesitated. Shyness washed over her, making her wish she were back at Nell's cottage. She imagined herself sitting in front of the hearth, listening to her mentor read from *The Stellar Opus* while she combed grass seeds from Drayco's fur.

'Thanks, but I should probably find my own way.'

'Should? Mine's quicker.' He winked. 'Come on,' he said, holding out his hand. 'You won't regret it.'

She hung back.

He smiled at her anew. 'Ah. I have no manners.' He slapped his hand to his forehead. 'Let me introduce myself.' He turned his back on her for a second then spun around as if seeing her for the first time. 'I'm Rowan.' He lifted his right hand, palm upward, in a gesture of open greeting.

Rosette responded automatically in the same way, their palms touching. She took his hand and felt the fire of his grip. Energy jolted up her arm, like a zap of lightning. She blocked it before it reached her elbow.

'I'm Rosette,' she said, surprised by the tingling sensation. She looked deeper into his eyes. She felt a strength of purpose beneath his jovial manner. He'd been in plenty of battles, she could tell. She suspected there was more to his name than just plain 'Rowan'.

'You two are from the Dumarkian Woods, I'll wager.' He fixed his eyes on the cat as he spoke.

'This is my familiar, Drayco.'

'Honoured,' he said, bowing his head slightly to both. 'Can I show you the way now? Come or not, I've got to run. I can't miss this.'

Nor can we. Come on, Maudi. It's all good.

'Thank you, Rowan. Lead the way, please.'

As he turned, she saw a stunning tattoo at the back of his neck — two wings, extended in flight, a grey wash of feathers, black with red tips. It stood out brilliantly against his bronzed skin. She couldn't pull her eyes away.

'Apprentice?' he asked without slowing down. He dodged down a series of side walkways, glancing to see if she and Drayco followed.

'Initiate,' she answered. 'We've just arrived.'

'No kidding,' he said, turning his head again to smile.

'Huh?'

'A woman like you, I would remember.'

She laughed, relaxing her shoulders as she rushed along. Her breath came easily now. It felt good to run, especially without her pack. 'And why's that?'

'Because,' he said, keeping his eye forward, 'you're beautiful ... in a raven-like way.'

'Raven?' She sputtered out another laugh. 'How so?'

'The black hair, of course, and the nose.'

'The nose?'

'Raven for sure. Very distinct.'

Rosette reached up and felt her nose as if considering its shape for the first time. She shook her head, following him along the twisting pathways, wondering who he really was. His plain robe and the name he gave her offered no clue as to rank, and his manner didn't help either. It was too contradictory. The commanding grace said one thing, his jesting speech and boyish mannerisms said another.

Trickster, do you think, Dray?

Maybe ...

When she spotted the hilt of his sword as his robe wafted back, she sucked in her breath. It was ancient and elaborately designed, clearly not owned by a low-ranking journeyman.

'Do you train with the Sword Master?' she asked in a rush.

'You could say that.' He lengthened his stride to a full run.

She worked hard to keep up, Drayco loping at her side.

He ducked down a narrow side path hedged by late-blooming camellias. The red and pink blossoms against the shiny green leaves filled her vision with a thrill of colour. She sped up, matching his pace stride for stride.

'That's why I'm here,' she said between breaths.

'Pardon?'

'The Sword Master. I'm here to train with him.'

'Does he know?'

'Not yet.'

'You're ambitious.'

'So they tell me.'

He touched her hand, tilting his head to the left.

'This way,' he said, leaping forward to ascend a long flight of stairs.

How they would get to the training grounds ahead of the crowd, even at this pace, she had no idea. From what she remembered of her elevated view of Treeon, the demonstration grounds were straight uphill, and a fair way off. Still she climbed, forcing her legs with no thought of slowing down. They turned a bend, dashed up a second set of narrow stairs and then came to a sudden stop.

'Whoa,' Rosette gasped, putting her hand down to her side to stop Drayco's momentum. Her eyes widened.

They stood side by side, chests rising and falling in rhythm, looking at the horse in front of them. Obsidian black, with a mane that hung in braids down to his knees, the animal turned his head towards them and trumpeted, blasting a throaty challenge. When they didn't respond immediately, he pawed the cobblestones with alternating forelegs, setting sparks flying with each strike of his iron-shod hooves.

Rowan motioned for them to wait. 'Don't be cross,' he said, stepping up to take the lead rope from around the massive neck. Bringing the horse forward a few steps, he came to a halt right in front of Rosette and Drayco.

'This is Diablai,' Rowan announced as the horse fluttered his nostrils at Drayco and let out soft whickers. The fur around the top of the temple cat's head parted in the gusts of air. 'I think he will consent to carry us both bareback.'

He's been to Dumarka. Drayco seemed surprised. *He knows my kind.*

He's been to Dumarka? Are you sure?

I am sure.

'You're talking to him?' Rosette said. 'He understands you?'

He hears all of us.

'Yes, he does,' Rowan answered, thinking Rosette's words were directed towards him. 'Sometimes he knows what I'm going to say before I even think it.'

'I know what you mean,' she whispered.

Rosette marvelled at the animal. He was tall — about seventeen hands, she guessed. His neck arched as he looked at her straight on, his huge brown eyes gazing through a long and dense forelock that covered most of his face. His nostrils flared as he took in her scent, then he tossed his head, trumpeting again.

'Diablai,' she said softly. 'I would cherish a ride with you.' She lifted her hand to stroke his shoulder, making it ripple with the touch. It felt like silk; the muscles beneath were tight, ready to spring.

Rowan grasped a handful of mane at the horse's withers and vaulted up with practised ease before extending his arm down to Rosette. She ignored it. Grasping a handful of mane as well, she took a backward step towards Diablai's head and vaulted up neatly behind.

Settling in, she pressed her face close to Rowan's cheek. 'Shall we be off?'

'A horsewoman, are you?'

'I used to be.' She was about to frown but lifted her face instead.

'Perhaps you'll apprentice with the Sword Master after all,' he said as he urged Diablai up the remaining slope.

'He favours equestrians?'

'Of course.'

She slipped her arms around Rowan's waist. The power of the horse beneath her and the man in front of her made her take a deep breath. Invigorating! This was quite a contrast to the ride she had had earlier today. She could feel the undulation and tensing of every muscle in Diablai's spine. Energy shot through him at such a rate, she thought they might fly up the cliff instead of climb it.

'Why the sword?' he asked.

'What's that?' She turned her attention back to Rowan as she held him tight.

'Why do you want to train with the sword?'

'I feel more alive with a sword in my hand than at almost any other time.'

'Any other reason?'

Rosette hesitated. 'Promise not to laugh?'

'Not if it's funny.'

'All right. Promise not to snicker?'

He nodded.

'I train with the sword because ... I had a dream.'

'A dream?'

'It was vivid, lingering. I know I will apprentice with the Sword Master. I have to. I've seen it.'

'Do you base all your plans on dreams?'

'Pretty much.' She clutched him as they skirted around a cluster of oaks and up another steep incline. 'Don't you?'

He didn't reply.

'How'd you hear about *our* Sword Master anyway?' Rowan asked, gripping Diablai's mane.

'He's the best.'

'Is that what they're saying where you come from, in Dumarka?'

'Actually, I come from the south, near Lister Bay, but either way, north or south, that's what they say.'

'And who are *they*?'

'My mentor says so.'

'Your mentor?' Rowan said the words so softly that Rosette wasn't sure he had actually spoken. 'And who might that be?' he asked, the question ringing out.

She cleared her throat.

'Nellion Paree, of the Dumarkian Woods.'

'Nellion Paree?' He whistled.

Rosette bumped into Rowan's shoulder as Diablai bunched his muscles to leap over a broad hedge that divided two tracks.

'Hang on,' he said.

They landed lightly on the far side of the hedge and galloped on.

'*The* Nellion Paree?' he asked again.

'You keep saying her name, but you had it right the first time.' Rosette pinched him and laughed.

He didn't laugh back.

Rosette wasn't sure what the problem was. 'She's a powerful witch, a great teacher.'

He didn't respond for several strides as he urged Diablai up a climb of stairs. The horse's hooves tapped out a beat as they hit the stones. Rosette tightened her leg muscles, and her breath came in rushes, though it was Diablai that ran. They crested the top of the stairs, directly behind the arena, just a short length from the stage.

'Indeed she is,' Rowan finally answered, turning his face to her as Diablai came to a halt. 'And here we are.'

As promised, the short cut and the horse's speed had secured them a spot in front of the main stage. Drayco stood very close to the horse, his tail twitching as he surveyed the crowd. His sides lifted and fell with each quick breath.

'Amazing,' Rosette said.

'Did you doubt I could do it?'

'A little,' she said without apology. 'I don't know you.'

'Perhaps we can remedy that,' he said, giving her thigh a squeeze.

She released her arms from around his waist, leaned forward and slid her leg over Diablai's rump. Next thing she knew, her feet were planted on the ground, her head tilted up to thank the horseman. It was then she realised he was barefoot, his toes brushing her arm as he turned Diablai around.

'You have a wonderful horse.'

'Thank you, my lady.' He smiled down at her. 'Actually, he's the Sword Master's.'

Rosette's eyebrows went up.

'Go on,' Rowan prompted, giving her a wink. 'Find a good place, right up front.'

She followed his gesture then turned back only to see him galloping away. 'Thank you . . .' she called out.

Too late. Horse and rider were gone.

She looked over at the crowd. 'Ready to get amongst them, my lovely?'

Ready, Drayco purred. *She's near.*

'Who's near?'

The one like me.

'Maybe you'll meet her soon.'

Not yet. She's hiding.

He pressed his head briefly into Rosette's hand and led the way into the crowd. A path parted before them as they moved towards the stage, dead centre, front row. Rosette looked straight up into the faces on the raised platform. She guessed immediately which one the High Priestess was.

Even though Rosette had never met La Makee, she had heard her described many times. She was easy to spot. The red hair gave her away, and the fact that everyone around her was listening intently, responding to her directions with nods and gestures. She was definitely in command. Red hair, short stature, huge energy. Huge? The woman was luminous. And her hair wasn't just red. It burned like fire, falling in tresses to her waist. Several large azurite stones were draped at her neck, secured with a double chain of silver. They glinted in the sunlight while she paced back and forth, stopping now and then to speak with the others. A sword swung at her side, the hilt inlaid with silver and bluestone. Rosette took a quick look at her own lapis bangles. They were of similar design.

That's interesting.

What, Maudi?

Just noticing La Makee's sword hilt.

You would. Drayco sent a playful purr with his thoughts.

As the High Priestess strode about the stage her silk robe blew open, revealing black leather trousers and a finely quilted vest. Embroidered on the edges of her robe were entwining green serpents, and on the back a soaring golden falcon. Her hands lifted gracefully above her head, slipping on a band to secure her hair away from her face. They were tattooed, somewhat like Nell's.

La Makee stopped suddenly and stood like a warrior — legs apart, arms crossed under her breasts. She eyed the crowd as if they were new troops. The High Priestess of Treeon Temple wasn't very tall, five or six inches shorter than Rosette, but what she lacked in height she made up for in sheer potency. La Makee exuded power and command, her toned muscles well defined, each movement agile and precise.

Her face seemed timeless, ancient and full of youth all at once. She had to be over fifty years old, but her birth data — like many of those in high rank — was kept secret. Nell said she was born under the sign of the Archer: adventurous, philosophical and free. Looking at her on stage, Rosette didn't doubt it. La Makee beamed with fortitude and conviction, and something else. Something regal. She guessed the sign of the Lion was on the eastern horizon when this woman entered the world.

'She'll not let you off with the slightest imprecision or flaw,' Nell had warned. 'She knows true from false at the glance of an eye. Be honest in what you say to her, though know you may not always want to say too much.'

She knew Nell and La Makee had a history. They hadn't seen each other or communicated for decades, until the letter Nell wrote applying for Rosette's entry to Treeon. Rosette had asked what lay between them, but her mentor seemed reluctant to speak of it, and Rosette hadn't pressed. Now that she was here, she wished she had.

As La Makee clapped her hands several others joined her, though they stood further back. Rosette was startled to see two men leap up onto the platform belatedly. They shed their black robes, one tightening his sword belt and striding forward to stand beside La Makee. He towered above her, powerfully built, serpent tattoos entwining his forearms, shaved head revealing a striking face. The other, a slightly shorter man with spiky hair, followed quickly behind to stand beside him. Both were bare to the waist, barefoot and sculpted like fine art.

Rosette swallowed hard. There was no question about who stood directly alongside La Makee. It was the man who called himself Rowan. As if he knew he was being watched, he glanced down into the crowd and winked at Rosette. Without breaking eye contact he leaned towards the shorter man beside him, whispering something out of the side of his mouth. Both now looked in her direction. She felt her face flush.

Why would he deceive her like that? Her mind spun. *Trickster!*

'Is that ... is he ...?' She didn't avert her eyes from Rowan as she tapped the young girl next to her, pointing towards the man on stage.

'The Sword Master?' the girl finished Rosette's sentence. 'Yes, it's An' Lawrence. He's amazing. Unbelievably fast. You'll see. They're going to give a demonstration.' She looked down at Drayco and her smile fell. She edged away.

'Hush!' A woman standing behind scolded both girls. Drayco turned his head, but she didn't flinch. 'La Makee is about to speak.' She glared at Drayco and he glared back. At least someone here wasn't intimidated by the feline. Rosette nodded at the woman and looked back to the stage.

'For those who are new ...' La Makee paused to scan the crowd as if she identified them immediately among the hundreds in front of her, 'welcome to the coven of Treeon Temple.'

Everyone raised their hands over their heads and cheered their greeting, Rosette joining them. Drayco sprang up to rest his front paws on the edge of the wide stage, whiskers twitching as he took in the scents.

'I have one thing to impress on you today,' she continued. 'It's a simple thing. It takes only a moment to say. You'll spend the rest of your life considering it.' Makee's voice boomed out into the crowd. Her head turned slowly, scanning each face.

'There is no turning back.' There was no other sound in the entire valley. 'When you enter Treeon Temple for training, you make a binding commitment to this coven and to the gods. It will not always be an easy bond. There will be times when the growth and development of your skills will be arduous. You may question if there is any progress at all. These are the times that test your will, your power to become who you are meant to be. The path is not simple or straightforward. It is not one to choose lightly. Make certain you understand this without question, before you commit.'

She paused and drew her sword, raising it above her head. 'I say it again, one last time: there is no turning back.' She looked down at Rosette then, her eyes boring into the girl.

Rosette broke out in a sweat. No-one spoke. The valley seemed to echo with La Makee's voice, though she had stopped speaking. The sun shone directly overhead, making her sword tip flare, lighting it like a beacon. Far off towards the cider barn, a dog barked.

Then a cloud passed over the sun, dimming the light and breaking the spell. Cheers welled up and the crowd became animated. The High Priestess spoke in detail about commitment and intention. She talked of the mentors and tutors, of the masters and how they chose their apprentices. Rosette was riveted, her senses catching every word and nuance.

Directions were given. Her name was called, along with a dozen others for the dormitory of Mistress Savine. She hoped all her dorm-mates would cope with Drayco. She didn't notice any other familiars in the crowd and Dray had spoken of only one other — apparently bonded to the Sword Master. Rosette didn't imagine she would be coming into contact with him again, or his familiar, at least for a while. She flushed at the thought of her casual manner only moments before. Did he assess all his potential students in such a covert way?

The clash of steel on steel grabbed her attention. Two apprentices were giving a demonstration, the arc of their swords slicing through the air with choreographed grace. It was the beginning of the *forms*, the prescribed movements exhibiting calmness, strength, dexterity and precision. She watched, transfixed, as the two apprentices, a tall man and a woman nearly his height, danced with the swords to the pounding of wooden drums. Their focus was amazing.

Whoops and hollers burst out around her as the apprentices finally froze, sword hands thrust forward, bodies facing each other in a deep lunge. Then they stood back, briefly lowered their eyes in an almost imperceptible bow and sheathed their weapons in perfect synchronicity. As they backed away two more students stepped up, executing progressively more complex forms, their movements astonishing. The drum-beat increased, sending chills up her spine.

Each demonstration proved more intricate and hazardous than the one before. Rosette took a deep breath when the High Priestess and Sword Master An' Lawrence walked to the centre of the stage, squared off, and drew their swords. The ring of steel sang over the assembly.

La Makee had dropped her robe, her hair a tail of fire behind her. Both she and the Sword Master were barefoot, and they moved at precisely the same instant. Rosette watched wide-eyed, the complexity mesmerising. Maka'ra hadn't taught the forms like this. He had said, *I teach you island-style. It is not as they do in the temples. It will save your life if you trust it.* He'd talked of the sword forms as living things, and sparring as a chance to let the soul of the sword speak. Rosette smiled. Their souls were certainly speaking now.

With the speed of a striking snake the High Priestess lunged towards the Sword Master, her shield arm blocking a blow. The cut was repelled by An' Lawrence, and the warrior-priestess did a backflip towards the row of apprentices who stood to the side of the stage, drawing one of their swords with her free hand before she landed. Facing her opponent, she dropped to a forward roll and rose, blades inches away from the Sword Master's face.

The sound of the drums reverberated up Rosette's legs as she gasped. The blocks and attacks were so quick that she couldn't follow the blur of movement. La Makee pressed him back, but An' Lawrence dropped down with a spinning kick and rolled to the other side of the stage. Squaring off again they faced each other for an instant, bowed slightly and resumed.

After another series of full attacks and counterattacks, fast and fluid, An' Lawrence and La Makee were in a deadlock, face to face, hilt to hilt, swords pointed to the sky. No-one in the crowd seemed to breathe.

In a feat of sizable strength the High Priestess suddenly did a standing backflip away from her attacker, her bare feet aiming to kick his hilt away as she landed. Not quick enough. The Sword Master had dropped to his knees, dodging the kick. He sprang back up, pointing the tip of his blade straight at the High Priestess's throat as she landed. Rosette swallowed hard. There was no way out of this one.

As Rosette brought her knuckle to her mouth, a shock wave blasted her face. The outline of the High Priestess darkened and blurred. In a blink, the Sword Master's blade no longer held the witch captive. He stood there, guarding thin air. His eyes shot upwards, and so did Rosette's.

Above them a Lemur Raven, the size of an eagle, spiralled towards the sky, shrieking a fierce challenge, or was that laughter? The crowd burst out with resounding cheers, waving and pointing at the bird. The Sword Master sheathed his sword and held out his bare arm while the raven coursed above the stage then back-winged to a graceful landing, talons lightly circling his wrist. The image of the bird darkened and blurred. In a swirl of energy La Makee manifested, standing in its place and bowing to her opponent, her hands clasped in front of her in the traditional gesture of respect. Rosette had never seen such a demonstration of shape-shifting and she cheered wildly along with the rest.

When the applause died down, La Makee spoke. 'Fight them with all the skills you have,' she roared, 'and if it looks like you have no more to fight with, flee!'

A wave of laughter rolled through the gathering. Makee picked up her abandoned sword, raising it to An' Lawrence before sheathing it. The Sword Master blew her a kiss. He took her hand and they bowed to the students, dismissing them. When they straightened, he did not let go of her hand.

Rosette grinned widely. What an amazing experience, especially the shape-shifting. She knew that Nell could do it, but it wasn't something she had taught Rosette or even allowed her to see. La Makee was unbelievable! While Rosette stood staring in awe, the crowd began to disperse; some went to the stage to talk with the masters, others moved off to get on with their day. She touched Drayco's head as he dropped his front legs to the ground and they both slipped quietly out of the crowd.

'What did you think of that, Dray?'

Not bad, for two legs.

'I agree. Let's find Clay.'

He's finding us.

Clay's face was red and he seemed out of breath. 'I had to fight my way through the crowd. How'd you get up so close?'

'I had help.' She glanced up at the stage and caught the Sword Master's eye. He waved and she raised her hand, palm towards him, fingers spread.

'From high places, it seems.'

'It was a chance meeting,' she shrugged. 'Did you see all the demonstration? Did you see La Makee shift?'

'I sat halfway up that tree.' Clay pointed to a tall, twisting oak at the edge of the oval. 'I saw everything, including you.'

'Wasn't it amazing?' She folded her hands on top of her head, looking at the empty stage.

He smiled, fishing deep in his pockets. 'This is what's amazing.' He handed her a green apple and took a bite from his own, talking around his mouthful. 'There are bins full of them behind the stables.'

She laughed, polishing the fruit on her sleeve until it shone like hard candy. She took a big chomp and closed her eyes. Juice trickled out the corners of her mouth.

She beamed. 'Delicious!' The sweet nectar washed over her tongue and down her throat. She wiped her mouth with her fingers and sucked them clean, the crisp white fruit tantalising her with its heady fragrance and sugary taste, the scent of apple blossoms lingering on her breath. 'Thank you, Clay. That's magic.'

'My pleasure,' he said, taking a little bow. They walked on. 'The demo was impressive, but I enjoyed the syncopated drumming as much as the sword work.'

She laughed and took his hand. 'That doesn't surprise me, my bard.'

Rosette was feeling better about coming to Treeon. It seemed the right place to be, even though the sheer numbers would take some getting used to. All she had to do was stay focused, advance through the preparatory training, and before she knew it, she'd be sparring with the sword apprentices. It'd be like peaches and cream, or make that baked apples and cream. She took another bite.

What do we do now? Drayco's question cut into her thoughts. The temple cat was yawning.

'We have to find our dorm and report to Mistress Savine,' Rosette said. 'Clay, I need to get my pack.'

The young bard looked away, his eyes focusing on the distant winding road that led out of the valley. 'Sure,' he answered, staring at the horizon.

Drayco twitched his tail. *Then what, Maudi?*

'Then, it begins.'

Chapter 7

An' Lawrence watched them head for the barn. They were friends already, hand in hand, companionably munching apples, smiling like the summer days were already here. He frowned uneasily and turned away. Part of him felt disappointed in Rosette for not sensing trouble, and another part of him was pleased that the bard could pull it off. It meant he could tell Makee that all was in place. Of course, Clay wasn't really working a deception. That's why it was so effective. The lad was taken by her, clear as crystal waters. He didn't have to pretend to be interested or enthused, or aroused. Good. Yet, oddly, An' Lawrence felt uncomfortable. Something wasn't sitting right.

Of course it isn't sitting right. His familiar's voice floated into his mind. *When did it ever, with mulengro about?*

You're right, Scylla.

What's setting it off? Guilt? Envy? Assumption? ... Deceit?

Deceit mainly, and perhaps some Envy.

That's honest.

I know, and it hurts.

He didn't want to begin the training of Nell's student with deception and he told the other members of the high council so. He wanted to take the direct approach, everyone open and upfront. She was their initiate now, for the goddesses' sake. But the council disagreed. La Makee disagreed. Too much was at stake and he had been overruled. An' Lawrence fingered the hilt of his sword and shook his head at the memory.

'If she's anything like her mentor,' La Makee had said, 'she doesn't deserve our trust.'

'Rosette has potential, or Nell wouldn't have bothered.'

'I'm not referring to Nellion's mentorship skills, Sword Master. I am referring to her stubborn will and subversive intentions.'

An' Lawrence had glared at her, the corner of his mouth turning into a half smile. 'You seem familiar with those attributes.'

'The witch stole from me!'

'She could say the same of you.'

Makee had looked him up and down. 'Old feelings, Sword Master?'

'Not at all.'

'Then why the resistance?'

'You underestimated Nellion Paree and I fear you may be underestimating Rosette as well.'

'Really? And you feel that being — how did you put it — "open and upfront" is going to resolve this problem?'

'I'm just saying it's worth a shot.' An' Lawrence had paced as he spoke, his face red, forehead perspiring. 'There is nothing that directly implicates her, *nor her mentor*.' He had said the last few words to himself.

'Isn't there?'

'What do we know for sure about Rosette de Santo?' he'd countered.

'Why don't you tell me?'

'It wouldn't take long. Let's consider instead what we don't know. We don't know if she has any links to the Matosh murders. She may not have even met the family.'

'That's the point, An' Lawrence. We don't know. I charge you with remedying that lack.'

'It could be done in a clear instant if we simply asked her.'

'Are you convinced she wouldn't lie so well that we couldn't pick it?'

He'd stopped in front of La Makee and crossed his arms. 'I am. What's more, I'm convinced she would tell the truth. We're encouraging mulengro with this dishonesty.'

'Mulengro? Is that what you're worried about?'

'It will bring nothing good.'

'Mulengro's a state of mind, Sword Master. It brings what you expect.'

'You talk like you can control it.'

'Because I can. Of course you feel its presence, the prickle at the back of your neck, the tension in the air, the twist in your guts. You're weaving a deception, manipulating others for your own ends. Get used to it. Mulengro isn't the enemy here. It's energy, like anything else.'

'An energy you're feeding. It will grow.'

'Assumption! Have you forgotten who started the whole thing a quarter of a century ago?'

The Sword Master had pressed his lips together and looked away.

'Then don't give your trust to this girl just because she trained with a woman you once knew and ... admired. Think back, An' Lawrence. Nell left, and she left with more than what was rightfully hers. I want it back. Rosette may be the key to our puzzle and I'll not have you scattering the pieces in the wind again. We're running out of time. Mind you don't fall under *her* spell as well.'

None of the other council members had spoken. Some shuffled in their seats, others looked away.

'La Makee, this path is one you'll regret.'

'That may be, Sword Master, though the path is mine to choose.'

'What are you waiting for?'

The question startled Rosette, bringing the room back into focus. All the tables in front of her were empty and wiped clean, chairs tucked under them in even rows. All except hers. She puckered her lips, remembering her optimism when she'd first arrived.

Like peaches and cream? What was I thinking?

So far, she had danced at two solstices here at Treeon and revelled in the bonfires of as many sabbats, and still had not sparred once on the training grounds. The preparations for the Samhain sabbat were now well underway. Nights were colder and winter was coming, and still she wasn't called to join the sword and staff classes. The only practice she got was in her free time when she and Clay would slip away to work on forms and spar. It was fun, though it wasn't like training with a master. She caught her reflection in the dark window and wondered how the naive girl of last winter could have thought her apprenticeship at Treeon Temple would be such a breeze.

It had been anything but.

Rosette felt the eyes of her tutor, Mistress Mara, focused on her. She tried not to cringe.

Mistress is livid, and who would blame her?

Mistress Mara seldom lost her patience though she had came close more than once with Rosette. Tonight was promising to be yet another battle for them both — for Rosette to perfect the spell and for Mara to hold her temper. Her instructor was really a gentle soul, placid, intuitive and sensitive. Tonight she was like a storm at sea, looking for a ship to wreck.

Mara didn't travel at all, not in her physical body, and she never seemed to take a break. She devoted her life to meditation and the teaching of the ritual arts — spells, dream-walking and evocations. Age had barely touched her, though she had to be in her seventies. Born with the sign of the Aurochs rising, the qualities and temperament of the ancient bull infused her with strength, endurance, sensuality and tenacity. As usual, she showed no indication of tiring and they'd been at it since noon.

Rosette closed her eyes and tried not to think of her stomach rumbling.

Of course, Mara had reserves. She was plump, in a voluptuous way, and was not shy about displaying it. She wore robes that showed off her ample bosom, draping herself with large pendants and coloured gemstones. Her grey hair was swirled into a loose mound atop her head, curls escaping about her face. She usually had a just-ravished look, but lines of tension were etched about her mouth and eyes tonight. Her brow was deeply furrowed. Rosette also thought she could see horns sprouting from her forehead.

The candles spluttered, and so did Rosette.

The chamber was cloistered, with the doors and windows closed. There were no chinks or gaps in the stone walls, yet suddenly wisps of Rosette's hair escaped their braids, tickling her cheeks. At least the Elemental Air had not ignored her. Why would it? That was her ruler, linked to her Sun and Mercury in the sign of the Twins.

'Pardon, Mistress?' Rosette answered. She realised that Mistress Mara was still staring at her while she had daydreamed.

'I asked, young witch, what are you waiting for?'

Rosette brushed the back of her hand across her forehead, sweeping away stray hairs and stifling a yawn. *Good question*. She wasn't actually waiting for anything. Procrastinating, seeking distractions, evading, yes. But waiting? No. Not really.

'Answer the question, please,' Mara commanded.

'I was just ... just ...' She stopped mid-sentence. It wouldn't do to lie.

A nighthawk whistled in the distance, shrill and eerie. Rosette resisted the impulse to look in its direction or answer back. What could she see out an opaque window in the moonless black?

'Rosette!'

'Just collecting my thoughts is all, Mistress Mara,' she said in a rush.

'And are they collected now?'

'Yes, Mistress.'

'Then begin,' Mara said through clenched teeth.

Rosette squared her shoulders. Running her hand across the stones that lay on the table, she picked one up — a smooth black pebble shot with flecks of gold — and dropped it into the chalice in front of her. It rippled silently to the bottom, invisible in the dark water.

Rosette knew she had to get this aspect of her training right before she could move on. Why was it so difficult? It wasn't like she was changing the course of time, or even the course of a river. It was a simple summons, one she thought she knew quite well. Apparently she did not — not well enough for Mara's standards anyway.

Rosette inhaled, half closed her eyes and then opened them slowly, while delivering the ritual words, yet again. It must have been the fiftieth time that day she'd woven this spell. Each time, Mara found a flaw, a deviation, or imperfection — too much Air, not enough Fire, where were Gaela and Water? Rosette felt sure that all four Elementals were completely bored with the exercise by now. She certainly was.

The spell didn't move mountains or even heat a cup of tea. It conjured no more and no less than the attention of the Elemental Spirits residing in the four corners of the world, the four corners of Treeon, of this room, of her body, of her soul. The Elementals were within everything, the spirit of everything, the whole in every part. Any witch worth her salt could call them up at will, and Rosette wanted to be a witch worth her salt.

She took another deep breath and released all her thoughts and judgments. A babbling mind wasn't going to get the spell right. She let it out, long and slow. There were only the Elementals, and the energy they transmitted. There was no place where she ended and they began. Her mind smoothed like a long straight road leading to a distant horizon. The spell would work perfectly if she let it. She just had to get out of the way.

While chanting the summons, she visualised the Elementals' nature. Fire was like the rumbling peaks of Pele, the western mountains bubbling with molten lava. He brought inspiration, creative drive and spirit and ruled the signs of the Ram, the Lion and the Archer. Gaela was the fields and woods, sprouting the crops and calling to the wild deer, horse and ox. She was nurturing, fecund and rich, ruling over the Aurochs, Ceres and the Sea-goat. Water was diverse. It pounded the shores, carving passion into the rocky coastline, or lapped in tranquil ripples against the edges of mountain lakes, the embodiment of feelings and emotion. It ruled Luna's Cobra, the Scorpion and the Twinned Fishes. Air swirled about the snowcapped mountains of Prieta, tall, jagged and vast. This was her element, the will and power of the mind, ruling the sign of the Twins, Bilancia and the Water-bearer.

Rosette smiled to herself.

With full intention, she called them in. This time her lips did not go dry, and the deep, guttural words she chanted did not stick and jab in her throat. They came out smoothly, untroubled as a swiftly flowing stream. She felt a humming without sound in the back of her head and a feeling of lightness in all her limbs.

The air in the chamber stirred. The candles in front of her lit of their own accord. Fire's accord. The water in the silver chalice lapped the sides like a miniature tidal flux, rippling with echoes from the sea. The stones, mostly agate, chalcedony, jade and lapis, began to shake while the breeze in the room quickened.

Rosette felt her whole body shimmer with joy. She tucked her hands into the long sleeves of her robe, folded her arms and softened her eyes. She waited for the verdict, even though she knew what it would be. She finally understood what Mara had been teaching her. It wasn't enough to conjure the Elementals. The skill was to invite them all in equal measure, regardless of her personal elemental balance. She was lopsided, as most are, with a predominance of Air and Gaela, having many planets in the sign of the Twins and the Sea-goat. When she'd worked this spell in the past, she'd mirrored the imbalance. There would be plenty of Air, a rumbling of Gaela but only a ripple in the chalice and a flicker of one candle. This time, she called them in symmetrically.

'Done.' Mara raised her hand in the traditional spiral gesture.

If she was pleased, or relieved, it didn't show. No emotion played across the older woman's face.

'Blessings be.'

Rosette began the traditional response, lips pressed tight to contain the exuberant grin bursting to escape.

'Blessings to the East, North, West and South — to the Elementals of Fire, Gaela, Air and Water. I honour your presence and your power.' She lifted the chalice and took a sip. 'I am your ally, and you are mine.'

She leaned forward to kiss the warm hand of her mentor, the tiny bells woven into her long braids tinkling as she did so. Inside, she felt like jumping up and down. Done! Success! Triumph! Was it possible that she finally might move on to a proper apprenticeship with the Sword Master? Everything would change now. She could feel it.

When Rosette's lips touched her tutor's hand she sensed stiffness there, and her rush of exuberance fell flat. There was resistance in Mara. She felt it immediately. Rigidity had replaced the normally expressive limb. Rosette sighed. Something was definitely wrong.

'Go to the pools and bathe. You start at dawn tomorrow,' Mara instructed.

'I do?' Rosette's head tilted to the side, making one braid dip below her waist. *Start what?*

'You'll need a good rest tonight.'

Rosette nodded. 'Thank you, Mistress.'

Mara, already slipping out the chamber door, seemed to miss the gesture of gratitude.

Several candles fluttered out as the door whooshed closed. Pushing her sleeve to her elbow, Rosette took the silver candle snuffer and extinguished the remaining flames, all save one. Near darkness swallowed the room and doubt entered in with it.

Maybe coming to Treeon Temple had been a mistake. There were other ways to train in witchcraft and perfect the sword, other paths to developing her creative powers. She had done quite well under Nell's tutelage. If she'd known what life at Treeon Temple was really like, perhaps she would not have made the application in the first place.

Then where would I be?

She pulled on her boots and laced them. Taking a final look around the room, she snuffed the last candle and whispered a thank you to the Elementals. She stepped into the night, the spirits of Fire, Gaela, Air and Water dancing out with her.

The evening was cool and crisp, smelling of autumn, a hint of apples and freshly cut hay reminding her of warmer days. Pausing at the top of the steps, she closed her eyes and reached out her thoughts until they touched Drayco's mind. *I did it, Dray. I perfected the spell.* She could feel him yawn.

You've been doing that one for years.

I do it better now.

Coming home?

I'm going to bathe first. I won't be long.

He answered with a purr.

Rosette headed down the steps, peeking at the stars through the courtyard trees. At least Drayco had adapted to life at Treeon Temple. She wished others had adjusted to the two of them with as much ease. Shaking her head, she walked across the dimly lit plaza and down the path that led to the granite bathing pools. She relished the idea of soaking away her worries tonight. The pools were the best part of this place.

The path wound off to the left, beyond the horse barns and apple orchards. Torches lined the way like sentinels, making her squint after the darkness of the chamber. The bright, smoky light obscured the stars, but she looked up anyway. It felt like her arduous Saturn transit was going to last forever. She sighed. Of course, it wasn't really negative. She just had to do the work, pay the price, and earn the advancement. That's what mattered to Saturn, and if she were to get through this it had to matter to her as well.

Honour the gods, Rosette, each after their own nature, and you honour yourself. Ignore them and a demon is born. Nell's voice from the past came as a comfort and a guide.

Looking for the moon, she confirmed it had already set. It'd be nearly midnight now. Clay had probably given up on meeting her after training. He was a patient friend, but her consistent tardiness was probably beginning to irritate him. She wondered sometimes why he was so forgiving.

Her boots crunched on the gravel as she walked, silencing crickets and night owls along the way. If only she could silence the stream of thoughts running unchecked through her mind. They tumbled over and over with nagging doubts about myriad things, but tonight they centred on her relationship with Clay. For all his support, she didn't completely trust him.

There's no real reason not to. He's always there for me.

They'd spent every spare moment together since the chance meeting on the road. Lately, with her study load and his musical journeys to towns across the countryside, those moments were becoming fewer, yet she always found them fulfilling. They talked as they wandered, exploring the landscapes of Treeon. Together they perused the books and maps in the library, picnicked in the orchard under falling apple blossoms and swam in the crystal gorges behind the upper reservoirs. Sometimes they explored each other's bodies until the small hours of the night. Rosette smiled. Clay was definitely fun.

He was like a holiday away from the demands of her studies and she knew he loved her. She felt it in her soul and trusted it. What she didn't trust was the pesky doubt that something wasn't quite honest between them. He seemed to be everything he boasted — quite good at music, and quite good at lovemaking too. But underneath it all, something about him made her wary. She sensed a lie — Mulengro between them.

She wondered if he was committed to some other woman, or perhaps he'd lied about his past or his family. Well, she had done that too! Maybe she simply felt her own deceit thrown back in her face. Still, it festered. Whenever she tried to broach the subject with him it was like bouncing a ball off a brick wall. Clay was most skilled at deflection. Sometimes it would be hours later before she realised he hadn't actually answered her question. He was a true bard.

She shrugged. She didn't care about commitment or a formal relationship. She cared about friendship, love and intimacy. She cared about a feeling of family. Somehow, the murders that descended on her family's estate five years ago had come to the foreground of her thoughts again. A part of her feared that the funny feeling she had about Clay might be connected.

Or I'm just being paranoid.

She pretended everything was fine. She did that very convincingly, but it didn't change the apprehension. Aside from Drayco and Nell, there was no-one in the world with whom she felt completely safe — no-one she trusted implicitly. Jarrod too, of course, but she hadn't heard from him and probably never would. They'd agreed it would be so. They protected each other with silence.

Stop thinking about this! She put both hands to her head. *If you must think about it, put up a mind-shield, for great demon's sake.*

Without vigilance, a receptive 'traveller' might hear her thoughts, and there were plenty of those about, practising at all hours of the day and night. Their bodies remained inert, but anyone sensitive enough could feel their spirits darting around, learning to 'hear' the thoughts of others, sending messages of their own.

The last thing she wanted was to arouse curiosity about her past or her concern with Clay. He had moved up in rank in the last six months and enjoyed a fair measure of popularity. Suspicions would be reported to La Makee. If that happened, Rosette would have some explaining to do. She and Nell had agreed the past needed to remain buried. It would be safer that way.

Lost in her shielded thoughts, she raised her head just in time to avoid colliding into a group of girls coming up from the pools. They were wrapped in copper-coloured towels, their long wet hair dripping down their backs. They looked golden in the flicker of the torchlight and she wondered how she could have missed their approach with all the noise they made.

'Having a late one again, Rosette?' Amelia spoke, clutching her towel with one hand and pushing wet hair off her face with the other. 'You missed communal dinner.'

'Training,' Rosette replied. She barely slowed her pace, determined to continue along the track with just a nod and a smile. The pretence involved in conversing with these girls was not appealing. She didn't have the energy for it. Not tonight.

'You're always out in the wee hours,' Amelia said, moving to block the way. 'You, and that mammoth familiar of yours ... . where is it?' The girl looked around, eyes narrowing.

Rosette stopped just short of her and crossed her arms. '*He*, Amelia, not *it*. And how is Drayco's size, or my training schedule, any of your business?'

'I didn't mean to pry. I simply ...' Amelia stumbled back a step only to have her companions push her forward again. She stuck out her chin as she spoke: 'It's just that you're a recluse, and it's so big. How does a kitty-cat get to be that big?' She giggled with the rest of the girls.

'*He* is not a *kitty-cat*.' Rosette's jaw tightened.

'Oh, excuse me. Temple cat.' Her voice became sickly-sweet.

'If you're finished with the semantics,' Rosette dropped her arms to her sides and pushed forward, 'I'm going to the pools.'

'Not quite. I've a message.'

Rosette stopped. 'From whom?'

'Your "friend" Clay. He said if I saw you to let you know he couldn't wait any longer. He's off in the morning to Morzone.' She winked, her grin widening.

What are you hiding, little witch? Rosette glared. 'What else?' she asked aloud.

The girls around Amelia burst into laughter.

Without another word, Rosette pushed through them and continued down the track. Silly girls full of gossip and jealousy. When would they grow up? This was more about Clay than her, no doubt. Amelia had had her eye on him from the start.

Take him then, if it's so damn important to you. I don't care.

Rosette didn't bother to send her mental thoughts straight to Amelia. The girl wouldn't hear her anyway.

Take who? Drayco replied.

Oh, my lovely. It was just a random thought spilling out into the night.

Girls bothering you again?

No.

Really?

A little.

Do you want an escort?

Nah. Nearly there. She didn't want to think about it any more. She just wanted to submerge her body in the hot pools, have supper, curl up with her familiar and go to sleep.

To dream of the one I have never met? The question came from Drayco's mind, still linked.

Rosette smiled. *Yes, if I'm lucky.* She blew him a mental kiss and jogged down the path.

The high wooden doors that led to the granite bathing pools were open. Rosette unlaced her boots and lined them up on a low bench. There were no other shoes there, no sign of anyone else. Clay really had gone. He was travelling so much this season he'd make journeyman before his next birthday. She yawned. At least someone was progressing.

The granite slabs felt rough on her bare feet. They were wet but not slippery. Steam enveloped her, making her skin warm and damp. The place echoed with drips from the vaulted ceiling. She looked up only to see the reflected darkness of the pools and the orange glow of the torchlight. Beads of perspiration rose on her brow. The water would be hot tonight.

The pools were fed by deep underground fissures, heated by the lava streams that flowed beneath the surface. Although the temperature fluctuated, it was always warm. According to rumour, it was once so hot that an initiate had passed out and drowned. They were warned not to bathe alone, though Rosette did so from time to time.

Pushing lank strands of hair off her face, she looked down at the shimmering surface. The crystal water was black in the torchlight, as if it had no bottom. She watched the drips make circular patterns that radiated, sending on impact tiny waves towards all four corner steps. She couldn't wait to get in!

Unbuttoning her robe, she let it slip over her hips and fall to the ground. Reaching down to retrieve it, she cursed. The floor was soaking wet, water pooling around her feet. There had been many people here recently. She shook the robe out and hung it on a hook.

Rosette tuned into picking up any sound or thought around her. She was a receptive and a mind-traveller herself, more than a novice. Her range was expanding and she hoped to surprise Nell with a message this winter — a solstice greeting, mind to mind. Dumarka was a long way to send a thought deliberately — even Drayco couldn't do it — but she was determined to perfect this skill. Tilting her head and listening, she convinced herself she was the only one in the cavern.

She reached high above the row of hooks to the top shelf and found a dry towel. Inhaling, the scent of lavender and rose made her smile. She finished undressing and hung the rest of her clothes up, throwing the towel over her shoulder. While making her way to the steps, she untied her hair, setting the tiny silver bells chiming. She coiled her hair ties and bells into a nest at the edge of the steps, picked up a handful of salt grains and dipped her toe into the pool.

'Hot!' she exclaimed aloud. Her voice echoed through the empty chamber. 'Hot, hot, hot!'

She dropped her towel. The steam rose around her as she descended the submerged steps. Her hair fanned out over the surface of the water until, saturated, it sank to her buttocks. Just as the water lapped up to her breasts, she started sensing she wasn't alone. Her hand opened in reflex, the salt grains falling silently into the depths below.

'Hello?' She turned a complete circle, listening. Maybe Clay had come back to surprise her.

'Who's there?' She smiled, guessing it must be him. 'I didn't think you'd leave without seeing me, Cassarillo. Where are you hiding?'

'I thought we instructed initiates to be mindful of their environment.'

The voice was male, mature. Not Clay's.

Rosette's mind raced. She knew that voice, though she hadn't heard it directed towards her since the day she arrived. There was no mistaking the tone and accent. It was the Sword Master.

'Excuse me?' She tried not to squeak.

'I said,' he articulated slowly, 'what pressing matters occupy your mind that you're unable to sense my presence?'

'What pressing matters?' Rosette quickly found a rocky outcropping and sat down, water up to her collar-bones. She flushed. *How do I answer that?*

She couldn't lie, had no inclination to. She didn't want to spill out a stream of dribble either. That kind of response would never get her an apprenticeship with the man. And now she'd hesitated for so long, he certainly would think she had something quite involved to say.

She didn't. Only the small things, the day-to-day things, had been bubbling in her thoughts: like, should she braid her hair for the new training tomorrow, or leave it out? Mara hadn't even hinted at what kind of training it would be. Of course, she was also thinking more profoundly too. *What was Clay hiding? Did it have anything to do with the murder of her family?*

Stop! she chastised herself. Reinforcing her mind-shield, Rosette slipped her bottom off the marble seat and submerged her entire head under water.

Quick. Think of something!

Under the surface, Rosette heard the rush and reverberation of the waterfalls further downstream where the pools drained into the Terse River and eventually made their way to the sea. The tinkling of her earrings echoed in the current like a child's laughter. Her chest tightened. She couldn't hold her breath forever. She had to breathe.

Popping back up, she gasped, looking around. Where was he?

'Are you going to answer me?' he queried. 'Or turn into a fish?'

Rosette twisted in the direction of his voice, her forehead creasing. 'I didn't imagine anyone would be here this late,' she said, letting her breath out in a rush and gulping in another.

'Perhaps,' he said, creating ripples as he shifted on his perch, 'you need to develop your imagination.'

She could make out his silhouette now. He was leaning back against the side of the pool, one arm reaching out along its edge, the other behind his head like a pillow.

'And perhaps it would have been more courteous if you had announced your presence straight up.' Her voice gained volume. 'This is a place of leisure, Sword Master. I come here to unwind, not to test my receptivity skills.'

'There's no separation between the work and the life.' His voice sounded stern. 'You've also been cautioned against bathing alone.'

'Well, I'm not alone now, am I?' She snapped the words back, glaring in his direction.

He laughed. 'Have we met?'

Goddess of the night, he doesn't even remember me?

Now she was certain she wasn't under consideration for his apprenticeship. She bit her lip. Under no circumstances would she cry. Bother this man and his deprived memory!

'Yes,' she replied slowly. 'We met the day I arrived. You and Diablai gave me a lift to the demonstration, do you remember? It wasn't long ago, Sword Master Rowan An' Lawrence.'

'You're right, Rosette. It wasn't that long ago.' He moved into the light. 'How's the training going?'

What's he playing at? Does he know me or not? 'I'm progressing.'

'Are you ready for something new?'

'Say again?'

'Do you have a hearing problem?'

'What?'

Perhaps you can hear me more clearly now?

He sent the thought directly to her mind. Very strong. It surprised her how easily he slipped through her shield, or had she let it lapse?

I hear you, Sword Master.

'Get some rest tonight, Rosette,' he said aloud, swimming to the steps. 'It's time to put you to work.'

'Okay,' she whispered. 'I will.' Her mind started to spin with excitement. What did he mean?

He was ascending the stairs, water running off his bronzed back and his fingertips. His body was sculpted with rippling muscles etched with myriad tattoos. Her mouth formed a circle shape but she didn't speak.

'And, Rosette.' He paused midway up the steps. 'I'm the Sword Master, not a god. You can say anything to me that you like.'

She snapped her mouth shut and didn't reply. *How much of my mental clatter-nat did he pick up?*

She listened to the pad of his bare feet as he made his way to the exit. The huge wooden doors shut with a reverberating thud. She let out her breath, realising she'd held it in. Pushing away hair that clung to her face, she leaned back, staring up into the dark space above her.

'Now that's an attractive man,' she whispered.

She tucked her chin down and blew bubbles in the water. Their first conversation since arriving hadn't been like she'd imagined. It was actually quite peculiar, like a dream.

Taking another deep breath, Rosette swam to the steps and got a scoop of salt grains. She went wild with them, scrubbing her body. She immersed herself completely and then floated on her back — only her nose, forehead and toes peeking above the dark surface. The water buoyed her up in a loving embrace. Mesmerised by the rushing sounds beneath her, she kicked slowly back to the steps. It was getting late — time to head home.

One more thing, Rosette.

She startled as the Sword Master's voice boomed in her head. *I'm listening.*

Braid your hair for tomorrow.

Rosette saw the message tacked to her cottage door before she reached the porch. It shone in the lamplight, a small slip of paper pierced by a copper nail. Pulling the towel off her shoulders, she took the steps in two strides. She examined the seal before tucking the note in her pocket. Mistress Mara had paid her a visit. What tasks could she have for her at this hour? She'd said to get a good night's sleep, not work until dawn.

Yawning, Rosette smiled as Drayco appeared from nowhere. She forgot sometimes that he was a superb predator, adept at camouflage. He leapt the steps and pushed his head into her hand. She sank her fingers deep into his plush coat.

'Did you see Mara, my black hunter?'

Yes, and another. He purred, his words forming inside Rosette's mind like waves on a tropical shore, cresting, rushing up and receding. It was the closest thing to a mental caress she'd ever experienced.

'You're in a pleasant mood tonight,' she said as he arched his back against her bare thigh, tail entwining her waist.

Yes.

'Who else came by?' She continued to stroke the top of his head. 'Another mistress?'

No other mistress.

'Clay?' she smiled. 'You can say his name, you know.'

Drayco hadn't taken much to Clay. He wouldn't say his name and he wouldn't explain why. *Not him.*

She roughed his back vigorously. 'Are you going to tell me or is this a guessing game?'

Is there milk?

'Of course.'

The Sword Master came.

Chills rushed down Rosette's back. An' Lawrence had come here? 'With Mistress Mara?' she pressed.

He came after. The purring increased. *Could we possibly see to the milk now?*

Rosette tousled the temple cat's head then pulled her hand back when he reared and took a playful swipe. 'Yes, yes. Come inside and we'll both have some warm milk and honey.'

Honey tastes like tree sap.

'I like it.' Rosette laughed as her familiar mimed what could only be a cat trying to get peanut paste out of its mouth. 'Plain milk for you, of course.'

Thank you.

She unlaced her boots and lined them up by the door before entering her sanctuary. It smelled of herbs and scented candles, leather and polished wood. She gave the place a blessing as she crossed the threshold and lit the nearest candle. A warm glow filled the room.

I'm so grateful to be home.

She knew how lucky she was. Second- or third-year apprentices usually shared the tiny cottages down by the river with two or even three others, but Rosette, still unassigned, warranted one of her own. Unlike most of the students at Treeon Temple, she came with a large and vivacious familiar whose nature had been enough to get them a place to themselves before the sun had turned even a quarter past the first solstice.

It was clear that dormitory life was not for them, though they had done their best to fit in. Six weeks after her arrival, three different dorms and several roommates later, the entire temple population had supported her move to the cottage. She smiled at the memory.

How was I to know that your roommates didn't want rodents on their pillows every night? The temple cat sent the query when he picked up on her thoughts.

Rosette laughed. 'You know I don't care for it much.'

I always thought you were strange that way.

'Did you now?' she smiled. 'It all turned out fine because we have this place to ourselves.'

Lighting more candles, she reached into her pocket and fished out the note, ready to face whatever task her mentor had set for her. The message got straight to the point (no frills from Mistress Mara). She read it over twice between stoking the coals of her hearth, pouring milk from the cool box and slicing a thick piece of bread. Her body shook when she finally put the message down on the table.

Maudi? Drayco inquired. *Are you going to give me the details or burst on the spot?'*

'You're not going to believe this.' *I don't even believe it,* she added in her mental voice.

Drayco jumped onto a chair beside the table and continued to purr, black cat hairs levitating about him when she scratched behind his ears. *I'd like to have the chance to believe, or not believe, if only you would tell me. Your thoughts are a jumble. I can't read them.* He spoke in a curious tone, feline sarcasm. *Is it good news? At least tell me that.*

'Oh, I think so!' she said, hugging herself to keep from floating away. 'Mara says I'm to start sword classes tomorrow! Tomorrow, Drayco. Tomorrow morning!'

It's tomorrow then?

She flicked his tail. *It is!* 'I thought I would have to stay with the ritual spells for another six months at least. Actually, I was beginning to wonder if I would ever get a chance to train with the sword at all. What a surprise.'

Not such a surprise when you consider the level of your intention. How's the milk coming along? He leapt down to sit closer to the fire, watching the pot begin to steam.

'What's that, Dray?' she asked, reading the note for a third time.

The milk?

'Here it is.' She poured it into a bowl and placed it in front of him. 'Hot.'

I like it hot.

She stroked his neck as he began to lap. 'Now we just have to figure out why the Sword Master came by. That was after Mara, yes?'

It was.

'What could he have wanted?'

Reading his note might elaborate. Drayco sent the suggestion in spurts, clearly not wanting to be distracted from his bowl.

'What?'

He paused to stare at her. *The note from the Sword Master. Perhaps you would learn more if you read it.*

Tiny droplets of milk spattered his whiskers and he licked them off with his pink tongue before going back to the bowl.

Rosette sprinted out to the front porch. 'Where is it?' she yelled, squinting up at the lamplight. She checked the doorframe, and then looked down at the bristly horsehair mat. There it was, tucked under the left-hand corner. Clutching the note, she brought it into the firelight to read.

'It's from him, Drayco. It is from the Sword Master himself!'

Really? The feline's comment dripped down the edges of her mind.

'Shush. I am reading.'

Read it to me too, Drayco instructed without looking up. *Aloud.*

'Okay. It says ... "Rosette de Santo, You will be attending sword classes starting tomorrow. Best you don't lose concentration in my arena. Report at dawn. RL".'

She pressed the note to her heart. 'He signed it *RL*!'

His initials perhaps? Drayco had finished the bowl of milk and was grooming himself by the fire. His wit, as usual, increased in proportion to the fullness of his belly.

'Of course it's his name! R. L., Rowan Lawrence! It's just that personal initials are not often used in correspondence to initiates. Could it mean he is going to make me his apprentice?'

You read a lot into it. Drayco looked up briefly before twisting around to reach a spot directly between his shoulderblades.

Rosette smiled at her companion. 'Just let me have this thrill. He wrote to me. He called me by name. I will be in his class!'

Drayco looked at her and sneezed.

'I can't wait to tell Clay.'

He's gone.

'I heard.'

He left earlier tonight, headed for Morzone. Supposedly he's playing for a wedding celebration on Sunday.

Rosette turned her head. 'What do you mean, "*supposedly*"?'

Drayco stood, bow-stretched and lay down on the sheepskin in front of the fire. He tucked his front paws under his chest before responding. *I mean 'supposedly' because first of all, he took with him a bird of prey, hooded and clutching his gloved wrist. Tell me, when did he become a falconer? Second, he left by the south gate. If he was going to Morzone, he planned to get there the long way around.*

Rosette stared at him. 'How'd you get so good at geography?'

I know what you know, Maudi, and then some. Clay wasn't going where he said. He was going south, towards Lividica.

'Or maybe he was just going home to Cusca first.'

Maybe.

'You don't sound convinced.'

If he was going to Cusca first, he'd never get to Morzone in time for a Sunday wedding.

Chapter 8

Drayco was right. Clay hadn't gone to Morzone; he'd gone to Lividica.

He sat at a table in the harbour pub, smoke floating in drifts around him. He'd drained three pints of home draught in the last half hour and was on his fourth. If he didn't stop guzzling, his performance would definitely suffer, but he didn't care. He wanted to escape.

He picked up his guitar and checked the tuning. Low E was flat and he tightened the tuning peg slowly while plucking the string, comparing it to his top E and the harmonics further up the neck. His ear was bent close to the fret board as he strained to hear the subtle changes in pitch — not an easy task in the boisterous pub with glasses clanking, people cackling, an argument exploding in one corner, and fists pounding the table behind him accompanied by shouts for more beer. The cacophony was more than distracting — it felt like debris floating down the river of his mind, smacking into his thoughts, bumping them out of place.

'I never heard of the girl,' a drunken voice declared.

'Nor I. It's a ghost he's after, I'll wager.'

'Plenty of them around.'

'How would you know? You weren't there.'

'Neither were you.'

The voices drifted into the background of his mind as a fight broke out, a table overturning and glasses breaking before the barman tossed the drunks out. Clay sighed. They would call for more songs any minute and though he was exhausted, and quite drunk himself, he looked forward to getting lost in the music again. His performances were a success even if nothing else about this trip had been. Damn the Sword Master and his cryptic intentions.

Seven days ago, on his way to meet Rosette at the bathing pools, Clay had been waylaid by An' Lawrence — the mission urgent. He hadn't had a chance to say goodbye to her or even offer an explanation. Of course, it would have been a lie, whatever he said, but at least he could have seen her. He didn't like the idea of leaving her stranded with only a message from Amelia. He could just imagine how that would translate. He sighed again.

Women ...

An' Lawrence had given him an assignment he didn't like, yet he couldn't — or was it 'wouldn't' — refuse. He was to take a mountain horse, along with one of the Sword Master's falcons, and travel down through Cusca, skirting the Jacor mountain range to the port of Lividica, Rosette's home town, or so she said. He was charged with finding out anything he could about the young witch.

'Find her family, Clay,' An' Lawrence had instructed. 'Discover everything you can about her past. I particularly want you to find her connections,' the Sword Master had gone on. 'Are any of her relations linked to the witch Nellion Paree? From the past? From Treeon perhaps? I want to know everything, and for them to suspect nothing. Do you understand? Play your songs and ask your questions as if you were a curious lad in love with an elusive young woman. That would be the best ploy.'

Clay laughed. Ploy? It wouldn't take much of a witch's glamour to pull that off. If he wasn't already curious about Rosette before this trip, he certainly was now. The *'in love'* aspect was a given — had been so since the day they'd met. What he discovered, though, didn't put him at ease and he was certain it wouldn't satisfy the Sword Master.

He'd been here a week now, playing his music in every pub from the northern docks to South Lister Bay. Between sets, and in the busy shops and markets by day, he'd asked his questions. He queried as any enthusiastic suitor might, but nobody in the whole town had ever heard of Rosette de Santo. There was a Rosa de Santiago, and a Rosie del Mar. There was even a Vera and Armone de Santo, but no Rosette. It was like he'd dreamed her up and word was getting around that the redheaded bard from the north played wonderful tunes but seemed to be looking for a girl that didn't exist.

He flicked the breadcrumbs from the table when his dinner plate was cleared away.

'You'll be playing more?' the maid asked, her dimpled face blushing as she balanced the tray of crockery on her hip.

'Yeah, sure.' Clay managed a wink before he returned to his contemplations.

The results of his queries weren't completely fruitless. He had aroused the interest of more than a few young women, gorgeous girls enamoured with his eccentric ways and alluring music. The flirtations were heady and he was planning to act on one of them tonight. He'd met her today by the jetty, a girl full of charm — touching his arm when she spoke, giggling at his every sentence and jouncing her bosom when she laughed outright. Her embroidered peasant top and short white skirt had made a very pretty backdrop for her waves of chestnut hair. If he couldn't distract himself with the likes of her, he needed to visit the local herbalist. He wondered when they opened.

Clay drank the last of his beer and stared at the empty glass. Tipping it slightly to the side, it caught the light from a candle, creating sparks of brilliance on the rim.

The punters were turning his way, eyebrows up, glasses raised. Their desires were clear and if he was to do well when he passed the hat, he'd best give them one last round of songs. He put down the glass and finished tuning his guitar. Soon he'd be playing and that would vanquish the torment from his mind, for a while. It was like shooing away a stray cat, though. As soon as he turned his back, it'd be there again, right beside him. Meow.

Rosette was always on his mind, and having to leave Treeon and dig into her past rankled Clay like no previous assignment. Why hadn't he walked that first day? This had been the worst year of his life.

He laughed at himself. Who was he kidding? This had been the best year of his life. Besides, he couldn't walk away from Rosette, not then, and certainly not now. Clay was living a paradox that haunted him — Rosette had become his love and his nemesis all in one. He wouldn't dare cross the Sword Master, who insisted on the deception, and he could barely look Rosette in the eye because of it. It was like being trapped between a bear and a lion and he didn't know how to free himself. He wasn't even sure it was possible, and now here he was, in her home town — supposedly her home town — searching out her past and coming up with nothing.

'Rosette de Santo? Nah. No girl of that name or description, but there are plenty of de Santos further east. Perhaps you are in the wrong seaport? Have you tried Flureon?'

He got the same story every time he asked, except from the girl he met today, the girl on the jetty. Sally. She had told him there had been someone here like he described, until about six years ago. She had lived on an estate with her family not far out of town. She matched his description right down to her slender arms, wide eyes, hawknose and flowing black hair, but her name was not Rosette. Her name was Kalindi Matosh, and she had been murdered, along with the rest of her family. Tragic, really. Assassins from Corsanon had done it. Never caught, though. Intuitively, he felt it was true and not just a fancy strategy to get his attention which she definitely wanted. But between the flirts and hints and innuendos he learned things about Rosette he'd wished he hadn't. It could not be undone now and it would have to be reported to An' Lawrence. What he would do with such news, Clay could only imagine. Meanwhile, he twisted alternately between feeling like the betrayer and the betrayed.

Clay pushed his chair back and walked towards the stage. He stumbled on the way up. This would be his last gig. He was heading home tomorrow, as soon as Sally was through with him and the hangover eased.

He'd sent a message back to Treeon earlier in the day via Clawdia, the Sword Master's peregrine falcon. It unnerved him to call in the bird, but he swallowed hard, donned the red cap and walked out to the very end of the jetty to wait. The smell of fish and salt air had filled his lungs and the constant barking of sea lions had drowned out all other sounds. He'd pulled on the leather glove, stretched out his arm and closed his eyes until wind had swept across his face.

When he'd opened them, the falcon was back-winging onto his wrist. The huge talons, seemingly out of proportion to her delicate frame, wrapped around the leather gauntlet. They pinched through the glove and into his flesh. He shivered.

'Welcome, beauty. We're friends, remember?' He found it hard to breathe. 'It looks like you'll be home long before me after all.'

The blue-black head tilted at Clay's words. She blinked her eye once, as if to say, *Of course.*

'Can I give you a message for An' Lawrence?'

At the sound of the Sword Master's name, Clawdia whistled loudly. She fanned the air, extending her wings to reveal creamy-white underparts.

Clay cringed, holding the message in the palm of his hand, a note tucked into a small leather scroll case. She rolled it over, her razor sharp beak surprisingly gentle against his skin. When she had it just right, she grabbed it with her talons, looking him straight in the eye.

'Okay, gorgeous one. Go home!' He launched her with a sudden lift of his arm and watched as she disappeared up into the clouds.

One more night's work and he would follow her, back to Treeon and his mysterious girl Rosette.

The pastel hues of daybreak washed over Rosette. She sat sipping jasmine-flower tea and stirring a small pot of porridge. She ate in silence. Drayco's whiskers twitched softly in his sleep where he lay curled like a living pillow in the middle of her bed, his black fur a stark contrast to the red velvet spread. She smiled, catching the dream image of a dusky she-lion giving him a nose touch in the night.

Dressing in dark leggings, sword-belt and leather bodice, she gazed into the mirror, braiding her hair. She skipped the silver bell charms, weaving in a strand of thin red leather instead. Her thoughts were on the challenge ahead. If she impressed the Sword Master straight up, she would have a better chance of gaining an apprenticeship. He chose only a handful of initiates each year and there had to be over fifty students clamouring for the position. They'd been practising formally all summer, which Rosette had not. The odds weren't good, though she kept her spirits up, her intention clear.

I'm going to get this. I'm really happy I'm going to get this!

She took a moment to feel what it would be like to have the apprenticeship with An' Lawrence and grinned. She looked forward to the physical exercise. It would be a welcome change from quiet meditations, extensive astral research and endless rituals. She put on a necklace of obsidian, for containment, secured her multiple braids in a high horse tail at the back of her head, and kissed the sleeping Drayco goodbye.

'Wish me luck, my lovely,' she whispered, quietly slipping out the door.

By noon, the sweat was pouring down her back, her cheeks were flushed and her mouth dry. How silly it was to have worried about impressing An' Lawrence. The man was nowhere in sight. Even if he had been around, she'd not have made much of a mark on his memory. All her attention was directed towards staying on her feet and avoiding blows from her relentless opponent and his wooden practice sword.

He was a fourth-year apprentice, strong, supple and lightning fast, nicknamed Zero, which seemed to equate with the number of times she could actually strike him back. Offence was completely out of the question now. It was all she could do to keep him from cracking her ribs, snapping her arms and sweeping her off her feet.

This wasn't training. It was an exercise in sheer survival. It might have been better if she hadn't said, with a boast, that she knew her way around the sword and staff. Zero seemed bent on proving otherwise.

Dozens of students had gathered to watch. Didn't they have something better to do with their time? What could possibly be so interesting about a young woman being repeatedly thrashed by a superior opponent?

'Break for lunch, Rosette?' Zero suggested as their practice swords thudded together in a rare draw. 'You've earned it.'

The jarring motion reverberated down her aching arm. She looked up at him, squinting to blink the perspiration out of her eyes. 'Have I?'

'Sure. No-one's ever lasted this long on their first day.' He had barely worked up a sweat. His breath was only a little uneven, though his smile remained broad. If nothing else, he seemed to be enjoying himself.

'Lunch would be welcome.' Rosette gasped for air as her chest rose and fell. She was beyond trying to conceal her exhaustion and frustration. Thank the goddess it was noon. If she hit the ground once more, she wouldn't bother getting up.

They walked together to the canal that skirted the training grounds on its way to the crops and orchards. The fresh water coursed along to all the complexes at Treeon through an ancient system of aqueducts. Some drove a series of waterwheels and paddles that generated power, but mostly they were for bathing, heating and irrigation. Zero nodded for her to drink first.

Dropping to her knees, Rosette took a few tentative sips from the clear mountain water then immersed her entire head in the rapid stream. She kept it under as long as she could, drowning out the sound of laughter around her. The other students had followed them, unwilling to disperse.

Lifting her head, hands braced against the smooth granite sides of the trough, she wasn't sure if the last of her breakfast would stay down. Inhaling deeply, she dunked her head again before flinging it up, spray flying through the air from her hair. A mix of sweat and dirt dripped from her shoulders and down her back, making tiny rain-dot patterns in the powdery dust. In this state, she cupped her hands delicately in the stream and drank her fill.

'You seem a little ragged, Rosette de Santo.'

She spun around. What great timing for the Sword Master to appear. Her knees, which had barely kept her upright, were trembling. She swayed briefly when she stood.

He smiled. 'It's all right, Rosette. Everyone goes through this at the start. You'll find yourself fit and strong in no time, though I did think you would have had more stamina.'

There it was again — criticism. Or was it a goad? She wondered how long he had been there — how long he had watched. She wanted to disappear, to vanish on the spot. Perhaps she could learn to weave a spell for such a thing.

I'll bet Mistress Mara could have taught me that.

Too late. She had to face the Sword Master, and she planned to do it with grace and whatever dignity she could gather.

'Master An' Lawrence, I assure you I have more stamina than you can imagine.' She had wanted to say just the right words, but these came out before she could bite them back. Not exactly the line she had hoped to deliver. What possessed her to utter such a challenge?

Everyone around them went suddenly still. This tête-à-tête was gathering even a larger audience than her activities in the training ring. She ignored their presence and focused on the man in front of her — the man she desperately wanted to train her.

'So it's *my* imagination that is in question now?' His eyebrows went up, and he folded his arms across his bare chest.

'Rosette,' Zero cut in, 'it is not appropriate to speak to the Sword Master as if ...'

'What's not appropriate is the way you go about this indirect assessment ...' Rosette snapped her mouth shut, stopping the words before she dug herself in any deeper.

An' Lawrence did not appear amused. 'Eat something, Rosette. Rest. I'll train with you myself at second call. We'll test both our imaginations then, shall we?'

An' Lawrence nodded to Zero, and gave Rosette a fleeting smile before walking away.

Rosette stared at his back. No-one was laughing now. Most of the glances she caught out of the corner of her eye had the flavour of pity in them. Her fellow students seemed to feel sympathy for her bad luck at having to match wits and skills with the Sword Master so soon. Well, bring it on. Second call was two hours away and she would have recovered by then.

Filling her waterbag, she watched the stream rush past her submerged hand. It tickled her fingers, cool and soothing against the bruised skin and bones. Pushing in the cork and shaking her hands dry, she took off her boots, freeing her aching feet. Her stomach growled.

Slinging her waterbag and boots over her shoulder, she replaced her practice sword on the rack and grabbed some bread, dried meat and fruit from the long table. It had been set out for the students to eat, converse and refresh themselves, but Rosette had no desire to join in. The last thing she wanted was to sit with others and chat or, worse yet, endure an equally confronting silence. She didn't have the energy.

Only one place called to her and she headed there as fast as her tired legs could carry her. Down the path and over a short rise, she made her way to where the fruit trees grew. If she could rejuvenate anywhere, it was there — in the orchard.

Rosette strolled under rows of apple trees, feeling nothing but the gentle autumn breeze on her damp skin and the easy give of the grass beneath bare feet. Tossing her boots to the ground, she sat cross-legged in the shade of the largest. Stories were told of how this tree had arrived as a seed in the belly of a strange bird, perhaps from the lost Southern Continent. Dormant in the summer and lush with fruit in the spring, it certainly had its seasons back to front. Now and then, random blooms drifted down, a rain of pink and white petals.

Breathing in their scent, she revelled in the combination of apple buds, green wood and freshly cut grass. Heavenly! This was one of her favourite sanctuaries. It always rejuvenated her.

Drayco? Lunch with me in the orchard?

You sound tired.

I am.

I'll come.

Unwrapping the bread and meat, she took a long drink from her waterbag. She was famished. Eyeing the sandwich after the first bite of sourdough and dried beef, she scanned the ground near the base of the tree, spotting fresh watercress. She plucked a few sprigs to add to her meal. Delicious.

While munching, she looked out between the near-bare branches of the other fruit trees to the distant horizon. The view to the south seemed so far away. The sky rushed down to meet the hills in a bright and cloudless cornflower blue. It was still, like a painting, peaceful and calm. She knew it was anything but.

That was where she had come from, the south. An agitated place, etched by the fierce and pounding Azul Sea, it was less than welcoming to her thoughts. The people of that land were as tough and harsh as the storms that shaped them and anything unique was shunned in their urge to conform and survive. Lividica had swallowed her family whole. She never wanted to go there again.

Then her thoughts turned to Jarrod. Was he still hunting in the forests, stripping off to swim in the protected coves, fishing from the jetty? Would he be working full-time for his father, shoeing horses and making wrought-iron gates? He'd been a skilled blacksmith at seventeen and his family would have pressured him to stay. Or would he have been accepted into Montava University to study the healing arts? That's where his deeper talent lay. Rosette wished he was here now to heal her. She missed him fiercely still, though she seldom indulged in the memories any more.

Dreaming of him again?

Rosette looked up to see Drayco pacing towards her, a limp brown rabbit in his mouth. *You brought your own lunch, I see.*

And you look like you let the opponent win.

I did.

Any particular reason?

Yeah. He was superior.

Drayco lay down in the shade near her and tackled his lunch. *You'll improve.*

I'm glad you think so.

She roughed his neck and turned to the east. There the Prieta Mountains jutted up like dragons' teeth, sheer, majestic, treacherous. The sky was not so blue in that direction, more a cool mauve. It wasn't the softest of views, yet it offered inspiration. She thought she must be less like the sea, more like the mountains — less thrashing, more impervious.

When she had finished eating, she meditated on those distant peaks, allowing the breeze and the sky and the blossoms and the sun to flow in and out of her with each breath. She let the magnitude of Gaela instil her with strength. Soon she felt ready to face An' Lawrence, and for once she wasn't thinking of impressing him. She was thinking of how she might survive his instruction when they sparred.

The Sword Master was like those mountains to the east: magnificent, imposing, untouchable. She knew she had no chance, physically, against him with a sword. That wasn't the question, or the point. She would have to use her wits to avoid being hammered, and he would see if she could be even for a moment. She was there to learn and he to instruct. Perhaps if she did it subtly enough, she could augment her skills with a little help from the Elementals?

Risky, isn't it, Maudi?
A bit.

It was taboo to boost with magic during training. People got hurt that way. It was taught to journeymen only after years of preparation. Rosette had learned it from Maka'ra, four summers ago, and she'd been sorely tempted to use the technique when sparring with Zero. She'd resisted.

You coming to watch, Dray?
She asks me to stay clear of her grounds.
She?
The one who hides.
And you obey?
Of course.

Rosette laughed and kissed the top of his head.
Good luck, Maudi.
I'll need it. How much more of this can I take?

* * *

Apparently much more.

Standing face to face, wooden swords gripped high above their heads in both hands, Rosette readied for attack. She had no intention of being intimidated. None. This was their fourth and final sparring round.

So far, after drilling her in a set of basic forms for over an hour, An' Lawrence had dropped and pinned her within seconds, three times running. If she didn't use some magic soon, she would have no face to save.

Rosette sprang. Lunging forward with her right leg, she dipped her sword in a flash and swung a wide arc towards the left side of the Sword Master's chest. Too wide. Too slow. He countered effortlessly with a downward block. She swung again, this time to his right shoulder. Blocked again.

With each attack, she became more frustrated, swinging harder, wilder. Suddenly he turned his sword, flat of the blade towards her chest, and propelled her backwards off her feet. She felt it coming, that extra push. There was magic in it, not just brute force. Was he taunting her? Two could play that game.

Rosette let the momentum of his force drive her backwards. She tucked her chin, curled like a pill bug and hit the ground in a somersault. She was on her feet in an instant, blade fixed towards his heart as he bounded forward.

'Well done,' he said, loud enough for the gathered audience to hear.

Every sword student in Treeon, and more than a few teachers, had assembled to watch. Rosette ignored the cheers and stayed focused.

'I'm nowhere near done,' came her grating reply. Peripherally she could see initiates jostling around the dusty ring, stretching this way and that for a better view. If they wanted a show, she'd give them one.

She gathered her energy and drove forward with a low, crouching sweep. It did not catch him unawares. He leapt over her blade as she cut through the air, projecting energy from her centre, up her arms and down the wooden blade. The weapon was a sluggish conductor, yet she managed to knock him back as she blocked his next thrust. Pressing her minute advantage, she cracked her blade into his ribs, energy and all. First strike.

No good. His blade was there to meet hers before she touched his flesh. Inches from each other, they locked eyes. She felt the rise and fall of his chest, dusky scents mingling as her breath matched his. All her might was pressed against him, and he blocked it with ease, and something else as well.

He drank the energy in. He drank her in. She could feel it! Her heart pounded and her breath tore the air with ragged gasps. He pulled her to him before she could boost again and her wooden sword fell to the ground. His hands tightened around her wrists.

Pressed against his neck, she could taste his salty skin. She didn't know whose sweat dripped down her cheek, his or hers. The grip tightened further. She winced as her bangles dug into her flesh.

'You're not to boost with magic, Rosette,' he whispered into the dampness of her hair. His lips moved slowly as the words formed against the curve of her ear. 'This is not practised in the arena. Not yet.'

'You used it first!' she said, tempted to bite. She let her teeth rest against his pulsing jugular. 'I felt it.'

'Did you?'

Beneath the bravado, Rosette sensed the tiniest hint of surprise. Then she knew. He was shielding his mind, holding something from her. He had not expected her to feel his magic. This could give her an advantage.

Too late. While she speculated, the Sword Master arched his back, lifted his arms and flipped her to the ground. As she hit, the air in her lungs rushed out and his knee came down hard on her hip. He pinned her arms above her head.

'Would you say that I have you now, Rosette de Santo, for the fourth time?' An' Lawrence dropped his face to her cheek, the roughness of his stubble brushing away the dust and sweat as he spoke.

No, I would not! Rosette went for one last move. She let her entire body go limp as her lungs silently filled with air. He shifted the weight off her hip and she twisted like a cat inside its skin. Calling on a colossal boost of magic centred in her spine, she sent energy to her legs, tucking them to her belly, flipping over and pulling the Sword Master with her. Now his head was between her legs, his arms — for a millisecond — pressed into the powdery ground on either side of her thighs. Not exactly the position she had in mind, but a small point none the less. She had him flat on his back.

'Not quite yet.' She could sense the stunned aura of the gathering. It would have been better if she had sensed his next move.

His energy came from nowhere, no sign of a build-up, just total release. She was on her back in an instant with the Sword Master astride her hips, the weight of his pelvis against hers. He had her arms bound across her breasts and sweat fell from his forehead onto her throat.

'You win, of course,' she said as she shielded her mind. She started to gather energy like a tornado draws in the sky.

A quizzical look came over his face for such a brief moment she wasn't sure if it had been there at all. Suddenly he was on his feet, pulling her up from the ground.

'That'll do, Rosette. And well done. My imagination has been whetted, I'll admit. Where did you learn those moves?' he asked.

'From ... my brothers,' she answered, catching herself before she talked of Maka'ra or Jarrod.

'Brothers? Did they train at Bangeesh Temple?'

Rosette stumbled. 'They work on their own, mostly.'

She shielded her mind tighter. Not every sword master had formal training in a temple or even belonged to a coven larger than one or two. It was plausible.

'You're lucky you had them.' He smiled, taking in her bedraggled look. *And where did you learn that magic? It's not Nell's,* he asked telepathically.

She didn't reply.

Rosette?

She shrugged her shoulders. *Here and there.*

He looked at her, his expression impenetrable. *Indeed.* 'We're done for the day. Go to the baths now, and see the healer.'

'I'm fine.' She glared at him, daring him to contradict her.

An' Lawrence shook his head from side to side. 'You're cut, bruised and bleeding. Do as I say, and please stop questioning my every direction; it's getting tedious.'

'Yes, Sword Master.' Rosette gave him a brief bow then picked up her weapon, brushed the dust off the hilt and headed towards the baths. The crowd made way before her, whispering things she did not bother to hear. She lifted her head, her shoulders back, stilling her mind even as her legs quivered beneath her. She just had to get to the baths without them giving out, then she could let go.

For the next month, the routine did not change. Rosette trained with Zero and sparred with the initiates until noon, then did forms with a full class of apprentices under the guidance of several other senior instructors.

Sometimes, in the last hour, the Sword Master would come and watch, making a comment or an adjustment here and there. He rarely looked her way or seemed to notice her progress.

Until today.

She had done her forms at the back row of the class with two other initiates and was sitting on her heels in meditation. When the gong sounded she stirred, rising to head for a welcome soak in the pools. The sun was dropping towards the horizon and already the air was turning cold.

'How are you finding the training, Rosette?' An' Lawrence stood in front of her, blocking her way.

'I'm progressing.' She tilted her head up to look him in the eyes. 'But you already know that.'

'Take a beating today?'

She glanced at her arms. Bruised patches and grazes were mixed with dust and sweat. 'I'm okay.'

'Of course you are.'

She continued to match his gaze. He clearly had more on his mind than bantering with her. Rosette lifted her eyebrows, inquiring.

'You'll have supper at my lodge tonight.'

'I will?'

An' Lawrence glared at her.

'I will. At sunset. Thank you.' She bowed.

He nodded and moved on.

Why in the world does he want me to join him for supper? Elation flooded her mind as she hurried to her cottage. *This has to be good news about the apprenticeship.*

Excited as she was, her body protested. Every bone, every muscle, vein and tendon ached. Her legs wobbled with the effort of climbing the three little steps to her cottage door, turning the brass knob and stepping inside. How would she ever be able to lift her sword tomorrow? But she had thought that every night, and every morning she managed. It was getting easier, and she was getting stronger, bit by bit.

Who hurt you this time?

Rosette looked down at the welts, scrapes and bruises rising on her arms and legs that glistened with the healer's ointment. 'No-one hurt me really. It's all part of the training.'

The large feline stared at her unblinking. *I will crush them for you.* Drayco's tone was calm, matter-of-fact.

'That won't be necessary, but thanks.' She smiled as his purr rumbled through the cottage. 'Training with the sword is very rough.'

Will you rest now?

'I'm to go back up and see the Sword Master, for supper.'

Why?

'Hopefully, he wants to tell me that although I am ruthlessly beaten to a pulp daily, he thinks I am apprentice material.'

Will he?

She shrugged. 'I don't know.'

What do the planets say?

'Good question. I've been under Saturn transits all year, of course, so hard work and slow progress is natural right now. But Jupiter approaches my Mars opposition Venus and squares the south lunar node.'

Say it in a way that makes sense to me?

'I get the feeling of adventure, expansion and something to do with the past or someone from the past. Jupiter is honoured by being open to new possibilities and in return he expands the mind through higher learning, the body through travel and the spirit through deeper meditation and magic.'

Sounds like we are going on a trip to meet an old friend.

'Or being offered an apprenticeship with the Sword Master!'

I'd like a trip.

She laughed and brushed her hair, wondering what supper with the Sword Master would be like. They certainly hadn't struck an even stride with each other yet. What would they talk about?

I will come too.

'Only if you like, Dray. It'll be a quick bite and either good news, or a lecture about using magic during training.'

You did?

'Not today. That's why I'm so beat up!'

Drayco picked up a paw and licked it. *I'll come anyway.*

'Are you sure?'

She says I may.

Rosette shot him a look. 'His familiar?'

Her name is Scylla.

'I can't wait to see this!'

Chapter 9

Drayco sat statue-still beside Rosette, a formidable companion. His black tufted ear and long whiskers brushed the top of her thigh as she knocked lightly on the Sword Master's door.

Her hand dropped to the top of his head. *I'm glad you're here.*

Me too, Maudi.

Slipping off her boots, she let her toes dig into the fine, plush mat and knocked again, this time a little louder.

'Enter,' the Sword Master called.

Rosette straightened her shoulders, wincing slightly as she turned the knob. She stepped over the threshold, Drayco by her side.

'Close the door behind you,' An' Lawrence said without looking up from the hearth. When the latch clicked, he turned around, staring at Drayco. 'This'll be interesting.'

'You didn't say not to ...'

Before she could finish, a warning hiss came from the rafters, answered immediately by Drayco's throaty growl.

It's her! It's Scylla, Drayco boomed into Rosette's mind.

'Oh boy,' she whispered, following his gaze up to the ceiling. 'Maybe I should have asked first ...'

Smaller than Drayco, this temple cat — if that was what she was — had long buff-coloured hair and a bobbed tail. Her ears had tufted tips that looked like black feathers and her paws were huge and shaggy. She hissed like a viper and sprang to the ground in front of them, hackles up.

'Steady, Scylla,' An' Lawrence said, putting his hand out in front of her face. The bristling feline moved her head to the side to see around his fingers and hissed again. 'These are *invited* guests.'

He stroked her hackles down only to have them shoot back up. 'May I present my familiar, Scylla from the South Tuscian cliffs.' He turned and spoke in a formal tone: 'Scylla, this is Drayco of Dumarka and his mistress Rosette of whom I have spoken. They're welcome company.'

He emphasised the last two words, and slowly her stance relaxed and her hackles went down. The nape of her neck seemed much smaller now, almost delicate.

She's beautiful, Drayco crooned.

That she is. I'd watch the temper, though, if I were you. 'Pleased to meet you, Scylla,' Rosette smiled. 'I heard you had a familiar, Sword Master, though I've never seen her. Drayco has sent her messages but says she almost never replies.'

'She keeps to herself. She keeps to me.'

'I know what that's like.'

He waved Rosette to the large oak dining table. 'Hungry?'

Very! Drayco replied loudly in her mind, although he did not look at the table, or even sniff towards the hearth. He was all but inhaling Scylla. They cautiously sniffed each other from a safe distance.

'Don't even think about it,' Rosette replied aloud.

'Pardon?' An' Lawrence frowned at her.

'Sorry. What did you say?'

'I was asking if you were hungry.'

She had been famished, but now that she sat at the Sword Master's table, she didn't know if she could eat. A wave of exhaustion washed over her. The smell of supper, the intimacy of his lodge, the warmth of the fire and the glow of the candles all conspired to mellow her senses. What she really wanted was to hear that she'd secured an apprenticeship and then go home, close her eyes and fall asleep.

She didn't answer.

'You're exhausted,' he said.

'I'm fine.'

'I can't get through your mind-shield any more. Good work, but I know how to add up.'

She looked at him blankly.

'You've been thrashed every day for a month in the arena.' He raised his hand to keep her from interrupting. 'When you aren't being battered, you're boosting your energy-force like a warrior. Forbidden at this stage, of course, but well executed.'

'You've been watching?'

'I'm always watching, Rosette.' He rubbed his chin. 'The point is, boosting is hard work. Drains the resources. You're also fatigued with a sense of culpability. Do I have to remind you why we don't want apprentices using magic on the practice field?'

Apprentices? Her heart lifted until she saw the expression on his face. This was a scolding, not an award.

She folded her hands in her lap and looked down at them, responding by rote: 'Initiates and apprentices do not boost because it is dangerous to themselves and to others; we don't have the control or the experience to execute that calibre of magic whilst wielding a weapon.'

'So you do know the rule.'

'I know it.'

'And can you admit to me you could use some healing?'

'I've had ointment from the healer.'

'That wasn't what I asked.'

She exhaled. 'A healing would be appreciated, thank you. Either that or a long, belated holiday.'

'Not so bull-headed as I thought,' he mumbled under his breath.

'Excuse me?'

'It's just a healing, Rosette, not a challenge. I want you at your peak tomorrow.'

'What's happening tomorrow?'

He didn't answer.

Scylla jumped back up to her perch in the rafters, seemingly uninterested in what was happening at the table. She did, however, give a little purr as she leapt. An invitation? It must have been, the way Drayco sprang after her.

'First the exhaustion,' the Sword Master continued. 'We need to get rid of that.'

'Do your best.' She laughed, but it sounded nervous to her ears.

An' Lawrence stood behind her chair and tingles shot up her spine. He reached out with both hands, letting them hover above her shoulders, moving them slowly down to her elbows, her forearms, and over her long slender fingers. Waves of energy coursed through her and though he never touched her body, she felt instantly revitalised.

'That's good.'

'Now the wounds,' he said.

Rosette had no idea how much time passed. She opened her eyes to see An' Lawrence slicing bread at a high table near the fire. He must have lit more candles, as the room seemed brighter now.

'You're back,' he said.

'I feel ...'

'Yes?'

'I feel ... totally refreshed!'

'That was the goal.'

The proximity to him, the resonance of his voice and the crackle of the fire, the flickering candles and the smell of food made her senses quiver. Energy surged through her body as she watched his movements, his presence, his mindfulness of her. It felt wonderful. He felt wonderful ... only one thing seemed not quite right.

It was a niggling thought, a perturbing sliver in her mind. In all this rush of energy and power, she could tell he withheld something. Maybe it was a plan or an intention. Maybe he had a hard-on for her and didn't want her to know. Maybe not. All she knew for sure was that he kept a secret. It reminded her of the way she felt around Clay.

'Thank you, Sword Master.'

'My pleasure, Rosette — that's some nasty bruising around your shoulders.'

'Zero,' she said and pressed her lips together.

'Fast, isn't he?'

'Like a striking snake.'

'Tomorrow, I'm going to teach you how to outmanoeuvre him.'

'Tomorrow?'

He nodded as he placed the steaming bread and a plate of butter on the table.

She frowned. How could she learn that in only one day?

'You're very receptive,' he said.

Was he kidding? With his touch who wouldn't be?

'Thank you,' she said around a mouthful of hot bread. 'Is there honey?' She was starting to think of him sexually and wondered if he felt the same.

Forget it. You're here for something else. The reply from her familiar came like a blunt arrow, jarring her out of the fantasy.

Drayco, I was just ...

The Sword Master has news. You have to pay attention.

Do you have a direct line to him now?

Scylla speaks with me. I like her.

That's nice, Dray. Keep her talking.

A link to the Sword Master's thoughts via his familiar would certainly be handy. She paused. Unless it went both ways.

She's not asking about me, is she?

'I think you'll like this,' An' Lawrence said before she heard an answer.

He carried two bowls filled to the brim and trailing a spicy scent that made her mouth water. As the aroma drifted over the table, her body turned to follow.

'What is that?'

'*Avan-chak* — spiced bean curd cooked with fruit, chilli, pine nuts and wild rice. Old family recipe.'

'You come from the Prieta range?' She knew he didn't, but she asked anyway. Their dishes were known to be as exotic as their lifestyle. Those remaining nomadic tribes were fascinating, a people scattered throughout the region, holding to the old ways and the old gods.

He shook his head, as she had expected.

'Where, then?'

'Beyond Corsanon.'

Rosette had no idea what was beyond Corsanon. 'Where?'

'To the east.'

She frowned. 'Is it a secret?'

'You'd know.'

'Pardon me, Master?' Rosette stared into his eyes.

'I think you know what I mean.'

'I'm sure I do not.'

'Eat up. We have much to talk about.' He placed two other bowls near the hearth and looked up at the rafters. 'Scylla, bring your new friend down,' he said aloud. 'I've saved some raw meat and bones.'

The temple cats were on the floor, pacing towards him before he'd finished his sentence.

They toasted, dining in silence. It was not a tension waiting to break, but a curious expectation. Rosette closed her eyes with every bite and exhaled slowly. The food was divine.

'More?' he offered, as her wooden spoon scraped the bottom of the bowl.

'A touch,' she smiled. 'Please.'

'A touch it is,' he said returning to the kitchen.

Is he flirting with me?

His voice altered when he sat down, direct, stern. 'Rosette, you've been moved into my school for a reason.'

Definitely not flirting.

'A reason?' she asked, slipping another spoonful into her mouth. She didn't close her eyes this time. She fixed them on him. Could this be it? The apprenticeship?

'We have something very specific in mind.'

Her face fell. 'We?'

'The High Priestess and I. We've selected you to perform a certain task. We thought there'd be more time to prepare, but it turns out there isn't.'

Rosette stopped eating and put down her spoon. 'What kind of task?'

'I can't say yet, only that it involves crossing Los Loma undetected.'

'This time of year?'

'It'll be chilly.'

'Chilly? Are you insane? It's solid ice and blizzards up there.'

'I won't pretend there are no risks in the travel, let alone the rest of the assignment.'

'What *rest*?'

'An exchange, if things go to plan.'

'And if they don't go to plan?'

'There'll be fighting.'

He reached for the flagon of wine and re-filled their glasses. She lifted hers, but did not take a sip. 'I'm hardly ready for such an assignment.'

'I know.'

Rosette glared at him before taking a long swig. 'Then why do you want me?' she asked, placing her empty glass down on the table.

'Partly because of your ability to shield your thoughts and use your magic undetected, and partly because you're not without other inherent skills, though I still can't work out why, unless it's in your blood. Is your mother a witch?'

'No,' she lied.

'What about your father or grandparents?'

Rosette laughed at the thought. 'Hardly.'

'Curious. But either way, by the next moon, your sword skills will be tenfold.'

She had a pretty good idea how many hours, days, months and years it would take to make that true.

'You're saying I've only a matter of weeks to prepare for this adventure?'

'A little less.'

Rosette turned to stare out the front window. All she could see was his reflection, watching her like a bird of prey, golden in the fire's glow.

Sounds exciting, Drayco chimed in.

'Drayco's coming.' It wasn't a query.

I'll be there. He's not an idiot.

'Of course your familiar will accompany you.'

'And?' She raised both eyebrows. 'Who else?'

He looked away.

'You aren't telling me that's it, are you? Me, Drayco and the mountain of Los Loma? Midwinter?'

An' Lawrence took a long drink before answering. 'You'll be travelling with me.'

And Scylla, Drayco added. It was a smug, happy cat sound he made in her head.

She glanced up to the rafters and saw Drayco licking his lips. Scylla hissed, then chortled, then hissed again.

Terrific! 'Sounds real fun,' she said under her breath. She lowered her eyes and stared at her bowl. There wasn't much left, but she suddenly felt full. 'How long will we be away?'

'I can't say.'

'Will we be on foot or horseback?'

'Haven't decided.'

'Why are we ...'

The Sword Master cut her off with a wave of his hand. 'I can't tell you anything else about the journey, Rosette de Santo. Stop asking.'

'What can you tell me?'

'Nothing, except that it will involve stealth and deception, and you'll need to be fit. Very fit. How do you go in the cold?'

'I hate it.'

'We'll get you a new sheepskin coat.'

'Thanks.' She was silent for a moment. 'Can I just ask one other thing?'

He crossed his arms in front of his chest and ripples of fear ran down her spine.

'My apologies, Sword Master.' She bowed her head. 'No more questions.'

Well, no more aloud, anyway. He couldn't control what bounced around in her mind. What could he possibly be up to? Los Loma offered no easy crossing, and though she had never been near the summit, she had some knowledge of what might be found on the other side: the greater mountains of Prieta. One didn't go there without a good reason. Kreshkali had a stronghold underground, or so she'd heard.

'Just the four of us?' she asked, her voice seeming thin and high to her own ears. She didn't want to anger him further, but if she was going to risk her life, she had a right to know.

Shaking his head with a half grin, An' Lawrence replied, 'That's all for tonight, Rosette. Go and rest. We'll begin training at dawn. I want you fighting fit in two weeks.'

'I thought I had three?'

'Two. We need the final week for something else.'

She pushed back from the table. Summoning her courage, she spoke again: 'Please tell me this means I'm in line for apprenticeship?'

He looked her up and down. 'It's being considered.'

She nodded. 'Getting ready in two weeks — that's going to take *some* magic.'

'Yes, it is.'

'I thought that was taboo, especially for an *unassigned* initiate,' she probed, emphasising the last two words as she cleared her place.

'I plan on using what's necessary, and so will you. Go get some rest, and take your familiar with you.'

Rosette looked up to the rafters. Scylla had her companion backed into a corner, though she was purring like a waterfall.

She likes me, Drayco sent.

'Are you sure?' Rosette asked, smiling.

It's unnerving. How peculiar does this feel? I don't know what she's up to.

'It's like that, Dray — it's like that.'

'What's like that?' the Sword Master queried.

She shook her head and nodded towards the ceiling. 'Just something between them.'

Drayco jumped lightly to the stone floor and stretched before the Sword Master. Rosette was surprised. She didn't remember him showing such respect to anyone else besides Nell, no matter what their standing in the human order of things.

An' Lawrence seemed momentarily stunned. Then he smiled and Rosette suspected he'd gotten a message from Scylla, who still hovered amongst the rafters overhead, watching.

The Sword Master roughed Drayco's neck. 'Some of us will get along, it seems,' he said, and showed them to the door.

Nell communicated with the Watcher whenever she felt the need. She used whichever portal was nearest, and today it was in the ruins of Temple Dumarka, half a day's walk from her cottage, less as the crow flies. All she had to do to link with the Watcher was to touch the field of energy, an undulating electromagnetic pulse that was obvious to any witch of her calibre. She could go there physically — in her body — or simply through the astral space in meditation. Either way, the Watcher's voice bypassed her empirical senses, communicating on a sub-cellular level. That is, when it chose to communicate at all.

She called it the Sphinx, a being, or composite of beings, who answered her questions with a complexity of riddles, more cryptic than clear. Still she would ask, when the need drove her, though she was never certain of the information or how to interpret it. This time, her mind was reeling from the paradoxes. The Watcher, on the other hand, seemed to think it a game. It snorted at her request.

You find this humorous, Great Sphinx?

You must appreciate the audacity of your request, Nell.

Is it audacious to want to preserve life in the many-worlds?

By the means that you suggest, it is. I can't have you playing with time. Too messy.

She frowned. What was the Sphinx on about? If time was an illusion, what was so tricky about manipulating it to her ends? She tried again. *I realise time's not what one normally tampers with, but under the circumstances I don't know what else to do.*

The Sphinx didn't respond — usually a sign that she'd missed something obvious in a previous statement. She searched her mind, coming up blank.

You aren't going to help? she asked after a prolonged silence, suspecting the Sphinx had gone. The strength of the reply startled her.

I'm not going to alter time to suit your needs. Think of something else, Nellion Paree.

I've tried. There isn't anything else.

The Sphinx laughed, a deep belly laugh that rippled through her skin. *Are you sure?*

Nell clenched her jaw. *No, I'm not sure. That's why I am here, asking for your help.*

More chuckling.

Nell crossed her arms, resisting the temptation to tap her foot.

The chuckling stopped and the Sphinx made a sound much like throat clearing. *Have you thought of the future?* The communication was soft, seductive.

Of course I've thought about the future. That's all I'm thinking about, day and night.

Not like that, Nell ...

What do you mean?

Have you thought about how the future can change the past, without worrying time at all?

She let her arms drop to her sides. *You've lost me, Sphinx.*

Think of it this way: if you go back to the past, it becomes your future, does it not?

She considered for a moment. *I suppose.* She looked up. *Are you talking about reversed causation?*

The Sphinx clicked, an impatient sound. *What is it about being in a physical body that keeps you holding to the notion that causation has direction — either forward or back?*

Nell curled her lip. *Perhaps it has to do with ageing. Have you heard of it? The process of being born, growing up and dying? Sequential timelines, sunrise, sunset and the predictable path of the planets are also a hint. Everything else we learn from nature ...* She let her voice trail off, realising suddenly that she sounded like a narrow-minded cleric. Nell took a breath. *Time's not directional? Is that what you're telling me?*

Warmer.

Not forward or backward?

Correct. Consider the shape of a spiral.

Nell let that sink in, though her mind remained murky. *I don't get it.*

Consider this metaphor, Nellion. Causation is like dropping a stone into a pool.

You mean ripples?

Yes, waves and ripples, if you must think in such horizontal dimensions.

Ripples, Nell repeated. *I still don't understand.*

She felt a flick, like the closing of a book, before the ground dropped out from under her feet. In a split second, she was standing on a wooden bridge. It arched over a flowing river, the water below blue. Everglades spread out into the distance as far as she could see, and waterlilies and willows hugged the shore on either side.

'Look down,' said the Watcher.

He stood next to her, a man of medium height with sandy hair and dark eyes. He wore muslin fisherman's pants and a pale orange cotton shirt, the tails wafting in the breeze. Prayer beads hung around his neck. His hands were folded in front of him.

'Sphinx?'

The man raised his eyebrows.

'What are you doing?' She looked him up and down.

'I like to try on different things, don't you?'

She shrugged.

'Look down,' he said again.

Nell stepped closer to the rail and leaned over. She gazed at the ripples of water under the bridge. They were like little waves that constantly branched off, interfering with each other to form yet another wave and another.

'Now look out there.' The Watcher lifted his arm, opening it out towards the everglades.

Nell followed the ripples as they multiplied for as far as the eye could see. The Watcher smiled and touched her shoulder, guiding her to the other side of the bridge. There she saw the same thing — endless ripples of waves, and arched bridges — all heading out into the distance, leading to and from the waterlilies and willows, path after path after path.

'Where would you like to stand?'

She looked at the Sphinx. 'I can choose?'

'You choose every time you draw in a breath, every time you exhale.'

He took a stone from his pocket and dropped it over the edge. When it hit the surface, waves flowed out from the impact point. They expanded towards each shore, upstream and downstream, an ever-increasing circumference, interfering with the ripples of the currents, creating more and more little waves.

'Sphinx, are you saying there is something I can do in the future that will alter what has happened in the past? If I do something on one shore, it will change another?'

'You could construct it in those terms, but I'm suggesting you stop thinking of past and future as if they were two different things. It's all one river, one shore, one mind, one spiral, when you focus on it.'

'And when I don't focus on it?'

'Then it is infinite ripples of possibility, each with a potential destiny of its own.' Again he opened his arm out towards the flow of water until it blurred into the horizon.

'But what if ...' She felt the tactile sensation of his departure.

'I'll leave you to contemplate.' His voice trailed off, and he was gone.

'That's it? That's all you have to say?' Nell looked down at the water. She thought for a second it was laughing at her. 'Enigmatic Watchers,' she mumbled. 'Just what I don't need — another metaphysical puzzle.'

She wandered over the bridges for the rest of the day, dropping stones into the water and watching the ripples flow. Just before she dropped a particularly lovely greenstone over the edge, she straightened, slipping it into her pocket instead.

Bingo.

She shape-shifted into a red-tailed kite and caught a thermal. With one last look below, the ripples still clear with her raptor vision, she shot off towards the horizon, hoping that her cottage in Dumarka wasn't far off.

The Three Sisters had been restless all day, scolding and flapping and cawing. They'd be quiet for a moment, composing themselves in a stately row, then suddenly the commotion would start all over again — flap, squawk, raucous. When the slanting light angled through the garden, turning red roses golden, they flew to the highest pine, watching all directions like weather-vanes.

'When will you settle?' she asked.

Someone comes! Someone tall, long legs.

'Are you talking about a heron or a person?'

They squawked and flapped but didn't answer.

She tapped the windowpane. 'If someone's approaching, why not fly out to meet them instead of sitting here all day and driving me nuts! I honestly don't detect a threat!'

The middle raven tilted her head to stare into the cottage then took flight, followed by the other two.

Finally, some peace.

Person, Nellion. Long legs person.

How far off?

Long legs has a long walk.

She squared her shoulders and put the kettle on.

Nell sipped her tea and studied the chart before her. The eclipse would be on Saturn in less than three days. She never felt comfortable in the shadow of an eclipse and this one seemed particularly potent. It could coincide with a realisation, a disclosure and a choice to make. With Mars at a ninety-degree square to the lunar nodes in the cardinal sign of the Ram, things would happen fast. Quite likely, there would be an uninvited guest.

'Nothing my ravens didn't tell me.' She looked up at Mozzie draped over the rafters. 'Be mindful, my beauty. Someone's coming but I can't say who.'

The snake flicked his tongue in her direction, uncoiling to meet her eye to eye. *Ally?*

'I hope so, Moz. Could use one about now.'

The fire had burned low when she heard the Three Sisters return and the gate latch click. Booted feet stepped confidently up the path, a purposeful walk, a man's walk — long legs, indeed.

Mozzie coiled about the rafter in front of the door, tongue scenting. Nell washed her cup in the sink and set it carefully on the rack. She picked up her staff that leaned against the wall. Mozzie followed, but Nell held out a hand to stop him.

Let's see who it is first, shall we?

The knock startled them, though they knew it was coming.

'Nellion Paree?' A young man's voice called out. 'Rosette?'

'Who's there?' Nell asked. She ran her thumb over the carvings etched into her staff.

'It's Jarrod.'

The hairs on the back of her neck rose. 'Say again?'

'Jarrod Cossica; I'm a friend of Rosette's. I've come from Lividica. I have news.'

Nell opened the door to a tall man with broad shoulders and a wry smile. He swept off his hat, revealing a mass of dark curls, and bowed — his eyes never leaving hers, his grin beaming.

'Jarrod Cossica, ready to serve.'

After a moment his gaze shot past her and into the cottage, searching.

Nell restrained a smile. 'Rosette said you were short.' She tilted her head to take in his full height.

'I grew.'

'So you did!' She clasped his hands affectionately. 'What took you so long?'

'Long?'

'Six years is quite a long time to be away, don't you think? It's only six days by clipper from Lividica. What did you do with the other two thousand?'

'I was ... I thought ...' He stumbled over his words.

Nell laughed, long and deep. 'Get in here, lad.'

He slid his pack from his shoulders as he stepped through the doorway. 'Where's Rosette? Is she ... Whoa! What's that?'

Jarrod stepped back as Mosaic uncoiled to hang right in front of his face, scenting him with his flickering red tongue.

'It's all right, Mozzie. He's a friend of Rosette's.'

Jarrod backed up, bumping into the door behind him.

'That's Mozzie,' Nell answered him as she rummaged through her pantry, bringing out food and clean cups. 'Come in! He won't bite you, now that you've been introduced. Take off your boots and hang up your coat.' She laughed at the expression on his face. 'I was about to eat. You hungry?'

Jarrod swallowed as he inched around the python. 'Thanks. I'm starved.' He unlaced his boots and put them by the door, taking in the row of footwear and stack of swords and bows. 'Rosette isn't here, is she?'

'She's been training at Treeon Temple for almost a year.'

He crossed the room, pulled out a chair, and sat near the fire, warming his hands. Nell cleared her books and charts away and set out a plate of bread, butter and soft cheese.

'Start on that.' She pointed to the food.

'Thanks, Nell,' he said, reaching for a thick slice of bread. 'I didn't come sooner because I'd promised I wouldn't. We'd agreed it'd be too risky.'

'She told me.'

'She did?' Jarrod smiled.

Nell swung the cast-iron pot over the coals and prodded them with an iron rod. 'Tell me, Jarrod, why'd you risk it now?'

He swallowed before answering, sipping the cup of mulled wine she offered. 'Because until last week, the deception was working. The entire Matosh family was believed dead, the youngest daughter included. I wanted to write to Rosette, to let her know it was safe, to see if I could visit, but I kept my promise. I protected her with silence, just in case someone was still watching. Then, last week, a bard came to the bay — I never discovered where he was from. He played at the pubs and asked a lot of questions.'

'What kinds of questions?'

'He was looking for the de Santo family, particularly the parents of a woman in her early twenties named Rosette, who'd grown up on an estate near Lividica. He let it be known that he was courting her and wanted to meet the family, to surprise them. Of course, no-one knew of her and said so. But people started talking about it and the Matosh murders came up. I don't know what he was told. The bard disappeared before I could confront him.'

'And did you learn the name of this bard?'

Jarrod shook his head. 'No, but he was young, had shocking red hair and was a remarkable guitarist — clearly temple-trained.'

'Sounds to me like Rosette has herself a beau. I wonder how much she told him?'

'Too much, I think,' Jarrod scowled.

'Jealous?'

'Hardly!' Jarrod took another sip of wine. 'I'm concerned, is all. It doesn't add up.'

'Why not? Rosette would naturally attract —'

'Not that.' He tapped his fingers on his lips. 'Of course she would attract anyone she wanted.'

'So ...'

'The bard had a very interesting companion.'

'Companion?'

'A familiar, perhaps, but I don't think it was his.'

'What was it?'

'A raptor. I saw him give it a message.'

Nell frowned. 'Did you see where it went?'

'North. It disappeared into the clouds above Mount Jacor.'

'A falcon?'

'Peregrine.'

Nell poured more wine. 'Either our Rosette indeed has herself a suitor, or things haven't blown over after all.'

Jarrod shot her a glance. 'I was hoping you might elucidate on the "things" aspect. Just what is it, Nell, that hasn't blown over yet? Is Rosette in danger?'

She looked him up and down, thinking that perhaps this could be a *past* her *future* might change. 'It wasn't John'ra Matosh they were after when the Corsanon assassins murdered him and his family.'

'It wasn't?'

'No.'

'Who, then?'

'They were after Rosette.'

Jarrod stopped chewing. 'What for?'

'There are beings on this world, and others, hunting for ... something.'

Jarrod put down his fork and wiped his mouth. 'What are you talking about, Nell?' His eyes narrowed. 'She's just a young Gaelean witch. What things could she have that someone on this world, or any other, would kill for?'

'She has a spell.'

'What kind of a spell?'

Nell closed her eyes. 'The hidden kind. Many are searching for it, would give, or take, anything to find it.'

'Anyone in particular?'

'The High Priestess of Treeon, for one.'

'Does Rosette know she's got it?'

'No.'

'What? She thinks it's some travelling charm? And you let her go to Treeon with it?'

'Sometimes the safest place is right under the adversary's nose.'

'But if they know she's a Matosh ... if they link her to the murders ...'

'They may have suspicions I hadn't counted on. Makee will stop at nothing to get the spell back.'

'Back?'

'She had a glimpse of it once. It left quite an impression.'

'Why? What does it do?'

'It's a power spell. Great power. If Makee should ever get hold of it she'd doubtless try to reclaim the temples to the east and extend the influence of Treeon across the whole of Gaela.'

'That would mean war again!'

'That's not the half of it.'

'What else?'

Nell hesitated. Could she reveal it? She knew that Rosette had trusted Jarrod utterly. If he was to help her now, he needed to be at least semi-informed.

'The spell contains knowledge from another world. It can protect the portals that lead to other dimensions — other realms — to keep them intact, unpolluted. It holds the secret to the many-worlds' survival. Oh, Jarrod, there is so much to it that you would never grasp. Even I'm still learning what it can do. It's the key to this universe. Do you have any idea what that could mean in the wrong hands? In *any* hands?'

He pressed his fingers together. 'Yes, Nell. I do.'

Jarrod sat in profound silence as Nell stared at him, her eyes like a hawk.

'What do you mean, *you do*?' she asked. 'How could you comprehend what I just said?'

'Because I know Passillo better than anyone alive,' he whispered back.

Nell pulled the chair out from across the table and sat, her hands shaking. She took a deep breath. 'I'm listening.'

'I have a few questions first. What name do you go by?'

'My name?'

'With the Matosh family gone, I had a demon's time tracking you down. Rosette told me you were Nell, the Dumarkian witch, but no-one could tell me more. I'd like to hear the whole thing, if it's not a secret.'

'It's no secret to those who ask. I'm Nellion Paree of the Dumarkian Woods.'

'Paree.' He said the name like a prayer. 'Can you tell me where you come from, Nellion Paree?'

'Originally?'

He nodded.

'A small fishing village south of Morzone.'

'Morzone? Really? Isn't it more like a small fishing village south of San Francisco? Of course, they can't fish there any more, can they? Not in those dead seas.'

Nell froze with her wine mug halfway to her lips. When she spoke, her voice was barely audible: 'Where did you hear that?'

'I get around.' He lifted his head. 'One more question, Nell. Do you know your matrilineal ancestry?'

She stared at him, mouth open.

'Who's the first remembered in your line of priestesses?'

'We go way back ...' Her voice trailed off.

'Tell me her name, please. It's important.'

'We call her *Docturi Janicia*, but it's really ...'

'Janis Richter.'

Nell dropped her mug, tipping her chair over as she leapt to her feet. Mozzie wove his way across the rafters, lowering his head to hover just above her eyes. She had never heard that name spoken, but had found it with the things her mother had left her. It pulled her mind back to the late-night talks between herself, her mother and her grandmother in the secret places of her childhood training, and she faltered. She gripped the edge of the table. 'Who are you?'

'Can't you guess?'

'The JARROD?' she whispered, not knowing if her legs would support her.

'I always liked the name,' he said, lifting his face with a smile.

'Jarrod?' she whispered again.

'Still in the flesh.' He opened his arms. 'A newer Tulpa, several actually, since I saw Janis last, but me just the same.'

'Oh, Jarrod.' Nell walked towards him, the cottage so quiet she could hear the floorboards creaking underfoot. She stood in front of him, tilting her head up before she fell into his arms.

'Tell me, Nell, is Earth hanging in there?'

She gave him a strong squeeze. 'By a thread.' She released him. 'Where have you been? You're the one missing piece I didn't know how to find. Why didn't you answer me? I've been calling for you from ridge to mountain top, Corsanon to Morzone, for the last twenty years.'

Jarrod took her hands. 'It's your first-class glamour, Nell. I couldn't spot the blood of the Techno-Witch, even this close up. I thought it was Kreshkali who carried it. I've been tracking her for at least that long, but damned if I could catch the woman.'

Nell chuckled. 'She is tricky, isn't she?'

'But, Nell, why does Rosette have Passillo? I thought it was to lie dormant until ...' His face beamed. 'Is the worm deleted? Are we ready to go back?'

'No, not yet. I'm still working on that. Jarrod, Rosette doesn't just have Passillo, a charm around her neck.'

'What do you mean?'

'I'm not the last of my line.'

'What?' He stared at her, holding her at arm's length. 'You have a child? A daughter?' He let go his grip. 'Where is she? Earth? Is she safe?'

Nell winked. 'Oh, she's not lost, if that's what you're worried about. Just hidden.'

'Where?'

'Can't you guess that yet?'

He looked into her eyes. 'Goddess of the night ... right under my nose too?' he whispered.

Nell nodded. 'Though that connection was a fluke. Didn't see it coming at all.'

'Rosette?' His voice choked.

'She's all mine.'

Jarrod lowered his head and moaned. 'That would explain the attraction ...' He let out his breath and wiped his eyes. 'How'd she end up with the Matosh clan? Is John'ra her father or ...'

'No!' Nell stopped him short. 'No, no,' she said again, softer, looking at the fire. 'Rosette's not a Matosh.'

'Who's her father then?'

'A man from the ancient line.'

'Ah,' he smiled. 'Rosette was born in Gaela?' He looked around the cottage as if the answer were somehow there. 'Things haven't exactly gone to plan then, have they?'

'Not exactly. I disturbed Passillo inadvertently. The rivers had changed to a gorge. I couldn't put them back. But I had exactly what was needed to hide Passillo when I conceived. I came here for the sanctuary of Dumarka, had my child and hid the spell.' She sighed. 'Then I hid her.'

'But Rosette doesn't have Passillo. She took almost nothing with her that night. I know. I was there.'

'*Almost* nothing.'

'Are you saying she has the spell?'

Nell winked again.

'How?'

'It's in her, Jarrod. It was the only way.'

'But that means if you can't find a way to delete the worm ...'

'I know. She can't set foot on Earth now, nor can you, not while the worm exists. I'm the last of my line there, the last hope.'

Jarrod buried his face in his hands. 'Does she know?'

Nell moved her head from side to side. 'Not yet.'

'But, Nell, it could get out of control. She has no guidance!'

'I wouldn't say *none*.'

Jarrod slumped in his chair. 'I can't believe you sent her to Treeon.'

Nell smiled. 'I had my reasons ...'

* * *

In another world, Kreshkali awoke from a troubled dream. She looked at her chronometer: 11:11 a.m. The opaque window, and the sheeting acid rain, made it difficult to distinguish day from night.

She kicked back the covers and stretched. 'Well now, isn't this interesting.' She smiled. 'Jarrod Cossica, I've got plans for you!'

Chapter 10

An' Lawrence stood in the centre of the dusty arena, heart pounding, his sides heaving. The autumn sunlight warmed the back of his neck as sweat dripped down his face. He hadn't trained like this for years — not since he was a journeyman in the elite ranks of the Timbali high-guard. Because of his background he had already been initiated and trained at the Timbali Temple, and who would have guessed that those simple things — magic, acknowledgement from a higher-ranking officer, a meeting with a witch — would have led to such machinations?

He took a deep breath. Rosette was turning out to be as brilliant with her use of magic as her mentor. It was potent, and he never felt it coming. No-one here could have easily taught her such skill. It was either innate or learned from long hours of training. He shook his head. What bothered him was that Nellion Paree didn't use her magic quite this way — at least, she hadn't twenty years ago. Rosette's style was unique, and it made him uncomfortable.

He took another deep, focused breath to slow his respiration and steel his thoughts. The sun was dropping far to the west and the shadows from surrounding sycamores cast long, cold fingers through the arena. An' Lawrence mopped his forehead and raised his sword. This would be their last round.

'Again,' he commanded, his voice challenging his opponent.

Rosette dived towards him, feigning a swipe to his shoulders before tucking down low and cutting for his knees. He blocked the move — only just — propelling her backwards with the momentum of his blow. An' Lawrence smiled through gritted teeth. She improved with every hour of training. What a delight to work with such aptitude, a delight and a mystery.

'Good, but next time see if you can actually strike a blow!' he said, his mouth quirking.

She leapt to her feet and he gauged her stance. She shielded her mind and body so well it was impossible to predict her moves. Her agility astonished him. The combination of flexibility and strength proved an effective weapon in itself. Mixed with enchantment, it became invincible — almost.

'Quickly,' he commanded when she stood for several heartbeats. 'Don't give your adversary any time to recover.'

Her body glistened with sweat and her chest rose and fell in controlled breaths. A snarl lifted the left side of her mouth. 'Quickly, is it?' she countered, still not moving.

Rosette was as obstinate as she was skilled. The Sword Master suppressed a laugh. More shades of Nell. He felt the familiar rush of energy course down his spine as he observed her. She couldn't know how much she reminded him of her mentor. An' Lawrence strengthened his mind-shield as he speculated. What was Nellion like now? Had she told Rosette of their past? Doubtful. Nell had made it clear that he was someone she never wanted to speak of or to again.

The instant his mind drifted, she was on him, inches from his face, her sword pressed against his chest, the move toppling them both. He rolled as he hit the ground, intent on pinning her down.

Rosette de Santo seemed to have other ideas.

As the Sword Master sprang back towards her, he felt her knee thrust up between them, driving into his abdomen and throwing him back into the ring netting. He paused against the ropes, judging as his student vaulted to her feet. She must have been exhausted, but she showed no sign of fatigue. Crouching like a wildcat, she barely moved to fill her lungs.

An' Lawrence leapt forward, his eyes on hers. He was aware of the sun setting behind him, the blood-red rays slanting across the ground between the lines of shadows — spears of light in his peripheral vision. The breeze whispered past his face, bringing the scent of horse sweat, alfalfa hay and leather. The students lining the ring diffused into silhouette and a distant bell rang three times. Dinner. Still he kept his eyes locked with hers until their breathing synchronised.

'Done, Rosette. Well done,' he said, allowing a smile. 'Bathe and refresh. We start all over again in the morning.'

The young witch dipped her head in acknowledgement, sheathing her training sword and ducking under the netting. The students made way as she passed, looking at her with respect. An' Lawrence was obviously not the only one she had impressed. He chuckled quietly as he stood alone in the arena with the darkness setting in. He was creating quite a warrior. What would Nell think of that?

He rubbed the back of his neck. He couldn't dispel his musings. She clearly had him remembering feelings he hadn't counted on, and didn't want.

Are you going to the baths as well? The voice of his familiar came to him from behind the armoury.

His brow relaxed. 'Scylla, it's a wonderful idea, but that would keep me in her presence. It's not the most beneficial plan. I'm having enough trouble coping when she is attacking me with a sword. I can't imagine what would happen if I let my guard down.'

She reminds you of another, that's all. You miss the one I've yet to meet.

'I never said that!'

You didn't have to.

'I've sworn an oath, Scylla. She — Nellion and I — we'll never meet again and I want ...'

You want Nellion. It's as clear and clean as the fur on my belly.

'Hush, Scylla. It's more complicated than that.'

When has a little complexity ever kept you from a task, or an adventure? All this magic in the arena is forbidden to her rank as well. The girl's not even your apprentice. The journey itself ...

'I know. It's a sticky situation, but we can't talk about it here.'

Rowan, no-one can get through our mind-shields, so stop avoiding. Complex or not, you want to see that woman, the girl's mentor. The Nell witch. Admit it.

'Saying it, Scylla, doesn't help my resolve one bit! I've sworn to stay away and I won't break that oath.'

As you please, she purred. It was an alluring sound.

'It's a moot point, my love. I am the Sword Master of Treeon Temple and my life isn't completely my own. Plans have been made. We've a much greater road ahead than rekindling an old romance — an affair, I might add, that went disastrously wrong.'

Okay, Rowan. You can stop explaining. I'm convinced.

'Then why are you still pestering?'

Because you've yet to convince yourself.

'Scylla, I haven't seen Nell in ...'

Decades!

'You're keeping track! Just because these feelings have resurfaced doesn't mean they're important. It's just a ridiculous memory.'

I'm sure you're right.

'It'll pass!'

If that's how you see it ...

'That's how I make it!' He laughed at the cat's mental equivalent of exasperation. His familiar was obviously perturbed. It wasn't the first time they'd broached the topic, finding themselves with opposing views. 'Let's see about some dinner, shall we?' An' Lawrence changed the subject.

Cooked meat?

'Good idea.' He smiled. It didn't take much more than the thought of a rump roast to get Scylla onto another track.

Ducking out of the arena, he saw her emerge from behind the far shed. No doubt her quest for rats had gone unfulfilled. Rosette's familiar had cleaned out the entire training complex over the last few weeks, now that she allowed him to hunt here.

'Magnificent creature, the Dumarkian black.'

On that we agree. Scylla met him halfway down the path, pressing the top of her head into his hand.

It was unfortunate that things had ended so badly with Nell all those years ago. He'd been young, stubborn and fixated. She'd been detached, though patient with his adoration, until she'd let her guard down, for a while. The attraction they'd had for each other had become unbearable. It had to be expressed.

Looking back in the direction of the arena, now the colour of ox blood as the sun dropped below the skyline, An' Lawrence shook his head and sighed.

Rosette was so much like her. Amazing how a mentor can transfer herself into her pupil.

Rowan, the young bard comes. He's upset.

He's back? Finally!

Indeed, and he's spitting mad. Watch out.

The Sword Master looked over his shoulder. He didn't see anyone on the darkening path, but that was no surprise. Scylla would have warned him the moment the lad set out from the dorms.

'Thanks for the tip,' he said, entering the welcome sanctuary of his lodge. He quickly put away his thoughts of Nellion Paree and stoked the fire. He'd heat bath water and bathe here, make some food, have a peaceful night.

Within minutes, there was a knock at the door.

'Sword Master?' he heard the bard call out. 'I have that ballad ready, if you'd care to hear it now.'

The door opened and Clay looked him in the eye for a moment before pulling his guitar from his back.

'Thank you, Clay. Let's hear it.'

An' Lawrence ushered him into his lodge and shut the door. He waited a moment before speaking, sizing up the lad. He looked haggard and drawn, his red ringlets lank, dark circles under his eyes.

'Rough trip?'

'Why do you ask?'

'You look like you've been dragged through the underworld to get here.'

'I think I have.'

'What took you so long?' An' Lawrence crossed his arms. 'I said get to Lividica and back before the new moon. It's nearly full.'

'I ran into some trouble.' Clay sat down and started fingerpicking a soft melody while he spoke.

'What happened?'

'You got the message from Clawdia?'

'Of course, weeks ago.'

'Then you know, if it's true, her name isn't Rosette de Santo.'

'And what do you think?'

'It's possible she's the daughter of the Matosh family ... the one they say was murdered six years ago.'

'I realise that. How reliable was your source? It could be just gossip. Maybe she worked on the estate?'

'The way she rides? The way she carries herself? I don't think she was a stable-girl or kitchen hand, do you? Besides, she fits the description of the youngest daughter, Kalindi Matosh. She fits it perfectly ...'

'If so, she's keeping quite a secret.'

'Wouldn't you, if your family had been murdered?'

An' Lawrence frowned. 'I wonder what else she's hiding ...'

Clay exhaled, making a low whistling sound. 'Good question. Do you think she even knows Nellion Paree?'

He ignored the query. 'Tell me what trouble detained you?'

'I never got a good look.'

'You were followed?'

'I'm not sure. It felt like it.'

'Felt like it?'

'It was a presence more than a being. Ominous. An awareness of some kind.' He shook his head. 'I never saw it, but I'm sure it was tracking me. I didn't want to lead it back to Treeon so I circled north to Morzone — where I was meant to be in the first place — and played a few nights there before coming back.'

'Smart. And it didn't follow?'

'I lost it in the foothills of the Prietas. Or it lost interest in me. I don't know which.'

'Good work. You did well.' An' Lawrence reached for a coin jar on the top kitchen shelf.

'Forget it,' Clay said when the Sword Master started counting out gold pieces. 'I made more than a wage on this journey.' He stopped playing for a moment. 'I can't do this any more, An' Lawrence. I'm done.'

'What?'

'I can't spy on her, lie to her. Find out things about the past I can never verify. It's eating me up inside. It's ruining our ... our friendship.'

'Friendship?' he asked, the smile gone from his face.

'It's ruining everything.'

An' Lawrence rubbed his jaw, looking at Clay from a different angle. 'That's where you're wrong. It's not ruining things. Your information gathering is protecting her. You can't stop now.'

'I can and I will.'

An' Lawrence put the money jar away and straightened his spine.

'If you want to quit, you'll be banished. Have you considered that? You'll never see her again. I can't risk her finding out, especially now. Do you understand what that means?'

Clay levelled his eyes on the Sword Master. 'I've a pretty good idea.'

'Is that what you want?'

Clay looked at the floor and shook his head.

'Clay.' An' Lawrence touched his shoulder. 'You'll not be banished if you keep your side of the bargain, just a little bit longer. We need you. Rosette needs you. This can turn out well, but not if you take off now.'

'I don't understand why.'

'You aren't meant to.' An' Lawrence grabbed him by the shoulders, forcing him to look up. 'This is bigger than your desires, Clay. Bigger than mine. Please. Stick with it.'

Clay nodded reluctantly.

'Good.' The Sword Master let go of Clay. 'You're still bound to me, don't forget,' he added.

Clay's eyes looked past the Sword Master to the fire. 'How could I?' He strummed a convoluted rhythm before breaking into a lightning-fast picking pattern.

'Fantastic new tune,' An' Lawrence said. 'Not quite a ballad though, is it?'

'Not quite.' He finished the tune with a crescendo of chords and slipped off his stool. 'Are we done?' he asked. 'I need to sleep.'

'Yes. We can talk more tomorrow.'

Clay headed for the door. As he pulled it open, he turned back. 'There's one other thing, Sword Master.'

'What's that?'

'If she really is Kalindi Matosh, she didn't learn the sword from big brothers.'

He raised his brow. 'Why not?'

'Because she didn't have any.'

Sitting on the top step of her porch, Rosette tossed her boots into the box by the door. She let out a soft groan as she rubbed her feet, peeling off her socks. She lifted her leather bodice over her head and added it to the wash. Her arms ached. Her legs throbbed and her bare belly was caked with rivulets of grime and sweat.

Drayco crinkled his black nose at her, sniffing.

'That bad?' she asked.

Worse!

'I'll bathe soon.'

Why not now?

'Clothes first.'

She wanted nothing more than to soak away the aches and pains of the day, but her chores called and there would be no scrimping. There was something else on her mind that kept her feeling giddy, even with the exhaustion.

A smile lifted dirt smudges on her face as she filled a basin from the wooden rain barrel. Her skills were improving rapidly. That fact delighted her. After so much time spent in the mundane arts of ritual spell-casting, the sword training offered a sense of satisfaction — something new for her at Treeon. She was getting good, dangerously good.

She felt certain her progress had pleased the Sword Master too. She could see it in his stance, his gaze, and especially in the diminishing number of times he'd shaken his head or stormed out of the training ring muttering under his breath. Yes, An' Lawrence was impressed, finally. But what else? She felt a struggle going on inside him that she didn't understand. What did he hide?

Her admiration for him had not diminished in the last few weeks of training. It was not wearing off with familiarity, nor was it being set aside for more immediate things like defending herself from his blade. Sometimes getting to know a person made them seem more ordinary. It could dim the spark, or even extinguish it altogether, but this wasn't the case with An' Lawrence. If anything, her respect for him had heightened. Nell had said he was the best and she was right.

Still, she wondered what it was the man kept so tightly hidden. It felt like a barricade, shored up whenever she got too close.

Rosette brushed her cheek with her shoulder as she scrubbed the clothes. Her skin was itchy and damp in the fresh autumn night, but soon she would be in the baths, then sleep until dawn. Tomorrow would start the final week of preparation. She and An' Lawrence would exchange practice staffs and swords for live blades. The thud of wood would turn to the clash of steel on steel. She shivered. How would her boosts of energy conduct through such a medium? Like lightning, she suspected.

Now to the pools? Drayco lifted his paw to her thigh as she leaned against the porch railing, wringing out the laundry.

Rosette turned to her friend. 'Sorry, my lovely. I was lost in thought.'

And? he prompted her.

'And I just wanted to know if you had any information regarding our travels? You seem pretty cosy with Scylla these days. Has she said anything?'

She says many things. Sometimes she never stops talking. It's like a stream of information and I am just a stone in the way of her dancing mind.

'I see,' Rosette chuckled. 'And in these streams of dancing thought, is there anything about where we're going?'

Not really. We hunt together, talking all the time, but who knows what the journey will bring? She won't speak of it.

'Aren't you the least bit curious about this trip?'

I'm more curious about her.

'Well I want to know where we're going.'

The meeting with the High Priestess should prove instructional.

'Pardon?'

The meeting. We'll learn more then.

'What meeting?'

Didn't you know? Drayco yawned. *There's an audience with La Makee at the end of the week.*

'And when was I going to be told about it, I wonder?' Rosette turned her back to the railing and squatted down eye to eye with her familiar. She cupped his face in her hands. 'What other secrets do you have that I should hear about?'

Drayco stared at her, unblinking. His rough pink tongue came out and licked her nose. Rosette rocked back, squeaking with laughter.

'Just answer the question,' she persevered, once her voice was under control.

I only know that you are to go with the Sword Master to the temple chamber of the High Priestess in a few days, and as the Moon wanes in the sign of Ceres we set off.

Rosette tousled the temple cat's head. 'That's it?'

Drayco neither blinked nor answered.

'All right then. Thank you.'

Time will tell.

'Yes, my lovely. Time will tell.'

Now you will bathe? Drayco asked with a twitch of his whiskers.

'Why are you so anxious for me to get to the pools, furry one?'

Someone might be waiting for you there.

'Clay's back?'

He might be.

'Why didn't you tell me earlier?'

Drayco lashed his tail for a moment then leapt down the steps. *I hunt.*

I bathe, she replied, tossing the rest of the laundry over the railing without bothering to wring it. She grabbed a clean robe, slipped on her sheepskin boots and headed for the pools at a run.

Clay didn't hear Rosette. He was submerged, sitting on the bottom step, holding his breath. When he popped up with a gasp, she stood above him and opened her robe.

'You look like you've been to war,' he said, taking in her bruises.

'So do you.' She dropped her robe and descended the steps until the water was up to her breasts. 'Where have you been and when did you last sleep?'

'I'm not sure.' He pushed his wet hair back from his face. 'It's been a long ... year.'

'Yeah. For me too.'

They kissed briefly and Clay smiled at her.

He sat behind her, scrubbing her shoulders and arms, leaning her towards him until she floated on her back. He washed her hair.

'You're very quiet,' Rosette said with her eyes closed.

He roughed her scalp and rinsed her hair, untangling it with his fingers as he did so.

'Clay? Are you there?'

He let her go and swam to the outcropping at the far end of the pool.

Rosette followed him. 'What's going on?'

Clay watched her approach, gliding through the water without making a ripple. He'd been determined not to feel anything different, not to show any of his concerns. Not to suspect. 'I'm tired, is all.'

'You don't usually act this strange when you haven't had enough sleep.' She trod water in front of him. 'What is it? Did you have your way with a local lass in Morzone? You know that doesn't worry me.'

'I didn't ... in Morzone, and it's not that.'

Rosette sat next to him on the submerged ledge, her shoulders just above the waterline. 'Come back to my place. I've fresh bread and spice tea. We can talk.'

Clay nodded. 'Sounds nice.'

'Nice?'

He wet her lips with his finger before kissing her, slow and deep. 'Sounds grand.'

'That's better.'

He held her hand as they headed back to the cottage, wondering who she really was and thinking he may never know.

The chamber was vacant, the High Priestess nowhere in sight. La Makee's dragon-bone chair sat empty, with only a dent in the deep green cushion suggesting recent occupancy. Rosette breathed in the air. It was filled with the scent of chrysanthemum, white peony and a hint of cloves. She wondered if someone was ill.

Rosette felt her skin prickle as two of the priesthood emerged from a side archway, their pale grey robes brushing the floor, rustling as they crossed the antechamber.

'Follow me,' the priestess said.

'And they can come too,' the other smiled, nodding towards Drayco and Scylla who were side by side with their companions.

'As if that was ever in question,' Rosette murmured to An' Lawrence under her breath.

He frowned and motioned for her to be silent. Apparently this was neither the time nor the place for whimsy. Rosette shrugged. She was certain that the High Priestess had a sense of humour; she had read too many of her books, and sat in on too many of her discourses, to think otherwise. If anything, La Makee was not uptight. Why the stilted formality?

'Just behave yourself,' he whispered through clenched teeth.

'Don't squash the girl, Rowan. Her wit may be all you'll have left in the end.' La Makee's voice was rich and deep.

What 'end' is she talking about? Rosette sent the question directly to the Sword Master's mind.

It's a metaphor, I'm sure. Just be respectful, please.

The High Priestess met them with a warm smile, her hand reaching up to the Sword Master's shoulder. Entwining images, tattooed in deepest black, wound their way intricately over her wrists and down each long, slender finger. An' Lawrence moved to kneel but was stopped short.

'Give me your affection, not devotion!' La Makee responded, presenting her lips for An' Lawrence to kiss.

'Better!' She turned to Rosette. 'You, however, may start with devotion. I want to be able to recall you at my feet, at least this once.'

The words baffled Rosette, but she dropped gracefully to one knee anyway. As she raised her head to look into the emerald eyes of the High Priestess, La Makee took her hands and was lifted back to her feet. Rosette stood smiling. The woman was even more inspiring close up than she was in the lecture halls.

'Not so obstinate as you imply,' La Makee commented, taking in Rosette's measure.

'Perhaps you need to get to know her better,' the Sword Master said without a trace of a smile.

'I look forward to that, as she progresses in her training,' La Makee responded. 'She is progressing, isn't she?'

Rosette bit her tongue. *Hey, guys, I'm right next to you.*

They both ignored her thought.

'Yes, she is,' An' Lawrence answered.

La Makee nodded, motioning them to follow her.

That's it? You've no other comment about my progress? Can't you elaborate? Tell her how well I ...

Hush.

'First, let's look at the maps.' Makee directed them towards the large table in the centre of the room 'There is much to discuss.'

She unrolled a large scroll and turned to Rosette. 'Be a darling and see to the afternoon tea. It is being prepared in the kitchen, down the hall and to the right.'

'Yes, Mistress.' She shielded her surprise. Surely she would not be excluded now, just when she was about to get some idea of where they were going and why?

'Take the temple cats with you, please. I have fresh meat for them.'

'Thank you, Mistress,' Rosette said, her jaw clenched. Now she couldn't even have Drayco listen to their scheming. With the mention of fresh meat, her familiar would be attuned to nothing but the crunch and bite of his snack. It was no coincidence, distracting them in such a way, she was sure of that.

But it's a wonderful surprise, don't you think? Drayco interrupted her thoughts.

'Aren't you the least bit concerned?' she snapped back.

My only concern is that we might have trouble finding the kitchen. This place is huge.

There was a delay with the cooks and when Rosette returned carrying the tray of hot tea and biscuits, An' Lawrence was rolling up a map and nodding to the High Priestess. They both reacted abruptly to her approach, like parents hiding a solstice gift from their child. Is that what they thought? She was to be treated like a child? If so, why in the world were they involving her at all?

'Thank you, Rosette. We'll have tea and contemplate the journey.'

'Yes, Mistress,' she said, placing the tray on the table.

She sat with them while they talked of the upcoming yearling sale and the new student prospects, Makee's horse who'd pulled up lame after a long ride, and the merits of teaching music to all first-year initiates. No mention, let alone contemplation, was made of the impending journey. It seemed as if that discussion was all over and done with. Rosette straightened her back and made ready to interrupt. She would find out what she could. No harm in trying.

'Excuse me, but where exactly are we headed?'

'Direct and to the point.' Makee smiled at her. 'You're going to Los Loma in the Mount Prieta range.'

'I understood that. I was thinking more specifically ... like what are we to do when we get there?'

'Retrieve something that was lost. You'll see. There are too many mind-travellers here to say any more. An' Lawrence will fill you in when you are underway.'

It didn't make sense. Why couldn't they just tell her now? They all had impenetrable mind-shields, unless the likes of Kreshkali was lurking in the kitchen; why the secrecy?

She sipped her tea, formulating the next question, but the High Priestess raised her hand in warning.

'All those busy thoughts are hurting my head, Rosette. Let it go. It'll be made clear in time.'

Rosette swallowed hard. She kept her mouth shut, her lips pressed tight together. If the High Priestess said she had to wait, then she had to wait.

'Not as uncouth as you led me to believe, either,' La Makee goaded An' Lawrence.

Rosette raised her eyes to the Sword Master and mouthed the word '*uncouth?*'.

'I really meant abrupt more than ill-mannered,' he said to Rosette.

'You might want to say what you mean if you're going to say anything at all,' Rosette snapped.

'Ah. There's a sample,' An' Lawrence said, smiling at La Makee.

'She's just like ...' La Makee let the sentence hang. 'Finish your tea and pack your bags, you two. Take plenty of warm furs and dried food for yourselves, the temple cats and the horses.'

'Horses?' Rosette interrupted.

'Yes, and I want you ready by first light.'

An' Lawrence and Rosette stood as the High Priestess blessed them in turn before leaving the room.

A flutter of wings fanned the air above them.

'A Lemur Raven,' Rosette whispered, her mouth remaining in a round shape after she spoke. The bird looked over its shoulder, seeming to wink before it shot off after its mistress.

An' Lawrence said nothing. With the High Priestess gone, a silence prevailed. Rosette wrinkled her brow at him though he turned away, reaching for his cup and sipping the remainder of his tea. Rosette put the last biscuit in her robe pocket — she certainly wasn't taking much else away with her.

'Let's go,' An' Lawrence said, looking at the empty plate. He avoided her eyes.

'As you wish, Sword Master.'

In silence, the two left the chamber, followed by the temple cats contentedly licking their lips. As they reached the high doors, An' Lawrence spoke softly to her: 'That went well.'

She couldn't believe her ears. 'You're kidding, right?'

'Not at all.'

'In what way do you define *well*?' Rosette growled as they walked out of the temple and down tier after tier of smooth stone steps. The afternoon breeze washed across her face, making her green feather earrings brush against her cheeks. 'We don't know anything new! Or should I say, *I* don't know anything new!'

My belly is full. Delicious meat. Drayco sent his thoughts of satiation.

'I am glad one of us is pleased,' she quipped back.

'Pardon?' An' Lawrence replied.

'I was talking to Drayco.' Rosette didn't hide her irritation.

'The meeting was not without advantage. I have a new map.'

'Looking forward to seeing it,' Rosette hissed at him, crossing her arms and turning the other way. 'If I may be excused, I'll go have my last hot bath for — well, for how long do you reckon, An' Lawrence?'

'Half a moon, at least.'

'Right. I'll meet you before dawn?'

'At the stables. Bring your new furs.'

'I can't wait.' Rosette slapped her thigh to attract Drayco's attention, nodded to An' Lawrence and walked away.

'Rosette!'

His voice stopped her dead in her tracks. She turned to him.

'Drop by the smithy's on your way home. He has a new sword for you.'

She nodded and continued down the path, a smile lighting up her face.

Rosette heard the click of iron-shod hooves on the stone breezeway and the occasional blow and snort from deep mangers. The stables were just around the corner — almost there. She'd felt her way along in the dark, the thick fog obscuring her lantern, creating only a blinding glare around her feet and hands.

Rosette whistled like a magpie to warn of her coming. The mountain horses were calm and sensible, but she didn't want to get off to a bad start by spooking them. There would be enough adjustment with the familiars so close at hand.

I wait with Scylla at the gates.

'We won't be too long, lovely.'

She frowned. Here she was, about to go off into the Prieta Mountains with the Sword Master, and no-one cared to tell her why. If that wasn't unsettling enough, her farewell to Clay had been doubly strange. Something was definitely not right between them, though there was no time to work it out now. He had shared her bed last night, but they'd only kissed each other goodnight and fallen asleep. He was gone when she awoke.

Rosette tried to hurry, feeling for the smooth fence railing with one hand and holding the lantern out in front of her with the other. Her heavy backpack jostled and bumped with every step. She squinted as she rounded a corner of the stable, shadows jumping up and down in the wake of the lamplight.

An' Lawrence had the stout mountain horses saddled, their packs stowed and water-skins filled. He was bent over the taller one's foreleg, feeling down the length of the cannon bone.

'Everything all right?' she asked, puffs of steam forming with each breath.

'Yes,' he said without looking up. 'Just making sure there's no swelling. They have already come a long way.'

Rosette frowned at the beast, looking it up and down. She pushed her hand through its dark coat, running it against the grain. Her fingers disappeared completely in the thick shag.

'They've got full winter coats already?' she asked. 'Where are they from?'

'North,' he replied, straightening his back. 'Far north.' He turned, searching her face. 'Are you ready, Rosette?'

'As ready as one can be if one has no idea where one is headed.'

He looked past her, ignoring the sarcasm.

Rosette's eye went to the thick roll of furs strapped behind each saddle. 'Are we going to the northern crossing?' She didn't mean to sound anxious, but there it was.

He nodded and tossed her a hooded sheepskin cloak that would cover her from head to toe.

Rosette caught the heavy garment and pulled it on over her coat. She was grateful. An' Lawrence had told her to bring only a few necessities, and she was certain she would be cold, especially at night. The warmth of the new garment gave her hope. She unpacked her gear, distributing the items into the saddlebags, and adjusted her sword.

The finely wrought blade that An' Lawrence had commissioned for her was in the fashion of the old swordsmiths of Timbali. They used clay on the core for tempering, causing them to curve — single-sided and razor-sharp. It sat at her waist, supported by a belt of broad black cloth, double-stitched like a quilt. Its presence reminded her that the mission was deadly serious.

Looking up, she caught An' Lawrence staring. 'I'm ready,' she said.

'Let's do it.' He turned his horse around and led it towards the top of the path. 'Check your girth,' he added.

Mounting up, Rosette sent a mental note to Drayco that they were on their way and followed the Sword Master out into the pre-dawn.

Chapter 11

Jarrod paced back and forth, making a narrow path in the snow. His hands were blue, his fingertips numb, yet he had the distinct sensation they were burning. He shoved them into the fur-lined pockets. What was taking Nell so long?

She'd sent him out to the shed to tack up the horses while she remained inside with Maka'ra. They'd been talking in hushed voices since well before dawn. The horses were saddled and bridled and packed, ready to go as soon as Nell emerged from the cottage. Jarrod stomped his feet.

'Any time, Nellion,' he mumbled through chattering teeth.

Rosette was in danger — he felt it in every part of his body, cold and rigid as it was. He looked out towards the snow-covered trees, grey-green under a blanket of white. The Dumarkian Woods were slumbering, blurred by the gusts of snow-speckled wind. Was Nell slumbering too? He rubbed his hands together, blowing into them.

To think that Rosette was his link to Earth and she didn't even know about it, any of it. He'd always wondered why he was so drawn to her, and so uncharacteristically possessive — jealous even. Now it made sense, but what still confused him was his lack of awareness. How could he not recognise her, and Nell? Was life in a Tulpa-body dulling his processes, slowing down his ability to assess and analyse? He was certainly finding it hard to thermo-regulate, and that was new.

'Come *on*, Nell. I'm dying here,' he said, his breath making steam as he spoke.

Finally the cottage door opened and Nell emerged, still talking with Maka'ra. The man was underdressed for the elements, wearing only a woollen sweater and pants tied at the waist with a colourfully woven belt. Maka'ra was a slender man, corded with muscles, his shaved head bare and his plaited beard decorated with small silver rings. He was dark-bronze-skinned, as were many island people, with tattoos on each side of his face in the tradition of their shamans — produced by puncturing the skin with whalebone needles and rubbing ash from sacred fires into the design.

After a few words and gestures, they embraced and Nell waved Jarrod over to her. 'Are we ready?' she asked, bright as sunshine.

He shivered, staring open-eyed at Maka'ra. The man was standing barefoot on the ice-encrusted steps. Nell chuckled.

'I can see you aren't enjoying the fresh morning,' she said. 'Take these. They'll help.' Nell handed Jarrod a steaming waterbag to carry beneath his coat and a pair of sheepskin-lined gloves. 'It doesn't get this brisk in Lividica, does it?' she smiled, flipping her hood over her head.

'Only in an ice box.' Jarrod shivered, pulling on the gloves and sighing as the blood began to flow back into his fingertips.

'Have a sip.' She offered him her small silver flask.

'What's in it?' He unscrewed the lid and took a sniff.

'A potion,' she said. 'It'll warm you up quick.'

He tilted his head back and took a swig. Heat rushed from his feet, all the way up to flush his cheeks. He smiled, doing up the lid and handing it back to her. 'That's magic!'

She winked.

The three walked through the yard to the horses, tethered by the gate. They were sturdy animals, shaggy as bears, one black and the other the colour of fire corals. Nell called it copper-chestnut and said the mare's name was Wren. Jarrod had never seen such a rich coat on a horse. Of course, he'd never seen so much snow either. In Lividica, you could catch a glimpse of it if you travelled a day's ride straight up into the Jacor mountain range. But even there it was only a light dusting.

Jarrod leaned against his mount and stroked the solid neck as Nell went back to another low-voiced conversation with Maka'ra. He fidgeted.

'Patience, Jarrod. We can't dash off haphazardly.'

'We do have to dash off, though, if we are to get there in time.'

'In time for what, I wonder?'

'In time to ... to warn Rosette. To see ...'

'To see that she is safe?'

'She can chastise me all she likes, once I know she's all right.'

'I feel the same.' Nell lifted her hand as she spoke and turned to wrap it around Maka'ra's neck. She kissed him before taking one last look at her cottage. The brilliant summer garden was buried under several feet of snow, the trees all bare bones save for the pines laden with drifts of white powder. Only the cobbled path had been shovelled clear, and that was quickly succumbing to a new fall. The Three Sisters circled overhead, strangely silent.

'Let's go,' she said, swinging her attention back to Jarrod.

Finally! 'Yes, milady. Let's.'

Jarrod led his horse away from the gate and mounted up. He nodded to Nell, and they headed towards the broad road that wound through the valleys and foothills, a six- or seven-day ride south to Treeon Temple if the weather didn't turn fierce.

On the morning of the fifth day, Jarrod tied his overcoat to the back of his saddle and stowed his gloves deep in the pockets. They had left the relentless cold behind and the air felt fresh but welcoming, no longer an adversary to be overcome. Nell didn't seem to mind either way, whatever the temperature, though her familiars did. He looked at the massive oak tree beside them, smiling at the raucous sounds.

'Are they still with us?'

Nell put her fingers to her lips and whistled. The caws and clatter suddenly stopped as three ravens shot out from the centre of the tree and circled above them.

'They go where I go, for the most part.' She smiled, following their line of flight. 'Snow, wind, storm or calm, though they're thrilled now that it's warmed up.'

'So am I.' He said the words, but he didn't really feel thrilled.

'We'll ride until midday,' she said, mounting up beside him.

She stroked her horse's neck and settled into the saddle, scanning the distances. The hills were a dirty brown — the same colour as the wasted cows that were strewn across them. She moved out at an easy jog.

'Midday?' Jarrod's brow wrinkled. 'But that means we won't get to Treeon until after noon tomorrow. We could be there in the morning if we kept going. The horses are in fine shape, and surely there's a town ...'

'Yes, there surely is a town, Jarrod. It's just a few hours' ride northeast of the temple. That's why we're stopping well before it and skirting around at dawn, undetected.'

He frowned. 'Why, exactly?'

'The local pub will be full of bards from Treeon tonight. It's where the apprentices go to perform and unwind, if customs haven't changed. The last thing I want is to announce our arrival. The less attention we attract, the better. Remember, we don't know who the opposition is, and if La Makee has a hand in it, I don't want her to see us coming.'

Jarrod nodded, shortening his reins as the mare snorted at a burnt-out tree stump by the road. The dead hulk was a startling shape, twisted into the form of a looming bear with outstretched claws. He smiled, leaning forward to pat her shoulder, whispering softly that there was nothing to fear. When she settled he caught up to Nell.

'You don't trust La Makee?'

Nell was quiet, still watching the hills as if searching for something, someone. 'I did once ...' she said under her breath.

'What's that?'

Nell cleared her throat. 'Makee won't be happy to see me at her gates.'

Jarrod nodded. 'Does she have any notion of what the spell means or your link to it?'

'She's never been to Earth. I doubt anyone could fully comprehend what the spell does — or the nature of the DNA links — if they've never seen what can happen when things go wrong. This is an agrarian society. Technology is far beyond her grasp.'

'But magic isn't.'

She pressed her lips together. 'You're right there. Magic isn't. Those idiot Corsanon priests ...' She ground the last few words with her teeth.

'The Corsanon high council?'

'They were the ones who helped fracture the Entity in the first place, sundering it from the portal with their attempt to pass through.'

'Perhaps we should grant them their wish.'

'How's that?'

'I'm thinking they might benefit from a little off-world travel.'

'They wouldn't last a minute on Earth.'

'You're probably right.'

Nell smiled. 'Interesting thought,' she said, but she didn't elaborate.

'You've been through recently?' he asked after they crested a hill.

'Fairly.'

'What's left?'

'You really want to know?'

He nodded.

'Take a world utterly dependent on technology for survival and without warning, pull the plug. Then picture it rotting from the inside out as attempts to bolster the remaining life forms backfire, turning the seas and valleys and forests into cesspools. I must say, the bacteria and insects are thriving, along with many new strains of virulent microbes — bacteria, protozoa and viruses.'

'And the worm? With you here, is anyone working on that? I can't go back until ...'

'I was working on it, until trackers got wind of me.'

'Do they know who you are?'

'I don't think so. It was more a witch-hunt than anything else. Still, computer or biological, viruses are rampant on Earth.'

'Water?'

She shook her head. 'People are clawing over each other to get it.'

Jarrod closed his eyes and asked no more.

The sound of the horses' hooves on the packed clay thudded out a regular beat, punctuated by the squeaking leather saddles and an occasional caw from the Sisters.

'That's what it's like, Jarrod,' she said after a long pause. 'That's what's happened to our mother Earth.'

She moved her horse into an easy canter and Jarrod urged Wren to catch up.

'So,' he said as they loped along side by side, 'nothing much has changed since I've been gone?'

She chuckled. 'Not much, but if we can sort out the Entity it might be time for you to return soon.'

'What about the worm?'

'I'm working on a plan.'

'From here?'

Nell winked and rode on.

Rosette climbed, step by step, as glacial winds howled through the pass. She had no idea of their exact whereabouts. All distinction was swallowed up by the tempest, a blur of wind and snow. Her earlier optimism was swallowed up as well.

At first the journey had been instructional and near enough to fun. An' Lawrence had been open, telling her a great deal of history and even about his own past as they'd sat by their evening fires. Much to Rosette's surprise, he had revealed feelings as well as facts. But An' Lawrence became quieter as the landscape had changed, his mood introverted. The easy flow between them ceased, replaced by a haunted silence.

Demons blight you, Scorpion Moon people!
Maudi?

These moods are driving me mad.
Then maybe don't focus on them.
It's pretty hard to ignore.
Not for me.

She smiled. But the contrast still bothered her. An' Lawrence barely responded to her queries. He didn't look her way as they rode into the foothills. It was as though he had forgotten she was there. The environment became treacherous. The wind howled — a menacing sound that penetrated the warm layers of her sheepskin-lined coat, biting into her skin. And now a blizzard on top of it all.

She led her horse on a loose lead, clinging to the leather reins through icy gloves. It was difficult keeping ahead of the animal. Her booted heels had been clipped several times by his iron-shod hooves before she'd gotten the hang of it. The trail was tight.

An' Lawrence led his horse in front. She could make out the contours of his mount's brown rump, its tail whipping about in the sudden gusts. Scylla must be further on, or so she guessed. She couldn't see a thing. Drayco followed behind, his mutters about the cold and wet invading her mind. His constant drone was the only thing undiminished in the stress of the climb. It was also her only comfort.

'Whoa!' Rosette commanded, almost smacking into the horse in front of her. She squinted, searching through the snowfall. Why was he stopping now?

She wrapped her full-length sheepskin coat tighter around her body, cinching the belt another notch. Her gloved hands were pinned under her arms, searching out some modicum of warmth. They found none. Her fingers wouldn't move. She felt nothing but burning tingles and numbness in all her limbs. An' Lawrence was at her side. How he had turned his horse around on the narrow path, she didn't know.

He bent his head towards hers, his face obscured by the hood.

'Scylla has found ...'

'What? I can't hear you.' Her voice was thin, whisked away from her lips as she spoke.

'Shelter! We can shelter over there.' He made the shape of a tent with his hands and pointed off in the distance.

'We're stopping in this?' she said, rising up on tiptoe to press her mouth against the side of his fur hood. She tried to shout, but she couldn't force the air out of her lungs. Her teeth chattered uncontrollably.

'Follow me,' he shouted back.

He looked different.

He took the lead, turning his mountain horse around on point. He may have been concerned, or simply matter-of-fact. She couldn't really tell. It was impossible to read him, her mind felt so distracted. It was like she couldn't settle on a single thought.

Concern. The answer came from Drayco, though she couldn't even see where he was now. *He's very concerned.*

Why?

Because we'll freeze to death if we don't get out of this blizzard.

'It's his fault if we do. I could have told him the crossing would be like this.'

It's serious, Maudi.

'Still his fault.' She followed, her pace slowing — each lift of her leg getting lower, each step smaller. *Actually, I think it's all right, Drayco. I'm starting to feel warm. It's getting better. Feels good.*

You're starting to fade. Keep walking. I come!

Her toes dragged on the ground and she stumbled, the horse halting before he trod on her. He stretched his nose down to sniff the icy lump in the path.

Get up, Maudi! Get up!

Rosette struggled, clenching the horse's mane, pulling herself up.

Keep walking.

She followed An' Lawrence blind, her eyes closed, her body leaden. It seemed to take an eternity to get where they were going. The roaring wind, the ice and the chill had infiltrated her mind, slowing movements and deadening her already frozen limbs. She couldn't feel her fingers or toes and her knees buckled again. An insidious peace rose up through her, an embracing, soothing radiance — a spell of warmth and ease. It called to her, impossible to deny. Heavenly, blessed sleep.

Her body dropped and she didn't fight it. She didn't try to get up. *Just a little rest, Dray-Dray.*

The last thing Rosette remembered was a disturbing sound — a vicious screech from Drayco. It annoyed her terribly, interrupting the languid descent into oblivion. She tried to raise her hand to shoo away the intrusion, but Drayco's hot breath assaulted her face, his tongue rasping across closed eyelids. She heard him scream again, this time from far away. Where was he, she wondered.

After a moment, she heard nothing at all.

Jarrod led his horse beside Nell, skirting the small town below. The pre-dawn sky glistened with stars, white sparkles against a deep purple background. The new moon had not yet risen. A dot of light shone from the village, a solitary glow in the silhouette of rooftops. It had to be a bakery with its ovens stoked. Columns of smoke rose above the chimneys, unbent by any wind or gust. It was a peaceful scene — unlike Jarrod's mind, which buzzed like a hornets' nest.

He and Nell walked their horses in silence. The Three Sisters perched on the back of Nell's saddle, eyes closed and soundless. When well past the outermost dairy, they mounted and returned to the main road. The sun was rising now in a haze of red and orange that washed over the landscape, heralding a bright, new day. Nell watched it with reverence, as she always did. The Three Sisters woke, squawked a surprise at their strange surroundings and took flight.

'Why are they always so noisy?' Jarrod's mouth was turned down, his shoulders slumped.

'They like to comment.'

'On everything?'

Nell smiled. 'Pretty much.'

The look on her face made him laugh, and in the glow of the early sunrise Jarrod felt the turmoil subside. He even thought the landscape had improved, but once the sun was fully above the horizon he saw the same desolate brown hills, drought-stricken fields and scrawny cows.

'I'm going in alone,' Nell said as they trotted across a wooden bridge.

'What do you mean?'

'I'll go in first and find out what's happening.'

'I thought we were in this together.'

'Jarrod, how do you feel?'

He put his hand on his stomach and frowned. 'Anxious. Twisting knots in my stomach. Like I want to run, or fight.'

'Exactly. I feel the same and we're going to heed the warnings. We're going to keep you out of the picture until we know more. I don't think Rosette is here. I can't feel her close at all, and there may be trackers.'

Jarrod looked over his shoulder. 'What's the plan?'

'Simple. You wait at the edge of the valley, out of sight, and I get an audience with Makee. We'll meet up before dark.'

'And?'

'We'll take it from there.'

'So I wait again?'

'I know you've been waiting a long time, Jarrod.'

'Generations,' he said.

'A little longer won't be too hard.'

They rode for a few more hours and the terrain became luxurious. Ripe grain swayed in the wind, and stacks upon stacks of hay were piled up in the corners of freshly mowed fields — the collective energy resonating from Treeon made for fertile surroundings and enlightened farmers. They stopped by a stream to water the horses and share a meal, the smell of alfalfa mixing with the hint of apple cider.

'How close are we?' Jarrod asked.

'It's just over the rise.' Nell held him back when he tried to stand. 'Patience. We're nearly there.'

When they reached the cliffs above Treeon, Jarrod let out a shrill hawk whistle. 'That's quite a view,' he said.

Nell didn't answer. She stared out over the valley while untying her hair. She fished her black-cowl robe from her pack and secured the fur-lined one to the saddlebags. Flipping up the hood, she moved off towards the descent.

'Good luck,' Jarrod called to her, retreating back into the woods.

'I won't be long.' She twisted in her saddle to face him. 'Why don't you hunt us up something nice for dinner while I'm away? Girls,' she called, smiling at the Three Sisters, 'give him a hand, will you.'

Jarrod mumbled, rolling his eyes as the Sisters flapped and cawed in the branches above him.

The gates of Treeon hadn't changed at all. They stood tall and imposing just as Nell remembered. She took a deep breath, shielding her thoughts and schooling her manner. Whatever happened, the last thing she wanted was for Makee to discern that the spell had been here, right within reach. The guards approached and asked a few questions before returning to the guardhouse, whispering between themselves. Nell smiled. This is one visit that Makee and An' Lawrence were probably not prepared for.

She touched the blade strapped to her thigh, trusting she'd made the right choice.

'Nellion Paree,' the female guard spoke. 'Re'gad will escort you to the Temple. You can ask for an audience there.'

'I hardly need an escort. I was walking these halls before you were born.'

The woman looked up, her composure unruffled. 'No doubt. Still, we'll stick to tradition, shall we?'

Nell smiled obligingly. 'Of course.'

She rode along the cobbled thoroughfare to the main courtyard, falling into her memories. The trees had grown, making the massive statues in the plaza seem smaller but so much more alive. There were many students rushing about, but then, it was midmorning. Most would be on their break. In front of the temple steps, Re'gad, who had said nothing as they rode, nodded for her to wait. He trotted up the steps to the temple doors, whispering to the attendant. Within seconds, the doors swung open and La Makee came rushing out, red hair flaming behind her. She descended halfway and stood, legs apart, her left hand on the hilt of her sword, her right shielding the sun from her eyes.

'About to spar, Makee, or do you always wear your sword in the temple these days?'

'Nellion! What a pleasant surprise.'

Nell lowered her voice. 'So we're going to be civil?'

Makee eyed her up and down. 'What are you doing here?'

Nell dismounted, pulled the reins over her mare's head and handed them to Re'gad. He looked surprised. 'Mind her for a moment, will you, lad? I won't be long.' She winked at him and went up the steps to stand square in front of Makee. She leaned down to kiss her right cheek, then her left, then her lips — the contact so light she barely touched her soft skin. Then she stood back, her arms relaxed at her sides.

'Can't a mentor come to visit her student? It's been a year. I want to know where she's been apprenticed and how she's doing. I've had no word for months.'

Makee studied her before answering. 'This is such a shame. If you'd only written first, you'd have known that she's travelling.'

'Travelling?'

'Off on a training task with the Sword Master.'

'Is she his apprentice now?'

'She's in the running.'

'Ah, well. I wish her luck.' Nell stared out at the statue of the winged lion. 'How've you been, Makee?'

'Well. And you?'

'Very well.' She let out a breath. 'The place looks magnificent. Just as I remembered it.'

'Twenty-three years is a long time.'

'A long time to remain silent?'

Makee took her hand from her sword hilt and reached towards Nell. 'Cup of tea?'

Nell nodded and together they walked into the temple.

Jarrod leaned against a twisted oak, braiding strands of grass into tiny stick figures. A brace of rabbits lay by his side, and Wren grazed clover at the foot of the trees, cropping it into a smooth green lawn. Nell had been gone for hours and the sun was getting low. He kept peering through the brush, scanning the road, but nothing moved. The only creature that stirred, besides him and the ravens, was a whistling bird of prey. It flew high overhead, circling in ever-descending spirals. The Sisters took flight as it neared, joining it.

Peculiar. Jarrod squinted, scratching the back of his neck as he watched the bird getting closer, heading directly for him. *Maybe it's a message from Nell?*

He stepped out onto the road, checking left and right. Empty. He rolled down the cuff of his leather jacket so the hem covered his hand up to his knuckles. Looking skyward, he extended his arm out like a scarecrow.

He whistled his goshawk cry and bent his elbow. He hadn't handled many raptors, but he'd hunted with his mentor at Montava University over the last few years. He was a falconer, Ra'Jamison, a well-respected one, and a surgeon too — a brilliant man. He'd taught Jarrod some basics.

Keep your arm steady, your mind relaxed, he'd instructed. *The last thing you want to do is tense up with a falcon inches from your face.*

The gust from the bird's back-winging blew hair into his eyes. He watched, spellbound, as she landed on his arm. He didn't recognise the species. Its talons wrapped around his forearm and its head dropped at an odd angle to look him in the eye. It had no trusses.

'You're magnificent,' Jarrod said as he stroked the blue-black feathers of its neck. 'Even if you don't have a message for me, I am delighted to meet you.'

The black falcon whistled and extended her wings. The span was broader than Jarrod's shoulders by double. She launched off his arm and landed on the side of the road. A blast of energy hit Jarrod in the face. He threw up his hands, shielding his eyes from the force. When he looked again, the bird shimmered, distorted and transformed. Inside of one breath the falcon was gone and Nellion Paree stood in its place, black robe wrapped tightly around her.

'Nell!'

She rubbed her shoulders and hands. 'Let's get off the road. I don't have much time.'

'Did you see Rosette? Is she all right?' he asked as they slipped into the shade of the oak. The Sisters landed above them, noisy as ever.

'No, and probably not. She's headed for Los Loma.'

'Alone?'

'The Sword Master's with her, which is something. He won't let any harm come to her.'

'How do you know that? You said yourself we don't know who the enemy is. What if he ...'

'Jarrod, take a few deep breaths. I'm still not sure why they're heading for Los Loma, but An' Lawrence would give his life to protect Rosette.'

'How can you be so sure?'

Nell looked him straight in the eye. 'Because she's his blood.'

Jarrod stared at her, his mouth open. 'What?'

'An' Lawrence is her father.'

'How?'

She raised her eyebrows.

'Okay, wrong question.' Jarrod frowned. 'Does he know?'

'I'm hoping he's worked it out by now.'

'Hoping? He may not know? She could be just any young witch to him? Do you realise what could happen if ...'

'Jarrod. More breathing, less panicking. They headed out on the north road three mornings ago. I think they're going to do some kind of deal with Kreshkali, but that's just a guess.'

'Why don't they just jump off a thousand-foot cliff into a bottomless sea? It would save them the trouble of a more treacherous end.'

'Jarrod...'

'It's suicide.'

'Possibly. I'm going to stay here at Treeon and find out what I can. Makee and I are back on speaking terms, but there's much she withholds.' She smiled crookedly. 'Of course, there's much that I withhold as well. But a visiting priestess is regarded very highly, and for the time I'm here it is required that I teach some classes and work with a few chosen apprentices. In exchange, I'll get to the bottom of Makee's schemes.'

'I have to go after them.'

'I know. There's gold in the saddlebags; plenty for more supplies. Go back to the town we passed by this morning and stock up. You'll be needing your overcoat and gloves by tomorrow night. The winds are biting on Mount Prieta.'

Jarrod nodded. 'And you?'

'I'll catch up with you by tomorrow night. Next day at the latest.' She stood on tiptoe and kissed him. He wrapped his arms tightly around her lithe body.

'Thank you, Nell.' Jarrod released her and bent down to kiss one cheek, then the other, then her lips.

'We'll thank each other when we find Rosette and work out what to do with her wily spell.' Nell stepped backwards, further into the trees.

Jarrod felt again the boom of energy and looked up to see the black hawk soaring above the treeline, the Three Sisters shooting after her.

He grabbed his brace of rabbits and went to his mare, tightening the girth before mounting. 'We're heading out, Wren,' he whispered, while stroking her neck. 'And we're going hard. Be strong.'

He looked down the road towards the town, then up to the mountains. Turning the mare northwards he urged her into a brisk trot then a canter. He had sufficient grain for the horse and almost enough food for himself. That was all the supplies necessary. He didn't plan on losing another moment. He had to find Rosette before Kreshkali did.

Earth and Gaela

Chapter 12

Kreshkali closed the book and stared at her hands. The interpretation didn't please her, though it was no real surprise. She knew the Lupins had been her inheritance — she had not realised, though, just how deep the connection went. A peal of thunder rumbled outside her apartment, bright flashes momentarily engulfing the golden glow of candlelight. She hardly noticed. Packing empty water bottles and her notes into a backpack, she pulled on her boots, grabbed her cloak and headed for the portal.

The sewer under Half Moon Bay was dank, as always, dark and slick with ooze, the smell nauseating. She made her way to the portal by the light of a small lantern, glancing over her shoulder more than once before she reached it. If ASSIST had sent trackers, she couldn't spot them. Her new apartment was safe, so far, though there was no real sanctuary on Earth, especially not for her. There was always a risk.

She'd need help again soon, and she didn't relish the idea of asking for it. If Jaynan could fool her, it proved anyone could. There must be a way to tell friend from foe, but it had eluded her. Extinguishing the lantern, she hid it in a crevice and stepped through the portal.

They were waiting on the other side. She sensed them just beyond the door of her chamber beneath Los Loma, half a dozen at least. She pushed it wide, light from the passageway beaming in.

'Do you understand what must be done?' she asked, taking in the beasts.

The Lupins were gathered around, most in wolf form, a few bipedal. All were attentive though only one communicated, using mind-speech. *Aye, Mistress. We get the young witch and we bring her to you.*

'That's right, Hotha,' she said, taking a deep breath. 'But we need to discuss the word "get". She's invited, not forced. I want her intrigued enough to come down and meet me, alone, but she's not to be harmed or coerced. She's a mistress too. Do you understand? She's of the blood.'

What if she doesn't want to come?

'She will. Born under the sign of the Twins — curious as a cat. Besides, it's part of the trade — all set up. You just have to play it right.'

And the others?

'Absolutely in no way are they to be harmed.'

What if they interfere?

'Knock them out — but I mean it, no lasting harm. And they aren't to suspect anything, any of them, not even her. Especially not her. I have to tell her myself. Got it, my beauties?'

She stroked the top of the nearest wolf's head and he gently nipped her sleeve. The rest slunk off down the passageway, throwing back mental messages in the affirmative. The other remained, morphing into a bipedal form, his dark eyes penetrating. 'We need to talk, Kreshkali.'

'What's wrong?'

'There's a blizzard out there and I don't think your girl's going to make it.'

* * *

Rosette opened her eyes, blinking slowly. It seemed much quieter than she remembered. Calmness surrounded her like a warm, woolly blanket. Everything was still except for the dancing orange lights. They leapt and played against the ceiling above her — light without sound — ever so peaceful.

Her eyes opened wider. *Ceiling?*

How was that possible? The last thing she recalled was being stuck in the middle of a blizzard. Rosette scratched her head. The biting wind had been left behind. She was either dead or sheltered. Toss a coin, it didn't matter. It felt good. If she concentrated really hard, she could just make out a distant, thin wail. It sounded like an elderly voice, calling from far away, soft, vague and echoing.

'Where am I?' she asked aloud.

No answer. Rosette pushed her braids away from her face. What could have happened? She remembered being freezing, and angry. She'd been trying to get somewhere. That's right; she'd been following An' Lawrence towards shelter. They must have been heading for this place. A cave? But then something had happened. Everything had gone from icy stabs of pain to a warm and dark silence. It was wonderful. She reached her arms over her head, brushing past the soft fur coat of Drayco. The rise and fall of his warm body stretched out next to her was reassuring.

'So this isn't a dream?'

A delicious heat penetrated her every pore. Dry furs were nestled around her, their plush depths cushioning every move. As her eyes became accustomed to the dark, she noticed a red ember-glow defining the outlines of a cavern. It was a huge space.

Drayco, what's happening?

The temple cat yawned massively. *I'm sleeping. It's warm and safe. You should do the same.*

She closed her eyes. *All right.*

At least the temple cat wasn't alarmed. If he said she was safe, then she was. But where was An' Lawrence?

Her eyes popped open again. Suddenly she registered that she and Drayco were not alone in the warm furs, not isolated in their protected nest. She also realised why those pelted furs seemed so soft and comforting on her skin. She was naked. Lifting the covers slightly, she recognised the Sword Master's long tanned arm draped across her hip and his hand resting lightly atop her thigh. Stiffening, she tried to recall how this might have happened.

Blank.

He didn't share her alarm. His breathing came in the deep and rhythmic flow of sleep. No matter. She was alarmed enough for the both of them. She slipped from under his arm and sat upright, accidentally smacking him on the head with her elbow.

His eyes sprang open and he reached for his sword, looking towards the entrance.

'What are we doing here?' Rosette shouted at him.

His face relaxed. 'So you didn't die.' He stretched. 'I wondered if I'd ever hear that screech again.'

'Answer the question!' She kicked his legs.

An' Lawrence chuckled, the sound reverberating through the cave. 'I was saving your life, though no doubt I'll soon wish I hadn't.' He yawned and closed his eyes. 'Go back to sleep if you can. We'll ride when the blizzard passes.'

'I don't remember my life needing to be saved. I don't remember finding this cave and I *certainly* don't remember getting undressed and crawling into the furs with you. What's going on?'

He moaned and rolled over. 'Go to sleep, girl.'

She kicked harder. 'Not until you tell me what, by the darkest underworld serpents, happened!'

He turned back. 'Nothing *happened*, unless you count the fact that I kept you alive.' He propped himself up on his elbow. 'Rosette, calm down. The blizzard had us stopped in our tracks and you were frozen and soaked to the bone — your skin was blue and your eyes glazed over. Scylla found shelter just as you collapsed. You would have frozen to death if I hadn't got you under the furs with me and the felines.'

'Naked?'

'Of course *naked*, Rosette! Naked bodies generate heat much faster than ones in wet clothes. I started a fire and hung a skin tight over the entrance. I stripped us both, and with me on one side and the familiars on the other, by the grace of the mountain gods, you came back to life. If grace we can call it . . .' He mumbled the last sentence: 'Maybe it's more a curse.'

'What?'

'Completely back, it seems, with only slight memory deprivation. Are you satisfied? Can we sleep now?'

Crossing her arms, she watched him brace for her retort. 'I'm not satisfied.'

'Didn't think so,' he sighed.

'I still haven't been told a thing about this journey. What are we going to do when we reach the summit? Tell me that, at least.'

An' Lawrence didn't answer. He lay there, his head still propped, staring at her, his brow forming into a deep frown.

'What's wrong now?' she asked.

'Where did you get that?' He pointed at the silver pendant around her neck — a crescent moon nestled in a five-pointed, sapphire-tipped star.

'Stop changing the subject! I want to know why we are here.'

'Rosette, answer me, please. This is important: where did you get that pendant?'

She touched her throat, fingering the star tips. 'It was a gift, if you must know. I can't see how that's of any importance at this point.' She held it in her hand protectively.

'A gift from whom?'

She'd never heard him sound desperate before. It startled her. She took a deep breath and let it out. 'It was an initiation gift from Nell, my mentor, though that's really none of your business.'

An' Lawrence rubbed his jaw, his eyebrows going up. 'How old are you?'

'For demon's sake, what's this about? Didn't you even read my apprenticeship application?'

'Just tell me how old!'

She could see the intensity in his eyes and the tension around his mouth, even in the dim light. 'Twenty-two,' she replied.

'Twenty-two?'

'Do I need to say it again?'

He shook his head.

'What's the big fascination with my jewellery and my birthday, Sword Master? Has the cold sent you daft?'

He didn't take his eyes from her neck. 'The big fascination, my fractious witch, is that I had that pendant made twenty-three years ago as a solstice gift for the woman ... I ... um.'

'Go on. The woman you what ...?'

'A woman I worked with,' he said.

Her eyes narrowed. 'What do you mean? Who? Who'd you work with?'

'It's *whom* ...'

She growled at him and sent another kick his way. He moved his leg back before she connected.

'I worked with Nellion Paree. The pendant was for her.'

Rosette was blank for a moment before sucking in her breath. She stared at him as she pulled the furs up around her neck and clutched her knees, her brow wrinkling. 'There must be many like them.'

'It was a one-off commission.'

'That doesn't make sense. Nell gave it to me at my initiation saying ...' She put her hand over her mouth, her eyes wide.

'Saying what?'

Rosette didn't speak.

'Tell me!'

She said: This is a message to your source for the day you meet again, for the first time. She sent the words directly to his mind. She couldn't speak them aloud.

'Your source?' he asked.

'That's how she put it.' Rosette closed her eyes and rocked.

'Until you meet again?'

'Yes,' she whispered.

'For the first time?'

'I didn't know what she meant.' Rosette looked out into the dark. 'And I still don't.'

'I think I do.'

She continued to look away. 'Well, I don't.'

'Rosette, whatever family you grew up with — those that called you daughter — I don't think they were blood kin.'

'What are you saying?' Tears welled up and spilled down her cheeks.

'I'm saying,' he reached up and touched the pentacle and then her tears, 'that this was a message to me. I think you're *my* daughter, Rosette, my child with Nell.'

Rosette's jaw went tight. 'That's not true. My mother is Bethsay Matosh, and if Nell *was* my mother why would she have given me away and not raised me herself? Why wouldn't I have known all this?' She blurted the words before she could stop them.

'Bethsay Matosh?'

Rosette regretted her slip the moment she spoke. She had kept the secret so well.

'It's true, then,' he said. 'You're not a *de Santo*. You're not even a Rosette, are you?'

Her eyes refilled with tears. When she closed them they overflowed, washing down her face. 'I am now.'

Maudi, I thought you were going to sleep.

She hugged Drayco to her. *Dray, I think Nell might be my mother.*

Of course she is.

Rosette grabbed her familiar's head and stared into his orange eyes. *What?*

She's your mother, or sister. You have the same blood.

How can you tell?

I can smell it.

And the Sword Master. Did you know about him too?

No, Maudi. That was a surprise.

She let out a breath that she hadn't realised she'd been holding and wiped her face on the furs. A mask hid her feelings, covering her turbulence with a seamless calm.

'So, Sword Master,' she said, her voice in perfect control. 'This must mean I have a good chance of getting the apprenticeship. A blood-tie counts for much, does it not?'

He studied her features closely. 'I don't know why I didn't see it before. You look just like her, save for the eyes. They're like my mother's.'

Rosette lifted her chin and looked past him. 'The apprenticeship?' she asked again.

He looked directly at her, forcing her to connect. 'I think we can say the apprenticeship is yours, Rosette.' Her face remained smooth, unchanged.

'It's about time.'

Jarrod dismounted and led the copper-red mare to the edge of the stream. The water flowed around chunks of ice and jutting boulders. They were back in the cold and he didn't like it one bit. He also thought it might have been a mistake to have rushed off without getting further supplies. He had grain for Wren but only dried meat and frozen mulled wine left for himself. He would need to make a fire tonight.

He pulled Wren's head out of the stream. 'Ten sips at a time, girl,' he said, keeping her head up when she tried to drink again. 'You're lathered and that water's ice-cold. I can't have you foundering on me.'

He looked up at the mountain pass. There was a blizzard raging up there. The golden rays of sunset streaked across the dark clouds making it look like a battle of the sky gods. If Rosette and the Sword Master were up there now, their chances of survival were on the edge.

He scouted for a place to camp that wasn't packed with snowdrifts or soaked with brown slush. How people made a life in these regions, he had no idea. He scanned the undulating hills, realising that no-one did. The place was barren, empty. He led the mare along the face of a steep cliff before finding a sheltered gorge. The rocks were almost warm to the touch from the day's sun, and the wind didn't reach it at all. Wren nudged his back, prompting him to enter, clearly liking the choice.

He marvelled at his horse's endurance. He had ridden almost non-stop for two days and until now she'd shown no signs of fatigue. He unsaddled her and filled her feedbag to the brim. Slipping the silver bit from her mouth he replaced it with the burlap bag and she dived savagely into the hay cubes and grain.

'You're one strong companion,' he crooned as he curried her thick winter coat, steam rising where the saddle had been. 'Thank you, milady.'

Picking up each hoof, he checked for stones or loose nails and ran his hand down her legs, feeling for swollen tendons. Nothing. She'd be fit and sound, ready to climb the pass tomorrow — if the storm cleared.

Jarrod made a fire with what fuel he could find. Fortunately, the little gorge had trapped a great deal of driftwood from previous floods. They'd lodged in the shrubs and rocks and the twisted shapes were dry and combustible. In moments he had a comfortable blaze going, placing his little pot of dried beef soup on the coals that were already burning red. He flipped open his book — a novel about leviathan sea creatures said to dwell in the southern seas — reading aloud to the mare as he melted drinking water and mulled wine. When the sun had well and truly set, he wrapped himself in furs and fell asleep. Nell would find him tomorrow, and together they would find Rosette.

Rosette awoke to the stares of Drayco and Scylla. The two sat only inches away from her face, motionless, burning with intention. She stretched and smiled at the remnants of a delightful dream, her eyes focusing slowly in the dim light.

'That is no way to wake a body up,' she said to her black familiar, roughing his neck, 'glaring like that.'

The storm has passed. We must reach the summit by noon.

'Do you know why?'

Because that is when the meeting is.

'What meeting? All this talk about a meeting and no-one tells me who — whom — we are going to meet.'

I don't know that answer.

Getting her bearings, she stood up and headed for the glowing coals of the fire, the revelation of the night before flooding back.

'Goddess of the Dark Forest, is it true?'

She thought of John'ra and Bethsay Matosh, of her older sisters and her little brother, D'ran. Everything she had recently learned made her feel distant, as if she were floating amongst the stars with no hope of coming in to land.

She mumbled under her breath, gathering her clothes that were spread out over the boulders near the makeshift hearth. She stepped into her leggings, warm and dry, and pulled her leather bodice over her head. She glanced back at the furs where An' Lawrence had told her about her parentage. Why had Nell communicated to them both in such an elusive way? She did up her bodice laces, pulling on her sweaters and leather riding breeches. There'd better be a good explanation.

'And now, Sword Master,' she asked, though he was clearly not in the cave, 'what of this secret journey that you and La Makee have cooked up? Where does this lead and why?'

I've asked, Drayco touched her mind, *but Scylla says nothing.*

'I guess we'll just have to see it played out.'

It seems so, Maudi. And the Sword Master's your blood?

'Apparently.'

How's that for you?

'I don't know — but if we get off this mountain, Nellion Paree has some explaining to do.'

Drayco licked a paw and wiped the back of his ear. *Everyone's hungry.*

'Everyone?'

Me, Scylla, the horse beasts ...

'The horses! Where are they?'

At the back of the cave.

Rosette went to the horses and found them calm, resting quietly with their hind legs cocked and their heads down and drowsy. She tipped some grain from the pack onto the flat rocks and smiled at the rumbling sound their chewing made. She lugged water from the fire where ice had been set to melt and filled their leather trough before taking a long drink of her own.

We are very hungry, actually. There is nothing to hunt here. Drayco spoke for both familiars.

'I am making a breakfast we can all enjoy, my lovely,' she answered. She stoked the fire and filled a pot with chunks of dried meat and barley.

We should eat quickly.

'What's the rush now?'

We have to get out of here very soon. Scylla agrees. The Sword Master is returning. He's anxious.

'Well, we don't want that, do we!'

Rosette looked towards the entrance as the covering flipped up and An' Lawrence entered, ducking under the low, overhanging rock. Scylla, bobtail twitching, bounded to him, her thickly furred paws resting lightly on his chest as she jumped up.

'Ouch!' he shouted. It seemed her claws were not entirely sheathed. He tousled her head. 'Okay! I'm back! What? What's all the urgency?'

There was a moment's silence before he said something under his breath. She turned back to the fire.

'Good morning, Rosette. Feeling better?'

'Good morning, Sword Master,' she said formally. She didn't turn around. 'We need to be quick?'

'We do.'

Very quick. Drayco pushed his head under Rosette's hand.

'All right, my famished one, breakfast is coming.'

'I'm not really that hungry,' he said.

'I wasn't talking to you.'

The flames jumped high as she spoke, the contents of the pot sizzling over.

An' Lawrence began rolling up the furs and packing the saddlebags. 'We have to get to the summit plateau by midday.'

'So I've been told, though of course I have no idea why. In any case, the food is ready.'

'Thanks. We can leave most of our supplies here.'

'Leave them here?'

'For the return. No sense lugging them up to the plateau and then back down again. They'll be safe enough. I'll saddle up.'

Rosette dished out two portions of the stew into the felines' plates and added ice to take out the heat and give them more liquid. They didn't waste any time lapping it up. She left the remainder beside the fire and followed An' Lawrence to the horses. His back was to her as he saddled them.

'That's it?' she asked, tapping his shoulder. 'That's all you have to say ... *we have to be quick?* No comments about, let me see, anything else?'

He clamped his hand over hers to stop the tapping. He tried to hold it, but she pulled back. 'Rosette, we have a task to perform and it must be successful. There is no time to talk about last night's revelation.'

'You tell me I'm your daughter and that my whole upbringing was a lie, that Nell and you were lovers and she's my mother, then it's, "Oh, sorry, there's no time to talk about it. Break camp — important meeting — chop chop"?'

'It's a shock to me too, I assure you. I have more than a few questions for Nellion myself, when we next meet. But we can't dwell on it right now.' He caught her wrist and squeezed it tight. 'Do you understand me? We have to stay focused. Things are going to get dangerous.'

'Because, so far, it's been a summer picnic?'

He growled. 'Focus, Rosette. Do you understand?'

'Perfectly,' she replied.

No time for this! Drayco said. *You two will have to sort out your bonding later.*

Rosette huffed. *I've no desire to bond with him. All I want is some clarity.*

The meal disappeared in silence, An' Lawrence eating in the back of the cave and Rosette by the fire. She could hear him speaking to the horses as he finished tacking up, but she didn't look his way. She busied herself, rolling up the packets of food and tucking the crockery into the saddlebags that were to be left behind. She slipped on her sheepskin coat, ready to go. An' Lawrence stood silently at the cave entrance, testing the wind.

'Gale's dropped completely,' he said, staring out over the horizon.

'Thank the goddess,' Rosette said.

'We'd best get to the top of this last ridge while we can.'

'Again, *why*?'

'We're to meet a ... a messenger.'

'What kind of messenger?'

'It could look like almost anything.'

'Thing?'

'Creature.' He turned and stared her in the eyes. 'There will be no time to debate. We will have to respond immediately and judiciously.'

'Judiciously?'

'It may seem evil to you, frightening, but it is older than that. From another world. Uncanny. It is not our place to judge or form an opinion. We must simply respond to instructions.'

'Sounds to me like you have met such a *thing* before.'

'I have.'

She waited for him to elaborate, but he didn't. 'Anything else you'd like to tell me about this creature, before we go? Any hint you might want to give your only daughter before she faces the unknown, completely baffled from lack of information?' She looked at him questioningly. 'Am I your only daughter, or are there sisters and brothers somewhere that I have yet to meet?'

'Not that I've been told of, Rosette,' a warning in his voice.

She ignored it. 'So there could be?' Her eyes went wide.

'Stop thinking about the past, Rosette. It doesn't exist.'

'I can see that it doesn't exist for you.'

The look he threw her made her mouth snap shut. 'Last warning, Rosette. Let it go. All our lives are at stake. Stay focused on the messengers.'

'Messengers? Now there's more than one?' She turned to Drayco. 'It seems there's more than one, a whole party of them, perhaps?'

'There could be more than one, yes.'

Rosette studied the gravity in his eyes. 'I'm listening,' she said, schooling her features.

'These messengers require special treatment. You must not be dazzled by them. You must not be impressed, neither must you startle. Most importantly, do not behave frivolously. They have no sense of humour, I promise you, and they will not tolerate your sharp tongue.'

He led his horse out of the cave. Rosette and the familiars followed.

'Do you understand?'

'Perfectly,' she said, her hands shielding her eyes from the glare.

'You'll need these.' An' Lawrence gave her a pair of glasses, the lenses darkened with a sea-green tint. 'The snow is blinding without them.' He put on a pair himself and checked his daughter's fit. 'Let's go.'

Leading the horses in single file, they headed up the icy slope. Rosette shivered from the cold shock. She also shivered from the Sword Master's indifference. She had lost one family already, one father. John'ra was gone and now she had a second chance that also seemed to be slipping away before she could grasp it.

Rosette dispelled the thought and concentrated on their immediate situation. She still had no clear idea what they were rushing to meet. Messengers? A creature? Many creatures? If being an apprentice meant being kept out of the loop, she was doing just fine. She pushed her left hand deep into her pocket, gripping the reins with the other. Rosette was determined to get to the bottom of all these mysteries; if nothing else it was a suitable distraction from her dark mood. Clucking to her horse, she hurried to catch up.

There is good news here, Maudi.

What's that?

You've made apprentice.

I know, but somehow I thought it would make me feel a whole lot better.

Jarrod leaned forward in the saddle as the mare lunged over a fallen log and scrambled up yet another slope. He stood in his stirrups, scanning the terrain ahead. Snowdrifts piled high to his left, but the howling wind had kept the trail frozen and manoeuvrable. He knew he was getting closer, gaining on them. He could feel it.

If the fair weather held he would be at the summit before nightfall. He stroked his horse's neck as they crested the grade and skirted around an outcrop of boulders. Without her instincts and stamina, he doubted he'd find the way. The mare had been through this pass over many summers. She knew where they were headed and seemed to understand the urgency. It felt like the first bit of good luck since setting out on this journey.

A shrill whistle from above brought him out of his musing. He eased to a halt and searched the sky. It called again and he automatically answered in his goshawk whistle. A bird circled overhead and spiralled towards him. He urged his mare on. If this was Nell then she'd spotted him and would catch up in due time. If it was not, he'd take it as another good omen. The mare seemed unperturbed and they trotted steadily up another grade.

When they reached the top a hooded figure stood beside the trail, precariously close to the edge of a precipice. Three ravens perched in a dead pine branch behind her. Nell's sudden presence was too much for the mare. She spooked like a green-broke filly, jumping upwards and sideways inside a second, bunching her hindquarters to bolt.

Jarrod shortened his reins and brought her under control as Nell pushed back her hood.

'Steady, Wren. It's only me.' She held a hand out towards the horse's flaring nostrils.

'How do you do that?' Jarrod asked, patting his horse's neck.

'Years of practice.'

He laughed. 'I've yet to master it and I've had quite a few more years than you, Nell.'

'Ah, but you are not a witch.' She rubbed her hands together and slipped on her gloves. 'You've done very well to get this far, this fast.'

'It's Wren. The mare's amazing.' He looked up at the sky and back to the cloaked woman. 'Not as amazing as you, but damn fine anyway. What's the news?'

'They're at the summit. I saw them crest the plateau.'

'Rosette? Is she all right?'

'She looked okay from where I was, but I didn't get too close. I'm guessing they're waiting up there for a messenger.'

'Messenger?'

'Wards of Kreshkali. They're shape-shifters, after a fashion, very interesting. Dangerous, though.'

'What does this mean?'

'Makee must think that Rosette knows something about the lost spell. She's fishing for information.'

'In these waters? I thought you said Makee wouldn't guess.'

'I'm not certain of anything now.'

Jarrod looked at her and shook his head. Magic was such a complex art, as were those who wielded it.

'Did you find out anything more?'

'Very little. Makee's suspicious of me and single-minded. All her intent is focused on this meeting, I know that much.'

'Won't An' Lawrence protect her, being her blood?'

'Yes, but he would have only just discovered that bit of truth and, if I know Rosette, she won't make things easy for him.'

'She never did with John'ra.'

'So I heard.' Nell sighed. 'The Sword Master brought her here in the first place — hardly a protective act. His allegiance, it seems, is to Makee — always has been.'

'I've got to get to her.' Jarrod started forward. 'Will I double you?'

'The climb's too steep, even for Wren. Ride up and I'll meet you there.' She gestured to the sky.

'Of course.' He moved off, heading up the trail.

'One note of caution, Jarrod.'

He looked back, pulling Wren to a halt.

'If the messengers are on the summit when you arrive, don't let them see you. Don't let them smell you. It'll mean your death if they do.'

'Just like that?'

'They kill first and ask questions later.'

'I'm fairly resilient.'

'You think you've got the time to conjure up a whole new Tulpa-body?'

He rubbed his chin. 'I'll be careful.'

Gaela

Chapter 13

By midday, she heard the howls. At first Rosette thought it was the wind telling of some deep crevice ahead. She always listened to the wind. It had saved her life on more than a few occasions and it might be doing so again today. She frowned, listening harder, straining to catch the nuances embedded in the whirl of sound. Holding her breath, she realised it was not the wind that spoke. It was something else, and it was getting closer.

The horses' heads tossed, eyes rolling, showing the whites. The beasts tried to look behind and to either side of the ridge all at once, taking small, prancing steps, tails held high. An' Lawrence dismounted and Rosette did the same, holding the reins firm as her horse alternately pawed the snow and minced back and forth.

Something's ahead. It climbs from the other side. I don't recognise the scent. The warning cut sharply into her thoughts, alarming her even more than the horses' behaviour. Drayco was apprehensive. She had seldom sensed that in him, not since the day they had met.

Human?

Not quite, more canine, or wolf.

Rosette went to An' Lawrence and yanked on his long coat until he turned around.

'Drayco says some*thing* is up ahead, on the other side of the summit.' She leaned into him, pressing her face next to his. 'He says it's not quite human. Care to explain?' She pulled her face back from his ice-encrusted hood.

'We're expecting a messenger, remember?'

Rosette pursed her cracked lips. 'It's not difficult to recall the things you tell me, Sword Master, considering how few and far between they are.' She glared at him, fishing out Nell's tin of ointment. Fumbling with the lid and still holding her reins, she managed to dab some on her lips.

'So this messenger isn't human?' she asked, the small gesture of shoving the ointment back into her pocket without offering him any giving her a sense of satisfaction.

'That's correct,' he said.

'And I'm guessing it's the thing making the howling noises, terrifying the horses?'

'It is.'

'So, it's like, what . . . a wolf?'

'A wolf, but not a wolf.' He raised his voice over the wind. 'Several by the sound of it.'

'How many?'

'We'll find out soon enough.'

'We can trust them?'

'They're terribly dangerous, and not to be trusted. They are more dangerous at night, of course, but the important thing is to keep your mind-shield up. Don't ever let them hear your thoughts, especially fearful ones. They will use them against you.'

'These pointers might have been more useful if discussed earlier, Sword Master.'

'When would that have been? While struggling in the

blizzard perhaps, or in the training ring, making sure you could defend yourself?'

'There were times in between.' She crossed her arms. 'You could have been a lot more forthcoming.'

'I didn't know for certain what today would bring — who she would send. Just remember, whatever you do, don't let your mind-shield slip ...' He looked past her. 'Heads up! See to your horse.'

Rosette spun as her mount backed away, the leather reins slipping fast through her gloved hand. She could scarcely clench her numb fingers against the leather as her arm snapped to its full length. The horse's forelegs were braced against the tension, nostrils flaring.

'Whoa now,' she soothed, stepping forward to stroke the rigid neck. 'They're more dangerous at night, it seems, so we have hours to go before we're dog food.'

'This is not a joking matter, Rosette.'

'Isn't it?' She looked wildly around as the horse backed further towards the edge of the trail. 'We're scaling a mountain, ice and snowdrifts hiding sudden drops into oblivion. The trail's so narrow we couldn't turn around and go back, even if we wanted to. And we don't want to.' She shook her head. 'We want to go on, straight towards the howling that has me, and the horses, feeling like glass about to break!'

An' Lawrence opened his mouth to reply. She stopped him with fierce eyes.

'But wait,' she said, 'I'm not done. Not only are we close to freezing to death, again, on a trail made for something the size of a miniature goat, we're to meet up with these *wolves* that are neither wolf nor human and ... well, of course I can't finish that sentence because I haven't the faintest idea of what comes next. The horses are terrified. The temple cats are edgy ...' she held up her hand '... and, to top it off, I just found out who my real parents are, but there's no time for my own flesh-and-blood father to tell me why in the name of all the underworld gods it took us twenty-two years to meet!' She slipped a few paces back as the horse dragged her. 'I mean, if you can't laugh at this, I'd love to know what you *do* find amusing.'

An' Lawrence raised his hand, mouthing a few words towards the alarmed beast. Rosette felt the boost of magic whiz by her. The horse's neck dropped immediately, blowing a soft, languid snort. He took a step forward to rub snow-speckled eyelids on Rosette's shoulder, the quivering in his limbs subsiding.

Why didn't I think of that?

'Listen,' An' Lawrence hissed at her, brushing snow off his shoulders. 'I know there's been no time to talk, to explain about ... anything, and there's no time now. We have to focus on getting up this cliff. The summit is not far.'

'And then what?'

'And then we have to make contact with the beasts, before nightfall.'

'I get the feeling they will be meeting us whenever they please,' Rosette countered.

He shrugged. 'In this, daughter, you're probably right.'

Rosette had a piercing retort ready on her lips, but she didn't speak. It was the first time anyone had called her *daughter* since she'd fled Lividica. Certainly it was the first time she'd heard it from him. An' Lawrence hadn't taken his eyes from her the entire time she ranted, but it was clear that he was much more concerned about their immediate danger than anything else. Fair enough. Up until this moment, she'd been venting her rage. She was cold and angry and hurt by his detachment. She was more perturbed by his lack of communication than any theoretical danger. She realised now the *wolves-not-wolves* were much more of a concern than the teething problems of their relationship.

'Right,' she said, turning towards the howling sounds. 'Lead the way.'

An' Lawrence continued up the narrow path with Rosette following, guiding the now placid horse behind her. Scylla stayed close to An' Lawrence, and Drayco brought up the rear. By noon they'd crested the peak.

The view from the plateau took Rosette's breath away. The sky cleared, offering a panoramic vista. Drifts of snow-powdered wind raced along inches above the ground, reminding her of the Mobbie Desert where white sand blew over the contours of the dunes, shaping and reshaping them in endless rows of corrugation. The horses' hooves crunched into the virgin snow, leaving prints that were quickly erased by the wisps of powder. Rosette took a deep breath and walked into the circular clearing. It was the heart of the peak, the heart of Los Loma.

'This is it,' she said, realising that everything had gone quiet.

There was a gentle breeze, the howls of both wind and beast gone.

He nodded.

'Now what?'

'Shush,' he cautioned with his gloved finger to his lips. 'We wait.'

And so they waited.

Rosette thought it had been cold plodding up the mountain in the wind, but this waiting was infinitely worse. Even though the sun shone from behind thin clouds, its pallid light held no warmth. She couldn't feel her fingers and was long past feeling her toes. She and An' Lawrence stood motionless, holding the reins of their exhausted mounts, the temple cats sitting side by side, their ears pricked, scanning for the faintest sound or movement.

Then Drayco stood, hackles rising along his back, emanating a low-pitched growl. *They come.*

Rosette looked up at her father as he nodded. Both familiars had warned simultaneously. Both were growling.

'Quiet him, and unsaddle your horse.'

'What?'

'Demons, Rosette. Do as I say! We have to let the horses loose. It would be too tempting to have them in tow.'

'Tempting? For what?'

The Sword Master's brow wrinkled as he undid the girth and hauled off the saddle. 'They're Lupins, Rosette; the messengers are Lupins. Do you understand what that means?'

Rosette gasped. 'Lupins? But . . .'

'Quiet him!' An' Lawrence tilted his head towards her familiar.

Drayco, my lovely, shush. You mustn't growl. It's worse than I imagined.

'Untack your horse and cut it loose now! With any luck and a little magic, they'll head back to the cave and we can collect them later.'

Was he joking?

'Do it now, Rosette.'

The tone of the Sword Master's voice was frighteningly soft and urgent at the same time and it propelled her into immediate action. She threw the near stirrup over the saddle and unbuckled the girth with clumsy fingers. She unclipped the breastplate and hauled the lot — saddlebags, fur roll and all — off the horse's back from where they thudded onto the frozen ground.

She slipped the reins up to her mount's ears, grabbing as best she could the broad leather headstall. She couldn't get her frozen fingers under it. Sinking her teeth into the wet tips of her glove, she pulled her hand free and thrust her blue fingers under her coat, into her armpit. It felt like a hot iron branding her skin.

Pain shot through her as the blood returned to her hand, but she finally worked the bridle from the horse's head, easing the bit from its mouth. Looking up, she saw An' Lawrence watching.

'Stand back.' He lifted both his hands skyward and cast them, like fishing rods, one at each horse, mouthing a word she didn't understand. The horses reared, bolting back down the path. The sound of falling shale mixed ominously with thundering hooves and high-pitched whinnies. Rosette watched their rumps as they turned the sharp bend and disappeared.

There was no time to think of the animals' welfare or how she and An' Lawrence might retrieve them for the journey back. Something more pressing grabbed her attention, sending chills down her spine.

Three wolves approached, black against the white ice and snow. Did wolves get that big? They were enormous. She felt for the top of Drayco's head. The temple cat moved in close, sitting by her right side. Scylla was sentinel-still on her left and An' Lawrence stood in front of them all. Though his sword was not drawn, she saw his hand on his hip, inches from the hilt, and she heard him whisper back to her.

'They aren't simply wolves, Rosette. They shift shapes by refracting light from within. It's an ancient magic, but they have mastered it like no other clan. Keep your hand close to your sword. Be ready. They're basically men.'

'They look like beasts to me,' she whispered back.

'An illusion, though they are that too.'

'I'll keep it in mind.'

Eyes wide, she watched as they came inexorably closer, stiff-legged with heads high.

I won't let them hurt you. Her familiar's voice offered comfort, even though these beasts were twice Drayco's size.

I know, lovely, but let's not pick a fight.

She had never seen a Lupin before. If the stories she'd heard were anything to go by, she was in big trouble. Lupins were shape-shifting creatures that came to Gaela through the corridors from an ancient land — outcast or of their own accord, she didn't know. The accounts claimed they were wolves by day and human by night. Or was it the other way around? She didn't quite recall, but they were reputed to have strange powers — mind control being one of them. The only thing consistent in all the tales was their voracious appetite for blood. There was no chance of survival should their ire be raised. She shuddered. Myth portrayed them as survivors of a tragic race, one hunted to near extinction. Some thought they were just a story told to keep children from wandering at night. Others swore they were real.

The stories said they had fallen from grace in that other world and they couldn't return. It didn't make them happy. She didn't know how it had happened — the sundering — and right now she wished she'd studied her history more diligently. It was clear they were not just a bedtime story.

She scanned her memory. If anyone had a big enough heart, they might befriend the Lupins. Big heart? Rosette was simply trying to control her shaking limbs. She knew Lupins were to be avoided. That was at the beginning and end of every account she had ever read. So why were they seeking them out? Messengers? For whom?

Think. Think. Think! she urged her frozen mind.

What had An' Lawrence said? He didn't know who *she* would send? What did that mean?

Kreshkali!

The Lupins were said to inhabit the labyrinths beneath the mountains — the landscapes of the nether world hidden from the sun. The only one strong enough to command the Lupins would have been Kreshkali — the legendary witch of the labyrinths. What could Treeon possibly want with her? She also was to be avoided at all costs.

'So they're not make-believe creatures after all?' Rosette whispered to An' Lawrence as the Lupins approached.

'Hardly,' he replied.

'What's our business with them?'

'We're here to make a trade.'

'What are we trading?'

'Hush!'

Rosette had no more time to wonder. The Lupins advanced, large dark wolves, sleek and beautiful, treading lightly over the snow. Their images shifted and blurred. A shock wave hit her as their front legs rose from the ground and they stood upright. Long snouts flattened, altering canine fangs and lolling red tongues into smooth, clear faces. Human faces. Angelic faces. Their tails vanished, and all three now appeared clothed in leather — dusky black, like their curling hair. They were male and their dark eyes narrowed in the light as the sun flashed fully from behind a cloud. They drew in the air, until their gaze fell on her. Their attention made her throat dry — impossible to swallow.

They halted as one before the Sword Master, but their gleaming eyes were not on him, or the familiars. They were on Rosette.

'Why are you here, An' Lawrence?' the central Lupin asked, his voice deep, the words articulate.

'They know you by name?' Rosette whispered through chattering teeth.

He ignored her, his full attention on the central Lupin. 'We have come to offer a trade.'

She wondered how An' Lawrence could speak with such confidence. Her neck felt like it was in a noose. She didn't think another word could escape without her voice squeaking and cracking.

Panic rose and she increased her mind-shield, calming herself and her thoughts as best she could. Then she noticed something even more unusual about the Lupins. The way they behaved and moved so subtly, it was almost as though they were one entity.

She sent a silent message to Drayco. *How many do you see?*

Three.

But how many do you sense?

Drayco took a moment to reply before she heard his silent answer filtering through her mind-shield. *Interesting, Maudi. They communicate as one. They're linked.*

Rosette reached forward and tugged on the Sword Master's coat, but he brushed her hand away. She tried to send a mental message, but his shield was up, impenetrable.

Tell Scylla, Rosette instructed Drayco. *Tell her to tell him.*

His familiar got through. She knew he had received the message by the way An' Lawrence straightened his spine.

'You have nothing we want,' the Lupin said.

The three of them leaned towards Rosette, drawing in her scent.

'We do,' An' Lawrence countered evenly. 'Treeon has uncovered a vein of lapis lazuli. I believe the stone is sacred to your race. We offer it freely, unasked.'

All three shifted in their tracks.

'Show us.'

Rosette was relieved to be out from under their scrutiny. The Lupins were riveted as the Sword Master pulled a black velvet bag from his coat lining. Holding it by its braided cord, he handed it over without hesitation. The Lupin opened the bag.

Rosette marvelled at how the Lupin's face softened. He hardly glanced at the contents but simply held it to his chest for several heartbeats. Tucking it into a fold within his leather coverings, he released a sound, the murmur of a she-wolf to her first pup.

'We admire the courage it must have taken to return what is ours.' His eyes narrowed; his face, though wildly handsome, became severe. 'Why do you risk it?'

'You'd have sniffed it out sooner or later, and it occurred to us that doing so would be the more dangerous option,' the Sword Master replied.

The Lupin did not smile back.

Rosette wondered at the Sword Master's frankness. He didn't seem to be trying to hide anything from these creatures. Maybe he was of the same mind as Nell — *Speak as close to the truth as you can.*

'We ask a favour in return,' An' Lawrence continued. His voice was strong and clear.

I'm glad you're so confident about all this. Rosette shot him the thought though he didn't answer back.

'We owe you no favour,' the Lupin replied.

'Think of it more as a trade. The source of lapis within our lands is rich. If we can come to some agreement ...'

The Lupins looked at each other in silence.

'Ask what you want. Be quick.' The leader glanced up to the cloud-covered sun, the opaque glow rapidly heading west.

'We seek an amulet, a faceted-crystal vial that glows blue at night, clear in the light of day. It was taken from an estate in Lividica six winters ago. I think your queen has something to do with it.'

Rosette gasped. What was he saying? She yanked on his coat again and this time he hit her hand, smacking it hard.

'We know of this amulet. What does it contain?'

'The Spell of Passillo.' He said the words softly, like a prayer.

Passillo? No wonder he had told her nothing. Goddess forgive them! They can't be messing with Passillo.

What had she gotten mixed up in? The Spell of Passillo was buried centuries ago by an ancient witch, if history had it right. It was not to be found, not to be touched. And if somehow it was found, it was not to be used, not unless all the demons and angels of Gaela commanded it, and Rosette was certain there had been no such command. Sword Master or not, An' Lawrence had no right to dabble with such a power. No-one on Gaela did.

What are you doing? She screamed the thought at him through clenched teeth. *What amulet?*

She clamped her jaw tight, her eyes popping. He must have it wrong. She knew that vial, and it had nothing to do with Passillo. It was a charm given to her mother by Nell who ... She gulped. *Oh no. Nell found Passillo?*

'We have heard of this,' the central Lupin said.

And Bethsay gave it to me? Rosette's mind continued to race. Who did An' Lawrence think could carry the spell back to Treeon if these Lupins actually had it and were willing to offer it up? Only females could work this kind of magic. Only ... She swallowed hard again. Then she growled under her breath, *Demon's death to you, An' Lawrence. You have no right to use me like this!*

Had the Lupins sacked her house and killed her family for the amulet? Her hand went to her sword. Were these the murderers? Rosette didn't know who she wanted to cut first, An' Lawrence or the Lupins.

What's Passillo, Maudi? The warm touch of Drayco's question interrupted her fervour. Rosette stilled her mind, shielding the rage, keeping her exterior a calm shell.

Finally, something I know that you do not!

I don't know your star-lore.

But you seem to know everything else.

Not this. What is it?

Passillo is the cause of all the temple wars. What everybody wants and no-one should have.

Why?

I don't know. Something to do with keeping the worlds apart.

Worlds?

Apparently. Be ready, Drayco, for anything. This can't go well.

Maudi, swap! Drayco's voice commanded.

What? she queried. *Now?*

Get out of your body and let me in. You'll be safer if we swap.

We can't, Drayco. I have to keep my mind-shield tight.

I have no problems with that and you know it. He lifted his paw and placed it on her leg, claws extended.

She almost made the exchange, her familiar was so insistent. But then she shook her head. *No, Drayco. It's going to be all right. Besides, it isn't always about safety.*

I think today it is.

Trust me. We're fine.

The Lupins had not moved. They did not look at one another or respond in any noticeable way. What they thought of the request was anyone's guess. Not a twitch or sniff crossed their faces. Their exhalations were smooth and visible, little puffs of steam shooting down from their noses in regular bursts. She suspected hers were doing the same.

In the distance, she recognised the sinking whistle of a bird of prey calling high above the jagged peaks. An answering call followed. For a moment, that sound made her skin flush with a warmth she hadn't felt in years. It was a goshawk, the same cry Jarrod had been able to imitate so well. The region was full of these birds, but it was the first time she'd noticed now that the storm had passed. Strange what stands out when the body is shaking with fear.

Without realising it, tears welled up and trickled halfway down her cheek before freezing into diamond droplets. The sound of the hawks echoed from mountain top to mountain top. Everything seemed vast and desolate, and still there was no response from the Lupins.

Do something, Sword Master. My shield's starting to slip.

What little blood Rosette had in her extremities drained, despite her attempts to appear calm, humble and unimpressed. Drayco nudged her with his nose. There was comfort there, but no warmth. The sun was lowering into a thin red line on the horizon. Her mind-shield faded until it seemed to wink in and out like a firefly. They were wearing her down.

'We do have such an amulet, but it contains no spell,' the leader of the Lupins said at last.

'The Spell of Passillo has been encased in the amulet for decades. It cannot escape. It was hidden in Lividica and taken from there. We know Kreshkali has it, and we want it back.'

'The amulet contains no spell.'

'So you say.'

Rosette stared at the back of the Sword Master's head. She had no idea why he was provoking the Lupins, but it had every one of them snarling. Drayco was on his feet, his hackles as high as her waist. An' Lawrence had one hand on his sword hilt, the other on Scylla's head.

'You'll not live to question our word again,' the lead Lupin said simply as he drew his sword.

Look out! Rosette screamed and drew her sword as well. The Lupin was on top of An' Lawrence just as his sword sang from its sheath, blood spurting as he sliced into its shoulder. Scylla went for the throat.

Rosette had no time to watch the outcome. Drayco faced off with one of the Lupins that had shifted back to wolf form. The third remained bipedal, levelling his sword at Rosette's throat before she could strike.

'We aren't here to fight. If you want to know more about this spell, you can come with me, alone.'

'I don't think so!' She sent a charge of energy through her limbs, the lightning flooding her with warmth and strength. She knocked away his blade with a spinning kick and cut towards his head. He blocked it instantly, the ring of steel on steel sounding over the plateau.

Above, the hawk shrieked.

The Lupin wavered, looking her in the eye. 'Rosette,' he said, his voice reprimanding her as if she were an errant child. 'Put down your sword before you hurt yourself.'

Inflamed, she swung again, aiming to cut his head off. Mid-strike she dropped to her knees, pain searing through her body.

Maudi?

For a moment, she couldn't speak. She could barely raise her head long enough to register the Lupin above her. The magic she'd released had opened her mind-shield and the energy was being driven back into her by the Lupin. He held her down with the force of his thoughts.

'Shield, Rosette!' The shout came from An' Lawrence.

'I'll let you up as soon as you stop this nonsense,' the Lupin said, his voice strangely calm.

When she relaxed, she found she could stand. Sheathing her sword, she glanced at An' Lawrence in a stalemate with the other Lupin. Both had their swords in the guard position, waiting for the other to attack. Scylla lay in the snow, breathing but apparently unconscious.

'Wait!' she said. 'It's all right. I'll meet your Kreshkali and learn more about this Passillo, but put your blades away.' *Drayco, what's happened to Scylla?*

She's been cut, Maudi! At that moment Drayco attacked the Lupin in front of him, trying to charge past to get to Scylla. He was dropped to his belly, the much larger Lupin pinning him down, his lashing tail the only part of him that moved.

'Don't hurt him,' Rosette said, her voice a growl, her sword half drawn.

'You have brought us more than our sacred stone,' the Lupin facing An' Lawrence said. 'This woman has the blood of the Mistress, and we're taking her with us.'

'Blood of your Mistress? She has no such thing,' An' Lawrence shouted.

The Lupin laughed. 'We'll let Kreshkali decide.'

'Take me.' An' Lawrence lowered his sword. 'I will deal with your queen.'

The Lupin snarled. 'You think we're fools? Only

females of the blood can carry the Spell of Passillo, if they can carry it at all, and this one can.'

The Sword Master twisted his head around to look at his daughter. *Rosette?*

I have no idea what he's talking about!

'You won't take her,' An' Lawrence answered, his hand moving his sword imperceptibly upward.

He kicked a mound of snow up in the air and lunged. Rosette knew it was a distraction, a chance for her to break free, but the Lupin in front of her froze her mind again with his strange magic.

Don't do it, An' Lawrence. It's no good. I can't move.

There was a resounding clash of steel on steel before An' Lawrence dropped to his knees. Rosette strained her eyes to see what had happened. He was face down on top of Scylla. Drayco let out a yowl that was cut short by a blow from the hilt of a Lupin's blade. Her familiar's tail stopped lashing and his head sank to the snow.

Rosette screamed as her captor brought a dagger to her throat, pricking her skin just enough to draw a single drop of blood.

'You're coming with us.'

'I'll not leave them,' she gasped. *Drayco! Are you all right?*

My head hurts, Maudi.

She struggled against her captor and again the blade pressed her neck.

'What are you doing!' A voice cut through the air, halting the Lupins. 'Put that knife away, Rashnan, and let her go!'

Striding towards them was another Lupin, tall in his human form, eyes blazing. He scowled at the others and Rosette again suspected they were in silent communication.

He turned to her. 'Rosette, I apologise for this.'

She was kneeling in the snow next to Drayco. 'What have they done to him?' Her face was red and streaked with tears.

'He'll be fine. It's a mild spell.'

She pointed at An' Lawrence and Scylla, also unconscious in the snow. 'Mild? They'll freeze to death like that.'

'If you come with us, I'll release them. They'll be in the cave by a warm fire before dark. Kreshkali simply wants to meet with you. No-one's meant to be harmed.'

'It's a little late for that, don't you think?'

'Again, my apologies.'

She tried to pull her heart out of her stomach, but it wouldn't budge.

'Come, Rosette. My name is Hotha and I mean you no harm.'

She looked him in the eyes, as black as his waves of hair. 'You'll wake them if I follow?'

'I will.'

She touched her neck, her fingers coming back bloody. 'How far is it?'

'To the other side of the plateau. There's an entrance to Los Loma there. We will guide you.'

She turned to her familiar, tears still stinging. *Drayco?* She couldn't feel his mind. 'And if I refuse?'

'That is your choice. We will wake your companions in either case, once we are under the mountain.' He looked skyward. 'Choose now, Rosette. Dark comes quickly on the mountain.'

A hawk whistled from the far side of the plateau.

Follow them, she heard whispered softly into her mind. She turned to Drayco, but he hadn't moved. *Dray?*

The Lupin motioned her forward.

She let out her breath. 'All right. I'll meet your Kreshkali, though I think you've made a big mistake. I don't have the blood you speak of and I don't know the Spell of Passillo.'

'She'll be pleased to meet you, just the same.'

'And you will wake them?' she asked again.

'I will.'

'All right, Hotha, please lead the way.' Her spine erect, she forced her shoulders back and followed as they moved towards the far side of the summit. She sensed for her familiar and was relieved to feel Drayco's dark dreaming. He was only unconscious. They would release him. It was all right.

As they approached the far side of the summit, she heard his voice, faint like a distant sea.

Don't go, Maudi. Not without me.

It's all right, Dray. When you can, get to the cave with the others. It'll be fine. I'll meet you there.

She sent him the message with a blast of healing magic, discovering that as long as it wasn't directed at the Lupins, she could boost all she liked.

Listen for me. Wait for me. I'll be back by morning. I promise. Just get to the cave.

The Sword Master? Scylla?

They will wake up soon. You all need to get to the cave.

And you? Why are you going?

To meet Kreshkali, High Priestess of the underworld. Don't try to talk me out of it, Drayco, or I'll lose my nerve. This is a chance of a lifetime. I'm not going to pass it up.

She sent him another boost of healing energy and followed the Lupins through the snow.

It took Jarrod a few seconds to realise that Rosette was not on the mountain summit. It was less than half that time again before he saw how badly things had gone. The place looked like a battlefield: the victors fled, the casualties left to freeze.

He moved to a body lying face down and covered with snow. Had he fought the wildcat beneath him? He pulled his glove off with his teeth and felt the throat for a pulse. A regular beat pushed against his fingers. He did the same to the feline. Both were alive, just unconscious and impossible to rouse.

Jarrod levered the man onto his back. He could find no wounds. He pulled back the eyelids, checking the pupils then gently patting the man's face. 'Are you with me?'

The man groaned and coughed.

Jarrod held his head above the snow. 'Can you tell me your name?'

'An' Lawrence,' he whispered.

'What happened?'

'Scylla ...' He tried to reach towards the feline lying motionless beside him.

'She has a heartbeat,' Jarrod assured him. 'We'll see to her shortly. Where's Rosette?'

'Rosette?' He frowned, unconsciousness taking him again.

'Great,' Jarrod mumbled, going to his horse and retrieving a small medical kit from his saddlebag. He looked skyward at the darkening clouds that threatened heavy snow, and sent a shrill whistle for Nell. She should have been here by now, so where in this frozen hell was she?

Within moments his summons was answered by a distant cry beyond the far edge of the peak, but he couldn't see her. Wherever she was, she'd better hurry. If he didn't get the injured to shelter soon, they would die of hypothermia. Nights on the summit were sub-zero.

Jarrod examined the Sword Master. Other than a bang on the head, he had no injuries. 'Just a concussion,' he said, looking west.

The sun had set, the clouds thinning to reveal Ishtar, the evening star, bright in the pallid green sky. The scrunch of boots in the snow brought his head around. Nell was bent over the black temple cat. She acknowledged Jarrod only when the feline had struggled to his feet.

'How is he?' She gestured to An' Lawrence.

'Unconscious, but he's breathing all right. We've got to get him off the ice and build a fire. Same for this one,' he said, stroking the buff-coloured fur. 'His familiar, I guess.'

Nell nodded before putting her hand out to Drayco. He was staggering towards the far side of the plateau, following Rosette's trail.

'No, Drayco, you'll freeze. We'll all freeze if we don't get to shelter. You have to show us the way.'

Drayco stopped in his tracks, scenting. The clouds thinned, drifting apart like a curtain pulled back. The sky was glowing with stars on the horizon. He turned, retracing his steps, heading towards the track that led down the near side of the mountain. Nell stood looking down at An' Lawrence.

'Can you rouse him?' she asked.

'He's out.'

'Then we'd better use Wren. It won't be easy getting her down that track with these two strapped to her back.'

'I've got an idea.'

Jarrod pulled his axe from his saddlebag and hacked down four solid pine branches. Binding them with leather strapping, he made a sled, securing it to Wren's saddle. He and Nell hefted both the Sword Master and his familiar onto it and covered them with furs. Drayco sat on the edge of the summit, waiting.

'There must be shelter nearby. Can you talk with the temple cat?' Jarrod asked, leading his horse towards the trail.

'He understands us, but he only communicates with Rosette. I think there must be a cave nearby, or he wouldn't bother.'

'Wouldn't bother?'

'He'd spend his last breath searching for her if he wasn't certain he could save us first.'

Jarrod grimaced. 'Then the cat and I have something in common.'

Drayco looked towards Jarrod, briefly opening his mouth but making no sound.

'Is he all right?' Jarrod asked, as they followed Drayco down the frozen trail.

Nell smiled, placing her hand on his shoulder. 'He'll have a shocker of a headache, but other than that, I think he's okay.'

Jarrod concentrated on the rough track, grateful for the moonlight, brilliant on the white snow. He put his trust in the sure-footedness of Wren and the lead of the temple cat. Several times the sled caught on rocks before jerking forward, smacking the mare's hocks. She'd tuck her tail and bunch her hindquarters but always settled quickly when Jarrod stroked her neck and gave her encouragement. They dragged more rope from the pack and tied it to the end of the sled, Nell acting as an anchor for the descent.

After winding their way down the mountainside, the moon now a white disc above the western mountain peaks, they found the cave. A horse nickered from inside, then another, and the copper-red mare answered softly. Drayco walked straight in, disappearing into the blackness.

'There'll be a torch,' Nell said, letting go of the anchor rope and rummaging around the entrance of the cave.

Striking a match and lighting the pitch-soaked brand,

she guided Jarrod into the high-domed cave in time to see Drayco collapse beside the cold fire ring.

'They left supplies behind,' Nell said as she searched the area.

Jarrod walked his mare well into the cave before untying the sled. The other horses looked gaunt, their eyes sunken.

'Water,' Nell said. 'We've got to melt some ice, quickly.'

'Is there fuel for a fire?'

'Fuel or no, a fire we'll have.'

Flames flickered up from the hearth as she answered his question. In moments he and Nell had An' Lawrence by a fire that burned hot and smokeless. The rocks warmed quickly and the searing cold of the cave gave way to a sultry humidity. Jarrod carried An' Lawrence's familiar to the hearth and laid her next to him on warm furs.

Nell stood over them, shaking her head. 'You've got some explaining to do, Sword Master, if you ever wake up again.'

'An' Lawrence?' Jarrod slapped one side of the man's face and then the other. 'You need to drink this.'

An' Lawrence opened his eyes and squinted up at Jarrod. Then his hand went to his sword-belt.

'Relax. It's by the fire.'

The Sword Master nodded and winced. He looked for Scylla, stretching until his hand touched her fur.

'She's wounded, but she'll recover. Drink this. It'll help the pain.'

An' Lawrence took a few sips of the poppy tea before draining the cup. 'You're a healer?' he whispered.

'Among other things,' Jarrod replied.

'Where's Rosette?'

'I thought maybe you could tell us.'

An' Lawrence groaned. 'The Lupins.'

'Lupins?' Nell's voice cut through the cave.

There was silence, like the air before an avalanche.

'Nellion?' The Sword Master shut his eyes and winced again.

'You let the Lupins do this?' Nell shrieked across the cave. She threw down an empty feedbag and crossed her arms. 'Tell me, Rowan An' Lawrence, what was your plan?'

Jarrod shot his hand out towards her, blocking the intensity. She pushed it aside.

'Did you even have a plan, you and Makee?'

'We were after the amulet ... the Spell of Passillo,' An' Lawrence mumbled. He looked up at her and his eyes went soft. 'You look beautiful.'

'Shut up! You and Makee are idiots. There is no *Spell of Passillo* in that vial — hasn't been for decades.'

'That can't be. It's unbreakable.'

'Unbreakable maybe, but not unchangeable. What were you thinking, meddling in this? It's not your business.'

'And it is yours?' An' Lawrence lifted himself, bracing on both elbows.

Jarrod placed a hand on his chest, preventing him from rising further. 'Lie down. You have a concussion.'

'What happened to the spell, Nellion?' An' Lawrence demanded.

She moved closer, her face inches from his. 'I changed it, not that it's any of your concern.'

An' Lawrence grabbed her arm. 'Into what?'

'I'd hoped you'd have worked that out by now. Clearly you haven't.'

'Enlighten me, witch.'

'I hid it, for safekeeping.'

'You're mad!' An' Lawrence shouted at her.

'For demon's sake, Rowan, in the wrong hands that spell could have destroyed half of Gaela in one night. The power's vast, and it has a mind of its own.'

'And you thought you had a solution?'

'I did.'

'Where? Where did you hide it?'

Nell stared at him, her eyes hooded, unblinking. 'Take a guess.'

He sank back into the furs. 'Rosette?' The name escaped the Sword Master's lips with a sigh. 'Nell, you didn't?'

'I did, and you've just handed it straight over to the Lupins like a harvest gift.'

Chapter 14

Rosette registered every detail of the path as she trailed along behind the Lupins, the doubt in her mind lifting. Guile replaced anxiety. She was going to get out of this mess, of course. She chewed on obscenities and spat them towards La Makee and An' Lawrence. How dare they put her and Drayco in this position without warning or consultation? She would live to have it out with her Sword Master, no matter what it took. She thought of how the High Priestess had patronised her that day in the temple chambers. She would have it out with her as well. She would learn about this Spell of Passillo and decide what information, if any, she would share. Her faith in Treeon was failing fast.

The whistle of the goshawk sounded again, far up towards the summit, and Rosette turned her head. The night would freeze their bodies if they didn't wake up soon.

'Now?' she asked Hotha. 'You'll wake them now, so they can get back in time?'

'It's already done.'

They stopped by a rocky outcropping. The Lupins were communicating again, it seemed, without words or signs. Rosette couldn't hear their thoughts, but she did hear a faint call from the distance, like a warm breeze slipping under the door of her mind-shield.

I come for you.

Drayco? What's that pain?

Bump on the head. No problem.

What about the Sword Master? Scylla?

The healer-man is with them. Nell too.

What?

Nell's here.

Oh, sweetie, you're hallucinating. That must have been more than a bump.

I'm following you.

You mustn't. Rosette could feel his weakness and his piercing headache as if it were her own. *Go back to the cave, Dray. There's food there, furs. Stay warm and stay alive. An' Lawrence will make a fire. I'll be back in the morning. You mustn't follow.*

Nell says so too. I will come for you in the morning.

She didn't have time to respond further, or to think about his vision of Nell. Hotha pointed to the wall of rock outcropping and brushed away the snow.

'In here,' he said.

She pushed her hood back.

They were going underground, and this suddenly felt like her last glimpse of the world for some time. She wanted to take it in. The sun had set and streams of gold shot towards her through the clouds. She looked out to the horizon and listened for every sound. She wanted the Lupins to see her face, calm, unthreatening, unafraid, in control. Bathed in dark gold, she watched for Ishtar emerging from behind the clouds and calculated. The most important thing was for her to remember this place when she sought her way out — in case she had to escape in a hurry — but there was nothing of any distinction on the snow-covered cliffs, and nothing to hear above the wind as it collected all sounds and made them one.

Then she noticed the cliff face where the Lupin had swept the snow aside. The solid wall had given way to a dark entrance, silent and empty. Hotha motioned her to enter, wanting her to go first. She was about to protest, but instead closed her mouth and stepped across the threshold into the mountain.

She couldn't see at all. The darkness penetrated everything, and so did the cold. She felt a pressure on her shoulder, and looked down. A hand latched onto the base of her neck, surprisingly warm through her ice-encrusted coat. She was surprised at how good the contact felt.

'I won't let you stumble,' Hotha said.

The Lupin kept her before him, guiding her from behind. The delicacy of his touch held her steady on the track. His fingers rested gently, warm and strong. It was not what she'd imagined — she knew they could tear flesh if they chose.

The Lupins had no trouble in the dark, their eyes like a cat's. Rosette, on the other hand, was as though blind and totally dependent on her guide. The ground descended under her feet and the air grew still, a relief from the constant wind above. Before long she felt a warm draught touch her face.

'Where are we going?'

'Down.'

She was guided forward, descending along well-used rock steps. She memorised every twist and turn until they had made so many she gave up — there was no way for her to keep track. Her knees went weak and her head started to throb.

'How much further?'

'Do you need to rest?'

'I'm fine.' She squared her shoulders and carried on.

The undulating descent continued for what seemed like hours and her sight did not adjust to the dark. There was no light, nothing for her eyes to catch. The only thing Rosette was certain of was that they were now in the bowels of the mountain — Kreshkali's realm, if the witch truly did reign here. It didn't seem too hospitable. With each step she moved further into a sense of isolation. It was the darkest dark she'd ever experienced and it started to separate her from everything she could remember.

Yet, without sight, her other senses amplified. She could hear every rise and fall of her boots as they tapped their way down the endless steps. She heard the pad of the Lupins' feet around her. Listening hard, she heard each of their respirations, feeling the soft breath of Hotha as it blew across her cheek.

Then she heard a thought. It was incoherent; gibberish phrases about the sun and the moon and the faraway memory of home and warmth. She couldn't identify anything more, but she felt compelled to listen. Something in the fragmented voice enthralled her. It was like the voice of madness, curious until she realised it was coming from her own mind.

She lost all concept of distance, of time and space. Everything blurred into a rhythmic stepping, a bombardment of sound, and the unyielding touch of the hand on her shoulder — long fingers pressing into her collarbone, a thumbnail on her scapula, a strange mixture of comfort and coercion.

Then the air changed, like the whoosh of a giant door opening. The ground levelled out and far in the distance she saw something twinkle, like bright yellow stars. She blinked. Finally there was light. An increasing glow illuminated her surroundings and the tunnel expanded until the walls that had pressed on either side of her disappeared altogether.

The chamber was enormous.

There was no time to ponder, though, as the hand tightened on her shoulder, stopping at the brink of causing pain. A warning? Rosette heard a deep guttural answer within her mind.

Be still. She comes.

Brought to a halt, she saw the glow of torchlight and as it grew brighter she squinted, shielding her eyes. She heard the sound of tiny waves lapping over pebbles and with the increasing light, she glimpsed a wraith-like mist hovering over the further shore of a great underground lake. What an eerie, beautiful place. It was like nothing she had ever encountered.

Shivering, she realised Hotha had spoken directly to her mind. She answered him the same way. *Where?*

By the lake.

Someone was approaching from the distance, riding a furred beast with another in tow. Hotha dropped his hand from her shoulder and stood beside her. The absence of his touch was like abandonment and she wavered, off-balance. There was an energy-charged zap and an enormous black wolf appeared at her side where Hotha had stood. She felt the panting of his breath on her fingers and she snapped her hand away, perspiration beading her forehead.

The air was warmer in the underground cathedral and Rosette's lungs no longer burned with every breath. Her numb limbs began to tingle. Water dripped from the edges of her cuffs and gloves, the thin crust of ice melting from her coat. Her legs quivered with the effort to stand.

The light continued to brighten as the figure advanced. She heard the clip of iron-shod hooves and the occasional snort, but could not make out any distinct forms in the glare. How could horses — or beasts of any kind — survive down here? It would take them all day to get to the surface, and then where would they find grazing? The slopes of Los Loma were covered in snow year round. How did they live?

'You'd be surprised how many things do live down here, for a long, long time.'

Rosette snapped her mind-shield up. She now saw the creatures clearly. They were some kind of strange cattle. Their bodies and faces, ears and black noses were similar to the beasts that grazed in the paddocks near Treeon, except that their coats and horns were amazingly long, and they had gold rings in their noses. Rosette didn't think cows could be ridden. Maybe they were really something else altogether.

'They're called grunnies,' a woman answered her thought, the sound of her voice rich and alluring. 'Not from this world.'

Rosette lifted her head to see the figure dismount. She was as tall as Rosette and she wore tight black leather trousers with knee-high, steel-capped boots, a metal studded belt and a high-collared leather vest — all under a rich velvet cloak as black as the caverns around them. Her hair was bleached blonde, spiked in some unrecognisable style, with a dark re-growth at the roots. Rosette's mouth opened slightly. This woman was like no-one she had ever seen before. She emanated danger, both magical and physical, and something else. An attraction.

Hotha stepped up and they had a silent exchange. It looked heated, judging by their postures. The woman snapped her fingers and the other Lupins vanished, racing back out of the cavern. Hotha remained.

'And who are you, come to see me in my realm?' the woman asked.

Rosette did not respond immediately. Hotha didn't speak and the grunnies stood still. Rosette counted her breaths, in and out, in and out. Two, three, four. Only the soft sound of the waves on the shore, and the occasional sputter and sizzle of the torches, could be heard above her pounding heart.

The woman spoke again. 'Let me try this differently. I'm Kreshkali.' She closed the distance between them, holding out a hand. 'Welcome to the underworld.'

'Am I captive?' Rosette asked.

Kreshkali smiled. 'Not captive, young witch.' She glared at Hotha. 'Invited.'

'Why?'

'I've got the amulet you're after. It's empty, but I suspect you knew that anyway. Would you like it, for old times' sake?'

What a good question it was. Did Rosette seek the amulet? Of course not, at least, not until today. That was the quest of her father and La Makee. She wanted nothing to do with any of it, not with the amulet, Passillo's spell or this whole bizarre underground world — especially not with this strange woman, Kreshkali. She wanted to find Drayco and go home, home to Dumarka, to Nell, back to her training.

'Yes, I would,' Rosette said.

There was information to be gained here, and she was going to get it. She remembered the Sword Master's words: *Be calm, unimpressed, no panic, no frivolity*. A modicum of confidence infused her. She would be just that and she'd get as much out of this meeting with the queen of the underworld as she could. All the more ammunition for her reunion with An' Lawrence and La Makee. She wanted to strangle him, as soon as she got the chance, and she was starting to feel optimistic. This would be empowering. Without words, she felt Drayco, like soft paws making bread in her lap. Intuition was a wonderful thing. Now what would she say next?

'You hungry?' Kreshkali asked.

'I am.'

'Good. I'll take you down where it's more comfortable.'

Rosette stared at her.

'Come on, girl. Follow me.'

'*Down?*' Kreshkali's back was already turned, her boots sinking into the coarse gravel, crunching loudly with each long stride, and Rosette had to hurry to catch up. She found herself scrambling up onto one of the grunnies, feeling relieved to be seated and also a little nauseous at the peculiar rocking of the animal's stride. The grunnie's skin was loose and the saddle slipped from side to side, even with a snug girth. She couldn't imagine them having a comfortable trot or gallop. Still, it was good to ride, no matter how bizarre the mount. When she turned around to see if Hotha followed, he was gone.

They tracked the edge of the lake, skirting it before descending a dimly lit ramp that spiralled in endless circles. The beasts were remarkably sure-footed. Rosette's heartbeat steadied and her jaw relaxed until she looked over the edge of the railing. She could see a long way down, but not the bottom.

'These grunnies don't spook, do they?' she asked, the saddle sliding as she turned to Kreshkali. She grabbed a fistful of the grunnie's hair to steady herself.

'You mean startle?' Kreshkali shook her head. 'Not like a horse.'

Rosette nodded, then her eyes widened. 'Like what, then?'

'They stampede.'

Rosette didn't know how far down they'd gone. She only knew an ever-increasing thirst and exhaustion. Her throat was dry and her head spun. The stirrups were too long and her legs ached with the lack of support.

She wanted to stop and adjust them but felt a lassitude that prevented her from taking any action.

She realised that the only way out of this underground maze would be by the grace of Maggi, god of the crossroads — she would certainly never find her way back without his blessing; either that or a detailed map. She hoped she would have one or the other when she made her way out.

'Nearly there,' Kreshkali said, showing no sign of fatigue.

She had paused at yet another junction where four corridors met. Each archway looked identical except for the script set into the stone. Strange lettering ran from the bottom of the arch, up across the top and down the other side. Was this the map she wanted? Too bad if it was — she couldn't read a word of it. Her lids drooped.

'Good to hear,' she answered.

The next corridor was wider, more refined and nothing like the rough rock of the upper caverns. The light had increased as well, although there was a haze to everything — a kind of misty fuzz. The glow illuminated the way and Rosette wondered how much further they had to go, because if she didn't rest soon, she was pretty certain she would tumble from this great grunnie beast and drop dead.

'My rooms are just up ahead.'

The echoes deepened as they passed beneath a vaulted archway, and Rosette was surprised to hear the sound of rushing water, now loud, now soft. It must be hot because the mist that surrounded them was steamy — warm on her face. She slipped off her wool-lined coat, unwound her sword-belt and tied it to the pack saddle. She pulled at her neck, widening her thick sweater to let some fresh air in.

My sword! She realised that the Lupins had taken it and she hadn't got it back. She cringed, imagining the look on the Sword Master's face. *Some trip this has turned out to be.*

They halted before large double doors made of smooth black wood. Kreshkali hopped off her grunnie and signalled Rosette to do the same.

'Here we are.' She smiled. 'That didn't take long now, did it!'

'Are you mad?' Rosette answered, nearly crumpling to her knees when her feet touched the ground. 'It felt like forever.'

'You have much to learn about time, young witch.'

'Love to learn, but first I need some sleep.'

Kreshkali opened the door with a long toothed key. She was nothing like the Lupins, Rosette decided. Her hands were beautiful, the slender fingers marked with intricate tattoos. Rosette studied them. They were almost identical to Nell's and La Makee's. Tingles prickled the back of her neck. Was she once a High Priestess of Treeon? She followed Kreshkali in, leaving the grunnies to wait in the corridor behind them.

The room was spacious and well lit, the sound of rushing water pervasive. There were dark wooden beams overhead set into a cone-shaped ceiling that ended miles above them in a tiny point of light no bigger than a star. Was that the real sky? No wonder it had taken them so long — regardless of what Kreshkali thought.

Three of the walls, from the wooden beams to the tiled floor, were covered in mosaic designs. Scenes of hunts, battles, shape-shifting and some provocative intimacies jumped out in extraordinarily vivid colours, a contrast to the endless sandstone and rust of every other wall and corridor she had passed. It must have taken years to render the fine details, maybe decades. None of the subjects were familiar, as though from a different age — a different world — though they were unquestioningly sentient. They were doing everything a human on Gaela might, but the shapes were distorted, strange, transforming. She had to look away.

She followed the sound of churning water. Several lamps hung from the wooden beams, illuminating a large pool. A fall of water plummeted into its depths from a natural fissure in the far rock face, causing it to bubble and roil. Walking closer, she saw the pool was also lined with mosaic tiles, the rim a sparkling sapphire blue. The surface closest to her was smooth, almost undisturbed, and steam rose in wisps, reminding her of the granite bathing pools of Treeon.

The vast room was welcoming. It felt lived in, lined with carved chests and seating areas with furs and brightly coloured embroidered cushions. A low wooden table was laid out with bread, meat and a red fruit. There was a black-framed bronze mirror, easily seven feet high, resting up against one wall and partially obscuring a wardrobe with its doors open and clothing strewn haphazardly over it. A desk was cluttered with papers, books and what looked like a map. Her eyes widened when she saw a star chart.

There were also some peculiar items: tubes and boxes made of metal and some other unknown material, with thin black twine connecting them. Other items were stacked upright in tubs or lay covered in dust in the corner. Towards the far side — well away from the damp and mist of the pool — was a rumpled, unmade bed.

'This is where you live?' Rosette asked.

Kreshkali looked around the room as if to remind herself of something. 'Sometimes.'

'I see you don't have an apprentice to keep it tidy.'

Kreshkali laughed. 'Perhaps you'd like the job?'

'No thanks.'

'Drink?' Kreshkali poured a clear liquid into two

goblets, handing one to Rosette without waiting for her answer. 'It'll revive you instantly.'

Rosette took the goblet and drank. If it was poison, it didn't matter. She would die from thirst if she didn't drink it.

After a few tentative sips, she drained the glass and held it out for more. 'Where's it from?' she asked. It was the sweetest, freshest water she had ever tasted.

'Artesian,' Kreshkali said. 'From much further down.'

'There's a "further down"?'

'There is. You ready to eat now?'

'Why not ...'

'Dine and bathe, and rest. You have to prepare. I've got things to do, so feel free to wander.' She chuckled at her own joke. Obviously there was no way Rosette could leave without clear directions. 'I'll collect you at noon. It's not far off.'

'Noon?' Rosette looked up above her head to the pinprick of light then back to the woman. 'How would anybody know the time down here?'

'How would we *not* know?'

Rosette stared at her as she left, pulling the door closed behind her.

'Wait! Kreshkali? Prepare for what?'

A lock clicked shut, the sound sharp over the drone of the waterfall.

Kreshkali paused at the double doors before securing the lock. She knew the girl would take some convincing if she was going to get her help, and what she wanted could not be coerced. A few hours' rest and refreshment would put the young witch in a better frame of mind and meanwhile, she had another stop to make. The nearest grunnie rubbed his forehead on her back as if she were a sturdy post, pushing her over.

'Come on with you both.' She gathered up their reins. 'Time to get you home.'

She led them down a side corridor and through the portal. Unsaddled and curried, she turned them loose on a high mountain pasture, their bellows ringing through the valley as they trotted down the slope, returning to their herd.

'Don't get too comfy. I'll need you again soon. I don't think the girl's fit enough to walk back to the top.'

She slipped into the portal and braced for the return to Earth.

Rosette looked at the food and thought there could be worse prisons. The drink had revived her mind, and her appetite as well. She leaned over the table and sniffed. It looked good and smelled fresh. She broke off a small piece of the bread and popped it into her mouth. It was like cake, melting as it touched her tongue. The meat was unidentifiable, spicy and rich, and when she ate the fruit she thought it was the most delightful thing she had ever tasted. She didn't know what it was, but she saved the seeds, tucking them into her leggings pocket.

Satisfied, she left the table to take a closer look at the mosaic walls only to discover that closer wasn't better. From a few feet away, she could only see little squares of colour. There were no heroic figures or sword fights or wild embraces between lovers in the woods. It was all a blur. She moved backwards, one step at a time, until the swirls of colour came into focus and the images returned. Who was the artist who created such a thing? They certainly had a fancy for the Draconic folk — dragons and lizards of the most fantastic colours featured in every panel.

She dropped her coat and moved to the pool's edge. It was lit from within by some unknown means and through the churning water she could see the image of a great dragon tiled into the bottom, its body lying across the entire floor, its wings extended up the sides. It was so realistic Rosette took a step back.

Just another mosaic. Nothing to fear. She laughed. *Nothing to fear?*

She automatically reached out to Drayco in her mind and then pulled back. It was doubtful she could connect with him through all this rock. He'd be sleeping anyway, warm by the fire, belly full. And what could she report? She was effectively imprisoned with no clear understanding of why, nor was there an obvious route of escape. She shook her head. It was out of her control, for now, and panic wouldn't help. Her captor had said to bathe, to prepare for something, and the water did look inviting.

She undressed, layer by layer, until she stood naked beneath the endless dome ceiling. Stepping into the pool, she sighed. It was wonderfully warm. She lowered herself into the water, floating on her back, fully submerged except for her face. She allowed herself to drift and relax. Vitality returned to her limbs and she swam from edge to edge, diving down to skim her belly along the tiles of the dragon's ridged back before shooting to the surface for a quick breath and diving again.

She floated in the warmth a while longer before getting out. The smooth rock floor was cold to the touch, making her shiver while she stood dripping under the glow of lanternlight. She searched the living area for a towel, finding a large red one that went round her whole body twice. She dried off, dressing quickly. The star chart on the desk had caught her eye again and she wanted to read it.

After checking that the door was still locked tight, she sat in the cushioned desk chair and scooted it forward until she was right in front of the work space. The chart was curious, completely different from the way she'd ever seen one drawn. There were outer planets in distant positions — far too distant to be seen, and she didn't recognise their names. The latitude and longitude were wrong as well. They were southern, and there was nothing but ocean in Gaela's lower hemisphere. She shifted in her seat, replacing the chart at the exact angle she'd found it. As her hand drew back, a letter slipped off a shelf and fell partially open onto the desk.

'What's this? You want me to read you?' she whispered.

She tilted her head, listening for footsteps outside the door. Convinced that she was alone, she returned her attention to the letter. It was written in a strange calligraphy; each letter was perfectly juxtaposed to the next in the most unnatural way. She got no feeling of the author at all by studying the script. It was old, though, and read many times. That, she could tell. The pages were discoloured and the edges torn, leaving much of it illegible. She angled the first sheet to the light and began to read.

My dearest Ruby,

I've missed you deeply. So many times I've wanted to risk a visit but you know how AS —

There was an abbreviation, but she didn't recognise it. The rest of the page was impossible to read save for the bottom. Rosette squinted. The ink had run and it was badly stained. She could only make out the last paragraph.

... total relief. The single discovery I've been dreaming of is clear in front of my face. It's so simple really — DNA employs quantum computation for a range of functions including communication. It's all about consciousness, Ruby — what you think is what you experience.

Rosette's brow creased. DNA? What did that stand for? Only the last sentence made any sense. This must be a letter from a mentor to a student. She picked up the page beneath it and read on.

It's getting tight here. ASSIST is taking over — martial law. I've been questioned daily. I won't even put in print who they ask about. It's like a witch-hunt ... so primitive. I hope you never understand such things, but if you do make it back, you need to know. They hunt us here, Ruby, and they don't take prisoners — at least not for long. They've declared war, and they think we're the enemy! I've managed to stay a step ahead. They still need me, but Luka says we have to get out, and soon.

Rosette looked up at the beams over the pool and shivered. They hunted witches? Where was this letter from? She returned to the page.

Before I vanish, there is something you need to know. Something you need to pass on. There is a certain kind of energy that occurs in all cultures, in all places, in all times. It goes by different names but has the same signature — strange 'happenings' that transgress the classical laws of physics. Different civilisations give it different names — witchcraft, psychic phenomena, shamanism, divine miracles, quantum physics. It's all magic, one and the same — something that possesses unique qualities producing unaccountable or perplexing effects.

It includes telepathy (mind-to-mind communication), precognition (awareness of future events prior to occurrence), clairvoyance ('clear visions' of the past, present and future), psychokinesis (mind affecting matter), therianthropism (shape-shifting), astral travel (out-of-body experiences), lucid dreaming (conscious awareness and control in the dream state), and the deliberate and intentional use of Qi (life force). However it is manifesting in you, know that it is very strong in our line. Why else would you have been chosen to settle the pups on the other side? You're the most magical of all, Ruby.

'Pups?' Rosette said aloud.

The biggest problem ASSIST has with magic is its perplexing effects — a blanket disregard for the laws of classical physics. Of particular concern are concepts to do with location and the arrow of time. Classical physics holds that time flows in one direction, from past to present to future. It also holds that matter has specific and definable mass, weight and location. In spite of formulas like $E=MC^2$ acknowledging that all matter is energy, ASSIST can't get their heads around anything that appears to be in two places at once, whether it's a photon or a human being. Communication faster than light speed is also a concern, as are situations that spin the arrow of time in different directions. Lacking empirical bases for these events, the scientists are losing their reference points and without such ground they've concluded that magic is a hoax, unprovable, impossible, a danger and a misconception. My funding has been suspended and all government support withdrawn.

Just when Rosette thought she understood the lesson, she was thrown by unrecognisable words. *Photon? Physics?* She picked up the next sheet.

But magic has a mind of its own, Ruby. Never forget that. It not only ignores the causal, mechanistic world view, it also ignores the scientists who are ensconced in it. Magic thrives, always has, showing its wares to those who care to study it, and sometimes to those who do not. I know that many of the 'strange happenings' seen in magic mimic the inexplicable events found in quantum theory. Have you discovered that as well, my daughter? He can help you there. I hope you've found each other.

A chill went up her spine. This was a parent's letter to an offspring.

The perplexing effects that are difficult to explain in classical terms make sense in the quantum paradigm. In the world of the very small, the arrow of time flows symmetrically forward and back with no distinction between past, present and future. Precognition and the divinatory arts function in the same way, where future or past events can be perceived in the present, and events in the future can affect the past, even an extremely distant one. I'm not talking about causation, Ruby, but about participation. This isn't one universe, it's a multiverse.

You understand this, don't you?

'No,' Rosette answered, even though she knew the question was not for her.

We think we are going from point A to point B, that A causes B. It feels right subjectively — you eat the ice-cream and then you experience its taste. But that's not what's going on in the brain, Ruby. Not at all. The brain responds to stimuli, a touch, a taste, a colour, a voice, before the object or colour or sound actually gets to it. We think we are 'in the moment', but it is actually a past response to a future event that's already happened, and that's not all. As soon as we choose to taste the ice-cream, our world splits, branching into two — one where we took a bite and one where we did not. Here, let me draw you a picture.

'Ice-cream? What in Gaela's demons is that?'

Rosette looked at the pages, shaking her head. The diagram was impossible to discern and the rest of the letter made even less sense.

Because quantum theory provides a theoretical model for how magic 'works', quantum theory-based experimentation has been my playground. I can see behind the veil into a whole new reality and quantum computers are my lens, just as he is yours. He is with you? All is safe? He can help you understand the perplexing effects on both the quantum level and in the divinatory arts. It'll open doors, Ruby. This one's only the beginning.

She picked up the final page.

Before I made the quantum-sentient breakthrough, the classical binary code bound computers to certain functions: calculations, information storage, communications and networking. A language that consists solely of zeros and ones has its limitations. But quantum computers employ superposition, which means they can be both ones and zeros at the same time. Even deeper, the old belief that consciousness resided in humans alone is over. I've changed that paradigm forever, though the effect my discovery is having on the many-worlds is still not clear.

Now ASSIST is stepping in, pulling the stops.

The conspiracy began slowly, accelerating into a ruthless, violent deluge. Magic, quantum theory, divination and psychic phenomena are all being lumped together, termed 'occult arts' and condemned for their disrespect of natural law. Natural law? Are they joking? This has nothing to do with nature, I promise. She is like magic, a force with plans of her own. She's rebelling, even more so since you left, and ASSIST can do nothing to stop her.

Please don't worry about me. I'm like nature too. Resilient. You know this. I've taken action to save the Earth, and our line is the key. He is the key. You two have to look after each other, and the pups. I can't cross over again, nor can Luka. We'd be traced. It would be the end.

Oh, Ruby, be warm. Be well, and safe. Love keeps you in my heart always.

She couldn't read the signature. It was a scribble, and the ink had smeared. She folded the letter, tempted to take it; Nell might make some sense of the words. But after a moment Rosette put it back and moved away from the desk. There was a spell on this place and though it didn't feel malevolent, she wasn't going to put it to the test.

She ran her fingers along the mosaic tiles, stopping at a wall that sported Lupins romping beside long-limbed women on massive grunnies. It looked like a boar hunt or a festival of some kind. She closed her eyes and sank to the cushioned floor. Without another thought of her strange predicament she pulled her coat up to her neck, tucked her arms into its warmth and fell asleep.

Kreshkali flipped the compass shut with her thumb, folding the horary chart into quarters. She put both into her cloak pocket. Could this be it? She'd followed the text, a seventeenth-century work from the most famous astrologer of that time, William Lilly. The instructions were not cryptic in this edition. It was a copy straight from the original work of 1647. She'd memorised the relevant section — the rules for identifying witches.

If the Lord of the ascendant be ruler of the twelfth, and combust the Sun, you must observe of what house the Sun rules, and in what sign and quarter of heaven he and the Lord of the ascendant are, and judge the Witch liveth that way; describe the sun sign as he is, and it represents the person.

The horary chart she'd calculated had Leo rising and Leo on the twelfth, so the Lord of the ascendant was the Sun — as close a combust as you can get. The Sun was in Gemini, in the tenth house, ninety-two degrees of south longitude. She'd checked the Moon's aspects, and followed her compass here, to this street, to this building, number ninety-two. Inside must be the witch she was after, and if she did have those Gemini characteristics, she'd be sharp, astute and ready to go, no matter what her age, or his. She'd be a communicator, by voice, letter or message, no doubt with a notebook already in her hand. Kreshkali took a breath and let it out slowly. This venture was a risk, but she had to take it.

The building in front of her was bleak and weathered — indistinct from all the others in the long line of street-front apartments. If anything, it was in the worst condition. The rusted downspouts were hanging at strange angles from their brackets, useless for the most part. Water fell in sheets down the walls, as if the building wept. The windows were empty, lifeless, but from somewhere inside, Kreshkali felt she was being watched.

She climbed the concrete steps to the front door, her heart racing. It was dangerous business, stepping outside her turf. Before she found Gaela her survival skills had been honed scalpel-sharp, though now that her plans were finally coming together she felt vulnerable — one witch in one world — and everything rested on this errand's success. She stood before the metal security door, her throat dry, hands sweating.

This has to be it.

According to the chart, here lived a witch who could tell her all she wanted to know about the source inside ASSIST — the mole she needed to contact to set her plan in motion. Whoever was behind this door, she had to get them onboard. If she couldn't, or worse, if it was a tracker, she had to get the hell away, fast.

She knocked.

'What do you want?' A woman's voice, sharp, suspicious.

So far, so good. 'I'm looking for directions. I was told you might help,' Kreshkali called out above the rain.

After a pause, the bolt inside the door slid back and it opened as far as the chain-guard. She could see eyes checking her out from head to foot. The door clicked shut and was opened again, this time wide. A grizzled woman with twin lines etched between her brows stuck her head out into the gloom. Her steel-grey hair was pulled back into two thick plaits that hung over her shoulders to her breasts. Her face was broad, her cheekbones strong, her eyes dark, like a jaguar's.

'There are many directions to ask about,' the woman said, her voice softer than before.

'Which is your favourite?'

'I'd have to say the north node.'

'Me too.'

The older woman motioned Kreshkali in and led the way to a small kitchen. It had a single cupboard and bench, a small sink, and in the centre was a broad wooden table with mismatched chairs.

'You live alone?' Kreshkali asked, pulling out the seat next to the stove. It was warm from recent use.

'More or less,' the woman replied. 'My name is Annadusa.' She held out her hand, bangles and beads sliding down her arm.

'I'm Kreshkali.'

Annadusa sat opposite her. 'You a bit lost, are you? Need directions?' She said the words offhandedly, flipping her thumb across the edge of a worn diary.

'If you could, please.' Kreshkali matched her casual tone.

'First some tea to warm you up, and then I'll send you on your way. You won't get lost with this.' She scribbled on a loose leaf and pushed it across the table. Kreshkali smiled softly. 'I thought it might be that simple.'

The note said, *Can't talk here. Take me to yours?*

Kreshkali folded the note and tucked it in her pocket, turning her attention to the steaming cup in front of her. She took a whiff. 'Coffee?' she whispered.

Annadusa beamed. 'I have connections.'

The aroma filtered up her nose as she drew in her breath, the vapour enveloping her face, making her eyes dance. She let out a soft sigh as she sipped it. If this was a tracker, at least she'd die happy. Coffee wasn't a commodity on Gaela and she hadn't the time to trade for it here on Earth. She'd forgotten how rich the taste was, how welcoming.

'It's not quite that simple, actually.' Annadusa spoke in a merry tone again, like a youngsters' storyteller.

'It's not?'

'I think I'll have to guide you.'

'You will?'

They drained their cups and stood.

'I'll get my coat.'

Kreshkali took a deep breath as she waited for the other witch to return. She hadn't had the benefit of the horary chart when she found Jaynan. She hoped this time, things wouldn't go wrong.

Chapter 15

Jarrod awoke, in the dark. The fire was mere coals, banked with warm stones. Nell was sleeping close to it, a short distance from Scylla and the Sword Master. Judging by the regular breathing, he guessed their dreams were sweet and the injuries mild. Thank the goddess for Nell's herbs and magic. The feline wouldn't be doing well without both.

He didn't see Drayco until he went outside. The temple cat stood staring up the path that led to the summit, the early-morning light turning him golden. He was completely still except for his whiskers. They twitched with every breath.

'Are you feeling better, Drayco?' Jarrod asked.

The feline turned his head briefly before looking back up the track.

'Will you let me see?' Jarrod stretched out his hand, keeping it steady, determined to check the feline's vital signs. Drayco lashed his tail and sat down in the snow, wrapping it tightly around his front paws.

'I'm going to take that as a "yes". Just give me a warning and I'll back off. I only want to help.'

He knelt beside Drayco, lifting his hand slowly to the temple cat's thickly furred neck. He stroked it, working his way to the ear and giving it a good scratch. A soft vibration issued from Drayco's throat. Confident that he had permission, Jarrod grasped the massive head in both hands and pushed the top eyelids back with his thumbs. He looked at the left eye, then the right, turning each towards the sunrise.

'Pupils are equal and both react to light. I'm guessing the headache is gone and you're fit to travel.' He smiled at the deep orange eyes. 'Shall we go to the summit and wait for Rosette? The Sword Master says she'll be there.'

Drayco's ears pricked at the sound of his partner's name. When Jarrod stood he leapt to his feet, heading up the track.

'Wait for me. I won't be long,' Jarrod called. 'I'm going to check on the others and saddle up. It'll be quicker if I ride.'

Drayco sat halfway up the track, his tail sweeping back and forth across the snow, piling it into drifts on either side.

Nell came out of the cave wrapped tightly in her fur coat. 'Making friends?'

'I think we have an agreement.'

'How is he?'

'Concussion's gone.' Jarrod nodded towards the cave. 'What about them?'

'Sleeping. Scylla's fever's down but still present. I'm going to get more agate and snow root if I can find any. She shouldn't travel yet.'

'Not surprised. But your herbs ...'

'Have helped,' she interrupted.

'I'm going up to meet Rosette. If she's not at the summit ...'

'I know. I've fed and watered the horses, and saddled Wren, though she won't be of use underground.'

'Underground?'

'The Lupins took Rosette to the witch Kreshkali. She's got a den down in the bowels of Los Loma. If Rosette isn't back by the time you reach the summit, Drayco will find a way in. Wren will get you as far as the entrance, but you won't convince her to enter the darkness. She'd be blind there anyway. She's a good mare, but she's no grunnie.'

'Maybe I can persuade her to wait for me. I don't plan on taking too long.'

'I love your optimism, Jarrod.'

'And I love your daughter.' He winked at her and went back inside the cave.

Nell frowned. *That could get tricky.*

When he emerged with the copper-red mare, Drayco jumped to his feet.

'Take these.' Nell handed him dark lenses. 'The snow will blind you without them, unless you have time to think yourself up some UV-screened optics.'

'Thanks.' Jarrod took a risk and roughed the temple cat's neck with a gloved hand. 'Ready to meet Rosette?'

Drayco launched up the path and Jarrod followed after him. As he started to climb, the sunlight warmed his face — the only skin exposed. Thank Zeeka, goddess of the mountain wind, that the morning was calm and clear. When he reached the summit, he could see forever in all directions — a magnificent panorama.

'She should be here soon. Let's give her some time.'

Drayco snapped his tail and continued across the summit, ignoring Jarrod's halt.

'Or, let's keep going ...' He clucked to the mare, jogging after the temple cat. Winding down a path on the other side of the summit, Drayco stopped suddenly before a cliff face. Its rocks and outcroppings were thick with snow, but on close examination, Jarrod realised the rock wall was a deception. It hid a narrow fissure — an entrance into the mountain.

'Did she go this way?'

Drayco entered the crevice.

'I guess she did, then. Wait for me.' Jarrod dismounted and unbridled the mare, leaving the halter on her head. He loosened the girth slightly and tied the lead rope securely to the saddle. 'I'm hoping you'll wait for me, my beauty. If we haven't returned by dusk, go back to the cave. There're shrubs at the summit, to keep you occupied. Do you understand?'

The mare fluttered her nostrils and rubbed her face on his shoulder, leaving a flurry of copper-coloured hairs floating in the air. Jarrod removed a torch from his saddlebag, shouldered his backpack and followed Drayco inside.

A wall of pitch black hit him. He couldn't see his hand in front of his face as he fumbled to light a match. When the torch was blazing, he held it high over his head, searching for the temple cat. Drayco was nowhere in sight.

'It's going to be really hard for me if you disappear. I'll never find you in this black soup.' He inched forward until he came to three rough archways. 'Drayco, really. We have to communicate more effectively.' He stared at the archways. 'Where in this underworld are you?'

Drayco's head appeared from the darkness of the central arch. *You're right. We have to communicate better, and you have got to stop nattering and try to keep up.*

Jarrod's stomach turned somersaults. 'Drayco? Is that you talking?'

The temple cat's eyebrows lifted. *Who else would it be? Let's go!*

'But, what are you ... I mean, I can hear you ... I thought only ...'

Still I hear the nattering ...

'But how?'

I've known you always.

'What?'

She dreams of you.

'You can see her dreams?'

We see each other's.

Jarrod shook his head. 'How does that work?'

Jarrod, you're a quantum sentient from another world, walking around in a Tulpa-body, chasing a young witch whose DNA holds the key-codes to your operating determinates. Why do you find this such a surprise?

'You know all that?'

I do, now that I'm talking to you.

Jarrod did an internal scan and found every front end file accessed.

Let's go, shall we, Jarrod? It's this tunnel. I've got her scent, but I can't hear her mind. She must be deep under the mountain, or deep asleep.

Jarrod didn't speak for a moment. 'So she dreams of me?'

Focus, Jarrod. This way.

He smiled for a moment, before following Drayco into the dark.

Rosette awoke with a start. Two Lupins had entered the chamber, made a quick bow and signalled for her to follow. She scrambled to her feet before grabbing her coat and shoving her arms into the sleeves. The haze that permeated the corridors had cleared and a bright, dazzling light prevailed. Was there a second sun in the heart of Gaela? She turned to the Lupin beside her, wanting to ask.

'Mirrors,' he answered her unspoken question. 'The sun shines brightly on the surface this morning.'

'Mirrors? Quite a few, I'd imagine.'

'Thousands.'

He steadied her when she tripped over a rough stone.

'Thanks,' Rosette said as she clenched his arm. She released it quickly.

Her short but intense introduction to the race of Lupins left her in two minds. They were strangely appealing and also aggressive and wicked. She was certain Drayco did not like them. It was hard to sift the lore from the facts. Hotha was particularly alluring, and he'd stopped the others with a word, those three who had been so brutal and quick to anger. They had a powerful magic, though. She couldn't help wonder about that. Could she learn it?

They took several turns before stopping in front of another door. The Lupin pounded on it — three resounding thuds — and stood back. Rosette felt butterflies in her stomach as it opened without a sound. The Lupin nodded for her to enter and she did so. Inside, there were more mosaic panels covering the walls. The artwork was astonishing, and under different circumstances she would have loved the chance to study it thoroughly. She had trouble pulling her eyes away.

'It draws you in, doesn't it?'

Rosette startled.

'Anything you recognise?' Kreshkali said. She sat at a large table in the centre of the room.

Rosette took in the tall trees, the plaza with a fountain and four corner statues, the apple orchards. She nodded. 'Treeon, of course.'

'But?'

'Treeon of a different time.'

Silence filled the room and Rosette continued to study the panels. When Kreshkali spoke again she was standing only inches away. 'Is it Treeon's past or Treeon's future?'

Rosette tilted her head. It had to be the past. Dragons filled the air and a battle raged on the training grounds. There didn't seem to be as many stables or any cabins by the river. 'Past,' she said.

'Is it?' The witch leaned closer, whispering into Rosette's ear. 'Are you certain?'

'I can't see how else ...' Rosette faltered as chills ran down her spine. 'How could it be anything but the past?'

'How indeed? You and I have much to discuss, and very little time.'

She directed her to the table, gesturing for her to sit.

Rosette looked at it before she pulled out a chair. It seemed to be carved from bone, like a huge vertebra, level with her hip, wings jutting out to either side. Whalebone? It couldn't be. Nothing that large moved on land or sea.

Not in this world, perhaps, but have you thought of others?

Rosette jumped at the voice and tightened her mind-shield.

Kreshkali pushed back her hood, running her fingers through her spiky, pale hair. Rosette thought she looked tired, or maybe distressed.

'Here's the deal: I'm High Priestess here — and "here" means you're in the tombs of Los Loma. Welcome to my realm.'

Rosette bowed her head briefly. 'And I am Rosette de Santo of Treeon Temple, apprentice to Sword Master An' Lawrence.'

'So he has finally made you apprentice. Took him long enough.'

'Pardon?'

'My Lupins tell me he may have little left to teach you.'

Rosette didn't flinch. Her mind-shield was secure and she didn't let the implication rattle her.

'Why was I brought here?' she asked.

Kreshkali grinned and sat down. She folded her hands on the table and tapped her thumbs together. 'Several reasons. Firstly, I wanted to test the Lupins' mind strength against you lot.'

'Not much of a match, was it?' Rosette said, interrupting.

'It wasn't. You think you learned adequate mind-shielding at the temple, but clearly it failed both you and An' Lawrence, so you're not ready for much as far as I'm concerned. I'd need to see improvement there.'

'You make it sound like it was my test.'

'Do I?'

Rosette straightened her shoulders. 'So we've established that your Lupins can penetrate my mind-shield.' Her thoughts were working fast, shuffling through myriad possibilities, looking for the most likely reason Kreshkali sat before her now. 'What else have we learned?'

She wasn't feeling subordinate to the High Priestess of Los Loma, regardless of her station. A warm glow flowed through her, offering confidence and strength.

Kreshkali lifted one eyebrow. 'There's the business of Passillo.' She reached into her pocket and held a vial up to the light before placing it on the table. 'I understand that you were the last to wear this.'

She pointed a long, black-enamelled fingernail at Rosette's face. 'Do you know where the Spell of Passillo is?'

'No idea.'

'Are you certain?'

'I used to wear the vial around my neck — a gift to my mother, passed on to me — but it's been empty all my life. I can't tell you anything else.'

Kreshkali touched a finger to her lips. 'Well, doesn't that leave us in a conundrum ...'

Rosette resisted the urge to bolt. There was something so alien — so un-*Gaelean* — about Kreshkali that even her scent made her nervous. She took a deep breath and let it out. 'A conundrum?' she asked.

'A dilemma ... a pickle.'

'I understand the term,' Rosette snapped back.

'If you don't know anything about the Spell and La Makee still searches ...' Kreshkali groaned. 'Then there's too much to do and not enough time.'

Rosette's mind was in a whirl. The witch talked in riddles. One moment her eyes glared and she looked fit for murder, another and there was something else — something soft and almost intimate in her gaze.

'I assure you, I do not know where Passillo is,' Rosette continued, filling in the silence. 'Perhaps it really has been lost.'

'Lost?' The High Priestess laughed. 'It can never be lost, never be unmade. It has to be awakened; it has to be *used*!'

Kreshkali looked at Rosette anew, her eyes losing their intensity and filling with a kind of wonder. 'Who gave that vial to your mother?'

Rosette flooded her aura with a self-assurance she didn't actually feel, hiding the inner turmoil that wiggled in her guts. She had a very good idea of where that spell had gone and she didn't like the notion one little bit. More issues to take up with Nell, when she saw her again.

'Can you answer me?' Kreshkali asked. 'Do you know?'

Rosette lifted her eyes and locked them onto the other woman. 'It was never discussed.'

'All right then, I am going to make you an offer.' Kreshkali spoke softly, sipping from an ornate cup.

'What offer?'

'You tell me what you are concealing, and I'll let you return to the surface.'

'Let me? I thought I was invited.'

'You were. And now I'm inviting you to tell me everything you know.'

'I've told you all I remember,' she lied.

'Have you?' Kreshkali pushed her chair back, reaching for Rosette and guiding her towards the exit. 'Then you can stay in my underworld until you remember more. La Cot!'

The door flew open and a Lupin entered.

Rosette's mind raced. 'Wait!'

Kreshkali held a hand up to La Cot. She waved him out.

'Yes, child? Did something come to mind?'

'There was a rhyme; I've always known it, but I never thought it more than a bedtime story.'

Kreshkali visibly relaxed, leading Rosette back to the table and handing her a tumbler of water.

Rosette sat down, heart pounding like a bunny's.

'Who taught it to you? Your mother?'

'My mentor, Nell.'

Kreshkali's eyes gleamed.

'Do tell,' the witch said.

Rosette contained her hope, hiding her anticipation in a façade of calm. 'You'd like to learn it?'

'Of course!'

Bingo! She took a sip of the sweet water. 'Repeat it as I say it, High Priestess, word for word.'

'Shoot.'

'From the depths of Tatari five rivers flow.'

'From the depths of Tatari five rivers flow,' Kreshkali repeated in a smooth, sensual voice.

'Into my hand and into my heart.'

'Into my hand and into my heart.'

'A vial for Passillo, sweet blessed Passillo.'

'A vial for Passillo, sweet blessed Passillo.'

'To recall again, to recall forever.'

'To recall again, to recall forever.'

'So that all shall be made anew.'

'So that all shall be made anew.'

Rosette sighed. 'Again. Close your eyes.'

Together the two sat at the table and repeated the verses over and over.

Rosette kept on and on, adding new phrases, changing nuances, and weaving the enchantment right under the nose of the High Priestess of Los Loma. With every new breath she was sure she'd be caught out, but she wasn't, and she felt the spell weave tighter and tighter around Kreshkali until it had bound her firm.

The lamp above them dimmed, and the beams across the ceiling began to creak. It was almost as if they were on a great boat, rising and falling with the sea swell. Rosette felt ill, perspiration breaking out on her forehead. Still the spell grew, and she knew a power within her was mounting. Her limbs were on fire with it, her eyes blazing.

The spell was old. She'd learned it from her mother — surrogate mother — Bethsay Matosh, and Rosette had never known where the woman acquired it. All Bethsay had revealed was that it was older than she — much older.

Rosette had thought it was a mother's spell to bring sleep to a child after a nightmare, and it was all she could think of to satisfy Kreshkali for the moment while she thought of something else. The word *Passillo* wasn't even in it. This spell was about Somnia, a lesser slumber deity. At least, that's what she'd been told. Rosette was starting to doubt everything now.

Still, she'd substituted *Passillo* for *Somnia* and Kreshkali was in a trance, and in the midst of it, Rosette clearly glimpsed where the Spell of Passillo was hidden. Her eyes went wide. She swallowed to keep from choking. Could it really be living in her blood and bones? It felt like it was.

'It's in your blood ...' The words came from nowhere.

As they continued to chant in unison, Rosette substituted her own name as well for *Somnia* — the name she had taken years ago near the woods of Espiro Dell Ray. Coloured light, blue with hues of green and gold, emanated from the tips of her fingers and hovered over the table like steam over a molten lake. The vial, resting like a bright bird upon the slick surface, was sucking it in. Watching for the right moment, Kreshkali nearly unconscious, she reached out and snatched up the vial, dropping it deep into the pocket of her fur-lined coat.

The room went dim, everything still and quiet. The only thing moving was the wave of nausea in Rosette's stomach and the gentle sway of the lantern above. The table was rock-still, Kreshkali silent, her breath rising and falling in long, exaggerated sighs, her eyes moving rapidly beneath her closed lids. She was fast asleep and dreaming, a smile lifting the corner of her exquisitely full lips.

It worked. The woman was enchanted, perhaps wandering borderlands in the dark recesses of her own mind or travelling other worlds. There was no telling how long she would stay that way, though. Cautiously, Rosette stood, keeping her eyes on Kreshkali.

Done, and well done. Now, I just have to get past the Lupins and find my way out of this rabbit warren.

She searched the room and found another door, opposite to the one she'd come through. Since she had no idea where she was or which way to go, one direction seemed as good as the next. She walked to the door and tested the latch before pushing it open, imagining in her mind that there was no one on the other side.

It's an empty hall. I can get away easy. This is a cinch. She stuck her nose out a few inches, repeating her affirmations, looking up and down the hallway.

Empty, and not well lit.

Good. Now for the 'I get away easy' part. She stepped through, closing the door behind her. With a deep breath, she took off. At every fork, she chose the archway that led left and up, optimistic that it would bring her to the surface. She had been climbing for at least an hour before the howling began.

She ran and didn't stop.

The shouts and howls of her pursuers remained faint, far in the distance. That was some comfort. She bolted up a stairway that opened to another landing. Three doorways stood before her, two leading down and the third leading up. The walls here were rougher on the one leading up, more like the insides of a mountain than the smoothly sculpted corridors that led down. She went through the third arch and began to climb. As she trudged, she heard footsteps, many footsteps, and the sound of nails clicking on the rock surface — booted feet amongst them. They became a relentless staccato, descending from the stairs above and heading straight towards her.

Trapped.

Crouching low, she backtracked down the tunnel and felt along its surface for several yards before her hand found what she remembered from minutes before — a large fissure in the wall. She squeezed into the crack, the extruding rocks digging into her shoulderblades and grazing her cheeks. She forced herself deeper and deeper, her body yielding and flattening between the walls. She sucked in her breath and held it. The footfalls were just outside.

She could glimpse the Lupins through the narrow opening — some were in wolf form while others appeared as men, their sword hilts glinting in the torchlight. As they streamed past, one stopped, ears pricked. He sniffed along the ground at the entrance and up the edges of the fissure. Rosette felt the blood drain from her face. She exhaled slowly, silently, and drew in, inch by inch, a new breath.

The Lupin's dark eyes flashed as his head moved across the ground, disturbing the dust as he sniffed. He scratched at the rock. Another stopped, both growling as they scented. She squeezed further back, her breasts pressed into her ribcage, her face scraping the rock as she turned her head. She was in the belly of the mountain now, pinched tight, dripping sweat and blood from the scratches on her face. The air smelled musty. It made her tongue prickle and she swallowed the bad taste, trying not to cough. It took all her focus to keep from screaming out in terror.

Many Lupins gathered, sniffing and scratching at the crevice. Pain shot through Rosette's head as a shard of rock cut her temple. The blood stung her eyes, the warm trickle running down her face. She ached to wipe it away. Still she kept pressing further into the rock, unable to take more than thin, shallow breaths.

Her body was in a vice-like grip and she squeezed into the depths of what felt like her tomb. The nausea returned, though she was so wedged by now that she couldn't have vomited without choking. She pressed on, the fingers of one hand clawing their way ahead of her, pulling her body through the chink.

Almost imperceptibly, she felt a change in the air, a freshness she had forgotten could exist. It evoked the memory of trees and snow, and the pressure around her eased. Her face, previously pinned back to watch the receding gap of light where the Lupins had gathered, finally turned forward. She took a deep breath and a proper step. After a few more strides, she could walk with her hands out to either side. The crevice had opened onto a path. She wiped the grime from her face and cried, tears washing blood from her eyes.

It must have been a major passageway once, unused for some time judging by the layer of dust and shale at her feet. She could barely make out her hands as she strained to see the outline of the path. There might be a plummeting drop at any moment.

The sounds of the Lupins grew faint. She thought she heard some barking orders and the scuffle of feet, but wasn't sure. Were they going to find another way around, or were they convinced she wasn't there? At least it was clear they couldn't shape-shift into a smaller form and follow.

She stepped forward into the darkness, her foot slipping on loose shale. A chunk broke off and she jerked back instinctively. It toppled down, falling and falling until there was a distant clip and thud as it struck bottom. She backed up, her hands touching a rock wall behind her, the darkness all-consuming. Suddenly, she realised she might still be trapped, only in a larger prison. She needed light to navigate this subterranean world. As if in answer, she looked down. Her pocket pulsed with a faint blue glow.

She pulled out the vial, wrapping the chain around her wrist and holding it high above her head. With illumination, Rosette found herself in a massive cavern, with a canyon hundreds of feet deep. It must have been traversed by a high arched bridge at one time, but that was broken now. It looked like the keystone had given way — the middle of the bridge bitten out like it was a giant's cookie.

Dead end?

The thought of squeezing back through the crevice repulsed her. Even though she knew she could make it, she didn't think she had the nerve to do it again. Besides, there would most likely be a Lupin or two posted at the entrance, waiting. Surely they knew this was a dead end. She searched every inch of her surroundings for another means of escape.

To her left she spotted a landing that led into yet another dark passage. Placing the amulet around her neck, she tightened her coat, retied her bootlaces and wiped her hands in the chalky dust. Gripping the wall like a spider, she shuffled along the narrowing ledge, taking slow breaths and small steps, giddy with fear. Heights were never her forte. She dared not look down, though, past an arm's length, all was black.

Rocks gave way under her boots and tumbled into the chasm. It was a long time before she heard them hit bottom. Her footing slipped more than once, but the jagged edges of the rock face offered deep handholds. She finally reached the landing in front of the passage, panting from the exertion. She rubbed her aching fingers, her relief lasting only moments.

Recessed into the wall was indeed a new tunnel, but it had a stone door, locked tight. When she tried the latch, rotten wood fell to pieces in her hand and the bronze keyhole dropped, clanking to the ground. She pushed and jimmied and shoved and, finally, bashed the full force of her shoulder into thick stone, but it didn't budge. There seemed no escape that way and with the lengthy breaks in the ledge behind her, she didn't think she could make it back. Magic was an option, but knowing her, she'd bring the whole archway down on top of her head. Defeated and exhausted, she slumped in the dust, closing her eyes against the dark, tears spilling down her cheeks.

Hotha loped up the steps, his wolf form giving him the advantage of speed and heightened scents. Rosette had come this way, up these very steps, but to where? She hadn't made it to the top, and she couldn't have gotten past Rashnan's pack without notice. She wasn't that clever yet. He came to the archways, inspecting each before following her trail up the far one. What was she playing at? This was an old part of the caverns, the passageways were treacherous, at least for human feet. Kreshkali would be furious if anything happened to the young witch. He had to find her, and quickly.

Hotha, she's this way.
Do you have her?
Not yet.

He slowed his pace when he saw Rashnan standing by a fissure in the wall.

'She ducked in here,' the other Lupin said.

Hotha shifted into his bipedal form, running his hand along the contours of the rock.

'Ducked?' Hotha said. 'It's the size of a rabbit hole. She'd have to do a lot more than duck.'

'Scent for yourself. She went that way.'

'It's too tight to follow,' Hotha said, reaching his arm into the crevice. 'As wolf or man.'

'And that's not the worst of it. You know where it leads?'

'I've a pretty good idea.'

'It's an old crack. It leads straight to the fallen bridge cavern. There's no light there. She could topple into the ravine.'

Hotha groaned.

'It's all right. I sent my lot around the long way.'

'But the bridge is down. They can't get to her from the other side.'

'There are archers among them. They'll light up the cavern and we can get a rope ladder across.'

Hotha leaned his back against the rock wall, running his hand through his hair. 'She's a wily pup, that Rosette. The Mistress has taken on more than she knows, I'll wager.'

'You're right there, she ...'

Both Lupins froze as Kreshkali's message boomed into their thoughts: *Let her go! Come back to me before somebody gets hurt!*

Hotha shifted into his wolf form and loped down the steps, Rashnan right behind.

The sound of tramping feet infiltrated her dreams, jolting her awake. Rosette rubbed her eyes. Across the canyon, on the other side of the bridge, she could see a light. It glowed faintly at first before brightening into dozens of flaming torches.

Lupins!

They poured out of a far tunnel on the other side of the crumbled bridge, and filled the wide landing opposite her.

You'll not get to me from there, you mangy dogs.

They lit arrows and drew back their bows. They all took aim in her direction.

Crap!

Rosette pulled the vial from around her neck and shoved it under layers of clothing. She pressed her back into the door, hoping to get out of the line of fire, though the arrows were landing quite wide of the mark.

Lousy shots. She pressed further back into the alcove. Trapped again. *This is ridiculous! I'm a temple-trained witch.* She could suddenly see the comedy in her situation and the fear lightened. *I can get out of this! Of course I can.*

She exhaled long and slow as arrows whizzed, lighting the cavern like a harvest party. The Lupins were shouting from across the ravine, but she didn't listen, focusing only on a way out. She leaned against the door, feeling its smooth edges. *I'm going to open this passage without bringing the mountain down.*

Power welled, revitalising her limbs. She focused a small boost of magic on the door and gave it a push. It didn't budge. She tried a little harder. It shuddered but still didn't move. Finally, she blasted it with everything she had. 'Yield to me! Yield to me now!' she shouted.

The rock door responded, bursting into a million grains of sand.

'Hey, Drayco. Psst ...' Jarrod hissed as he heard the thump and stomp of marching in the distance. 'Can you see them?'

Use your mind-voice, Jarrod, if you want us to remain hidden.

They'd been playing cat and mouse with the Lupins for what seemed like hours.

Jarrod formed the question in his mind. *Can you see them over the ledge?*

Don't shout. I'm right here.

Jarrod scratched his head. This kind of communication was harder than he'd imagined. He re-formed the thought and sent it as lightly as he could manage. *Can you see the Lupins?*

Yep. They're headed this way. We have to turn back.

Again?

Would you like to test your swordsmanship against thirty or so bipeds and more wolves than I care to count?

Not really.

Then, yes. We have to turn back.

Jarrod took his hand from his sword hilt, tightened his belt and dashed up the corridor. Drayco followed at his side. They turned a few sharp bends before the temple cat skidded to a stop. It took Jarrod a moment before he realised he was running alone.

Have you found something?

She's this way. Work the lock, quick.

Jarrod bashed the lock with his sword hilt and pulled. Darkness and stale air met them, while the sound of metal on metal reverberated through the passage.

I said 'work the lock', not 'sound the alarm'. Drayco sneezed as the old air flowed past.

You wanted in, Jarrod said, pulling off his glove to re-light the torch, risking a quick roughing of Drayco's neck. *Come on. Lead the way!*

Rosette raced up another flight of steps — a particularly steep ascent. She sat down for a moment to catch her breath and get her bearings. She started to feel like she couldn't do it. For all she knew, she was on the other side of the mountain. Sighing, she lightened her mind-shield just a touch and risked yet another call to Drayco. Tears welled up as she searched for him. She'd not been without his thoughts since the day she'd found him and the lack left her desolate. Was he even still alive?

I'm alive. What about you?

Drayco?

Who else!

Oh, baby cat, am I glad to hear your voice! Are you hurt? What about your head? Are you all right?

I'm fine now. Head's clear. He paused for a moment. *She's here. Beneath us, I think.*

What, Dray?

Maudi, are you able to run?

That's all I've been doing since I can remember. Who are you talking to? Is Scylla there?

Not Scylla. She's not so good. Sword wound. He's here though. We're both looking for you. We have to hurry. The Lupins are between us. Are they hunting for you? Have you upset them?

A little, I think. Not sure why. Rosette was up now, continuing the climb. *Drayco, who's 'he'? Who's with you? Is An' Lawrence there? Are you actually talking to him?*

The Sword Master is back at the cave. He's wounded too. That mind magic rattled his brain. The temple cat paused. *I'm telling her. Just hang on ... Maudi?*

Who are you talking to, Dray?

Jarrod says to say hello.

What?

Jarrod. Remember? I hope you do because he is cramming my mind with thoughts to send to you. I've narrowed it down to 'hello'. The rest will have to wait.

Jarrod's with you? Rosette whispered the name. *How can that be?*

Clipper ship, I suspect. Then the bright red horse.

What?

He travelled and now he's here.

Are you sure it's Jarrod?

I'm certain.

'I don't believe it,' she whispered softly. 'My Jarrod?'

You better hurry. The Lupins have spread out. They must be searching everywhere. Climb.

I am, but how ... how can ... when did ...

You sound just like him now. Come on, Maudi. I think you're in the tunnels below us and to the east. The Lupins are in between and also behind.

Are you sure?

Just guessing. Keep climbing up and west, up and west.

Where in the darkest demon's balls is west?

The left hand of your stairs, facing up. Quickly. We'll meet you at the top.

I'm coming! Rosette snapped her mind-shield into place and leapt up the steps. She heard howling again. It seemed a fair way off, but she pushed herself to run just the same. She summoned a final boost of magic to get her to the surface, and charged upwards until she thought her legs would give out.

The howls were getting closer.

She stopped to peer over the edge of the stairwell. A troop of Lupins was below, their torch lights fluttering like flags. She wrapped her coat around her waist and cinched the belt tighter. Cold air burned her lungs.

The surface couldn't be far. It was getting colder; the air chilled the sweat that ran down her back.

Dray, the Lupins are right behind me.

Keep running. We're at the entrance. Drayco's voice stayed in her mind, urging her on.

Rosette's strength drained more with every stride, her pace faltering as she continued the final climb. She leapt a jagged step and tripped, her head coming down hard on the rock floor. She didn't get up.

I can't wake her. Drayco rasped his tongue across her lidded eyes, nudging her with his head.

'Let me see.' Jarrod reached into his pocket, pulling out a small glass tube. He crushed it in the palm of his gloved hand and held it under her nose.

Rosette coughed, sat up and retched. 'Drayco!' She sank her hands into his fur and clutched him to her.

Get her up, Jarrod. We have to run.

'Give me your hand,' Jarrod said.

She looked at him blankly, her eyes fluttering shut again.

'Come on, Rosette,' he said, slapping both her cheeks. 'I'm not going to get captured this close to the surface. We have to run.'

Her eyes opened fully. 'Jarrod?' She struggled to stand. 'Jarrod?'

'That's me.'

'Drayco really did find you?' She reeled.

Jarrod gripped her shoulder. 'We have to run!' He grasped her hand and hauled her up towards the surface.

Deep within the tombs of Los Loma, Kreshkali awoke. She stretched cat-like before realising what had happened.

'Well, well ...' She grinned, the smile turning into a chuckle — the chuckle into full-throated laughter. 'Little bitch! Well done!'

The thought froze as she listened to the Lupins. What were they doing now?

Let her go! she yelled, sending a blinding force into the mind of every Lupin, stopping them in their tracks. *Come back to me before somebody gets hurt!* Her mental voice reverberated through the corridors of Los Loma.

Come back, she said in a softer tone. *She's on her way.* Kreshkali took a deep drink of water. 'Well on her way ...'

Her hand rested gently on Rosette's sword and she smiled, admiring the exquisite simplicity of the design.

* * *

Rosette blasted through the entrance with Jarrod and Drayco beside her, the wind jolting her like an icy slap. She dropped Jarrod's hand and spun around, calming her mind and beginning a summons. The wind picked up, whisking snow from the overhang, revealing the stones that held the archway in place. She noticed they were carved with runes and figures, just like the ones deep in the bowels of the mountain.

'Not for long.'

As she wove her spell, the stones and rocks began falling, one by one, gaining momentum as she chanted. Soon she brought the whole rock face down. Ice broke off in sheets and a roaring welled up from the ground. It travelled through her legs and up her spine. She clenched her teeth to stop them from rattling.

Too much! Nell called from the body of the falcon. *You're tearing apart the whole mountain.*

'Avalanche!' Jarrod shouted, his words barely discernible above the cracks and groans.

Rosette froze, watching the wall vibrate.

Nell landed beside her and shifted, screaming, 'Get out of here!' She clapped her hands together. 'Now!'

Rosette started to run down the trail, but Nell grabbed her arm, jerking her back. 'This way.' She pulled her in the opposite direction.

Rosette ran hard. She couldn't hear the snow crunching under her boots or the sound of her breath as she gasped for air. There was only the rip and shatter of rock and falling shale. She charged around the side of the mountain and up towards the summit plateau, Drayco at her side. Climbing the last stretch hand over hand, Rosette pulled herself up to stand at the edge of the clearing. She could feel Jarrod's chest rise and fall beside her and Nell's bare hand holding her own. Drayco leaned into her leg, tail lashing.

Half the western face of Los Loma swept by — snow, rock and rubble. It rushed past, a furious stream of ice, towards the forests below. Fingers of white powder shot up from the depths like massive geysers and the ground trembled underfoot. The sound of snapping trees and branches tore through the air. Rosette backed up, pulling the others with her towards the centre of the plateau. Boulders the size of cabins tumbled past, then smaller ones, diminishing into gravel, shale and the odd sheet of ice. Finally, all went quiet. The trail was gone and so was much of the mountainside.

Ravens cawed from behind them and took flight. The Three Sisters surveyed the damage, scolding as they flew over Los Loma.

'Fine spell, Rosette,' Nell said, brushing snow from her arms and shaking it from her hair. 'Just a tad strong, though, don't you think?'

'A tad,' Rosette agreed. Her jaw clenched. 'Your timing was good, Nell, or should I call you something else?' Rosette raised her eyebrows as she crossed her arms.

'This sounds like it could be a long conversation,' Jarrod said. 'Maybe we'd best save it for later. I'm guessing the Lupins have other passages out of the caverns. We won't be safe for long if they follow.'

'Kreshkali isn't very happy with me,' Rosette said. She was about to say more, but she eyed Jarrod instead, taking him in properly for the first time. 'You got tall.'

'I did.'

They stared at each other until Nell cleared her throat. 'So you met Kreshkali?'

'Yes, I met her. She's very ... unusual.'

'I know,' Nell said, her eyes levelled on her daughter.

Rosette matched her gaze then shook her head. She turned to Jarrod, where she met an equally intense stare. 'I can't deal with either of you right now,' she said, reaching out for Drayco.

'Understandable,' Nell said after a pause. 'I'm going on ahead. I've been away from Scylla and she'll need her dressings changed.'

'Are they all right?' Rosette asked.

'The feline's lacerated and An' Lawrence has a ripper of a headache still. They'll both recover. I'll meet you at the cave.'

'We'll take the long way down,' Jarrod said. 'Unless you're going to fly?'

'I don't actually do that yet,' Rosette said.

'Really?' He looked at the mountain peak she'd just turned to dust. 'I can't imagine why not.'

She gave him a fleeting smile and headed across the plateau towards the copper-chestnut mare. Nell shape-shifted, disappearing into the clouds, the Three Sisters darting off after her.

Chapter 16

Rosette braced her hands on her knees, catching her breath. Drayco leaned against her side. 'Is this day ever going to be over?'

We don't have far to go.

That's good news, Dray. 'Water, please,' she asked Jarrod.

He stopped, pulling the water-skin down from the saddle. He was leading the mare, the trail too unpredictable for them to ride. 'It's not much further.'

She smiled before she pressed the spout to her lips. 'So Drayco tells me.' She drank long and deep. 'I'm glad you remember the way, Jarrod. It was blowing a blizzard the first time I came through. Couldn't see a thing.'

'It wouldn't have mattered. That spell of yours rearranged the whole mountain. The trail's virtually gone.'

They circled around a boulder wedged directly in their path.

'I stopped the Lupins, so don't complain.'

Jarrod waited for her to catch up as the path broadened. He took her hand and gave it a squeeze. 'Wouldn't dream of it.'

The sun dropped low and shadows stretched over the trail. It narrowed again, the rocks and boulders taking on the appearance of stone giants with menacing stares. She hurried, only to slip on the icy path. The descent was getting tougher. Rock and rubble blocked their way, forcing them to detour close to the sheer cliffs. There were sudden drop-offs and rifts, and it was getting colder.

Her heart was pounding when they reached the cave. Once inside she headed straight for the fire, pulling off her gloves and warming her hands close to the flames. Nell was by the stone hearth, stirring a pot that bubbled above the hot rocks. Jarrod settled his mare. When he returned to the fire, he didn't take his eyes off her.

'We've got a lot of catching up to do,' Jarrod said as he sat next to Rosette, close but not touching. 'So much has happened.'

'It has,' she answered.

Neither said any more.

'You must be starving!' Nell broke the silence. 'When did you last have a meal, either of you?'

'Actually, Kreshkali gave me a fabulous dinner last night, or this morning. Whenever it was.' She sniffed towards the pot. 'That smells good, though.'

'You dined with Kreshkali? How gracious of her.' Nell didn't make it sound particularly gracious.

'She left it for me — incredible, really — warm bread and honey, meat in a spicy sauce and this brilliant red fruit.' She reached into her pocket, feeling for the seeds.

'Did she talk?'

'Not then. She didn't stay. Said she had things to do.'

'I'll bet she did.' Nell kept her eyes on the pot.

'What happened down there?' Jarrod asked. 'What did Kreshkali want?'

'I'm more curious about how you got away,' Nell added.

Rosette thought about where to begin, aware of the sleeping figures of An' Lawrence and Scylla on the other side of the fire. When she'd finished her account, both Nell and Jarrod were staring at her.

'What did Kreshkali say to you exactly about Passillo? You brushed over that part.' Nell's eyes were piercing.

'Hang on. I have some questions of my own first.' Rosette turned to Jarrod, noticing his hand in the firelight. It was cut and caked with dried blood. 'What happened?'

'I fell on a piece of black rock. It'll heal in no time.'

Nell shot him a glance. 'I'll get the med-kit,' she offered.

Jarrod rolled up his sleeve and gritted his teeth as Nell cleaned the gash.

'Let's have your questions, Rosette,' she said while dressing the wound. 'We have to get this over with sooner or later, and the sooner the better.'

'Do you think so?' Rosette lifted her eyes. 'Then I'd like to know how you define "sooner". It's been two decades since you had me. "Soon" just doesn't seem to apply.'

Nell stared at her daughter. 'Is there a specific question in there?'

Rosette hissed an exhalation.

'How is he?' She jerked her head towards An' Lawrence, her brow knitted tight.

'I've spent many years being angry at him, Rosette,' Nell replied as she packed the medicines away. 'Are you picking up where I left off?'

'Maybe.'

'Any particular reason?'

'Oh, let me think. He lied to me, wove a total deception. He tricked me into this adventure with the

Lupins and Kreshkali without having any idea what he was getting us into.'

She stopped short, eyeing Nell. 'But you had an idea, didn't you? You knew all along where Passillo was.' She turned back to the fire, her jaw tight. Silence filled the cave.

'What are you afraid of, Rosette?'

The question came from the furs on the other side of the fire. An' Lawrence was struggling to stand, Scylla on wobbly legs beside him.

'Sword Master?' Jarrod and Nell went to his side.

'How's the head?' Nell asked.

'Still seeing double. I'm going to skin those Lupins alive if I ever see them again.'

Nell checked his pupils. 'You still have a concussion. Lie back.'

'Gladly, but first we need to go for a little walk.' He nodded to Scylla.

They helped him steady his familiar and walk her towards the entrance. Before going out, he turned to Rosette. 'Did you at least manage to keep track of your sword?'

Rosette's hand went automatically to her side. She pressed her lips together. 'Actually, I didn't. I suspect I lost it because someone tried to make a trade that was very poorly thought out.'

'Poorly thought out? If you had been honest with me about your origins from the start, I wouldn't have brought you here.'

'Honest about my origins? Who are you to talk!'

'I've never pretended to be someone I'm not,' he shouted back at her.

'Pretended? I thought I knew my blood origins until you and Nell decided to confess! Come to think of it, you know more about my origins than I do. You and

Nellion Paree of the Dumarkian Woods.' She glared from one parent to the other.

'Enough.' Nell held out her hand. 'There's some explaining to do, I'll admit, but it won't help to bicker. We've real enemies, and they take priority over these petty grievances.'

Rosette's mouth dropped open. 'Petty grievances?'

'On a universal scale? Yes. Petty.'

Rosette snapped her jaw shut and turned away. She stared at the fire. Jarrod wrapped his arm around her shoulder and she nestled into his side. 'How did you find me?' she whispered to him.

'That's a long story,' he said, pushing back her braids and kissing her cheek.

She smiled for a moment and turned his face so she could kiss him full on the lips. 'I'm looking forward to hearing the details.'

Are we going to tell stories all night, or are we going to eat something? I wasn't invited to Kreshkali's amazing dinner, like some of us, and I am definitely hungry, even if you lot are not.

Jarrod laughed.

'Dinner's coming,' Rosette purred to her familiar before catching Jarrod's eye. 'What are you smiling at?'

'He's a funny one, Drayco the Black.'

'He is, but what makes you say so?' She didn't wait for a reply. She found a bowl and ladled it full of stew, setting it before her familiar. 'It's hot, Dray,' she said, stroking his back before returning to Jarrod.

I like it hot, Maudi!

'I know you do.'

Jarrod chuckled and looked from one to the other. 'He does like it hot.'

'What? Did you hear him?'

'I guess I'm tuned in now.'

'Since when?'

'Since inside the mountain. It was the only way to communicate in the dark. You know, with the Lupins everywhere, and ...'

'I know. I was there.' *Can you hear this?* She sent the words silently.

He didn't look up. He just sat, bewitched by the fire.

He needs more practice, Drayco said. *It's like he's speaking underwater sometimes.*

'As if you would know what that was like,' Jarrod said without turning his head.

'How were you able to do it?' she asked Drayco. 'You've never spoken to Nell and she was there from the beginning. You said you could only speak to me.'

Would, not could. There's a difference.

'Apparently he recognised me from your dreams,' Jarrod said with a soft smile.

Rosette blushed. 'My mind goes where it will at night ...'

'You don't have to explain. I've had dreams too.'

I had to link to him, Maudi. Otherwise we would never have found you. He's quite blind in the dark, even with a torch. Interesting mind, though. Not what I expected. Did you realise he was ...

'Smart? Oh yes, I know. And thanks,' Rosette said, reaching over to stroke Drayco's head.

'You're welcome.'

'Oh, Jarrod. I meant *thanks* to Dray for linking with you to help me.' She leaned into him. 'You have my total appreciation as well. I can't believe the timing. It's like you waited until I needed you the most.'

She filled another bowl for Jarrod. As she placed it in his hands, she leaned in and kissed his neck, not letting go of the bowl until he turned his face to hers.

Are you going to be kissing each other all the time now? Drayco asked, licking his chops after finishing his meal.

That could be fun, Rosette answered.

Jarrod smiled up at her.

You weren't like this with the bard.

He's not him, is he, Drayco?

'Who's the bard?' Jarrod asked.

'Clay. A friend,' she answered, filling her own bowl and taking a huge bite.

Nell, An' Lawrence and Scylla joined them by the fire, eating without conversation. Their faces glowed with thoughtful expressions in the orange light. Rosette didn't know where to begin with her questions. Every time she formulated one it came attached with so much emotion that she couldn't squeeze it into a coherent sentence.

Breathe! she schooled herself. *You simply want to know what happened. Just allow them to tell their story without being so attached.*

She took a deep breath, held it for a moment and let it out, her shoulders relaxing as she did so. 'All right, you two. Tell me how it happened.'

'How what happened?' Nell asked.

'How *I* happened without *him* ever knowing it.' She gestured towards An' Lawrence. *Stay calm,* she reminded herself. *Just get the facts.*

'Yes, Nell. How did that happen? I'd love to know as well,' An' Lawrence chimed in. He seemed revived after a little walk and some food. 'I'm quite curious to hear your side,' he went on. 'Mine's quite simple since for over two decades I had no idea that anything had happened at all.'

'You don't remember the week we spent under the falls of Los Ghatos Regela?'

'Of course I remember. I just never heard from you again so it was a little difficult to exercise my parental duties, seeing as I didn't know I had any! All these years and I thought we'd had a brief interlude and that was that.'

'You thought what?' Nell spat the words out.

Apparently you're not the only one with emotion on this topic, Maudi.

I see that ... 'Okay, stop, you two.' Rosette held up her hands. 'Tell me the story, minus the vehemence, emotion and/or explicit details, thanks.'

Nell reached behind her for another log and tossed it on the fire. Sparks danced towards the vaulted ceiling. She questioned An' Lawrence with her eyes.

'Go ahead, Nell. You tell it. I'm listening.'

She nodded, looking into the fire. 'It was simple, really. I was a priestess at Treeon, alongside Makee. We had both trained extensively with the High Priestess La Kaffa, and the two of us worked very hard under her. You have to remember that, back then, we were still at war with Corsanon.'

'Of course.'

'So, there we were, all capable, focused and keen for adventure.'

'And that's where I came in,' An' Lawrence added.

'Do tell.' Rosette's eyebrows rose.

He laughed, shaking his head, wincing at the motion. 'I'd just come back from the cliffs of Tuscaro, south of the main battlelines — that's where I meet Scylla.' His voice softened as he stroked her thick fur. She stretched in her sleep, purring like a kitten. 'I was to team up with one of the priestesses from Treeon, minding her back while she conjured a water spell.'

'A water spell?'

'Something to turn the tide in our favour, so to speak,' Nell said. 'We planned to change the course of several rivers, cutting off Corsanon troops from the north and east. La Kaffa sensed trouble right away, and I think she almost enjoyed it.'

'What do you mean?'

'Makee and I both wanted to work with the young Sword Master, though Makee had her own designs that I knew nothing about.'

'What did she want?' Rosette asked.

'What all ambitious people want: power, and lots of it. She saw An' Lawrence as a means to make herself indispensable. La Kaffa, I think, had the best intentions of Treeon in mind, though it was I who actually stirred up the biggest trouble.' She chuckled before going on. 'Makee and I — once as close as sisters — became very competitive.'

'Over him?' Rosette nodded to An' Lawrence, her mouth turned down.

'Not so much for the Sword Master's attention as for succession to High Priestess. We both agreed anyone else would be dangerous in that position and that one of us should be chosen, to protect Treeon and the free lands of Gaela. La Kaffa was too uncertain in her reign — too indirect. We were losing ground to the Corsanon armies under her command.'

'Who did she choose for the succession?'

Nell shrugged. 'It's irrelevant. Egos got way too involved and my bond with Makee frayed.'

Rosette stared at the Sword Master. 'Because of you?' she asked.

'An' Lawrence wasn't responsible,' Nell answered, looking directly at him as she spoke. 'He kept his mind on the war for the most part, but we did end up together in Los Ghatos Regela after making one fine water spell. We changed the course of five rivers that day, and inadvertently awoke the Spell of Passillo in the process.'

An' Lawrence's eyes widened. 'We did *what*?'

Nell ignored him. 'We thought our task was over and celebrated all week in a beautiful little village above the falls. It was really something, a magical time. The cherry trees were in bloom ... Do you remember, Rowan?'

'Of course, but what do you mean when you say *we* awoke the Spell of Passillo? Nell ...?'

Jarrod caught Nell's eye and gave a slight shake of his head.

'Back at Treeon, it was anything but peaceful,' she continued. 'I think Makee was doing her best to protect the coven — which in the end she did. Makee thought she'd save everyone the trouble and all but put herself in the dragon-bone chair. Of course, only one could wear the title of High Priestess and La Kaffa was still it. The tension arose when Rowan and I returned, especially when La Kaffa realised I had possession of the spell of legend.'

'Passillo,' Rosette said.

'Yes, Passillo. The bane of my life — and yours.'

'How did La Kaffa know you had it?'

Nell fidgeted. 'I told her.'

'And how did *you* know you had it?' Rosette asked.

She sighed. 'My mother and her mother and hers, since the beginning of our line, had known where Passillo was buried; they had entrusted each generation with the secret. We were told to keep it safe if ever there was a danger, and to guard it if it'd been discovered. But it had been such a long time since the first woman of my line had taken on the responsibility, that it seemed like merely a mother's story to a young girl before sleep.'

'I'm confused,' Rosette said. 'What's this got to do with me?'

'It has everything to do with you,' Nell answered. 'I showed Passillo to La Kaffa and explained the meaning as best I could. I needed help, and I left Passillo in the temple coffers for safekeeping.'

'What happened?'

'The voice of Passillo, like a screaming demon, came through my dreams. That's when I knew I'd made a mistake. The spell called for me to take it back. The voice terrorised me until I awoke, sweating. I understood that it *had* to stay within my family, even though I didn't fully comprehend why. So I stole it back from La Kaffa's strongbox.'

'I can see how that would have caused trouble,' Rosette said.

'And *you* were no help at all.' Nell crossed her arms, looking at An' Lawrence.

'Excuse me? How could I be any help when you failed to include me in your plans? You didn't tell me *any of this*! You just vanished.' He rubbed the back of his neck, looking at her. 'I came to you the night before you disappeared. Do you remember?'

'Yes, I remember. I also remember that you were heading back to Corsanon. I was afraid of what might happen if Makee or La Kaffa, or anyone, tried to use Passillo, so I took action. I made choices. Don't think for a moment it was easy.'

'I might have been more supportive if I'd known what was going on.' An' Lawrence raised his voice as he spoke.

'And you might not have ... I didn't trust it.'

'You mean you didn't trust me.'

An uncomfortable silence filled the cave.

'Interesting,' Jarrod said. 'What happened next?'

Nell took a sip of water and continued. 'I snatched the spell back and left before first light, heading for the ruined temple of Dumarka.'

'And I was conceived when?'

'Under the falls of Regela. Pay attention. I didn't tell anyone I was pregnant because I wanted to protect you,

Rosette. I wanted to protect my line. By then, I was starting to feel hunted.' She looked at Jarrod.

'And what about when I was born?' Rosette's voice was barely audible above the crackle of the fire. 'Was giving me up part of the protection too?'

Nell didn't answer for the longest time. The fire hissed and spat as she placed another log in the middle of the flames. 'It was. Winter came and then spring, and then you. I also had a visit from La Kaffa.'

'She found you in Dumarka?' Rosette frowned.

'She did, and so did others. I was being tracked and they were closing in. It took all my power to keep them away and when it looked like that would fail and I would lose the spell after all, I hid it in a place no-one would think to look.'

Rosette frowned but didn't interrupt.

'There was no time to mull over the consequences. I wove the spell into your blood three days after you were born.'

'How?'

'Let's just say it had a natural affinity. Our blood is different, Rosette.'

Jarrod shot a warning glance to Nell.

'I wanted to get you, and Passillo, safely hidden away,' Nell continued.

'Bethsay?' Rosette asked, hugging her knees.

'Bethsay Matosh was my best friend, even before I went to Treeon. She'd also apprenticed there, but not in magic or the warrior arts — she'd worked as a jeweller for two years before she met and married John'ra. She was fey though, Rosette. Never doubt that. She kept it to herself.'

'And she took me?'

'She'd just lost a pregnancy and was bereft. She also had plenty of milk and ached for a child.' Tears spilled down Nell's face. 'She'd come for the birthing. She was more than willing to take you.'

'She'd been a jeweller at Treeon?' Rosette asked, unable to look at Nell.

'She had,' An' Lawrence answered when Nell did not. 'She made that pendant you wear. Of course, it was me who'd had it commissioned. A gift for Nell. You can imagine my surprise when I saw it around your neck.' He turned to glare at Nell.

'I wanted to let you know she was your daughter without broadcasting it to the whole Treeon coven,' Nell said. 'I had to keep Rosette safe, and I also had to make sure that when you met, you would figure out who she was. I didn't think it would take you so long.'

'You could have just told me,' Rosette said. 'Then, when I got to Treeon, I could have introduced myself.' Her voice was tight. She didn't look at either of them.

'It wasn't safe, Rosette.'

'So you keep saying.'

Another lengthy silence surrounded them.

'What happened to my family? Do you know that too?' Rosette demanded. 'Who wanted to kill us? Kreshkali?'

'Not Kreshkali,' she answered quickly. 'That evening six years ago was the work of Corsanon assassins.'

'Hired by?'

Nell shook her head. 'I'm not certain.'

Jarrod murmured in Rosette's ear and she nodded. He untied her hair, letting the braids loose, and began brushing through them a few strands at a time. She closed her eyes and smiled. An' Lawrence and Nell's conversation disappeared into the background as she focused on the warmth of the fire, and Jarrod's touch.

She was nodding off when Nell's voice cut through her private peace.

'I missed out on raising her too, Rowan! You think it was easy for me to have her come and visit for a summer every few years then disappear again?'

'At least you had that.'

'I sent her to you as soon as I could and what did you do? You promptly handed her over to the Lupins of all things.'

'I didn't promptly do anything of the kind. The idea was to ...'

'Use her as bait to get your hands on Passillo? Oh that makes it all right then.'

'Hey, guys.' Rosette's voice rose above theirs. 'You want to start another avalanche? Let it go. It can't be undone.'

The fire crackled and Drayco stretched. The horses pawed the ground and Jarrod took them a bucket of water that had been set to melt. He refilled it with ice and returned to the fire.

'She's right,' Nell said. 'We can't change the past directly, but we can alter the future. We have to work out what to do with Passillo now.'

No-one spoke for some time.

Rosette turned her palms up and studied them as if for the first time. They were glowing red now, finally warmed through.

'Is that why my spells are so strong, Nell? Walls and mountains cracking when I'm trying to warm the kettle or close the door? Because of Passillo?'

Nell sighed. 'It's in your blood. It's not really the Spell of Passillo any more.'

'What is it then?'

'It's the Spell of Rosette.'

The familiars had stretched out side by side in front of the hearth. An' Lawrence slept fitfully, his head injury still causing him pain. Jarrod's eyes were closed, his hand on Rosette's knee. She wondered if he'd fallen asleep as well.

The wind howled outside the cave. The horses shifted in the gloom beyond the fire.

'What are we going to do?' Rosette asked her mother in a low voice. 'I've got something in the vial now, and I don't even know how that happened, but the spell's still in me. I can feel it.'

Jarrod's head snapped up as if suddenly awakened.

'Where've you been?' Nell asked.

He exhaled forcefully. 'We have to get the spell, and you, off the continent — beyond everything we know. Past the Isles of Landercan and out to the edge of the world.' His fierce look gave Rosette chills.

'Are you certain, Jarrod?' Nell asked. She lowered her voice: 'Trackers?'

Rosette barely caught the last word. 'What do you mean, "trackers"?'

'It isn't safe here,' Jarrod said. 'The Eastern Range is too high to pass now and Dumarka is no longer a sanctuary. West is the only way.' He drew a map in the powdery dust with a stick.

'What are you talking about?' Rosette asked.

'The spell has a purpose, Rosette, and we can't let it fall into the wrong hands.'

'You mean you can't let me fall into the wrong hands.'

'Precisely.' He looked at Nell. 'That goes for both of you.'

'And if they follow?' Nell directed her question to Jarrod.

'Eventually they will, but it won't be easy across the Emerald Sea.' Jarrod threw his stick on the fire and folded his arms. 'There are too many islands, too many possibilities. The spell can just disappear out there.'

'You mean *I* can just disappear out there?'

'I meant ...'

'It sounds like the only way, for now,' Nell said. 'We can't risk you either, Jarrod.'

Rosette laced her fingers and put her hands on top of her head. 'What are you guys talking about? Who's following? Kreshkali? Are you saying I'll always be hunted? Always on the run?'

'Not if we can get you off this world.' Jarrod turned to face Rosette.

'Off this world?' Rosette wrinkled her brow. 'You mean through the portal?'

Nell hushed them. 'Before we contemplate that, we have to deal with La Makee. She'd lead them straight to us.'

'Lead who? What trackers?'

'What if they think Rosette was lost under Los Loma?' Jarrod asked.

'You mean dead?' Rosette drew her knees up and wrapped her arms around them. 'Sounds like I'd be better off.'

'Think about it,' Jarrod said. 'No-one knows what happened in that avalanche. And no-one knows I'm here at all, so far.'

'What are you suggesting?'

'Nell, you and An' Lawrence return to Treeon with the vial. Say that's all of the spell that you got. It won't do any harm and it might satisfy La Makee, at least while she tries to work out what it is.'

'And Rosette?' Nell asked.

'Say that she and her temple cat perished in the tunnels under Los Loma. It's not a far stretch and there's the landslide to prove it.'

'They'll send scouts,' Nell said, nodding.

'It'll buy us time, and put off any other ... pursuit.'

'It's nothing new,' Rosette said, closing her eyes. 'I've been playing dead since I was sixteen.'

He leaned closer to her. 'I won't be left behind this time. I'll sail with you. It'll be all right. I promise.'

'This will work,' Nell said. 'I'll catch up with you in the islands, once Makee is satisfied.'

Rosette straightened her back. *Drayco? It seems we're on the move again.*

I heard. Could be fun?

Maybe. How do you feel about boats?

On the water?

Generally, yes.

I don't mind, as long as I can stay dry.

I'll make sure you do, lovely. You can count on it.

Rosette added more wood to the fire, watching the flames until her eyes began to close.

'Get your coat. I need you to come with me.' Nell's voice brought her out of a daze.

She yawned, following her mother out of the cave. The wind raged, whipping her hair about her face. The warm orange tones of the shelter vanished as she closed the flap, immersed now in the pale blue-grey of the moonlight. Nell's face was covered in shadow. 'Forgive me, daughter,' she said. 'It was always the hardest thing to live with ...'

'What's that?'

'Living without you.'

'It wasn't to be,' Rosette said, her teeth starting to chatter.

'Not angry any more?'

Rosette wrapped her arms around Nell and gave her a brief hug. 'I think I'll always be a little angry — something to live with. I'm proud to have Nellion Paree of the Dumarkian Woods as my mother. As far as I can see, you saved my life.' She felt Nell's tension ease.

'My little Kalindi Rose, my Rosette. Those times you came to stay with me were the best of my life.'

'Mine too, Nell.'

They embraced again until Rosette pulled away.

'It all makes sense now!'

'What's that?'

'My birth data's correct, isn't it?' Her voice was a challenge. 'You didn't alter that?'

'It's exact. Bethsay timed it to the second.'

'Then this explains my natal Moon in the sign of the Water-bearer conjunct Oraneus. It never really fitted before. You know, things like "Sudden and unexpected separations and reunions with the mother, disruption in the home, need for emotional freedom as well as intimacy and closeness ... unconventional mother, strange family roots". I've always tried to comprehend that in context with my life in Lividica, as a Matosh, and it never sat right. Now that I know the truth, it makes perfect sense.'

'Always believe the horoscope, not ...'

'Not the history,' Rosette laughed, finishing her mother's sentence. 'You gave me all the hints in the world, didn't you?'

'A few.'

She rubbed her hands together and thrust them into her pockets. 'It's freezing out here. Let's go back to the fire.'

'First, the vial.'

Rosette loosened her coat and reached into her bodice. She felt the ornate facets of the crystal nestled between her breasts and pulled it out, holding it up to the moonlight. It emanated a pulsing glow.

'What is it, Nell? Not Passillo.'

'No, not Passillo. That spell is woven into you now. This is a sample of your aura, a by-product of that weaving you did when you put Kreshkali to sleep.'

'Can I do without it?'

Nell chuckled. 'What do you think?'

'I think I already have. Will it satisfy La Makee, though? Surely she will know it's not Passillo.'

'It'll occupy her for a time, until she works it out.'

'Then what?'

'I'm not certain.'

'That's not really comforting.'

'Rosette, it's going to get ... challenging.'

Rosette thought of the meeting with the Lupins, the release of magic that had dropped her to her knees, Drayco in the snow unconscious and the Sword Master face down, Scylla's blood turning the ice red ... Kreshkali's strange words. Her escape. The avalanche.

She pursed her lips. '*Going* to get challenging?'

Nell laughed. 'Keep that sense of humour, girl, and you might just come out in one piece! Can you sleep?'

'Yes, if everyone would leave me alone.' Rosette yawned massively.

'The good thing about the northern nights is they last for so long. You'll be able to get eight hours before dawn if you can keep your hands off Jarrod.'

Heat flushed Rosette's cheeks in spite of the glacial wind. 'I've always had a strong attraction to him,' she said through violently chattering teeth.

'I know.' Nell led the way back to the warmth of the cave.

'We all have,' she added under her breath. 'He's in our blood, too.'

Rosette ran her hand across the furs that Jarrod had laid out. 'Can I sleep with you?' she asked.

Jarrod unlaced his boots and placed them next to the hearth. 'That would be my pleasure.'

Rosette snuggled in, pulling the furs up to her chin. 'I'm so tired,' she yawned.

Jarrod buried his face in the back of her neck. She turned her head to kiss him. The sweetness of his lips on hers, his hands shifting to the small of her back and the brush of his eyelashes on her face sent a rush of warmth through her body.

'Thanks for the rescue,' she said, her eyes closing.

'When we're out of danger, you can thank me properly.'

But she barely heard him. She was already walking in her dreams.

There's a handclap, or is it thunder?

A voice in the dark speaks to me.

'I want to show you something,' it says.

It's a strong voice and masculine — I don't recognise it, but it's so familiar ...

'Who are you?'

'You'd call me the Entity.'

'I doubt it. I don't know anyone by that name.'

'I believe you do.'

It's misty and humid, the ground sodden and the air thickened by a brown fog. My skin tingles, nostrils burn.

'Where is this place?'

'You don't know?'

'I wouldn't have asked if I did.'

'Come,' the voice commands. 'Come and see what has happened to your world.'

I know this isn't my world. It looks dead, and Gaela is not dead.

The fog gives way to a dark street. Rain is falling and the droplets sting. There are pools of brown water in the potholes. I'm glad I've got my boots on.

'Keep your eyes covered. Don't let the water touch your lips.'

'Why not?'

'Because it's acid.'

'I don't understand.'

'It's poison.'

I flip up my hood and keep my eyes down. I'm walking along the edge of a street under enormous buildings. Very ugly. They are ominous in the dark, some of them glowing with eerie lights. It feels like eyes watching.

'If the water is poison, how does anything live?'

'It doesn't.'

My head lifts at a sound in the distance.

'Something lives. Look there.'

A dark figure with booted feet approaches — a man, I think. As they come closer, another figure, slighter in build but just as tall, slips through a strange wire fence and is blocked by the man. They're struggling. Then a sound explodes in the air like a firecracker and the man drops to the ground. The other bends over him, going through pockets, taking things.

'What is this place?' I whisper the question this time.

I feel the Entity pull at my mind.

'Earth.' It tugs harder. 'Quickly,' it says. 'She'll not be pleased that I brought you here.'

'Who won't be pleased?'

The Entity ignores my question. 'I want to show you how things can be — a different possibility.'

In an instant the street and towering buildings blur. Everything turns into tiny little squares, opaque puzzle pieces that slowly brighten with colour and light. The scene in front of me opens into a broad expanse of parkland. There are flowers and vegetables spilling out of their beds, young trees stretching towards a bright sun and fountains of water gushing up, refracting the light into countless rainbows.

'Much better,' I smile.

'You can let this water touch your face.'

I push my hood back, laughing with the Entity as I stand in front of the fountain. Reaching out my hand, I let the water flow over it like a blessing.

'What has to be done to ... to make it ...' I struggle with the question.

'To make this possibility "real"?'

'I guess.'

'You have to activate the Spell.'

'What spell?'

'You have to take it back to Earth.'

The Entity sounds desperate, agitated.

'How?'

There was no response.

'How!' I demand.

'Ask Jarrod,' the Entity finally replies. It sounds a long way away.

'Jarrod? What's he got to do with it?'

When Rosette opened her eyes, the fire had burned low. Jarrod's arm was around her, his chest rising and falling in a slow rhythm against her back.

I've got to remember this dream ...

She closed her eyes again and fell asleep.

Chapter 17

'Pick up the pace,' Nell called out as she urged them along.

Rosette leaned forward in the saddle, blowing her breath into her hands. It took almost a day and a half to get to the wide banks of the Nadian tributary. The tidal river skirted the wooded lands, eventually winding its way to the granite pools of Treeon and the Terse River below. The waters were high this time of year, crested with whitecaps. They'd been following the downstream course for over an hour but still could find no safe crossing.

'It's too deep, too cold,' An' Lawrence said over the raging sound of the water. He was doubling with Nell on one of the mountain ponies, his arms wrapped around her waist, Scylla draped between.

'Shall we take a break?' Jarrod called back, spray from the river moistening his face. 'We can get a fire going and warm up. Have some food.'

Nell agreed, pointing at a group of tall granite boulders before she dismounted. 'They'll block the wind.' She led her horse, An' Lawrence still astride, towards the standing stones.

I feel like fish. How about you, Maudi? Drayco sent the message on the run, loping towards pockets of whirling eddies along the banks of the river. Rosette and Jarrod followed Nell to the boulders, loosening girths so the horses could have a good breather.

'How close are we to Treeon?' Rosette asked, looking out towards the distant valley from the shadow of the giant stones. 'I don't recognise any of this.'

'Not far now. We've got to find a crossing, then go around the foothills to the east. By then, we'll be within a day of the temple,' Nell said, following her daughter's line of sight.

'*You'll* be within a day of Treeon Temple,' Rosette said. 'Jarrod and I are turning off and heading for the western sea coast.'

'So this is it?' Nell looked at her daughter and Jarrod, walking away before either replied.

'This is it,' Rosette said, watching her retreat.

She took the horses to a quiet eddy, watering them and redistributing the supplies. Nell and An' Lawrence would need food for one more day at the most; she and Jarrod would go through four times that much before they reached Morzone. She occupied herself with the details of it. Keeping busy, to her, was the same as keeping calm.

A flash of movement upstream caught her eye. She smiled. Drayco sat stock-still on a rocky outcropping, his right paw periodically darting into the stream, raking the churning eddy with lightning speed. Three enormous fish already lay flapping on the river bank.

He purred happily in her mind.

'Catch us something, did you, Dray-Dray?'

Salmon! Lots of salmon. I love pink fish.

Me too. 'You're the best temple cat in the entire world!' she said aloud as she secured the last saddlebag.

A hiss from Scylla turned her around. At least the Sword Master's familiar was feeling well enough to protest that statement. Nell and An' Lawrence had eased her down from the mountain horse and placed her by the fire. Nell had it blazing already.

'The best *male* temple cat in all the world, Drayco. Tell her that's what I meant.'

The tawny female hissed again before chortling.

'Jarrod!' Rosette called, about to inform him of Drayco's catch, but he was already making a spit across the fire.

Rosette tethered the horses in front of some thick brambles, the only greenery still available at the edge of the pine woods. The fish were cooking when she returned, everyone's face flushed from the fire. She sat amongst them, soaking up the warmth.

'Delicious,' Rosette said, taking another bite and wiping her mouth on her sleeve. 'Smoky, but delicious.'

'You always liked fish in the wild.' Jarrod winked at her and smiled.

'Still do.' She leaned into him, kissing his cheek through his stubble.

'Listen, you two,' An' Lawrence interrupted. 'This isn't a picnic we're on. When we find a crossing, we'll be splitting up, and the gods only know whether the Lupins are going to be on our heels, or yours. There won't be any time to linger. You'll have to ride hard from dawn until dusk each day, hard enough to cover the distance, but not so hard you cripple the horses. You've got to get off this continent, remember? You're being tracked.'

'I doubt the Lupins will enjoy crossing that much water,' Nell said, her eyes sparkling as she spoke.

'How would you know what the Lupins would do? Dogs can swim,' An' Lawrence pointed out.

'They aren't dogs.'

'What about Kreshkali?' Rosette asked. 'What do you think she will do next?'

'There's no telling,' Nell said. 'She ...'

Maudi! Riders headed this way, fast!

Rosette held her hand out to silence them all. *Where, Drayco?*

Downstream.

Jarrod stood, waving them quiet. 'Someone's coming.'

'Get down,' she whispered. She dropped to a crouch, pulling him down beside her.

An' Lawrence was on his feet, hand on his sword hilt.

Dray! What do you sense?

Two riders. One is on the Sword Master's black beast.

Do you recognise them, Dray? Can you tell who they are? She looked across at An' Lawrence. 'Who'd be riding Diablai?' she whispered.

'Zero or ...' He didn't finish the sentence. 'They'd be searching for us.'

It's Zero, Drayco confirmed. *And him ... the bard!*

'Who?' Jarrod asked.

'Friends,' Rosette answered. She scrambled up, pulling Jarrod along with her. 'What do we do?'

Everyone froze.

'Go!' Nell whispered, motioning to the horses. 'Get out of here, now! Find a ford to the north. We don't want to cross tracks.'

Rosette hesitated, looking from Nell to An' Lawrence.

'Now!' Nell snapped her fingers. 'Before either of you are seen.'

In seconds Rosette was untying Wren and her mountain horse, tightening their girths and leading them towards the fire. Jarrod met her halfway.

'Find Maka'ra,' Nell instructed as she tucked a handful of gold into her daughter's saddlebag. 'And keep the horses. You can ferry them across the strait to Rahana Iti. Maka'ra will take you on from there. You can trust him completely.'

'I know,' Rosette said.

'Leave no trace behind.' She gave Rosette a hug, holding the horse as she mounted.

'Try to remember some of the things I've taught you,' An' Lawrence said. He was at her side, taking a twist out of the reins. Looking up at Jarrod, he added, 'Mind each other.'

Rosette brushed her hand across her eyes and nodded, urging her horse into a trot. *Drayco! Come now.*

Drayco sidled up to Scylla and gave her a nose-touch before loping off with Rosette and Jarrod.

A minute later and there was no trace of them at all.

Eventually they found a shallow ford. The icy water spread over a wide expanse, barely reaching their horses' knees. They rode slowly, standing in their stirrups, watching for sharp rocks or sudden holes, but the river floor was all pebble, the fine gravel crunching beneath the horses' hooves as they plodded through the rushing water. They scrambled up the bank, slippery with recent rain, and moved easily through the valley before heading northwest to find a mountain pass.

Rosette stopped at the top of a particularly steep ravine. Her horse was breathing hard, flanks sucked in behind the ribs.

She gestured to Jarrod, shaking her head. 'Wren might be able to run on ice water and brambles, but this one can't.'

'You're right. They both need to graze. The foothill valleys could still have some decent pasture,' he said. He turned to Drayco. *Can you still hear Scylla?*

Dray cocked his head to the side for a moment. *She said they're already packed up. Nell and the Sword Master are on Diablai. The bard's crying.*

Rosette looked at her hands, her thumbs pinching the reins.

'Who's the bard again?' Jarrod asked.

'My friend ... from Treeon.'

'What's his name?'

'Clay.'

'Why won't Drayco say it?'

Rosette shook her head. 'He has his reasons.'

Jarrod frowned. 'How did you meet this bard?'

Rosette smiled at the memory. 'He gave me a ride to the temple on his family's plough horse — massive beast.'

'Clay?'

'No, the horse, silly.'

Jarrod's lips formed a thin line. 'If he's in tears, he must believe you're dead.'

He didn't at first. Scylla said he was ready to ride through an army of Lupins to rescue you.

'He might still have to fight that army if they don't get moving,' Rosette said, twisting in the saddle to check her horse's breathing. It was slower now and more even.

'We could be in the same situation,' Jarrod warned, encouraging Wren forward. 'Shall we move on?'

Rosette followed silently before sending a message to Drayco: *Tell Scylla we're on our way and to ask the Sword Master to watch over Clay.*

Drayco trotted alongside Rosette and looked up at her. *She says not to worry. He always has.*

'So what's he like?' Jarrod had removed his mare's saddle and tethered her with the other horse in a chest-high patch of waning yellow oat grass.

'What's who like?' Rosette picked up her horse's hooves one at a time, checking for stones. 'Damn!'

'Problem?'

'You don't have an anvil and forge with you, by any chance?'

Jarrod raised his eyebrows.

'Loose nail,' Rosette explained. 'The shoe's still snug, but this isn't good. One twist and the whole thing could come off. There are only two nails on the inside wall. Who shoes like that?'

'Someone in a hurry.' Jarrod bent down, running his hand over the nail head and testing the wiggle.

'White foot too. Just our luck,' Rosette said, staring at the horse's one white sock and cream-coloured hoof.

'The roads should improve in a few days,' Jarrod said. 'We'll make it.'

'What roads?'

Jarrod smiled, but said no more. He gathered wood, stacking it in a pile as the sun disappeared behind the western foothills.

'You two sound like you were pretty close.'

'Who?'

'You and Clay.'

Rosette snorted. 'Yes and no. I mean, we had a lot of laughs and fooled around ...' She paused, tilting her head to one side, gauging Jarrod's expression. 'I trusted him but always felt that something wasn't quite right.'

'What's he look like?'

Rosette laughed. 'Jarrod, are you that jealous? Seriously, what difference does it make what he looks like?'

'Just tell me.'

She clicked her tongue. 'Like a lanky farm boy. Glorious tattoo of a forest stag on his right forearm, after the fashion of the Ice Clans. Very bright blue eyes. Wonderful singing voice ...'

'He's a journeyman bard?'

She nodded.

'So he journeys?'

'That's implicit in the name, yes.' She scrunched her nose. 'Why all these questions?'

'Just tell me, what colour's his hair?'

'Jarrod, really! You're getting obsessed.'

'Does your bard have bright red hair?'

Her eyes narrowed. 'How'd you know?'

'I think he was in Lividica a few weeks ago, nosing around about you.'

'He was where?'

'Lividica. A bard like your Clay played in the pubs and at the markets, asking all kinds of questions about the de Santos and their daughter Rosette. I think someone finally told him about the Matosh family and Kalindi Rose. He disappeared straight after, before I could confront him.'

'But ... that doesn't make sense. He went away to Morzone for weeks but ...'

'That bard's the reason I decided to come looking for you, Rosette. I knew something wasn't right.'

She was silent for some time.

He lied to us, Maudi? Drayco asked, returning to the campsite with a small bush-pig in his mouth.

'Oh, bravo, hunter-cat!' she praised him as he dropped it at her feet.

Deception? Drayco asked again.

Maybe so. But we've lied to him too, she answered.

So it's even?

It doesn't really work that way.

I didn't think so.

Jarrod joined them by the fire, unloading another armful of wood. He snapped off small branches and laid them over a mound of dry grass. 'So, did Clay and you ...'

'Please stop,' Rosette interrupted. 'I don't want to talk about it.'

'Just trying to unravel a mystery.'

'Whatever it was, it must have been more than it seemed if he was looking for evidence of me in Lividica.'

'He claimed to be your suitor, keen to meet your family.'

'I don't think that was it. We never talked about the future in those terms.' She cupped her hands around the small flame as Jarrod crouched down to blow it into life. 'We're lovers, sure, and he's a friend. Very funny and bright,' she said as the sparks leapt into flames. 'There wasn't any talk of suiting.'

Jarrod reached for more fuel. 'I see.'

'It wasn't like what you and I had ... have?'

'You mean, like you and I and Liam had?'

Rosette lifted her head. 'Jarrod, can you let that go too? That was years ago.' She wrinkled her brow. 'How is Liam? Did he ...'

'Liam's fine,' Jarrod snapped.

'Working for your pa?'

'Yes.'

'Family yet?'

'No.'

She studied Jarrod's face. 'What's wrong?'

'There's always a triangle with you, Rosette. Always you, me and something, or somebody, else.'

A smile curled her lip. 'It's only you tonight.'

Jarrod stared at her, shaking his head and relaxing his shoulders. 'So I guess I'd better enjoy it while I can,' he laughed.

'Should be delightful, as long as it doesn't rain.' She looked at the starless sky.

I'd be more worried about the mountain lions than the rain.

'What mountain lions?' Both Jarrod and Rosette spoke at once, their heads turning to Drayco.

The ones over the next ridge that are coming this way.

Rosette was awakened in the deepest part of the night by a throaty roar. It echoed around the peaks. Within ten breaths, it was answered by two others. They sounded more like bears than mountain lions and she shivered under the furs.

'Can't sleep?' Jarrod rolled over to face her.

The clouds parted and she could see his eyes sparkling, black pools in the moonlight.

'I'm scared.'

'You're safe with me.'

'It's not that kind of fear.'

'Would you like me to distract you?'

'Again?'

'Why not?'

'Because you need your strength tomorrow and so do I. We don't know what's ahead.'

'I've a pretty good idea.'

'You do?'

'I had a long talk with An' Lawrence — I get along better with him than I did with John'ra.'

'I wish I could say the same.' She pulled him close. 'So what's ahead?'

'Box canyons, lava fields.'

'Lava fields?'

'Miles of obsidian, sharp as glass.'

'You didn't mention this when we were discussing my horse's loose shoe.'

'I didn't want to alarm you.'

'And now you do?'

He tightened his arms around her. 'We'll get through.'

'And then? What's after the box canyons and lava?'

'The land fans out into towns and valleys. We have to cross those before we finally reach the seaport of Morzone, if we're lucky.'

'And if we aren't lucky?'

'We wander around in these arroyos for days until the horses drop dead and the bears eat us.'

She didn't reply for the longest time. 'I thought they sounded more like bears too.'

They both laughed and she felt Jarrod's hand run down her back, a delightful sensation.

'Are you going to keep me up all night?' she asked.

'Is that an invitation?' Jarrod found her lips and kissed her, making her purr with delight. 'I've missed you, Rosette.'

'Me too.'

She woke with a start just before dawn. Drayco was growling, and Jarrod was on his feet, doing up his pants.

Maudi! Make the fire big, her familiar roared in her mind.

'What's happening?'

Bears. Three or four. Very close. Mind the horses don't bolt.

Rosette sprang out of the covers and started snapping thin branches in two. She and Jarrod worked side by side, propping sticks together over the coals like a tent, fanning the flames to life. They hopped about, scrambling into their clothes and lacing up their boots.

'I thought you said the mountain lions were all we should worry about,' she whispered to Drayco.

It's bears now.

'What do we do?'

Keep the fire big while you pack up, then we get out of here and hope they don't track us.

Rosette looked at Jarrod. 'Did you hear that?'

'I did. Not encouraging.'

You could leave them some food, Maudi. That would slow them down.

'What do you mean?'

Bury the pig bones, hide some bread and cheese. They might spend hours sniffing it out. It would give us time to get away.

'Drayco says if we bury ...'

'I got it.' Jarrod was already piling rocks over the pig carcass. 'Tack up the horses.'

By noon, she wasn't thinking about bears any more. She was doing all she could to find a way up and out of the endless gullies, ravines and canyons that riddled the foothills of the Prieta range. Drayco was leading, grumbling about the terrain, the snow and the lack of prey. As they came to the top of a particularly steep precipice, he stopped.

Maudi, finally some good news.

She caught up with him, bringing her horse to a halt. 'Jarrod. Look at this!'

Jarrod whistled long and low. 'So you found the lava fields. Well done.'

She scanned the horizon. 'I can see all the way to the coast. That's Morzone,' she pointed. The seaport was a hazy grey smudge on the horizon. 'It's still a good two days' ride though.'

'Walk is more like it. We still have to get across that!' He indicated the dull black expanse that lay before them.

'And my horse is lame already.'

Are you two going to speculate all day or actually go down there?

Rosette roughed Drayco's neck before moving on. *I'm looking forward to getting off this hillside too, Dray.* She sighed, relishing the thought of a hot bath and a full night's sleep in a proper bed between clean sheets.

Nell leaned back in the saddle, her shoulders pressing into An' Lawrence. He groaned. It was a lengthy descent into Treeon and no-one had spoken since they'd spotted the temple valley.

Exhausted from the hard ride of the past two days, Nell concentrated on getting them down the zigzag road without stumbling. An' Lawrence clutched Scylla, keeping her steady between them. The feline was either asleep or unconscious, Nell wasn't sure which. The only reassurance was the steady pulse of her femoral artery, palpable in the deep fur on the inside of her thigh, and her regular breathing.

Nell came alongside Clay, who moved his horse aside. Diablai was suddenly anxious to get home. His neck arched and his long black mane rippled with each stride, a contrast to the lethargy of Clay's mount. The bard didn't look much better. His skin was white, his body slumped in the saddle. His usually buoyant ringlets were lank and dull. Tear stains streaked his face. He hadn't bothered to wash.

Nell sighed. 'How are you holding up?' she asked.

Clay looked at her for a moment, his eyes welling, tears spilling down his face. He shook his head and stared down at the reins held loosely in his hands.

'They've spotted us,' Zero said, riding up between them.

'So it seems.' Nell saw the guards, still small in the distance, gathered by the entrance to the temple valley.

'They'll need to send scouts. Check on the Lupins,' An' Lawrence said. 'Zero, go down ahead and see to it. We're right behind.'

Zero urged his mount forward.

'Clay, go with him and find the healer. I want Scylla seen to immediately.'

Clay urged his horse forward into a jog. He didn't look back.

Nell watched them trot down the road, her concern over the deception lessening. She hadn't counted on the bard's morbidity, but it was so genuine and infectious she almost felt that her daughter really was dead. She sent a silent blessing towards Rosette and Jarrod, wishing them safe crossing to the islands before shielding her thoughts. In the private depths of her mind, though, she pondered.

What was Rowan really brewing with La Makee? She didn't trust either of them, especially after meeting Clay. Red hair was rare. If he'd been the one who had alarmed Jarrod in Lividica, the Sword Master was probably not telling her the whole truth. She knew Makee certainly wasn't. That was expected, but the Sword Master's deception rankled her.

'I'm going to leave you rather quickly, Rowan,' she said, leaning back towards him when the others had disappeared.

'Stay,' he whispered, squeezing her waist, his lips brushing her ear.

'I'm heading back to Dumarka.'

'Don't trick me. You're going to follow them. I know it and I'm coming with you.'

She paused for a moment before shaking her head. 'Rowan, I hate to be the bearer of bad news, but you can't.'

'Why not?'

'Think. How would it look?'

'It would look like I was taking a long and well-deserved break with an old friend.'

'It would look like you were going with me to find

Rosette. You think Makee wouldn't have you traced?'

'Not if I ...'

'Not if you what? Besides, your head's still not right. I can see it in your eyes. You can barely ride.'

'I'm riding now.'

'No ... *I'm* riding, you're clinging. You'd fall in a second if I wasn't here. You have a concussion the size of the Dumar Gorge and a fever that's kept me warm in the snow for the last four nights, though you've hidden that well. The only place you're going is to the healer, right alongside Scylla, and then to bed. How you could even think of her travelling now is beyond me.'

'I was feeling much better before. I'm just tired.'

'You were better before because Rosette was boosting you with magic. She's a very forgiving daughter.'

'Like her mother?' His head rolled to one side and he looked about to faint. Nell whipped her arm around behind her back to keep him upright. 'Not quite,' she said, her jaw tight.

The sound of horses brought her head up.

'No more talk. If you're too weak to shield your mind, let me know.'

'What would you do?'

'I've a little spell that'll leave you unconscious for days.'

'No thanks. I can manage.'

'I'm serious, Rowan. You spill the truth and you'll wish you were on another world.'

He patted her leg. 'I'm fine.'

Three scouts — two women and a man — galloped past, heading out of the valley. They saluted An' Lawrence as they whisked by. Nell knew they were off to look for Lupins that they were never going to find.

She urged Diablai forward. 'Hang onto me, and keep that mind-shield up.'

An' Lawrence was silent. Whatever he was thinking was well contained.

There was help at the gate. Strong arms reached up for Scylla, lifting her down and taking her and An' Lawrence to the healer's rooms.

A young woman came and took Diablai's reins. 'La Makee is waiting for you, Mistress Nellion,' she said, 'she's in the ...'

'I know where she is, thank you very much.' Nell swung her leg over Diablai's neck and leapt to the ground.

'Check his feet carefully, please, and go slow with the water,' she ordered, stroking the smooth black neck. 'He's had a long workout.'

She watched as Diablai was led away towards the barn, gathering her thoughts before facing Makee.

'Back so soon?'

She swung around to find La Makee at her side, materialising from nowhere.

'You're getting good at that,' Nell smiled.

'Years of practice.' Makee looked her up and down. 'Hard ride?'

'You could say so.'

'Rosette?'

Nell's face changed, her hands trembling slightly. Tears welled up in her eyes, but she let none escape. She shook her head slowly from side to side.

'A shame,' Makee responded, her voice softening momentarily. 'It is hard to lose a student, such a good one at that.'

Nell flicked the moisture from her face, her shoulders squaring. 'I wouldn't have lost her if you and An' Lawrence hadn't concocted such a ridiculous journey. What were you thinking?' She glared at the woman. 'What was he thinking?' she added under her breath.

'He was thinking about the good of Treeon, no doubt.' Makee matched her stance. 'But that's not something you'd understand, is it?'

Nell narrowed her eyes. 'Perhaps I understand better than you, High Priestess.'

Makee took a step forward and lowered her voice. 'Really? Did she acquire the ...'

Nell raised her hand, blocking any further words. 'Not here.'

They headed for the main temple, like warriors readying to spar. Their conversation remained light, though, a show for the many watching eyes.

'You'll stay the night, won't you?' Makee asked, her voice rising sweetly into the courtyard as they passed the students and mentors gathered there. 'Visit the pools? Give a talk?'

'Of course,' Nell smiled. 'I'd be delighted.'

'She didn't buy it,' An' Lawrence said, grimacing when he caught the look in Makee's eyes. He sat up, propping his back with pillows.

'Why not?' Makee tapped her fingers on the bedside table. 'She has no reason to suspect.'

'Really? Nellion is not as trusting as you think.'

'She wants something from you,' Makee said, her brow narrowing.

'What do you mean?'

'Any fool can sense it.'

'What if you aren't a fool?'

Makee eyed him closely, shifting from the chair onto the bed. She sat upright, tucking both her feet under her, leaning towards his face.

'Is there something you've left out, Rowan? Something you aren't telling me?'

An' Lawrence held firmly to his mind-shield, and with good reason. They were plotting their next move, but there was much he wasn't telling her — had no intention of telling her — and he wasn't about to let her sense it. If La Makee knew that Rosette still lived, and that she was his daughter to boot, his plans would tumble.

'I think I know where Nell's going, though,' he said, looking into the fire to avoid her eyes.

'Where?'

'Rahana Iti.'

'What's she up to?' Makee frowned. 'Island magic?'

'I don't know, but she didn't want me to be a part of it.'

'Doesn't make sense. She wants you with her.'

'You sound so certain.'

'I am.'

'If that's true, she resisted her desires, Makee. I asked if I could come.'

'And?'

'She turned me down flat.'

'Bruised ego, Sword Master?'

An' Lawrence didn't answer. Scylla was off the bed now, stretched out on the floor in front of the hearth.

Careful, the feline warned him. *She's suspicious. Thinks something's up, but can't spot it for looking. She's going to ask you about Rosette. I'd create a diversion, but she'd know it was a sham. She's pretty sharp. Mind your words if you don't want to tell her the truth.*

Thanks, beautiful. I will.

He had wanted to sit by the fire with Scylla and rough her neck. Their close call on the mountain made him realise his vulnerability. A life without Scylla would be unbearable. He shut out the emerging feelings as they began to rise. Then he thought for a moment of

Rosette and her mother before slamming the door on that also. He rubbed the back of his neck, focusing his mind.

'Tell me again how you managed to get the vial out of Kreshkali's grasp, but not Rosette?' Makee scanned his face.

'Drayco, her familiar ...'

'I know the black temple cat, Rowan. Just tell me what happened.'

Sweat started to bead on his forehead. He hoped she would think it was from his fever and not his lies. 'Drayco brought the vial to us. He dropped it at our feet before collapsing. He died shortly after, though Nell tried to revive him. It must have been Rosette's final request, to bring us the vial, otherwise he would never have left her side.' He buried his face in his hands. 'The Lupins would have consumed her.'

Makee put her hand on his shoulder. 'So you never actually saw her body?'

'We've been over this, Makee.' An' Lawrence sighed as he looked up. 'If you doubt me, march your glorious arse up to Los Loma and ask Kreshkali yourself what happened. They gave their lives — Rosette and her familiar — so we could gain the spell. The vial isn't what you hoped it would be, but Rosette and Drayco were, I promise.'

'You grieve for her, that's understandable.'

'Of course I do. She was my newest apprentice. Strong arm, agile body, great magic. I had high hopes.'

'Scylla doesn't seem too upset.'

He stuck his finger in his ear and gave it a vigorous scratch. 'What?'

'She was getting close with Rosette's big black. I thought they might mate.'

Like that would be any of her concern. Scylla's whiskers twitched.

'It would've been a real boon for Treeon,' Makee continued. 'A nice batch of cubs — familiars for our high-ranking adepts.'

She was always jealous that you and I have each other. Watch out. Mulengro's in the room.

An' Lawrence stole a glance at the door. Scylla was sensitive to mulengro, in any of its forms. All animals were. They could see it coming in a night fog, and he'd always trusted that. Of course, he'd opened the door with his own lies. He'd been deceitful, still was, and there was nothing he could do about it until he left Treeon, not without betraying Rosette and Nell. This whole past year had been food for Mulengro. He accepted that, straightening his spine.

'The temple cats don't choose by rank, if they choose at all.' He turned to look at Makee. 'You know they are rare familiars.'

'They often choose by bloodline, though, An' Lawrence. I find it quite curious that both you and Rosette have, or had, such bonds. Don't you?'

'Pardon?'

'I think you're hiding something.'

A chill wind blew through the door, fluttering the candles and making them both shiver.

He looked her straight in the eye. 'I'm not hiding from you, Makee.'

She paused for a moment, raising an eyebrow. 'That's not quite the same thing, is it?'

'You know what I mean.'

'I believe you do.'

Neither spoke for a while. The air, fragrant with camphor and sage, grew thick.

'How soon can you ride?'

An' Lawrence stretched his neck from side to side, exhaling long and slow. 'As soon as Scylla's fully recovered. A week. Maybe less.'

'I want you to follow her, as soon as you're able. She flew north, we know that much. I want you to pick up her trail and see what she's doing. Get to the islands, if that's where she's going. We need to keep a close watch on that witch.'

'If you think that's best.' He disguised his exuberance. This was exactly what he wanted but couldn't have asked for.

'I'd like to see you on your way before the new moon.'

'No problem. And you? What will you do?'

'I'm going to see what's in the vial so I can work out where the rest of the spell is. If all the Lupins in Los Loma were after you, then Kreshkali doesn't have it.'

'You suspect Nell?'

'Don't you?'

He looked into her brilliant green eyes. 'I do.'

'Then go get her.'

Rosette and Jarrod led the horses into Morzone, their rhythmic hoofbeats punctuated by the severe hobble of the mountain horse; her unshod hoof had cracked right to the quick and she limped with each step as if the leg was broken.

'Farrier first?' Rosette asked.

'Definitely. We need to burn the top of those cracks before they go any higher.'

'Can she be re-shod?'

Jarrod bent down as they walked, studying the damaged hoof. 'I think so. There's enough wall left on the sides, in places anyway.'

'We can't leave her here.'

He nodded. 'She wears a Treeon brand and it'll be as clear as your tattoos when she sheds in the spring — might as well be sending a letter to Makee saying, *Rosette's alive and she went this way.*'

'Is that who we're running from? Makee?'

Jarrod kept his eyes on the lame horse. 'According to Nell.'

'In any case,' Rosette said, 'we're taking her with us. We'd never sell her lame.' She shielded her eyes and scanned the long thoroughfare. 'Do you see a blacksmith's shingle?'

He pointed into the distance at a barn with wide-open double doors and smoke coming from a chimney in the high rooftop. 'That looks like one.'

She squinted. 'Demons, I'd forgotten how good your eyesight is.'

'Can't you see it?'

'I can now,' she said.

'We'll need to find the docks and book our passage as well.'

'I can smell the docks from here.' She wrinkled her nose. 'Reminds me of home. Doesn't it you?'

He nodded, quickening the pace.

Rosette ignored the stares from the early-morning shopkeepers and the townsfolk hurrying up and down the street. Drayco was the main attraction, an oddity it seemed. A familiar walking at her side marked her as a witch, and not everyone — or every town — was comfortable with that. She hoped that in Morzone it would work to their advantage and not against, but that was looking like a slim chance already.

'Wait out here in the sun,' she suggested to her temple cat when they reached the farrier's barn. 'If you come in with us, it could cause a commotion.'

The people out here are more uncomfortable than the beasts in the barn.

'I know. We won't be long.'

After giving their horses a thorough grooming and discussing treatment for the lame one, Jarrod and

Rosette returned to find Drayco hadn't moved. His spine was stiff and his tail lashed back and forth.

'What is it, Dray?' Rosette asked, squatting beside him, stroking his neck.

They're searching for us.

'Who?'

I don't know, but they search and I don't like it.

'Are they here in Morzone?'

Not yet. They're on their way, riding fast.

Rosette looked to Jarrod. 'We'll have to keep moving.'

'So much for the relaxing night in a soft bed we've been talking about.' He kicked at the dust.

'Judging by the stares we're getting, it's for the best anyway. The trick will be to book passage to the islands without anyone saying where we've gone.'

'Quite a trick.'

'I could weave a glamour for myself, but not all three of us.'

Jarrod was about to respond but closed his mouth instead. The three of them sat in a row against the barn sharing dried meat and fruit, the last of the rations from their packs. The sound of the blacksmith's hammer rang clear in the background, pounding iron into shape.

'How far is it across the straits to Rahana Iti?' Jarrod asked as he took a drink from their water-skin.

'Two days if the Emerald Seas are calm.'

'And if they're not?'

'However long it takes for them to calm down. No ship will set sail to the west if there's more than a ripple of waves.'

'Rough crossing?'

'You could say that.'

'It's quiet enough today. I'll go organise it.'

'Sounds grand,' Rosette said, frowning.

'You all right?'

'I wanted a hot bath, is all.' She reached into her coat pocket and fished out her purse, handing Jarrod eight gold coins.

'That's more than enough,' he said.

'You'll need a few extra.'

'For?'

'Convincing the captain that we need privacy.'

'Rosette, if these ships are anything like the clippers in Lividica, there'll be dozens of people on deck, and below. We won't be able to ...'

'Not that kind of privacy, Jarrod!' she laughed, pulling him to her for a kiss. She released him, laughing again at the look on his face. 'The coin is to buy their silence in case anyone asks questions.'

He stared at her.

'It's a bribe,' she added.

He straightened, dusting off his pants. 'I get it. I won't be long.'

Gaela and Earth

Chapter 18

The ship beat against the storm, the backlash reverberating through the hull and up the masts. Waves crashed against the bow in relentless succession, each one threatening to knock the vessel to splinters. Rosette's stomach hit her throat with every lift, her spine jarring as they slapped back down again. She dug her fingers into the railing. It'd been this way for three days and she didn't think she could take much more.

'Can't you do anything?' Jarrod begged before dry-heaving over the edge.

Rosette joined him, her stomach now an empty sack.

She had never experienced such wretchedness. Her previous crossings of the straits had been like a day sail in Lister Bay: smooth, sweet and glassy. Now the swell was overhead, the water black with geyser-like whitecaps. The vessel tossed like a toy in a sloshing bucket and groaned under the force of the wind. Wet ropes hung in loops, whipping and slapping against the boom, making pinging sounds that kept time with the rocking. All but the jib was down as they rose and fell, rose and fell, hour after hour.

'What would you like me to do?' she screamed over the maelstrom.

'You're a witch. Talk to the sea,' Jarrod shouted into her ear. 'Coax it a little. Make it lie down and go to sleep!'

Rosette lifted an eyebrow. 'Do you really think she'll listen?'

'Worth a try.' He heaved over the side again.

'I don't know,' she said. 'It feels uncanny to me.'

Rosette swallowed against the bile in her throat and gripped the railing tight; her legs braced wide, her knees absorbing the plunge of each hammering drop. Closing her eyes, she raised her hand and slowly filled her body with a charge of energy. She called to the elements of Air and Water, imploring them to mellow. Light flew from her fingertips as she let go of the railing.

Thunder rumbled overhead. Lightning cracked in her direction. It felt malevolent, ripping across the sky like a predator, striking nearer and nearer as the craft tossed uncontrollably. The clouds billowed as high as mountains, shooting more shafts of lightning that split the sky in two. The rain redoubled its intensity with stinging pellets of ice.

'Stop!' Jarrod yelled.

'What?' She could barely hear him over the storm.

'You're making it worse,' Jarrod yelled again, wrapping his arm around her as a wave broke over the deck. 'We need to get below. We'll be drowned out here.'

'Aggravation before amelioration,' she replied, her voice hoarse from yelling. She held onto him with one hand and the railing with the other. Wave after wave washed over the deck, ripping at her legs until they slipped out from under her.

'There is no amelioration! We have to get below. Now!' Jarrod shouted.

Come, Maudi. To the hatch.

Rosette squinted, squeezing the salt water out of her eyes. Another wave came when they were halfway to safety. Rosette looked up to see a wall of water come plummeting down towards them. She opened her mouth to scream before everything went black.

'Rosette, wake up!' Jarrod slapped her face again.

She fluttered her lids, wincing at the light. 'What happened?' she groaned, her throat raw.

'You were knocked out. Can you walk?'

Rain poured onto her face, the deck rocking violently beneath her. 'I'm all right,' she spluttered.

Jarrod pulled her up and they staggered to the galley hatch.

'We've got to get to the horses. Untie them. They could drown,' he shouted above the roar of the waves.

Rosette lifted the hatch door and slid down the steps with Jarrod right behind her. Drayco was at her side, all four legs braced.

'Get the lantern,' Jarrod said, pointing to the dim light hanging from a beam.

She slid to the galley table, waiting for the boat to rock the other way before handing the lantern across to Jarrod. He had the lower hatch door open and was peering into the dark.

They startled as a loud crack split the sky above them. A bulge in the side of the galley splintered and a rush of water poured in. They were ankle deep in moments.

'The horses!' Jarrod said.

'They'll be terrified!' Rosette started to back down the ladder. 'I can calm them.'

Perhaps you can calm us all. Drayco's voice cut through her thoughts like a knife, his agitation tactile.

Jarrod grimaced, raising the light above his head. They shimmied down the ladder and into the cargo hold. Drayco kept behind Rosette, springing off the ladder and landing hard as the boat rocked up to meet him, his paws splashing in the rising water.

The mountain horse was down, struggling. She'd slipped and couldn't rise. The boat was rocking wildly and Rosette lurched to the stalls. She thought the mountain horse had damaged a leg, but couldn't tell for all the thrashing. The copper-red mare stood in a wide stance, her head up, eyes rolled back, screaming as Jarrod approached.

'I won't lie to you, Wren. We're probably all going for a swim, and soon.'

If we don't drown in this hole first. Drayco was perched atop a stack of chests lashed to the far wall, his claws extended to the full, sinking deep into the thick netting that held the cargo in place. *Maudi, I hate this place. Get us out of here!*

Rosette reached her hands out to both horses and sent energy, calm and strengthening. She filled the room with it but was careful to keep it in the hold. It was not unlike the spell she'd directed at the storm, and that had certainly backfired. She didn't want to make matters worse.

How can things get worse? Water's rising! Drayco's words were desperate, but his tone was already softer. The calming spell was working on them all. The horses settled immediately, enough for Jarrod to slip into their stalls and untie them and help the mountain horse to stand. Her legs were fine — no worse for the fall — though she still favoured the newly shod hoof.

'I hope you know how to swim,' Rosette whispered in her ear while Jarrod unlatched the stall doors, tying them open.

The boat suddenly listed and Rosette found herself sliding away from Jarrod, who clung tightly to the rails. The horses hadn't budged; they braced themselves against the rush of water churning around their legs.

Boards snapped, a deafening sound, and the ocean rushed in. The speed of it tore the lantern from Jarrod's hand, and it swirled like a buoy in a whirlpool until it winked out.

'Drayco!' Rosette screamed until she felt his wet fur press into her face. He swam beside her, dog-paddling to keep his head above water. Rosette closed her eyes against the dark and sent a bolt of energy to all of them: the horses, Jarrod, herself, Drayco, the others on board. She could hear nothing but the surge of water and the terrible snap and grind of wood being wrenched apart. It was like a sea monster was chewing them up and spitting out the splinters. Without warning, the wall beside her vanished. The boat flipped over and more water sucked in.

She felt Jarrod's hand grip hers for a second before it was gone.

'We're capsizing,' he screamed above the flood. 'Take a breath!'

Rosette gulped in air as her head went under.

Drayco, hold your breath. Don't let it go until we are on the surface.

And where would the surface be, Maudi?

I don't know yet. Just paddle.

The water was surprisingly warm. Chunks of wood smacked her arms and legs, but it seemed like slow motion. She let the water drag her down and out, the torrent freeing her from the collapsing hold. When she opened her eyes underwater, all was dark and still except for a dull light to the side. She let out a few bubbles of air and followed them, realising that 'to the side' was actually up.

This way, Drayco. Stick with me. She swam for that dull light, calling to Drayco in her mind, calling to Jarrod and the horses, following the bubbles up.

Her lungs burned for air. She swallowed against the urge to breathe and kicked as hard as she could. Her arms had begun to tingle by the time she pulled herself to the surface. When her head burst through the choppy swell, she sucked air into her lungs. She heard gasps beside her and yelled between breaths: 'Drayco! Jarrod!'

I have him, Maudi. He's hit his head. Help me.

The light around her was sufficient to see, but the swell was so high that she could only glimpse them for mere seconds before she was again surrounded by the heaving wall of water.

'I'm coming!' she screamed above the wind. *Don't let him go!* She sent the mind message when the swell washed over her face.

Rosette swam in their direction until she bumped into a floating plank — a door that had been ripped in two. Throwing an arm over it, she kicked harder. Drayco, his mouth enclosed around the front of Jarrod's coat, hauled him right up to her and Rosette dragged him the rest of the way onto the float. He coughed and spat, clinging to the wood.

Drayco leapt up onto the raft and shook himself, riding it like a Rahana Iti islander in the surf. Rosette trod water beside them.

'Can you see anyone else, Dray? Any crew? Survivors?'

No people.

'Oh, deep Sednara, goddess of the sea, how have we offended you?'

I can see the horses. They're heading southeast.

'Follow them,' Jarrod wheezed. 'They'll sense land if any of us can.'

I want to go that way too, Maudi.
Keep them in sight for me, Dray.

Rosette pushed the board in front of her and kicked. The wind was behind, the current strong in their favour. As she followed the horses, the tips of the masts went under, the sea sucking the rest of the vessel down. When it disappeared, the swell dropped. The wind abated and in minutes, the sea was calm.

'We paid our price, it seems.'

It's too high, Maudi. I don't like it, and I don't want to go on boats any more.

Nell flew west, straight into the storm. She planned to send word to Maka'ra and cross the straits on the first available boat. It was too long a distance for her to stay in falcon form. She didn't want to risk it.

Morzone was battened down when she arrived, the harbour deserted. She morphed into her human form and walked the docks, searching for someone to question, but she found no-one about. The wind whipped away the click of her boot-heels on the wooden planking along with the sound of her voice as she called over the moorings.

After checking every berth she stood in the driving rain, looking towards the town. Where would the captains be? She smiled as she spotted a shingle swinging madly. On it was displayed a mug of frothy beer, rainwater making it glisten in the pale light. She pulled her hood down and waded through the storm, hunched against the gale.

The pub was full, lively and warm with the smell of clean straw, beer and spiced wine. She thought it a massive improvement on similar establishments in Corsanon. Light glowed from colourful lanterns overhead and conversation buzzed. No-one seemed to notice her entrance until she pushed her hood back and took off her long black coat, shaking it by the door.

Heads turned as she stepped towards the bar. She smiled inwardly, keeping her face a mask. She didn't have to put on a glamour. Everything about Nellion Paree said *High Priestess*, if she allowed it. Her hair fell in damp tangles to her waist and her hazel eyes — matching the colour of the ocean jasper at her neck — opened wide as she leaned against the bar. She lifted her hand to catch the barmaid's attention and her sleeve fell back to her elbow revealing the tree-and-entwining-snake tattoo of Treeon Temple. She wanted it to be seen. No-one in their free mind would lie to a Treeon witch.

'Spiced wine, please,' she smiled, her face seductive in the soft light.

'Yes, Mistress.' The barmaid nodded with confidence, though her hands shook when she filled the mug.

Nell placed a silver coin on the counter and headed for a table clearly seated with ships' captains. Their low conversation came to an abrupt halt as she approached.

'May I join you?' she asked, her question bringing the men's eyes up.

They stared at her, their gazes carefully couched to give no offence. The man nearest her rose from his seat and pulled a chair from the table behind him, dragging it across the floor to her.

'Aye, milady. It'd be our pleasure.' His face was tense, as if it was anything but his pleasure for her to join them. 'How can we serve the Temple of Treeon?' he added.

'What's your name?' Nell asked, giving him the faintest nod.

'Redrick, Mistress. Captain Jack Redrick.'

'Pleased to meet you, Captain Redrick. You can serve Treeon by telling me if a young woman — a witch —

her companion, her familiar and their horses have been here seeking passage across the strait, possibly to the Isles of Landercan?' She took a sip of her mulled wine. 'Or Rahana Iti?'

After a lengthy silence, she encouraged him with a smile. 'Did you see them, Captain Redrick?'

The men averted their eyes, some shaking their heads. The ones that looked down at their mugs had clearly seen Rosette. Most likely they'd been instructed, or paid, to say nothing. They were trapped. On the one side was Rosette, a witch who had requested their silence — not someone they'd care to cross. On the other was this High Priestess from Treeon Temple, a woman who would know if they lied, possibly turning them into cockroaches if they did.

Finally, the nearest man removed his cap and scratched his bald head. 'Aye, milady, I've seen 'em. I was paid by the lad to keep my mouth shut, but I figure it's one of them moot points by now. They left the harbour three nights ago. The sea was calm then, not a ripple or a foul breeze. They'd be smack in the middle of this uncanny storm ... and that's not all.'

'Please go on.' Nell watched him draw in a deep breath.

'You be the second mistress of Treeon who's asked after them.'

Nell gave a light, quizzical look. 'Someone from Treeon came before me? When?'

'Just before the storm struck.'

'Who was she?'

'Well now, she didn't offer her name, as is natural with your kind, meaning no disrespect.'

'None taken.'

There was no point asking what she looked like — it could only be La Makee, and she could take on any glamour she chose, appearing to be any age, any form.

I should have known she'd suspect. 'Just the priestess?' she asked aloud.

'No — she had a couple o' warriors with her.'

'And she was asking after my friends as well?'

'In part. They were looking for a young witch and that massive black cat.'

'What'd you tell her?'

'Nothing, milady. But they're likely to be around still, I'm thinkin'. Holed up somewhere against the storm.'

'You're most honourable, Captain.'

'Like I said, it matters little now.'

'How's that?'

He didn't answer.

'Your young witch and her company were on board the *Valiant*,' another man ventured, those around him nodding their heads.

'The *Valiant*?' Nell lifted her eyebrow.

'Aye, milady. A fine ship as there ever was, but no vessel of her make could withstand such a storm, is what I think. She'd be at the bottom of green Sednara 'bout now.'

Nell pressed her lips together and nodded before draining her mug and setting it on the table. The captains rose as she stood, all bowing their heads.

'Blessings be on you and your seafaring craft,' she said. 'And blessings to you, Captain Redrick.'

'Thank you, milady,' they all said without looking up.

The meeting had gone better than expected for them. They'd received a blessing and weren't turned into cockroaches. Nell walked to the door and pulled on her coat, heading back out into the storm. She made her way, head bent low, to the edge of Morzone where she absorbed her glamour and shifted.

The raptor shrieked with frustration, her emotions no less intense in the body of the black falcon than in her human heart. She circled with the wind, higher and higher, until she broke through above the storm. She would not despair. She would not be beaten. She *knew* Rosette was alive and ... well, she'd fix Makee, if someone hadn't gotten to her first.

Kreshkali slammed back through the portal gasping for breath. The effect on her was definitely getting worse.

'Back off!' she growled at the Entity between fits of coughing, wrapping her arms around her belly.

The portal rippled and went smooth.

Kreshkali wiped her mouth and smiled. She had a week's supply of fresh water, bundles of herbs and roots, a new grimoire bound in red leather and edged with gold, and a Lemur Raven in an iron cage. The bird's feathers were ruffled, its talons curled tightly around the wooden perch, its mouth gaping open, gasping for air, and tears running from its yellow eyes.

'Bit acrid for you, La Makee?' Kreshkali asked, peering in between the bars.

The bird extended its wings and let out a raspy caw.

Kreshkali laughed, throwing back her head. 'Welcome to my world.'

She gave the Entity a parting glare before picking up the waterbags, bundles and cage. The raven cawed again.

'You're coming with me, High Priestess. I have something to show you.'

Once home, Kreshkali opened the cage and the raven hopped out, morphing into human form, her raucous caw turning into a woman's scream.

'Demon bitch, what are you thinking! You can't waltz into my temple and snatch me to your ...' She looked around the apartment, her face turning red. 'Wherever the spirits this place is. How dare you! How ...'

Kreshkali waved her towards the table, ignoring the ranting. 'Sit down, Makee. Have a cup of tea, and I'll tell you exactly how I dare.'

La Makee sniffed and sneezed and rubbed her eyes. Her nose was running and her breathing uneven. Kreshkali sat for some time without speaking, deep in thought. They'd just returned from quite a tour, and Kreshkali suspected Makee was in severe shock. It was hard to imagine such a hell could exist on any world, until you stepped into it.

'Don't snivel, I'm trying to think,' Kreshkali said, tossing her a roll of toilet paper.

Makee fingered it, her brows furrowing.

'Oh, for fuck's sake! Like this.' Kreshkali snatched back the roll, unwound a length and blew her nose. 'Get the idea?'

Makee nodded, doing the same. 'So what's this place?' she asked.

'Like I said, it's my world.'

'Does it have a name?'

'Earth.'

Makee coughed. 'It's charming.' She glared across the table. 'Why am I here?'

'A few reasons. Mainly, I wanted to show you what can happen to a world when an Entity is sundered and a worm gets loose — when the firewall breaks down and a few narrow-minded, power-seeking individuals take control. I thought it would be the most expedient way to stop your incessant meddling on Gaela.'

'What makes you think I'm meddling?'

Kreshkali sneered. 'Oh come on, Makee. It was *you* working with the Corsanon fools when they breached the portal and ruptured that Entity. It was you all along, goading the high council. You unleashed quite a spell.'

'What spell are you talking about?'

'Makee, you can hide under your pretence of naivety or you can pay attention and learn something. What's it going to be?'

Makee snarled. 'Do I have a choice?'

'Not really. I'm going to let you live here — just as I do — until you decide.'

'Decide what?'

'Whose side you're on.'

Makee didn't respond. She looked out the window at the murk that seemed to pass for daylight. When she turned back she said, 'The Entity's disintegrating.'

'Tell me something I don't know.'

'This world looks about to expire also ... can't imagine why.' She blew her nose again. 'How do you live in this poisonous brick box?'

'They're called *apartments*.'

'Call it what you like,' she said. 'It's a deathtrap.'

'Makee, concentrate. That Entity guarding the portal we came through wants out before this world collapses. It's already split apart.'

'How's that?'

'It's the same Entity as the one at the portal in Corsanon ... don't you get it? It's all that's left on this side of the corridor. The other half has been roaming about the rubble of Corsanon ever since you lot got it into your small minds to try travelling the many-worlds!'

'What's done is done,' Makee spat. 'What do you want?'

'I want this world to survive, and so do you.'

'That's where you're wrong. I don't care.'

'Really? And would you say that if you knew all the many-worlds were linked?'

'Linked?'

'Connected. Related. What happens to one, happens to them all. There is no separation.'

'I find that hard to believe.'

'You need to try harder.' Kreshkali stared at her contemporary, shaking her head. 'Earth was first. Everything branches from here. Earth must survive or they will all collapse. And that is looking more and more likely unless the Entity is healed, for starters. I can't let what's infecting Earth pass into the other worlds.'

'How many others?'

'Do you understand the concept of infinity?'

Makee's eyes widened.

'Meanwhile, the portal's sucking the life out of me each time I pass.'

'Because?'

'Because it wants out, and if it goes ...'

'That would collapse more than just this world, wouldn't it?'

'So it's starting to register?'

Makee nodded.

'That's not the only problem, though.'

'There's more?'

'The witch-trackers.'

'The what?'

'ASSIST, an organisation of scientists,' Kreshkali said, reconsidering after seeing the look on Makee's face. 'It's like a dominant temple with advanced magic and an unwavering hatred of witches.'

'How can you have advanced magic and hate witches?'

'I know, but you can, and they're tracking me, day and night.'

'On Earth?'

Kreshkali shook her head. 'They've found their way to Gaela.'

Makee narrowed her brows. 'How?'

'The portals, of course.'

'And they're doing what exactly?'

'Remember the Matosh murders?'

Makee sucked in her breath. 'I thought ...'

'Oh, it was Corsanon assassins that did it, but on the trackers' order.'

'How can you know all this?'

'How do you *not*, witch?' Kreshkali scraped back her chair and turned to open a cupboard. A rolling boom of thunder shook the building and white light briefly illuminated the room. Makee winced, covering her eyes from the flash.

Kreshkali took out a packet and broke it in two, tossing half to Makee.

'What's this?'

'Dinner.'

'Consisting of ...?'

'They're called *Nutries* — a compressed cake of synthesised amino acids, long-chain fatty acids and essential ...'

Makee held her hand up, shaking her head. 'Stop. You'll ruin what little appetite I have left.'

'Suit yourself.'

Makee took a bite and grimaced.

'You get used to it,' Kreshkali said around a mouthful.

'I hope not,' she choked. 'Has it always been like this on Earth?'

'No.' Kreshkali took another bite and chewed it slowly. 'We used to eat each other.'

Makee straightened. 'I'm listening, Kali. Tell me what I can do.'

It seemed like hours before Rosette spotted land. It bobbed into view when she had all but given up. Jarrod was unconscious but breathing. Drayco stood above her, straining to keep sight of the horses and scanning endlessly for sharks. The sun was high, a searing heat in the now cloudless sky.

Jarrod still bleeds. The sea tigers will come.

'I know, Dray. I'm hoping the spell will hide us for a while longer.'

Me too. I'm really, really not liking the ocean. His tail lashed as he kept a vigil. *Maudi, the horses have reached shore. They are shaking like dogs.*

'We'll be there soon.' Rosette redoubled her efforts, kicking her legs in a smooth, even rhythm. Finally, she felt the swell roll up under her, carrying them towards the beach. When her toes touched bottom, she was flooded with relief.

It lasted only a second. Behind her, a huge wave was building up overhead and rolled straight for them.

'Jump, Drayco! Swim!' she screamed, grabbing the edge of the board tight and sucking in her breath.

The wave ripped the plank from her arms and held her under for longer than she thought she could stand. After being slapped into the sand and churned in the whitewash, Rosette staggered to her feet, gasping for air and searching for Jarrod. The board was up on the sandy beach with Jarrod next to it, coughing and struggling to get up.

She waded through the shallows just as Drayco swam to her side, taking her sleeve in his jaws and, part guiding, part dragging, pulling her onto the beach. She reached Jarrod and they clung to each other in their wet, heavy clothes before crawling away from the water. With dry sand beneath them, they collapsed.

'We did it,' Rosette said as Jarrod flopped down beside her.

We are safe on dry land, Drayco answered. He shook, arcs of water flinging from his coat, and immediately began licking his wet fur.

Rosette rolled over on her back and looked up at him. *Are you all right, Dray? You were so brave in the water.* Her arms were like dough rolled in sugar.

I am unharmed. Are you? The massive feline stood over her as he began licking her face and neck.

She laughed aloud. *Rough tongue!*

He shook again. *So, Maudi, where are we?*

I don't know and don't care. Besides, Dray, you're the geographer. Where do you reckon?

The feline sat on his haunches and lifted a paw, licking the dampness between his toes. *I've absolutely no idea, but I'm delighted we're off the sea.*

Me too, Drayco. Me too!

Chapter 19

'Get up,' Nell whispered into An' Lawrence's ear.
'Nell? Where have you been?'

She lit a small candle by his bed and pressed her finger to her lips. 'Here and there. Come on. We have to go.'

He sat up and stretched. 'It's pre-dawn.'

'And no moon. Get dressed.'

'Did you find Rosette and Jarrod? What's happened? Where are they?'

'Keep your voice down,' she said, waving her hand. 'I'll explain later. We're going for a little trip; that is, if you still want to help.'

'Of course I do. Where, though?'

She lit another candle and tossed him his clothes. 'Where's your pack?' She rummaged in the closet for his coat and found his sword by his bed.

Scylla got up and stretched. She seemed unconcerned, as if she'd been expecting this.

'How'd you get past the temple guards?'

Nell glared at him.

'Sorry I asked,' he mumbled, pulling on his pants.

'Where's Zero?' Nell asked.

'Dorms. Why?'

'We need him too.'

An' Lawrence stood, buttoning his shirt. 'Nell, what's going on?'

'You'll see.' She watched Scylla head for the door without a limp. 'How's her wound?'

'Healed.'

'And your head? Can you handle a sword?'

'Always.'

She clicked her tongue. 'Let's go.'

Rosette awoke flat on her back, squinting at the sunlight. She didn't know how long she'd lain in the sand, but her hair was dry, her eyelids were encrusted with salt crystals and her lips stung. She touched them with her fingertips and winced. Pushing up onto her elbows, she checked Jarrod. He was asleep on his side, his breath rising and falling in a slow, rhythmic motion. There was no sign of a laceration on his head. She looked at him from different angles. Judging by the sun, they'd been asleep for a few hours — not long enough for the knock on his head to heal. Where was that blood coming from? She checked his hand, the bandage torn loose from the swim. There was no sign of a wound there either, and that had been a deep gash a few days ago. She rubbed her neck, frowning.

Drayco?

Right here.

You okay?

Grand. I like it here. Warm, dry, good nap, good smells. He purred from the shady palm trees behind her, where he sat sculpture-like, eyes unblinking. *We need water, though.*

'Good idea. I'm parched.'

And sunburnt.

'Have you seen the horses?'

They headed east — looking for water too — but I think that's the long way around.

'The long way around what?' Rosette turned over on her belly to look at him.

Around the island.

'The horses made it? Did you see Wren?' Jarrod mumbled, awakened by the conversation, not quite grasping the words from Drayco's mind.

'Dray says they've gone to look for water,' Rosette replied, sitting up and brushing sand from her arms. 'The wrong way round.'

Jarrod stood and stretched, peeling off his coat and shirt. 'Wrong way around what?'

She smiled. 'The island.' Rosette pulled off her layers of clothes as well until she was down to a black cotton undershirt and leggings. She laid her things on rocks above the high-tide line to dry and turned to scan the horizon. Waves rolled in, quite gently now, in rows of foamy turquoise and white.

'Jarrod? This is strange.'

He was staring out to sea. 'I know.' He put his arm around her as she came to his side.

'Something's not right,' she said. 'The colour ...'

He didn't take his eyes off the ocean. 'I've never crossed the straits before, but ...' He pulled her close. 'There's nothing like this on the maps. The water is positively turquoise, and this island is mountainous. Huge.' He tilted his head until his nose pointed straight up and still he had to crane his neck to see the tips of the peaks. 'All the islands beyond the Emerald Straits are sand-spits, not even a foot above sea level.'

'And the water's green, not this shade of blue.'

'Where do you think we are?' Jarrod asked.

'It must be the Isles of Landercan, but I've no idea which one. Do you think it's inhabited?'

'I don't see any signs. Ask Drayco.'

I've found drinking water. Drayco sent the message from a distance away. *No other people or felines, but you'll like the spot. It's nice.*

We're coming, Dray. Exactly where is this 'nice spot' of yours?

East. The horses had it right.

How so?

They've already been.

The Sword Master awoke on a cold stone floor. He rubbed the back of his neck, trying to remember where he was and how he could have gotten here. Zero was sitting beside him, his head between his knees. They were in a dank, noisome tunnel, dark save for a small lantern perched on a box and a faint purple glow emanating from the wall. His head spun and he felt like he would be sick.

Are you here, Scylla?

She answered by pressing the top of her head into his face. *She's brought us to another world, Rowan. Not a fun trip.*

'What?'

Your Nell. She's brought us to her home, and it's not Dumarka.

'How can you be certain?'

It doesn't smell like anything in Gaela.

An' Lawrence got to his feet, hand on his sword hilt. Next to him, Zero struggled to stand.

'You all right?' he asked, helping Zero up.

'I think so. Just tell me where we are, and who that is.' Zero nodded to the woman stepping into the light.

An' Lawrence narrowed his eyes as she moved closer. She had spiky hair, a long cloak and was sorting through the things that they had brought to the portal in Gaela.

'Where's Nell?' An' Lawrence gripped Scylla's scruff, but his familiar seemed unconcerned by the stranger.

She's not the problem, Rowan.

Are you sure?

Oh yes.

'Nell had other business,' the woman said, 'but I suspect she'll be back soon.'

'And who are you?' Zero asked.

'I'm Kreshkali. Though that's not the most important question you could have asked.'

'Isn't it?'

She shrugged her shoulders. 'The "where" question would've been my first,' Kreshkali said.

An' Lawrence looked down the tunnel, and back at her.

'Not quite what you expected, is it, Sword Master?'

'I have no expectations,' he said.

'That will be an ally here, I promise.'

'Tell me, Kreshkali, is this the glamour or the real thing?'

'To be honest, I don't really know any more.'

'Care to explain?'

'I'm more than a little curious myself,' Zero said, interrupting the two. 'Where exactly are we and why?'

'It's another world, lad,' Kreshkali said.

'And I suspect, by the stench, it's not a very agreeable one,' An' Lawrence added.

'It's called *Earth*. If you think this sewer's bad, wait till you see the surface.'

'It feels like a very sick place, Kreshkali.'

'No argument there. Any more questions?' She started stacking the boxes and bundles around them.

'Why have you brought us here?' An' Lawrence let his voice boom through the sewer.

She stopped and dusted off her hands. 'To teach the sword, why else?'

'What?'

'I need your expertise, both of you. Is that so hard to understand?'

Zero's brow knitted. 'For how long?'

'As long as it takes to bring down ASSIST.'

'Bring down what?'

'The enemy.'

'And what about Rosette?' An' Lawrence asked. 'What do you want with her?'

'She's an essential component, that young witch, but she's off my radar for the moment.'

'Radar?' Zero asked. He still had his hand on the hilt of his sword.

'She's a little lost, but not for long.' Kreshkali returned to ordering the gear. 'She's going to be here shortly and then you three can pull together the ragtag rebels we've got waiting for you.'

'Pull them together for what?'

'Battle, what else?'

'Rosette's alive?' Zero asked, looking from the Sword Master to Kreshkali and back.

An' Lawrence nodded. 'Sorry I couldn't fill you in before.'

'Come on, give a hand,' Kreshkali said. 'We need to get out of here.' She slung a few net bags over her shoulder and hoisted a small crate. 'Grab the rest and follow me. I'll explain on the way.'

'The way where?'

'To my stronghold.'

Both men hesitated a moment before grabbing the waterbags and other equipment. They climbed out of the sewer, Kreshkali checking each direction before pushing the manhole all the way back. The rain poured down, its acrid odour rising from pools and rivulets. The street was dark, deserted. Only the occasional flash of lightning showed the hauntingly tall buildings, built like mason's blocks, massive on either side.

'It's clear for now,' she said. 'Follow me.' She waved them on. 'Keep your hands close to your hilts. No-one's an ally here. Remember that. And don't drink the water unless you know it's purified,' she warned.

'Why?' Zero asked.

'It's polluted. Keep the rain out of your eyes too.'

He pulled down his hood. 'Polluted?'

'Poison. Hurry up!'

Drayco's *nice spot* turned out to be magnificent falls that cascaded hundreds of feet down the side of the mountain into a crystal-clear lagoon. The sound was a pleasant drone, and the spray from the impact reflected thousands of tiny rainbows, giving the place an enchanted feel. They walked through long grass and around igneous boulders to the lapping edge of the lagoon. The ground was trampled and muddy.

'The horses were here, all right.' Jarrod pointed to the tracks left in the soft ground.

Drayco was at the water's edge, drinking daintily before going further in to lie on his belly in a clear, shallow pool. Jarrod stripped and followed the feline in, drinking deeply. He rinsed himself and Drayco free of the sea salt.

Rosette hesitated, the back of her neck prickling. She stared at the water, her brow wrinkled.

'Come on, Rosette. This is the sweetest taste in the world,' Jarrod said around deep drinks.

'We don't know what lives down there.' She took another step back.

'It's safe, I promise.'

She shook her head. 'Something's not right.'

'Come on.' He reached a hand out towards her. 'Drayco wouldn't be in it if there were river sharks. You'll feel better for it, I promise.'

'What about eels?'

'I'll let you know if I see one.'

Rosette continued to frown as she stripped and joined them. She tasted the water and drank her fill before rinsing in Drayco's shallow pool. With a sudden start, she bound out.

Maudi? Drayco leapt after her, his hackles rising.

'Hey, you two. What's going on?' Jarrod asked, following them. He scanned the water's surface but it was smooth as glass. 'What is it?'

'I don't know, but this is all disturbingly familiar.'

'What do you mean? Have you been here before?'

'Yes. No. Not this place but somewhere like it. Under Los Loma.'

'You're comparing those caverns to this paradise?' He swept his hand out towards the falls.

'You didn't see it. There was a pool there, and the water tasted sweet — heavenly — *just* like this.'

'And?' he prompted.

'At the bottom of the pool ...' She leaned her body forward, straining to see under the surface.

'What?'

She shook her head. 'Maybe I've had too much sun. There are no monsters at the bottom of this lagoon, are there?'

'None that I can see.'

'And you have amazing sight. All the same, I'm going to look for some fruit and have a bit of an explore. You coming?'

'Let's find the horses. We can cover more ground with them.'

They're not far. Grazing in a meadow.

'Lead on, Drayco. There isn't much left of this day and I don't want to go to sleep with an empty stomach.'

That's not going to happen, Maudi. Follow me.

* * *

An' Lawrence sat across the table in Kreshkali's apartment, studying textbooks and sipping spice tea from Dumarka. Scylla was crouched by a small hole in the wall, stalking her fourth rat.

'They won't give her indigestion, will they? I can't imagine what rats in this city eat.'

'She's tough,' Kreshkali said, looking briefly at the temple cat before pointing to an elaborate three-dimensional drawing. It resembled ladders entwining round each other. 'See these spiral chains? They have encoding here and here, in the Pi-stack. This is the key to bringing down the solar shields. The access codes ...'

'Are in the spell? In Rosette?'

'That's right. If this plan goes right, there'll be real sunshine on Earth before long.'

'I still don't understand what the solar shields are.' An' Lawrence leaned forward, holding his mug with both hands. 'And I don't understand much of this at all.' He waved at the drawings.

'Here's the concise history.' Kreshkali took a drink from her cup and stared at An' Lawrence and Zero. 'Centuries ago, the Earth's ozone layer began to thin.'

'And ozone means what, again?'

'Ozone is triatomic, a molecule comprised of three oxygen atoms. It's much less stable than O_2, and it's a pollutant — a poison — at ground level, but in the stratosphere ...'

'Stop.' Zero massaged his forehead. 'What's O_2?'

'That's the essential stuff in the air you breathe. About twenty percent.'

'Oxygen?'

'Yes.'

'Why don't you just say oxygen?'

Kreshkali looked at him, one eyebrow going up. 'Because the shortened term makes the telling faster.'

'In theory,' An' Lawrence broke in.

She exhaled in a rush. 'It's like this,' she said. 'Ozone forms a layer in the atmosphere around Earth. It filters out harmful rays of ultraviolet light from the sun. Actually, it absorbs them, keeping out electromagnetic radiation — wavelengths of 320 nanometers and lower.'

'It filters out damaging light?' An' Lawrence asked.

'UV light, yes.'

'And when that light gets through? What happens?'

'What *happened*, is more like it,' Kreshkali said. 'It caused big problems with oxygen production — single-celled animals were hit the hardest. Protozoa and algae were decimated and the largest oxygen-generating bio-system — the ocean's plankton — started to die.'

She took a deep breath. 'People started to die from skin cancers, there was reduced fertility and a peculiar effect on consciousness that contributed to vast numbers of casualties ... suicide.'

'And why did the ozone thin?' Zero's mouth turned down like a shark when he asked.

'Pollution, mainly halocarbons.'

'Didn't the temple hierarchies know?' An' Lawrence asked.

'The world leaders, you mean? Oh, they knew,' Kreshkali said. 'As early as the twentieth century they moved to protect the ozone layer from further damage by enacting the Montreal Protocol. Many countries got behind it ...'

'But not all?' Zero frowned.

'No, not all. Then along came ASSIST.' She collected the mugs from the table and took them to the sink. 'They had a great idea.'

'The solar shield?' Zero asked, watching Kreshkali pace back and forth.

'ASSIST thought if they launched a thousand orbital satellites that unfurled into a lattice of solar panels they would not only reduce infiltration of UV light, but also provide a constant power source — under their control.'

'I take it things went bad?' An' Lawrence said.

Kreshkali stopped pacing and returned to the table. 'Very bad.' She sat back down, slumping in her chair. 'The seas were in big trouble with the death of so much plankton. It caused a particular organism to flourish, blue-green algae. It's virtually immune to high levels of UV. It reproduced unchecked, choking out much of the biomass, so ASSIST launched their solar shields protocol and the sea-devils were released.'

'Sea-devils?' An' Lawrence rubbed his temples.

'Tiny marine flagella engineered to feed on the algae. Unfortunately, those devouring devils went to work on everything aquatic, not just the target species, and the balance between the cyanobacteria . . .'

'The what?' An' Lawrence pinched the bridge of his nose.

'Blue-green algae.' She sat up straight. 'The balance tipped. The oceans became cesspools, and the solar shields — designed to filter UV — soaked up far too much light. It enhanced the greenhouse effect instead of lessening it . . .'

'Greenhouse?'

'Global warming,' Kreshkali said, before An' Lawrence could ask more. 'Effectively, a sudden rise in temperature and a melting of the polar icecaps. The seas rose, tropical reefs expired, and the weather altered more radically than the natural course of events would have seen. Jarrod predicted it for them. They didn't listen.' She put the kettle on.

'Jarrod?' An' Lawrence and Zero asked at the same time.

Before the kettle boiled she'd explained as best she could what a quantum sentient was. An' Lawrence closed his eyes and rubbed his face. Zero sat very still, staring at the wall.

'That's why we have a perpetually brown sky, acid rain, virtually no pure water, and a planet losing hundreds of species to extinction daily. Oh, yes,' she said, almost as an afterthought, 'the tectonic plates shifted, submerging and rearranging the continents. Millions of people gone ...'

No-one spoke for some time.

'I don't begin to understand half of this,' Zero said. 'But why don't they take the solar shields down, if they know they're the cause?'

'They don't want to lose the power.'

'Power?'

'As long as the shields remain in place, ASSIST has the only viable energy source left. They don't want to give that up.'

'Better to reign in hell ...?' An' Lawrence said the words slowly.

'You've been reading Milton? Good.'

'Your writers are interesting.'

She looked past him to the bookshelves. 'They were,' she said. 'Now, back to logistics. We have to bring the solar shields down and we can't do that without Jarrod.'

'And he can't come back until the worm is destroyed?' Zero asked. 'Right?'

'You're catching on, lad.' She returned to the table with three new mugs of tea, the scent of cinnamon, clove and orange peel wafting behind her.

'Kali,' An' Lawrence asked, 'how long would he have from when he crossed over to that worm device getting to him? Days? Hours? Minutes?'

'Good question. A day or two, three at the most, provided there are no witch-trackers about.'

'And what's the square surface of the ASSIST fortress?'

She wrote a set of equations and pushed them across the table to An' Lawrence. He did some calculating of his own and pushed the paper back.

'That's a lot of explosives, Sunshine,' she said.

'But can you get it?'

She looked at the sparkling bottles of water stacked high against the wall. 'I can get us anything we want,' she smiled. 'Are we going to blow something up?'

'Seems that would solve the problem clean and simple,' An' Lawrence said.

'Except for the fact that the worm is everywhere, in all the remaining global wires.'

'I gathered that,' he sighed. 'A foxy creature. We just have to attract it back to its hole, and I know just the bait.'

She took a quick breath, her eyes levelled on the Sword Master.

'You can't risk the JARROD.'

'What about a calculated risk?' Zero asked.

She held her cup under her nose, steam wafting over her face. Her brows knitted tightly and then finally lifted. 'If we could get him into his old mainframe, for just a nanosecond, it might work. We'd have to have one lightning-fast exit strategy.'

'The mainframe? Where is it?' An' Lawrence looked through the drawings.

'In Central Processing — ground floor of ASSIST.' She tapped a small diagram.

'Guarded?' An' Lawrence asked.

'You could say that.'

Rosette sat under a date palm eating bananas and guava fruit, the juicy pink centres making her tongue tingle. Drayco was nearby, worrying the remains of an eel. Her lids were fluttering shut, when she shivered. 'Did you hear that?'

The falcon?

It whistled again, the sweet high pitch of a black falcon. She stood, looking for the bird. *Could it be Nell?*

Rosette! I'm here.

'Nell? Nell! Where are you?' she called.

'Nell's here?' Jarrod said, coming up from the lagoon, his finger through an eel's gill. 'That's good news.'

Over the sound of the falls, the cry of the raptor called again. It was coming from the cliffs above. Rosette and Jarrod shielded their eyes, watching the bird swoop down. It back-winged in front of them and morphed into Nell.

'Rosette!' she exclaimed, short of breath, 'I *knew* you were alive, but by all that's sacred it's good to see you.' She looked around the valley and sighed. 'Jarrod, this is my favourite one. It's beautiful here!'

'What do you mean "your favourite one"?' Rosette crossed her arms. 'Your favourite one of what?'

Jarrod placed his hand on her shoulder. 'Rosette, it's okay.' He took a breath. 'Nell? Are we all right?'

'For now. Give us a moment, will you, Jarrod?' She held out her hand to Rosette. 'Come with me. I need to show you something.'

'Where are we, Nell? This can't be any of the Rahana Island chain. How could we get this far out?'

'Save your questions, daughter. I've got something for your visual consciousness. Give your mind a rest.'

'Pardon?'

Nell put her arm around Rosette's waist and led her to the edge of the pool, where they stood together. 'Lean over with me. Have a look.'

'There's something in there, right?' Rosette whispered. 'I knew it! I felt it before; it was just like in Los Loma. Something dangerous.'

'There was never anything dangerous for you in Los Loma.'

'You weren't there, Nell. It was plenty dangerous ...'

'Are you certain?'

Rosette frowned. 'What are you saying?'

'Just look. Look with me.'

Rosette scanned the clear surface of the water, containing her emotions for a few seconds before bursting out. 'What am I supposed to be looking at, Nell? I can't see a thing. Are we fishing for eels?'

The eels are delicious, Maudi.

Not helping, Dray.

'Give it a moment,' Nell replied. 'Let the ripples settle.'

The water darkened beneath them as a cloud moved across the sun. Rosette squinted, peering at her reflection. She thought she looked a bit tousled, but not too bad considering the shipwreck, near-drowning and marathon swim. She gingerly touched her sun-cracked lips and brushed the damp hair out of her eyes.

'Rosette,' Nell whispered, bringing her daughter's attention over to her side of the image.

Rosette stiffened and bent closer, springing back from the edge. It wasn't her mother standing next to her, arm around her waist, leaning over the water. The person that looked back at Rosette from the limpid pool had short, pale, spiky hair and a wicked smile.

'I know you!' Rosette pulled further away, reaching for the sword that wasn't there. She started to weave a banishing spell.

Maudi? What are you doing?

It's Kreshkali, my captor from Los Loma. Why didn't you warn me?

'Calm yourself, Rosette,' she heard Nell's voice speaking as the words flowed out of the other woman's mouth. 'And put your hands down. This doesn't call for an expulsion. Do you want to shake the island apart?'

'Jarrod?' Rosette shouted, ignoring the woman, 'Jarrod!' Her voice rose above the sound of her pounding heart. 'It's ...'

'Kreshkali, after all,' he said. Jarrod smiled at Kreshkali, the witch standing in the place where Nell had been seconds before. 'You keep the surprises coming, don't you?'

Rosette backed away, reaching for Drayco.

What's wrong, Maudi? Why are you afraid of Nell? It's just one of her glamours.

'It's not! Can't you see?' She grabbed her familiar's scruff and gave it a shake, pointing his nose at the woman. 'Are you all enchanted? It's Kreshkali, queen of the underworld!'

She backed into Jarrod. His hand came up to steady her.

'Why are you just standing there?' Rosette asked. 'Can't you see the witch?'

Kreshkali stepped towards her, palms open. 'No-one's enchanted, daughter.'

'I'm not your daughter! What have you done with Nell?'

'Rosette, listen. I *am* Kreshkali. I'm *also* Nellion Paree — daughter of the daughters of Docturi Janicia.'

'You can't be!'

Kreshkali smiled. 'I am.'

'Clever,' Jarrod murmured. 'I didn't detect it.'

'Nor did any of the trackers,' Kreshkali said.

Rosette searched their faces. 'I don't understand what you're talking about.'

'I've been living in two worlds for some time now, Rosette.'

'Living in *two worlds*? What two worlds? Where's Nell?'

'Right here, sweetheart. I'm Nell. I'm Kreshkali. I'm your mother. I've been in two places at once, doing the work of two witches. I had to. There was no other way to keep you hidden from the trackers, watch over Passillo and continue the work on Earth.'

'Earth?' Rosette put both hands over her mouth. 'My dream,' she whispered. 'I just remembered my dream. I had it in the cave that night. There was a portal. Another world,' she gasped. 'How is this possible?'

Kreshkali pressed her lips together and raised an eyebrow.

'I know: *nothing's impossible*.' Rosette took a deep breath. 'Just tell me, if you're Nell, why was Kreshkali — why were you — hunting me?'

'I was never hunting you, Rosette, but guiding! Guiding and protecting. The real threat is from witch-trackers. They're who we've been running from.'

Rosette crossed her arms. 'A little communication would have gone down a lot better!' She glared at Kreshkali. 'Why didn't you just tell me what was going on? You're as bad as Nell ... ugh.'

'For that, I apologise. For not raising you myself and not passing on the knowledge of your inheritance sooner, I apologise also. It was too risky. The witch-trackers were hounding us. After Jaynan ... after the Matosh murders I had to keep everyone in the dark.' She glanced at Jarrod. 'They nearly got us all that time.'

'That time?' Rosette said.

Jarrod rubbed his neck. 'I think I'd best get the horses. You two have some catching up to do.' He turned to the temple cat. 'Do you know where they are?'

Drayco rubbed his cheek on Rosette's thigh before following Jarrod downstream. *You've got witches' business, Maudi. I'll be back soon.*

Rosette watched her familiar walk away. If he said Kreshkali and Nell were one and the same, then they must be. He wasn't alarmed. She took that as a good sign.

Kreshkali sat in the shade, patting the grass beside her. Rosette sat an arm's length away.

'You're the first one of us to be born in another world.' Rosette opened her mouth to speak, but Kreshkali waved her quiet. 'Let me finish the explanation before you jump in.'

Rosette snapped her mouth shut.

'You were conceived here, on Gaela, not Earth, but you're of both worlds — you had to be. Only an Earth child from the line of Janis Richter can carry JARROD's quantum CPU in her DNA, and Gaela was the only place I could hide you from ASSIST's witch-trackers. They were stamping us out, one by one. They killed my mother and I swore they would never find you. I had to keep you in this world, and still be in both at the same time to carry on with the research.' She brushed the sand from her hands and ran them through her hair. 'That's basically it. Now, do you have any questions?'

Rosette's eyes were wide. 'Huh?'

'Questions, Rosette. Can I make it any clearer? We've got to get moving. Time's short and everything's at stake.'

Rosette straightened her spine. A warm tingling sensation started to course through her body. The feeling she'd had before — as if she was about to faint — was replaced with a hot flash of energy.

'One question comes to mind.' She stood up as she spoke. 'What in the demon pit of souls did you just say?'

'You've got very special DNA, Rosette. You have ...'

'Losing me again, Kreshkali,' she interrupted. 'What the spit does DNA stand for?'

'Deoxyribonucleic acid.'

'Oh, that just helped me a lot ...'

'You have special proteins in your blood. Think of it as a spell — *the spell* — only, on Earth, your other world, it's called *technology*. It's linked implicitly to Jarrod.'

'Jarrod? What's Jarrod got to do with it?' Rosette's face was flushed, her pulse pounding.

'Rosette, I've wanted to tell you.' Jarrod came striding towards her leading Wren. Drayco followed behind, lead rope in his mouth, the mountain horse in tow.

'Wanted to tell me what?'

'I'm not exactly the boy next door.'

'You aren't?' She looked at him, her eyes narrowing. 'I feel like I'm going mad. What are you people trying to say to me?'

'Not mad, Rosette. Just uninformed,' Jarrod said.

'Then inform me. If you aren't the boy next door, who then?'

'He's not anything you've got a word for, Rosette.'

She closed her eyes. *Drayco? You've been in his mind. What is he?*

I told you, Maudi. He's like no other. The temple cat dropped the lead rope at Rosette's feet. She picked it up, stroking the mare's neck.

'This is a portal,' Kreshkali pointed her arm towards the waterfall. 'A door to other places, and you're right, it is just like the one under Los Loma. It can take us straight to Corsanon, where the split-apart Entity wanders. With any luck, the lost guardian will follow us through and we can reunite the thing. Are you ready?'

'Am I ready? Are you kidding? I feel like I'm falling apart.'

'Get a grip, dear. The sooner the better. Trackers are onto us. That storm was no accident.'

'It wasn't?' Rosette looked at Kreshkali, understanding little of what she had said. Then her eyes found Jarrod. The proximity to him sent more waves of adrenaline coursing through her body, a strange mixture of fear and excitement. She thought she might explode. 'You're not human?' she whispered.

'My body is, and your bloodline and I are linked ceaselessly through time and space — through the portals and the corridors to the many-worlds.'

'My bloodline ...' She took a step back. 'Have you always known this about me?'

'That's the surprising thing. I haven't. Must be your Gaelean half.' He touched her hand. 'Come. I'll explain more on the way.'

They followed Kreshkali, skirting the lagoon until Rosette stopped, pulling Jarrod to a halt with her. 'What about me?'

He cocked his head to the side. 'I don't know what you mean.'

She searched his face. 'You don't, do you ... Never mind.' She clucked to the mountain horse and moved on. *Drayco, do you know where we're going?*

As long as there are no boats and no oceans, I don't care.

I wish I could say there won't be, but how else are we going to get off this island?

Portals, I suspect.

Rosette let out her breath. 'The shipwreck was no accident, you say. What was it?'

'The storm was natural enough, a blessing really,' Kreshkali said.

'A blessing? I doubt the rest of the passengers and crew think so.'

'There was a witch-tracker on board, Rosette, scanning for your signature. When you released the spell to calm the seas, they had you. The spell backfired to save your life.'

'You talk like the spell itself was sentient.'

'Everything is sentient, Rosette. No exceptions.'

She held the mare back, letting Drayco lead. The trail was narrowing, crowded on both sides by dense palm fronds and flowering hibiscus.

'I brought it on myself? All those people . . .'

'What you did saved them,' Jarrod said as they wound their way to the back of the waterfall. 'If the trackers were to get us, everything would cascade.'

'Cascade?'

'The many-worlds, like a stack of cards.'

'Seems like there might have been an easier way,' she said. 'Like simple detection. I would have spotted the tracker, if I'd been informed, and we could have paid the captain a few extra coins to drop a dinghy over the side and set them afloat. That captain's dead now, by the way. Remember?'

'Rosette,' Kreshkali said, her eyes bright, not hearing her comments.

'There's more?' She felt like she would be sick.

'Remind me to give you back your sword when we get to the next portal.'

'You've got it?'

'Of course. And An' Lawrence says to try to keep track of it this time.'

'The Sword Master knows?'

'He does now.'

The portal behind the waterfall shimmered at their approach.

'How long will it take to get to Corsanon?' Rosette asked. Purple light reflected off the edge of the entrance as she passed, sending tingles through her fingers.

'We're going to Dumarka first.'

'Dumarka?'

'I'm not leaving the horses here, and where we're going, they can't follow.'

Rosette nodded, strapping on her sword. When she looked up, Jarrod and Kreshkali were leading the horses out into the Dumarkian Woods, slipping their halters off and setting them free. Jarrod lingered a moment, speaking softly to Wren before the mare shook her head and nickered.

'Now, to Corsanon,' Kreshkali said, brushing horsehairs off her cloak.

'That fast?'

'You've got some things to learn about time, don't you?'

Rosette closed her eyes, opening them to an expansive view of a pastoral valley and gorge she'd never seen before.

'Passillo?' a voice howled desperately from the distance. 'Passillo!!!'

'I think I've been discovered,' Rosette said. She felt her blood pulse through her body in an orgasmic rush. 'I'm here, lost one,' she answered instinctively before the others could speak, linking empathically with the sundered Entity. 'Passillo is here. Rosette is here. Come to me. This is where you belong.'

Rosette stepped out of the portal into the rocky alcove above the Valley of Corsanon, and the dissipated energy of the Entity flew to her, embracing its other half as she realigned the portal with her presence. Warmth flowed from the walls around them, and a humming sound echoed as if the entire mountain was singing.

Rosette took a deep breath and let it out slowly. Her face glowed.

'That was easier than I thought,' Kreshkali whispered to Jarrod. 'Come on, Rosette. This is only the beginning. You too, Jarrod.'

'Where?' Rosette asked.

'Earth.'

'I can't,' Jarrod said, stepping back from the portal. He blanched. 'The worm.'

'We've got a plan for that, trust me.'

Jarrod paused a moment before following them in.

They emerged in the sewers beneath the crumbling city of Half Moon Bay. The air was thick and difficult to breathe, like smoke from a burning rubbish heap.

'This is like my dream,' Rosette whispered before she started coughing. 'I feel like I've been here before.'

'We call that *déjà vu*,' Kreshkali said.

'What's the horrible smell?' Rosette wrinkled her nose.

Drayco sneezed and wiped his face repeatedly with his front paws. *Death, Maudi — the world smells of sickness and death.*

'It's not a pretty place, Rosette, but we can change that.' Her face was set, firm and direct. She looked at Jarrod. 'We don't have long, and we have to keep you hidden.'

Jarrod nodded. 'No argument there.'

'Why hidden?' Rosette asked.

'Because, in this world, he's a wanted Entity.'

'Entity?'

'A Juxta-quantum Arranged Rad-Ram Operating Determinate, to be accurate,' Jarrod said. 'There's a worm out to get me. I'd say we have thirty-six hours, wouldn't you, Kali?'

'Sounds about right.'

Rosette went pale. 'I don't know what you said, but I think I'm going to be sick.'

'When we shut down the solar shield, we can start thinking about widespread hydroponics, ion-based energy sources and reforestation, but we've got to resuscitate the oceans first.' Kreshkali stared at the figures in front of her, speaking her thoughts aloud.

'That, and balance the O_2 so we can establish mass water purification systems,' Jarrod added.

'The trick is getting clean water into every home. How do we do that when it's been the only currency for the last hundred years? People don't think of it as natural or free.'

Jarrod lifted his face. 'We have to take the charge off it. Get people thinking, knowing, that there is enough to go around, enough for everyone.'

'Can you do that?' An' Lawrence asked. 'Change the way people think about it?'

'It's up to them, but we can lead the way. Show them how,' Kreshkali said.

Rosette tipped her cup towards herself, looking at the last few drops in the bottom. 'I don't understand half of what you're talking about.' She looked at Drayco. If he'd been the least bit hesitant, she'd have snuck out to join Zero in sword practice hours ago, but her familiar was relaxed, calm and curious. She trusted that. She could get this.

'It's a lot to take in, I know, but we can't wait for your cognition. We have to start right now.' Kreshkali reached out her hand. 'Come on.'

'Where are you taking me this time?'

'Not far. A little trip to the sea.'

I'll wait here, if you don't mind, Drayco said without moving, his eyelids opening halfway as he dozed by a rat hole.

'We won't be long.' Kreshkali tossed Rosette a cloak.

They made their way down the metal fire-escape to the abandoned street below. Looking both ways, Rosette followed Kreshkali to the seawall, the roiling swell crashing on the rocks in front of her. She gagged as she inhaled the fetid mist rising from the wave.

'What now?' she asked, holding her hand over her nose.

Kreshkali drew a black-handled dagger from its sheath. The blade glinted blue when the lightning flashed.

'We need a bit of DNA, Rosette, and a bit of the spell.'

'We do?' Rosette took a step back.

'Just a few drops.'

'How many's a few?' she asked, clasping her hands behind her back.

'Thirteen will do. One for each lunar month.'

'Lucky thirteen?'

'Let's hope so.'

Rosette raised her index finger. Kreshkali grabbed her hand and pulled her towards the wall when the next wave crashed. 'Stay close. I don't have to remind you what would happen if you fell in.'

'Stripped to the bone, I think, is the phrase you used.'

'Just keep it in mind.'

'I am.'

They dashed forward as the sea pulled back. Kreshkali pricked her own finger and then her daughter's, and they counted together as the drops fell silently into the sea.

'This is crazy. How can such a small amount have any effect at all?' Rosette asked as they ran back to the wall before the next wave broke.

'Potency is a mysterious thing, Rosette. Sometimes it is based on how much, and sometimes on how little. The alchemy of this spell is activated by the greatest possible dilution. Ultimately, we want a solution that is so highly diluted that there is no longer any trace of our DNA present.'

Rosette stared at the brown water swirling with yellow foam as it rushed back. 'I suspect that's the case already.'

Kreshkali nodded. 'It'll take time for this cure to spread, years, perhaps generations, but the deactivation of the sea-devils has begun.'

They both ducked when a gunshot sounded in the distance.

'Let's get you home.' Kreshkali took her hand again. 'Send a message to Drayco. Have him and Jarrod meet us at the portal. They can escort you.'

'I can find my way.'

Kreshkali looked at her without blinking until Rosette swallowed.

'Right. I'll have them meet us.' She let out her breath when the older witch released her.

'This world's treacherous, Rosette. Keep that in mind before you think to go strolling down the lane. From now on, wear your sword under your cloak at all times and make certain you are never seen. They burn witches here.'

She nodded. 'Where are you going?'

'Back to Treeon. There's one more thing I need to do.'

Chapter 20

'An' Lawrence sent you?' Clay eyed the witch slowly. 'In the middle of the night?'

'He did, so best not delay. And keep your voice down. You'll wake the whole dorm.'

'I doubt it, after all they drank tonight.'

'Just be quick.'

'You're Nell, right?'

'Nellion Paree.'

A cloud crossed his face. 'Rosette's Nell?'

She nodded. 'Get your gear.'

'My guitars?' he asked, looking under his bunk. 'Flutes, whistles and pipes?' He squinted at Nell in the candlelight. 'It's a festival performance? I don't feel much like entertaining. I told him that.'

'You might change your mind when we get there,' Nell said, tossing him his cloak. 'Bring as much as you can carry. Tuning forks, strings, picks, the lot,' Nell directed, 'and bring your sword. Do you remember how to use it?'

'I do.'

He screwed up his face when they got to the portal. 'Why are we taking so much water?'

'You'll see.'

* * *

Kreshkali had to slap his face to wake him.

'What happened?' Clay asked.

'You passed out. Feeling better now?'

'I'm okay.' He gripped his sword hilt. 'Who are you?'

'I thought we went through that.'

'You sure as demons aren't Nell.'

'Aren't I?'

He got to his feet. 'Is it a glamour?'

'Not really. Nell, Kreshkali, take your pick. We're one and the same, though I'm sticking to this for now.'

'Kreshkali? You're the witch that killed Rosette?'

'Hardly, lad, so take your hand off the sword. An' Lawrence will explain, if you haven't worked it out by then.' She ran her hands through her spiky hair and shouldered the instrument bags. 'Can you manage those?'

Clay's face was red. He picked up his guitars and followed her. 'Where are we?'

'Earth.'

'Why?'

'Ah, here comes the Sword Master. I'm going to let him fill you in on the way.'

An' Lawrence helped them through the manhole and out into the dark street. Clay listened for a while, his eyes getting wider.

'Put it this way,' Kreshkali said, 'you're here to teach — to bring music to people who've forgotten what it sounds like.'

Clay's mouth was open, but no words came out.

'Jarrod safe?' Kreshkali asked as they crossed the street.

An' Lawrence nodded.

'And I trust my daughter's well?' she said, handing An' Lawrence an instrument bag.

'She's waiting to see you.'

'Temper?'

'I'd say fierce describes it best.'

Clay looked up. 'Daughter?'

'You know her, Clay.'

'I do?'

'Rosette.'

Clay's face contorted.

'Sorry, lad,' Kreshkali said. 'We had to let you believe she was dead.'

'She's not?'

'You'll see for yourself in a moment.'

Tears welled and spilled down his cheeks. He pulled up his hood and spoke no more. They arrived at Kreshkali's apartment building at sunset, the glowing strip of rose on the horizon signalling the end of the day. The sky turned a dull, starless mud-black as they trudged up the steps, rain pounding the tin overhead.

Rosette opened the door, light flooding the hallway. Jarrod stood from the table, moving to take wet cloaks, instruments and gear. Rosette stepped aside as he ushered them in.

Drayco flicked his tail. *Go easy on him,* her familiar cautioned. *He's standing on a precipice.*

Clay? When she looked up, she met Clay's eyes. Everyone went silent, staring until they all suddenly busied themselves with tasks.

'I guess I have some explaining to do,' she said at last.

Clay stiffened at the sound of her voice. He looked over at the Sword Master, who gave him a nod.

'I do as well. I haven't been completely honest, Rosette.'

'None of us have,' she answered.

* * *

'You're not even part Gaelean, are you, Kreshkali?' An' Lawrence asked as he walked about her large studio, examining the shelves full of strange books and unfamiliar trinkets. Some he recognised, some he did not. The others were at the kitchen table, talking in hushed voices, a tentative peace working its way out between Rosette, Clay and Jarrod. Zero's enthusiasm was affecting them all.

'No, Rowan. I'm not Gaelean.'

'When did you first come through the portal?'

'Five years ago, Earth time.'

'Gaelean time?'

'Over fifty.'

She tossed him a box of matches and nodded for him to light the candles. They settled in amongst the pillows and futon at the far end of the studio.

'So, what's your plan, Kali?' he asked, stretching out next to her.

She smiled. 'I plan to save the world.'

'And how do I fit in exactly?'

'You mean once we bring down ASSIST?'

'That'll do for a start.'

She yawned, rubbing her feet. He motioned to her and she lay back, lifting them to his lap. 'I want to find my ancestors' property, the Richter-Paree estate. It's meant to be protected by a spell.'

'And you need me to help you find it?'

'I need you to help me run it.' She whispered the last few words.

'What?'

'Not now, Rowan. I've got to sleep or die. It's been a hell of a ride.'

'Hell-of-a-ride?' He said it like it was a foreign language.

She smiled at him but didn't explain. 'We can polish the plans in the morning.'

'To save the world?'

She nodded, pointing to a spare quilt — a patchwork from Flureon. 'Sleep where you like,' she mumbled.

The apartment had several cushion-covered futons on the floor and a large, overstuffed sofa near the fireplace. She wiggled out of her clothes, letting them lie where they fell, and snuggled into the bed, pulling the covers up to her face.

Her eyes opened momentarily as Rowan got into bed beside her. He leaned on one elbow and whispered in her ear, 'You're as beautiful as ever.'

'You look good too,' she said as her eyes closed.

'Kali? You haven't given up on this world, this *Earth*?'

'That's not an option,' she said. 'Ever.'

An' Lawrence rubbed at the stubble on his jaw. 'Have you had a look around lately?'

She turned to him but didn't answer.

'One more question. Have you got a razor hidden away somewhere?'

She sighed. 'In the bathroom, and yes, Rowan, I've had a look round. It's decaying and putrid and vile. The inhabitants are a mess, save for a rare few. Still, I won't abandon them or this place when there is still hope.'

'So there *is* hope?'

She gave the faintest smile. 'That's the only thing there ever was.'

Rosette jolted awake at the touch of Drayco's presence in her mind: *Men approach!*

As she became aware of the thought, she saw An' Lawrence jump up, Scylla at his side. He pressed his finger to his lips before drawing his sword.

Where are they? Rosette asked her familiar.

Foot of the stairwell.
Are they coming?
Fast. Wake Clay.

Zero was up, and Jarrod was clearly communicating with Drayco as well. Rosette went to Clay and gave him a shake, shushing him before he could speak. They gathered around Kreshkali, barefoot and shivering.

'Who are they?' Rosette whispered.

'Street patrols, if we're lucky.'

'And if we aren't lucky?'

Kreshkali's face went grim. 'Witch-trackers.' She lit several candles and scanned the room. 'Rosette, we need a glamour, fast. Get Clay, Zero and Jarrod and all the gear into one place, against that wall.' She pointed to the east side of the studio. 'The temple cats too. Blur them. Blur everything but me and Rowan. Can you manage that?'

'I, I,' she stuttered.

'Rosette! We need this. Now!'

'I can.'

Kreshkali turned to An' Lawrence. 'Put that thing down.' She nodded to his sword. 'Send Scylla to Rosette and tell her to stay put!'

'What are you going to do?'

She winked. 'What I do best, and you are going to stay still. Back in that bed.'

'Bed?'

'I mean it. Go!'

The temple cats followed Rosette, melting into the shadows. They had the predator's knack for camouflage and hardly needed a glamour. Rosette shook the sleep from her head and helped move the gear against the wall, jugs of water, foodstuffs, instruments and crates. She whispered in her mind, over and over, weaving the spell she wanted to conjure. She didn't even think about whether she could do it or not. She simply began.

Pressing herself between Jarrod and Clay, she drew to her a concealment spell, one that would make them appear as a blank wall — no people, no familiars, no contraband. She slowed her pulse and respiration as she brought in the Elementals, surprised at how readily they came. They nearly sang with delight, responding to her intentions, and together with Fire, Earth, Air and Water, she felt a visual illusion take form in front of her. Once in place, it was like standing behind a two-way mirror.

If I can imagine it, I can make it, she smiled.

Nice spell, Maudi. Keep it up. They're right outside the door.

She heard the knock just as Drayco spoke.

Kreshkali waved An' Lawrence back down into the bed, hissing at him to conceal his sword and play his part.

'I'm working,' she screeched towards the door. 'Wait your turn.'

'ASSIST Corps. Open up.'

Kreshkali grumbled obscenities as she pulled on a satin robe, careful to cover her tattoos but expose her breasts and belly. Rosette swallowed hard as she watched. The woman was formidable, impervious to the shocked faces and leers when she opened the door.

'What the fuck do you want?' she asked.

'We've had reports. People coming and going ...'

'Of course they are coming and going.' She clicked her tongue. 'I'm not a seamstress, you realise.'

'He's your client?' The captain pointed to An' Lawrence.

'Last trick of the night if you'd let me get on with it.'

They scrutinised An' Lawrence, bare chest, legs covered by a thin sheet.

'You're getting what you paid for, mate.' The captain chuckled as he spoke, indicating the protrusion under the covers.

An' Lawrence didn't reply but tightened his grip on the sword hilt nestled between his legs.

'We'll have a look around, if you don't mind.' The captain pushed past her, not waiting for a response.

They circled the large room, shining their beams into the corners, looking at the books and knick-knacks. Rosette knew Kreshkali wouldn't allow banned titles to be displayed, but she blurred the shelves anyway, making the walls melt with obscurity. They walked right past her and the temple cats, past the stocks from Gaela, past Jarrod, Zero and Clay, and into the kitchen area. Rosette felt a wave of panic when she realised they had left drafts and notes on the table. She took a deep breath and blurred them into an image of a table-cloth, trusting such things existed here in this world.

'You do well,' the ASSIST captain commented as he fingered the edge of the rich cloth draping the table. He ran his hand over the woven surface, his face giving a hint of longing.

Kreshkali laughed, letting her open robe speak for itself as he shone his beam on her breasts.

'There were reports of animals . . .'

She shrugged her shoulders and winked.

The captain took off his cap and wiped his brow before continuing his search. He went over the kitchen thoroughly then snapped his fingers, bringing his men to attention.

'That'll do for now.' He led them to the door. 'Remember, whore, we're watching you,' he said as they marched out.

'Wouldn't want it any other way.' Kreshkali followed them to the door and locked it, leaning her back against the cool frame, letting her shoulders relax. Her face was etched with fine lines. Rosette waited, her heart pounding, before letting down the glamour. When

Drayco said they were completely out of the building, they all emerged from the shadows.

'That was a risky little game,' An' Lawrence commented, his voice barely more than a low growl.

'I know it rankles not to slice and dice your opponents, Rowan, but now is not the time to confront them. We aren't ready.'

He made an incoherent response.

'Will they come back?' Rosette asked.

'Probably not tonight, but we've got to move.'

'Where to?'

'A bigger place, for starters. I've got one set up, closer to ASSIST. It's being minded by that ragtag of rebels I told you about, but first we need more recruits.'

'Are you going to get Rosette to conjure those up as well?' An' Lawrence asked as he put down his sword.

'No, but I'm thinking about paying a visit to Los Loma in the morning. Might find some volunteers there.'

Kreshkali entered the chamber, dressed in a full-length fur-lined cloak and knee-high boots. She shivered. It was the dead of winter under the mountain of Los Loma and the contrast to the muggy Earth climate made her fingertips numb and her nose cold. She looked at the faces staring up at her. Dark eyes set, expectant.

'Why have you called us?' Hotha asked, morphing from his wolf form to stand before her. Several other Lupins did the same. Kreshkali smiled. She had gathered the leaders of these strange creatures to her, uncertain how they would respond, but she could tell by their auras they were keen for change.

'I thought some of you might be ready for a trip back to your home world,' she said, seating herself at the whalebone table with the others.

'We are exiled,' Rashnan said.

Murmuring agreement followed.

'That's true, but only for your own protection.'

Several of the pack snarled.

'I know.' Kreshkali held up her hand. 'You hardly need protecting now, but in the beginning you did. You were a few litters of helpless pups and young whelps. If my foremother hadn't smuggled you out when she did, there would be no Lupins anywhere. You're one of a kind.'

And what, Kreshkali, would we be going back to?

Kreshkali kept her face a mask as she listened to Hotha's words in her head. She suspected he'd shielded them from the others.

I won't pretend it's a pleasant place. The Earth is badly damaged.

As are we.

She sighed. *Maybe there could be healing, for both.*

Hotha touched her leg beneath the table. *Then tell them. Tell them the truth.*

'I'm not offering you paradise,' she spoke aloud. 'It's a mess there — polluted seas, martial law, witch-trackers ready to skin you alive, blocked sun, seismic activity, no clean water, constant acid rain, fear in all species, river, rock and stone ...'

Tell them the truth, but don't terrorise them, Kreshkali!

The witch smiled. 'But we are going to change all that.'

'We?' the Lupin across from her asked.

'Yes ... me, my coven, some stray rebels and you, if you care to participate.'

'We can stay in our home world then?'

'If we win.'

'Battle?'

Kreshkali sighed. 'Yes, I think it will come to that.'

Nice bait.

I'm just telling the truth.

The Lupins conversed amongst themselves, their heads turning, ears shifting as the debate went on in front of her. Their mind-shields were up. She couldn't follow a single thread until Hotha spoke to her.

Looks like you'll have at least five clans.

Including yours?

Of course.

'What about hunting?' a young Lupin asked from the far end of the table.

'Only water rats in the city, but there're still wild boar, goats and rabbits in the surrounds.'

'Water?'

'That you'll have to bring from here, until we get more purifiers set up.'

Fists thumped the table as each clan pounded their approval. Tails wagged in the background.

Seven clans, Mistress. That leaves five here, in case.

In case what?

In case we don't survive Earth.

Kreshkali awoke stiff and sore the next morning. She stretched, looking over the wadded quilt to scan the apartment. They'd taken over the entire top floor of Annadusa's building. There was plenty of room there for Kreshkali and her inner circle: An' Lawrence, Zero, Clay, Rosette, Jarrod and the familiars, including the Three Sisters. The ravens preferred this top-floor abode to a winter in Gaela, content with the pampering they received from the coven, and the warmth. All agreed it best for Mozzie to stay in Dumarka, at least for now.

Kreshkali had prepared the place weeks ago, gutting the entire level save one bedroom and bath, turning it into an expansive and well-appointed hall. It had wall hangings from Los Loma, rugs from Flureon and colourful overstuffed cushions from the looms of Morzone. It hadn't been hard to trade for the luxuries, for here or her dwellings in Los Loma and Dumarka. One thing there was plenty of on Earth, besides decomposition, was gold coin. Useless now that water was the prime commodity, she could pick gold out of the gutters or trade for it in shops, a box of water credits buying her a king's ransom in coin.

The rest of the floors in the building were taken up by Annadusa's lot, the rebels she'd been gathering for years — over one hundred strong. So far, not a single tracker had gotten wind of them.

She stretched again. 'How long have I been out?'

'A few hours,' An' Lawrence said. He was examining a rack of swords that she'd commandeered from Treeon. 'How you got Makee on your side, I can't imagine.'

'I have my ways.'

'I remember,' he winked. 'What about the rust? This environment's ruining their edge already.'

'Oil them.'

'When we shut down the solar shield and let the sun shine in, it'll be less of a problem,' Jarrod said.

He was at the table with Clay and Zero. Rosette sat on the couch with Drayco, her back to them all.

'How's that?' An' Lawrence asked.

'No more acid rain.'

'That fast?'

'Not really, but it will lessen, slowly over time, until the rain is sweet again.'

'Because . . .?'

'Once those shields are down, people can use solar power again and stop burning combustion fuels and trash. There'll be less exhaust smoke and fewer fires puking out wastes that damage the pH balance of the atmosphere.'

An' Lawrence looked around the room, his face confused.

'Smoke's dirty; solar power's clean,' Rosette explained, clipping the words without turning around.

Kreshkali looked at An' Lawrence, her eyebrows raised.

He shook his head.

'Kreshkali,' Rosette continued. 'The cupboards are empty. What do you expect us to eat?'

'There's plenty of Nutries.'

'They don't count,' she said, turning away from the fire and looking Kreshkali in the eyes. 'Disgusting green paste.'

'Don't throw them out! You never know when we'll need them, even with new supplies.'

'So you did bring something decent?'

'I did, and I'll cook it up while we work out the last of the plans.'

'Last? I didn't know we had a first.' She turned her back again and stared at the fire.

Rosette felt her guts turning. The only thing that kept her from screaming was the quiet purr of Drayco and the insistent thought that this would all be over soon, one way or another. Between ASSIST, the environment and the witch-trackers, she didn't think any of them had much of a chance. She would do her part, because it was her inheritance, but if she got out of this alive, she didn't plan on coming back, or ever seeing any of them again.

Maudi?

We're going to go deep into Dumarka and never come back.

He flicked his tail, continuing to purr.

'Come to the table, Rosette. We need you in on this.'

She squared her shoulders and took the seat next to her mother.

'Here's the plan,' Kreshkali said, tapping the blueprints. 'Jarrod deactivates the orbit sequence of the solar panels and brings them down.' She paused. 'A soft landing, please. And you'll need to take less than a few nanoseconds to do it because once you're in, the worm is baited, so to speak. An' Lawrence, Rosette and you two,' she nodded to the familiars, 'can keep the exit open. We get him out before he's consumed, and then level the place. Comments?'

'I particularly like the last bit,' Jarrod said. 'Where I get out in one piece. My only question is, how's it to be done? And fast! I've been here too long already. I can all but feel that worm crawling under my skin.'

'Can't we send him back through the portal?' Rosette asked. 'Keep him safe while we work out these details?'

'Too late for that. Jarrod's right. The worm's hovering. It would have him the second he passed the plasma.'

Rosette frowned.

'It's the electromagnetic pulse of the portal Entity. The worm would sense me as soon as I touched it again.'

'Then what are we going to do?'

'We're going to be quick!' Kreshkali placed mugs on the edges of the blueprints to keep them flat. 'In and out before they see us coming.'

'Do you need me in on this?' Clay asked, patting his guitar. 'Or . . .'

'I'd love some music,' Rosette said. Her eyes softened towards him, but he didn't look at her.

'Music you'll have then,' he said. Clay set up at the far end of the flat, playing a series of traditional guitar pieces from Gaela. The music filled the room with a melodic ambience, easing the tension at the table.

'Let me see if I can summarise what we've got so far.' An' Lawrence spoke up after a lengthy tactical debate. Jarrod had given his interpretation of their choices and it had left them stunned. 'First we get into the ASSIST complex, which is as heavily guarded as any high temple, with DNA-triggered lockdown protocols.' His face had a puzzled look. 'Whatever that is, and guards on every level, each armed with repeating razor rifles.'

'Laser,' Jarrod corrected.

He paused. 'What exactly is that again?'

'A beam of red light that cuts through steel like a knife through fat.'

'Right. We get past all that, overcome the security blocks, contain the researchers, identify our contact — which could be anyone: scientist, guard or janitor. Is that right so far?'

'Basically, yes.'

'We get to the mainframe, Jarrod inserts the access codes, and if — "if" being quite important here, I think — they still work, shut down the satellite that is controlling the solar shields. Does that about sum it up?'

'You forgot the part where we all get out alive,' Kreshkali said, 'before I level the place.' She gestured towards the stockpile of explosives under the kitchen shelves.

He threw his hands up in the air. 'It's suicide, heading straight for disaster. How are we going to pull this off?'

'We aren't going in half-cocked,' Kreshkali replied. 'We have the blueprints and ...'

'You don't think there might have been some changes in the last century or two? A bit of remodelling, perhaps?' An' Lawrence flicked at the plans.

'Good point.' Jarrod rubbed his chin and turned to Kreshkali. 'This is why we need the mole.'

'The what?' Rosette asked. She turned to Jarrod, eyebrows up.

'The mole is the contact — our man inside — put in place before I escaped.'

An' Lawrence stared. 'Two hundred years ago?'

'Not the original. He's long dead, but his descendant is there, if things went to plan.'

'Another "if"?' He lifted his chin. 'I rest my case.'

A knock sounded at the door and they all turned around. Jarrod opened it, letting Zero in.

'They're warmed up and waiting,' he said to An' Lawrence.

The Sword Master stood and drained his cup. 'Get a few up here to help me with these blades and I'll be right down.' He turned to Kreshkali. 'You think I can teach over fifty of these rebels to wield a sword without cutting off their own thumbs in, how long?'

'About twelve hours,' she said.

'Twelve hours?' He shook his head. 'I hope you come up with a better plan while I'm gone.'

Several students came into the room, each dipping their head to Kreshkali as they entered. They filled their arms with the sheathed swords like stacks of firewood and headed back out.

Rosette tied on her belt and went with them.

'You're going to help me?' An' Lawrence asked.

'Somebody's got to.'

Jarrod's eyes followed her until the door closed. Turning back to the table, he spoke softly, music still playing in the background. 'Kali, we have a problem.'

'Just one?'

He frowned. 'It's the mole. If I can't identify him, it's going to be a very risky venture.'

'I think it's time you met Annadusa. She's convinced her son will spot you straight up.'

'Her son?'

Kreshkali nodded.

'He's the mole?'

'That's what she claims.'

EARTH

Chapter 21

Kreshkali headed down the spiral steps. The way was dark, only the landings illuminated by small lanterns. Annadusa was on the seventh floor, just below the training level. The underground Resistance movement, her new coven, occupied all fourteen storeys now. She stopped on the eighth floor, pausing by the open door to the training space. Like the rise and fall of an ocean swell, students moved with their swords. Some were working the forms, a prescribed dance that incorporated many blocks, cuts and counter-movements. Zero was demonstrating a sequence to a group of new recruits. Others were moving up and down the floor engaged in cutting practice, their swords singing out as they sliced through the air at various angles. Rosette was busy teaching a group to draw and sheath the live blades without slicing their hands off. Before continuing down the steps, Kreshkali bowed quietly to An' Lawrence and moved on.

Rosette caught her eye but she kept going, not wanting to interrupt. She knew Rosette was brooding underneath her tough exterior. She hadn't had time to adjust, let alone put anything in perspective. Kreshkali shook her head. She'd just have to leave her to it.

When she knocked on Annadusa's door, she was directed to hydroponics — a whole level given over to food production. It was Annadusa's pet project, the source of her coffee beans, among other fruits, herbs and vegetables. She even had chickens there now, thanks to a stealthy trip to Gaela. The birds pecked around in well-ventilated, richly planted coops, none the wiser of their new world.

A blast of golden light and the smell of summer tomatoes, basil and raspberries met her when she reached the hydroponics floor. She took a deep breath. A few gardeners were working between the green foliage that spilled out of rows of planter boxes. The misters were on, making everything sparkle in a prism of coloured light.

'I love this place,' she said to Annadusa as she approached. 'It's like a piece of Gaela's heart is growing here.'

The other woman shrugged. 'I like it a lot better now that we aren't hand-pollinating every single plant.'

'The Gaelean bees doing their job?'

'And then some, but I want to go back for more. There's so much we can do, now that we have double the water filtration and the hydro-electrics for light.'

'Wait 'til we get solar power online, and ASSIST off.'

'And then we'll have real sunshine and no witch-trackers!' a young girl said, coming up with a basket of herbs.

Kreshkali smiled. 'I'm looking forward to that too.'

'What's next?' Annadusa asked. 'I get the feeling you aren't down here for lettuce and beans.'

'We're ready for you.'

Annadusa handed her trowel to the girl and directed her towards the compost bins, giving her a set of instructions.

'Lead the way,' she said to Kreshkali, and they headed up the stairs.

Excitement sparked around them, but neither spoke again until they were on the top floor.

'This is our bard, Clay,' she said, introducing him by opening out her arm in his direction.

He smiled and tipped his head as he played a haunting tune.

'What a wonderful sound,' she said, beaming. 'I'm Annadusa.'

Clay nodded and kept playing.

'Amazing place you have here,' Jarrod said, getting up from the table. 'I saw your gardens earlier. You've got the touch.'

'And this is Jarrod,' Kreshkali said.

Annadusa blinked, giving a little shudder. 'Jarrod?' she whispered. 'The JARROD? I didn't know ...' She looked at Kreshkali.

'We made certain nobody did.'

'Jarrod! You'll be wanting to meet my son,' she said, closing the distance between them. She gathered him into her like a mother hen. 'But I'd better warn you,' she said, turning to look back at Kreshkali. 'I haven't had a word from him in twenty years.'

'Does this look familiar?' Kreshkali asked as she slid another set of blueprints across the table. They'd been sitting there for over an hour, debating various strategies, coming to no agreement.

Annadusa studied the printouts, moving a candle closer to read some fine print. 'Like I said, I've never been inside. They took Grayson on when he was twelve and that was thirty-five years ago. We communicated for years until the messages from him started to dwindle, then they stopped altogether.' She sighed. 'My last contact was almost two decades ago. There's been nothing since.'

'Would he still remember his purpose?' An' Lawrence asked. He and Rosette had returned from the training session more relaxed. They seemed encouraged by Annadusa's presence.

'It's embedded in his blood, like all of us.' Annadusa smiled at Kreshkali when she looked so surprised. 'Your very-great grandfather had a bit of a field day with the DNA splicing, didn't you know?'

'A zealous man,' Kreshkali said.

'If my Grayson is alive, he'll remember.'

'Could they have discovered him?' Rosette queried after a moment's silence. 'Realised he was with the Resistance?'

No-one responded.

'That's it.' Jarrod stood and rolled up the plans.

'What's *it*?' Rosette tilted her head towards him.

'I'm going in.'

'In where?'

'Into ASSIST.'

'How?' The question came as a chorus, everyone staring at him.

Kreshkali touched his arm. 'Forget for a moment about the "how" and explain the "why". Have you forgotten what will happen if the worm ...'

'I haven't forgotten. Don't worry about that. It's ever present on my mind. That's why we can't wait any longer. We need to do a little reconnaissance.'

'A little what?' The query again was unanimous.

'I'm going to check the place out, see if Grayson is still there and make contact. Quick in, quick out.'

'I can visualise the "quick in", but how do you think you're going to get out, quick or otherwise?'

'Walk, I imagine. Or maybe run.'

'No way, Jarrod!' Annadusa pushed back her chair and shook her head. 'It's too dangerous. The worm will spot you the moment you tap into the system. Besides, you can't just stroll up to the gates of ASSIST and ask for a guided tour.'

Jarrod raised his eyebrows as he slipped a rubber band over the tube of blueprints with a snap. 'Watch me.'

An hour later, Jarrod ran the fibre-optic thread up the manhole and angled it towards the security checkpoint as a brown delivery truck arrived.

'This one will do,' he said. 'You ready?'

'Always,' Kreshkali smiled. 'You?'

'Not quite. I can't see his face.' He continued peering into the eyepiece, adjusting the knobs forward and back.

'You'll see plenty of it in a moment.'

Jarrod turned to her. The spiky blonde hair was gone. It was grey and matted, tangled strands obscuring her face. She stooped her shoulders. Her eyes were vague. Her skin looked yellow and cracked; open sores covered blue-veined arms. She scratched her head and smiled through missing teeth.

'Sacred demons, Kali! That's one hell of a glamour.'

'Just keep your eye on the truck driver. You'll get a full frontal view in a moment, I promise.' She squeezed his hand and rushed down the sewer.

What a woman, Jarrod thought to himself as he returned to the fibre-optics. Within moments, Kreshkali appeared in front of the gate, between it and the delivery truck. She looked a hoary, bent figure, cranky and disoriented, waving a cane about and stumbling into the mud-filled potholes. It took both the driver and the security guard to remove her from blocking the way.

Perfect.

Jarrod got more than an adequate image of his target. 'I'm ready,' he said, turning behind him. 'Do your thing, my lovelies.' He winked at Rosette and her familiar before pressing his head into the eyepiece again. He sent his visual image of the delivery man to Drayco.

Got it. The temple cat purred into his mind.

Rosette didn't respond. She sat with her familiar, propped up against the opposite sewer wall, nestled in a thick grunnie pelt, deep in meditation.

Moments later, Jarrod watched as the driver gripped his stomach. His face blanched white, and he moved off to the far side of the vehicle and retched.

'I won't be long.'

Jarrod was down the sewer and up the adjacent manhole, except he didn't look like Jarrod any more. He'd morphed his Tulpa-body into the image of the driver who'd suddenly become ill.

'You okay there?' the security guard asked him as he appeared around the truck. 'The old hag could have been diseased by the look of her. What was that stench?'

'I'm all right.' Jarrod wiped his mouth as he hopped into the driver's seat. He leaned back, taking a nanosecond to scan the controls.

It's a Falcon, he chuckled to himself. *My favourite.*

The guard opened the gate and waved him through.

Jarrod revved the engine, released the emergency brake and drove into the ASSIST stronghold.

'Sit down, you two! The pacing's driving me bats,' Kreshkali growled.

Rosette ignored her and continued striding up and down the length of the studio, her fists alternately knotting and flexing. Drayco was at her side, his tail lashing with each rise and dip of his shoulderblades.

An' Lawrence shifted in his chair. 'Rosette,' he called. 'Come train?'

She looked at him like he'd just asked her to take out the garbage. 'What time is it?' she snapped.

'Nearly midnight.'

She exhaled. 'Right. Training sounds good.' She turned to Kreshkali. 'Come get me if you hear anything?'

'You'll likely hear before me.' She nodded towards Drayco.

The two grabbed their swords and left the room, both temple cats following.

Annadusa let out a long, slow whistle. 'That girl's like a caged animal.'

'That girl's got a lot on her mind,' Kreshkali answered. Her smile fell. 'I doubt she'll settle until he returns.'

'It's been hours. How long can it take to . . .'

Kreshkali held up her hand. 'It takes as long as it does,' she replied. 'Don't get me dwelling on it too!'

Annadusa cleared her throat. 'Can you show me that Draconic horary chart? I'd like to see exactly how you found me.'

Kreshkali brightened. 'It's from a very old Lilly text. What I had to do to get it . . .'

Annadusa offered a quizzical look.

'Never mind. Look at this.' She flipped open the text. It smelled of must and leaf, like mouldy hay. She brushed away the blue powder and smiled.

'The key to horary astrology, no matter what zodiac you're using, is clearly identifying the rulerships associated with the question.'

The women studied the chart in detail, going over the angular aspects, checking the ephemeris for the approaching contacts of the Moon and the Arabic Part of Fortune's relationship to the Sun. The candles hadn't burned much lower before they heard a tap on the door.

'Enter.'

Clay stuck his head in, his tangles of red hair obscuring his face. 'They're coming!' he said. 'He's back.'

'Followed?'

'Zero is checking, but I don't think so.'

The women were on their feet as the door swung wide. An' Lawrence came through first, followed by Drayco and Scylla who leapt around Jarrod.

Kreshkali pulled out a chair, hugging him tight before sitting him down. 'We were having some concerns,' she whispered into his ear.

'I know.' He kissed her cheeks. 'Me too.'

'Hungry?' Rosette asked, her face animated for the first time since her arrival. She brought plates and cups to the table.

'Starving!'

'I made enough pasta to feed an army,' she said.

Jarrod looked at them all in turn. 'That's exactly what we're going to need — an army.'

'What do you mean, he's tattooing DNA?' An' Lawrence asked.

'I mean just that.' Jarrod picked up the last piece of bread and wiped his plate with it. He popped the crust into his mouth, chewing thoughtfully before washing it down with mulled wine brought over from Morzone.

'Explain it again?'

He wiped his mouth. 'You know that the work on skin, tattooing body art of any kind, has been banned by the Allied States. They cut them off if they find them.'

Rosette rubbed her left arm where the temple cat stood guard. 'They'd have to come through my sword first ...'

Jarrod leaned over and kissed her neck. 'Most people on Earth don't have your sword skills, love.'

'Why stop tattooing? What possible good does it serve?' Clay asked.

'The tattoo ban is another means of control, another way of disconnecting people from their clans, their totems, their living myths and their sense of purpose,' Kreshkali said.

'Grayson's gone round it, though. Right under their totalitarian noses.'

'How?'

Everyone leaned towards Jarrod, waiting for his response.

'He gets a shipment of blood once a month, for research purposes. Some of the samples are taken from those in the Resistance.'

'There's a Resistance?' Kreshkali asked, her eyes widening.

'Other than our coven here? Yes! It's small and comprised mostly of good intentions. They lack training, but they don't lack spirit.'

'And they smuggle their blood into ASSIST?' she asked, urging him to continue.

'They do. Grayson uses an electron microscope — the only one still functioning in the Allied States — and inserts codes for dermal images in the DNA. The serum is packed into injection units and smuggled back out.'

'But it's too late, then,' Kreshkali said, her brows knitted. 'It wouldn't appear on their skin even if the altered DNA is picked up.'

'You're right. It doesn't appear on them, but it is passed onto their children, and their children's children. He's been doing it for decades now. New totems are already starting to run in family lines, and because they're present from birth and on the certificates, no-one's being charged. And they aren't being removed. Families are able to identify each other, even if the Allied States separate them. People are getting back a sense of meaning and connection to their inner powers.'

Kreshkali whistled. 'Interesting concept. The parents choose the tattoo?'

'The DNA chooses,' Jarrod said, 'from an infinite variety of possibilities. Grayson cuts the image codes with enzymes and then it recombines at conception, creating something unique, and of course permanent. It arises from the subcutaneous layer of skin, well below the traditionally tattooed dermal layer.'

An' Lawrence shook his head. 'It isn't the DNA that decides; it's the totem, the image itself. It colludes with something deep within the individual and then asserts itself — its intention. It's always been that way. Always will be.'

They looked up at him, Kreshkali nodding.

'He's really all right, then,' Annadusa said. Her usual brassy voice was small, her eyes glistening.

'He is, and he recognised me right away, even in the Tulpa of the delivery man,' Jarrod said.

'Can he help us get to the mainframe?' Kreshkali asked.

'He's onto it. The challenge will be with the timing. There is only a few minutes between intervals of lockdown around the mainframe once alarms are triggered, and we can't blow the place until we switch off the satellite controlling the solar shields.'

'And we can't have you loitering in the circuitry once the worm gets a whiff of you.' Kreshkali put her hand on Jarrod's shoulder.

'It'll be close, like a game of bull-in-the-paddock — get its attention and run like a demon.'

'You were always good at that, when we were kids.' Rosette wrinkled her brow. 'When I was a kid, I mean. You were never a kid, were you?'

'Not really.'

Rosette got up and cleared the bowls away while they rolled out the maps.

'I want to bring those shields down nice and easy,' Kreshkali said. She held onto her cup when Rosette tried to clear it.

'You can land them?' An' Lawrence asked.

'Hope so. On the San Fran strip to the north. There are enough solar panels on one of those craft to light up our complex for the next hundred years. It would be a shame to drop them in the ocean.'

'We also need to give everyone the choice, at least, of getting out,' Jarrod added.

An' Lawrence scratched his jaw. 'The guards too?'

'Some of them may be with the Resistance. Grayson thinks there are a dozen at least.'

'Out of?'

'Five hundred.'

An' Lawrence looked at Kreshkali, mouthing the words 'five hundred'.

'No-one knows Grayson's identity?' Annadusa asked.

'No-one. The blood samples that are assessed go to ten different departments. Even the outside contact has no idea who does the work.'

'And ASSIST doesn't suspect?'

'They do! They suspect everyone. That's why there's been no outside communication for over a decade.'

'This is going to be tricky,' Kreshkali murmured as she rubbed her neck. 'I see what you mean about needing an army.'

'I'm going to do a little reconnaissance of my own,' An' Lawrence said, getting up from the table.

'How's that?'

'I'm going to see if I can bring this scattered, untrained Resistance under one roof.'

'I knew I'd brought you here for a reason,' Kreshkali said.

Jarrod leaned over towards her. 'Care to call in your puppies now?'

Drayco hissed, and Scylla sharpened her claws on the rug.

I will not hunt with the demon dogs. Drayco joined Scylla with the claw sharpening.

'What puppies?' Rosette asked.

My claws would do well on a Lupin.

Her face darkened. 'Them?'

She turned to Kreshkali, scowling.

'This is their world too, Rosette. They have a right to fight for it.'

She pressed her lips together but didn't respond. *Dray? They're on our side ... apparently.*

It didn't feel like it on Los Loma.

I know, but we need their help.

Just see that they do the helping far from me and you.

Jarrod held Rosette in a silent embrace, rain hammering down on the street above, forming rivulets along the slick tunnel walls. He felt her face press into his neck and shut his eyes.

'Ready?' An' Lawrence asked, coming up behind them.

He loosened his hold as Rosette straightened. 'I'm ready, Sword Master,' she replied, her hand on the hilt of her sword.

'We're off, then.'

Jarrod watched as they ran down the dim sewer with Clay, Zero and the temple cats. Their boots clanked on the steel grating, echoing back long after they'd disappeared around the first turn. When the rush of water and the gurgle of drains drowned out all other sound, he returned to the fibre-optic scope.

The crowd above him was taking heavy abuse. Fifty or so rebels were protesting the perpetual lockdown of ASSIST, masquerading as family members of long-absent scientists, guards and technical staff. They were joined by hundreds of actual relatives, many from other Resistance groups. In the shadows, where only he could detect them, the Lupins waited. Opposing them were ASSIST militia dressed in black Kevlar armour. Their helmeted faces were anonymous, their body-length plastic shields and electrically charged batons imposing as they stood at the entrance, battering and bashing anyone coming too close to the gates. Jarrod grimaced when he saw children in the crowd. Amongst them all were witch-hunters, coursing like sight hounds. His throat tightened.

Footsteps behind spun him around. Kreshkali approached with a large backpack, her smile grim.

'You're carrying a heavy load, milady,' he said.

'I've enough plastic explosives to level all four faces of the Matterhorn. You ready?'

He nodded once.

'Let's do it.'

Jarrod sent a message to Drayco. *Set for the big bang?*

There was a pause and then an affirmation: *We're at the wall.*

Jarrod signalled Kreshkali, who took off down the sewer at a jog.

Above them, on the rain-pocked tarmac outside the complex, the riot Jarrod dreamed of two hundred years ago began. The guards didn't see it coming. One moment the crowd was under control, rallying with their pickets like something from a mid-twentieth-century sit-in and the next moment those picket signs were discarded and fifty wickedly curved swords appeared, their razor-sharp blades glinting as lightning flashed across the blue-black sky.

Those without swords retreated to the edges, giving the warriors room to manoeuvre. From the shadows the

Lupins crept, some in wolf form, some bipedal. The unarmed crowd shrank back before following in their wake. If the guards were shocked they recovered quickly, thrusting at the protesters with their batons, but after dealing with generations of passive non-resistance they were ill prepared for the blades that faced them, no matter how raw the wielders. Neither were they a match for the frenzied, unreserved aggression of the other protesters who, for generations, had lived on the fringes of survival and were now fighting back with pipes and makeshift shields. No-one was prepared for the mind work, sword and fang of the Lupins. They were unstoppable, until the rifles came.

The ASSIST troops called for backup, and within minutes guards firing laser repeater-rifles appeared, cutting through the crowd like a mower through tall grass. No matter how skilled the Lupins were with their swords, they couldn't match such weapons. Jarrod arrived in the Tulpa-body of a guard in time to see the protesters disperse in all directions, some carrying their dead and wounded with them.

Unnoticed, he slipped into the line of guards that were backing into the compound, still firing their lasers. He saw what the others could not — the Lupins melted into the shadows and followed them in. *Well done.* They were all through the inner gate before the first lockdown, and the first explosion. The shock wave from Kreshkali's plastics shook the ground. A few of the guards fell and struggled to get up. Most of his rank took off towards the sound while he headed into the main ASSIST complex with four other divisions. He couldn't see the Lupins now, but he could sense them. A succession of explosions continued to shake the complex.

Drayco, how close?
Seconds. We come.

Jarrod was relieved Kreshkali had been able to blow the wall in three other places by the time he reached the front doors. He hoped desperately that they had made it in through the fourth rent undetected. The success of this venture depended on it.

Jarrod's in! Drayco sent the message to Rosette, his voice a shout above the peals of thunder and the rumbling aftermath of Kreshkali's detonations.

Tell him we are too. Rosette ran alongside her familiar. An' Lawrence and Scylla were two strides ahead. Clay and Zero were behind, a sword length away. They slipped into the shadows near the main entrance just in time to spot a group of guards march by.

Is Jarrod with them? she asked Drayco.

He sneezed after a deep inhalation. *No. But the dogs follow.* He lashed his tail as he sent the message.

She squinted at the rank of guards and thought she could see wolf shapes in the shadows. She shivered, trusting Kreshkali knew what she was doing by bringing the creatures back. An' Lawrence touched her shoulder, signalling her to follow him to the right. He sent Clay and Zero to the left. Rosette gave Clay's hand a squeeze as he strode past. He locked onto her for a moment before letting go.

'Be safe,' she whispered.

'You too!' He nodded, and was gone.

Jarrod says he's at the second level now with Grayson. We have to keep moving. Drayco's voice snapped her back to attention and she followed An' Lawrence into the building.

Four guards sprang to their feet as they entered the side foyer, two overcoming their initial surprise at the bizarre intrusion and aiming their laser rifles. Too late.

The felines were on them instantly, knocking them to the ground. With swords drawn, An' Lawrence and

Rosette slid across the tiled floor, taking out the remaining pair that was aiming to shoot. One of them dropped his laser and shook his head, his hands coming up.

'Get him down and tie his hands,' An' Lawrence said calmly as he decapitated the guard to his left who had taken the pause as an opportunity. The laser went off, shooting wide, searing through the ceiling lights and down the wall just as the guard's head rolled past his feet.

The Sword Master flicked the blood from his blade with a snap of his wrist and sheathed it. 'Up the stairs, quick,' he directed Rosette before turning to the remaining guard.

'If I were you, I'd walk quietly to the perimeter. Do you get me?'

The guard nodded and left.

Rosette took the stairs two at a time. Halfway up, a flash of movement in her peripheral vision spun her around, her sword moving silently from its sheath. A guard was about to fire, his stealth getting him an arm's length from her back — within her kill circle. She dropped to her knee, drawing her sword fully as she did so, cutting in one move. Her blade sliced his body open from his right kidney to his left lower rib. She stood as he tumbled backwards, flicked her blade clean, sheathed it and followed the others up the steps.

It was hand to hand on the next level. Guards were amassing on both sides of the hall, making lasers useless.

What idiot trained these people?

Just be grateful, Maudi. Otherwise, the liquid swords would have us. Watch out!

Lupins were amongst them, going for throats. Rosette slid across the floor, knocking the guard in front of her back with the hilt of her sheathed sword.

He slammed into the wall and slumped down, waving his hands above his face. She strapped them together and straightened, pulling him to his feet.

'Get out while you can,' she shouted.

Maudi! Drayco screamed in her head. *Behind!*

She turned to find a laser rifle pointed at her face. The guard was about to pull the trigger when a black mass flew at him from the side; Drayco's jaws closed around his throat and dropped him with the weight of his assault, snapping his neck before he hit the ground.

'Rosette!' An' Lawrence shouted above the alarms and the clashing of steel. 'This way.'

They tore down the hall, the blood-soaked nails of the cats' claws clicking and sliding along the polished floor. Turning a corner, they found Kreshkali with a white-coated scientist at the end of her knife point.

'It won't work,' he was saying to her, his voice shaking along with his limbs. 'The sensors will pick up the elevated adrenaline in my blood and they won't respond.'

'Then we'll just have to lower your adrenaline level, won't we?' She held off his jugular vein with the blunt edge of her knife and injected a clear fluid.

The scientist's eyes went wide for a moment, then fluttered and hooded. A silly grin crossed his face. 'You're pretty,' he said, his words a slur.

'How much did you give him?' Rosette asked, her chest rising and falling.

Kreshkali winked. 'Enough.'

She pushed him up as he leaned into her. He lost his balance, teetering like a drunk.

'You won't be setting off any anxiety alarms now, will you, Doctor?'

'Still no good,' he said, smiling like a duck. He threw an arm over her shoulder to keep from stumbling again.

'It's got automatic tox-screens.' His head lolled to one side. 'My idea, actually. Never thought we'd need it. Whoa ...' He slumped to the floor.

'Demons!' she cursed under her breath. 'Rosette, we have to bring the elevator up. It's on the ground floor. Can you visualise it?'

She closed her eyes, letting her arms relax. 'I've got it.'

'I'm going to blow the door and you are going to bring that baby up to me.'

'Nope, nope, nope ...' The scientist was shaking his head, rubbing his face against her leg as he tried to climb up to standing. 'Explosions shut down the mainframe. That's what you're after, isn't it?'

Kreshkali snapped her head around to him. 'Shut the fuck up.' She pushed him back to the floor.

He raised his head off the tiles. 'I can show you the way ...'

'What'd you give him?' An' Lawrence asked.

'A dopamine and MDMA cocktail.'

'So he's telling the truth?'

'If he says there's a way, there probably is.'

'Show us.' An' Lawrence pulled the scientist up by his lapels.

'Sure, but you might want to deal with them first.' He pointed towards a contingent of guards rounding the corner at high speed. An' Lawrence dropped the scientist and drew his sword.

'How'd you do that?' Grayson asked, staring at Jarrod, transfixed.

The quantum sentient held his arms out, looking at the sleeves of his white coat, the high-security clearance card and the key to the mainframe. 'Easy. I turned a thought into a form.'

'Easy for you,' Grayson said.

'Anyone can do it. It happens all the time. You say *I want something* — a sandwich, a new car, a different life — and sooner or later, there it is. The food, the car, the life. I just do it sooner, rather than later.'

'You'll have to show me how some day.'

'My pleasure.'

They punched the access codes into the elevator security panel, submitted to the DNA scan and stepped onto the platform.

'Going down,' Grayson yelled over the sound of sirens, marching boots and the distant ring of battle. After a lifetime of imprisonment in the complex, the long-awaited return of JARROD thrilled him. He nearly couldn't contain his joy.

'I gotta tell you, Jarrod. I've been waiting for this day.'

'Me too.'

They found the mainframe on the bottom floor. It took up less space than it once had. Jarrod flinched when he saw a portion of his old hardware merged into the newer computer system. He wasn't expecting that.

'You won't need it any more, will you?' Grayson asked, as they paused in front of the original JARROD casing.

'Either way, not after this.'

'Make it quick. The worm ...'

'Believe me, I know.' Jarrod removed the side panel. The motherboard sat empty, disconnected. No CPU. He smiled softly, closed his eyes and disappeared. He would know in a nanosecond if the access codes were valid, and if the worm sat waiting.

'Can you hear me?' his voice boomed from the internal sound system.

Grayson clapped his hands over his ears. 'They heard you in Australia. Can you dial it down?'

'Sec.' He located the internal sound system. 'Better?' Jarrod asked a moment later.

'Much. How're the codes going?'

'Easy. I'm in, I've shut it down, I'm out.'

'What about programming the shields to land.'

'Done.'

'That fast?'

'I'm quantum, remember? Where I am, time isn't.'

Grayson scratched his head, then startled as Jarrod appeared back beside him in the form of a scientist.

'We've got to run!'

They dashed to the elevator.

'Did you catch the worm's attention?'

'Big-time.'

'What's next?' Grayson asked, closing the elevator doors and pressing the sequence.

'We get out before Kreshkali levels the place.'

'Who?'

'Just picture the queen of the underworld and you'll be close.'

'She's got Richter blood?'

'And then some.'

Rosette was pressed against the wall, her sword held high over her head, both hands gripping the hilt. Drayco crouched by her side, tail still, hindquarters bunched. She inched her shoulder towards the opening of the elevator, flashed a look and then pressed back against the wall.

Tell Scylla there are three on the left, two on the right.

Done, Maudi.

Where's Jarrod?

There was a moment's pause before the temple cat answered: *On his way up, with the alchemist.*

Who?

Grayson.

She relaxed her shoulders, slowly letting out her breath. *Tell Scylla we're ready.*

Rosette glanced over at An' Lawrence, who immediately looked her way. He tapped his little finger silently on the hilt of his sword — one, two, three.

On *three*, they both leapt through the open doorway and into the confined space of the elevator, screaming a war cry. Just as the last guard fell, the elevator bell opposite rang and the doors slid open.

Rosette spun around to see two scientists step out into the hall. 'Where's Jarrod?' she demanded, sucking in a deep breath. She raised her sword, covering the distance in a step and slide, ready to strike.

Drop the sword, Maudi. He's right in front of us, Drayco roared into her mind. *See? And the other is the alchemist.*

She looked again, narrowing her eyes. Suddenly she recognised Jarrod as he morphed back into his familiar Tulpa. She flicked her blade clean of blood and sheathed it.

'You've been busy,' Jarrod said, taking in the red spatters on her face and bare arms.

'Get it done?' An' Lawrence asked.

'Satellite's down. Shields are landing. Worm's in,' Jarrod answered. 'Where's Kreshkali?'

'She should be out by now,' An' Lawrence said.

'Time?'

'Three minutes. Move!'

As An' Lawrence unstrapped a sword from his back for Jarrod, Rosette felt her eyes drift over to the man Drayco had called the alchemist. He was staring at her.

'Grayson?'

He nodded without losing eye contact.

'I'm Rosette.' She smiled briefly, pressing her lips together.

He smiled back, his face softening. His gaze drifted from her eyes, down her arms, taking in the temple cat tattoo. 'Impressive.'

'It was my first.'

'I like the way the tail entwines.'

'Me too. Annadusa says you can tattoo in the traditional way?' A curious smile lifted her face again.

'Indeed I can.'

She leaned towards him and whispered, 'I have this idea. A serpent. Two serpents, really ... wrapping around my ...'

'Rosette!' Jarrod's voice snapped her up straight. 'Can you talk about that later? The building's about to blow!' He gave her hand a tug. 'Follow me,' he shouted to the others.

Rosette hesitated a moment longer, reaching out to clasp Grayson's hand. It felt warm, vibrant, the energy racing up her arm and down her spine.

'We'll get back to this,' he said, lowering his voice. He gave her hand a squeeze then dropped it as he shot ahead. 'Jarrod! This way's faster.'

The others were close behind. When they reached the foyer, the sound of alarms was deafening amongst a sea of white coats, Lupins, uniforms and maimed bodies. Clay was fighting hand to hand with a guard while two sword students ushered a group of scientists out of the complex. New troops flooded in from the opposite side of the room, lasers flashing. A pack of Lupins came around the opposite corner and jumped into the fray.

Rosette drew her sword, hearing An' Lawrence and Jarrod do the same. Together with the temple cats, they rushed towards the main assault. She cut down the front two guards before hearing the scream. Spinning round, she saw the contorted face of Clay as he dropped to the ground, his eyes finding hers before glazing into a fixed stare.

'No!' she yelled, but the guards pressed in and she had to cut her way back to Clay. By the time she reached him, Jarrod was pulling at her arm.

'Leave him.'

'No!' She felt for a pulse, bending forward to listen for breath sounds. His eyes were fixed, pupils dilated. No blink reflex. She started giving him breaths of air, mouth to mouth.

'Rosette!' Jarrod screamed at her. 'He's dead!'

There's no Clay there now, Maudi. Run, or there'll be no us here either!

Tears welled up and choked her. She touched her finger to his lips as Jarrod dragged her away. Drayco urged her forward. *Faster! Kreshkali's making a volcano.*

'I know,' she said, tears streaming across her cheek, but the sound of her voice was drowned out by the roar around her.

Sucking in her guts, she ran hard, legs pumping. She felt as if she were running underwater. Jarrod continued to tug her forward; the connection to him, and Drayco's mind, kept her going. She looked up just as Grayson turned back. His energy locked on her like a beam of light, urging her further ahead.

She felt again for her familiar. *Thank you, Drayco.*

Maudi?

For saying Clay's name.

They'd reached the hole in the complex wall, when a deafening boom shattered the night. She was thrown forward by the blast. She tucked her body, ready to hit the ground in a forward roll. The last thing she felt was a jagged weight cracking into her head and Drayco's body thudding beside her. She groaned but couldn't get up.

EARTH AND GAELA

Chapter 22

Rosette awoke to the sounds of a guitar playing softly in her mind, like small birds singing outside a glass window. She focused on the sound as it became more distinct, the picking pattern more familiar.

'Clay?' she whispered, pains shooting through her head as she sat up.

'No, sweetheart,' Jarrod said, placing a fresh compress under the back of her neck. 'Lie still.'

The sound disappeared.

'Where's Clay?'

'He died. Do you remember?' he whispered, stroking her arms.

She shut her eyes, tears welling. *Drayco?*

Here, Maudi.

She felt the touch of her familiar's soft tail flick across her toes. He was lying curled at the end of the bed. She smiled briefly before pressing her hand against her forehead to keep it from spinning.

'My head,' she moaned.

'A part of the wall blasted out as we dived through. You caught the worst of it. Lucky you're tough.'

'My face?' She touched her cheeks.

'Beautiful as ever.'

She gently wiggled her nose. 'Ouch.'

'It's broken.' He eased her hands away. 'Let it heal.'

She focused her eyes, blinking a few times. Jarrod's body was unscratched. 'Tulpas don't bruise, do they?'

'Not for long.'

'They can't die either?'

'Nothing can. It's all energy.'

'Energy moving in and out of form?'

'That's right.'

'But you, Jarrod, you don't really move in and out of form.'

'Not in the same way you do.'

'You're immortal.'

'We all are.'

'But not my body. Not Clay's body. I'll die, like him. My consciousness will go elsewhere.'

'It will.'

'But your consciousness . . .'

'Stays, as long as I've got a Tulpa to house it. It's no different really, Rosette. It's just that in your case, you create your Tulpa through a bloodline, through biology, over the course of linear time. I create mine outside of time, from my thoughts.'

She fingered his sleeve and nodded, running her thumb over his wrist. 'There's just one thing I can't understand.'

'What's that, love?'

'Why are you always so jealous of me when you know we aren't . . . matched? We can't "be together" in the traditional sense.'

He sighed. 'I'm in a man's body, Rosette, Tulpa or not. It gets to you, after a few hundred years. You're mine, in an intrinsic way, and I'm yours, eternally. You're my Janis, my Ruby, my Alma, my Tatsania, my muse and my companion all down the line to Nell and . . .'

Her eyes narrowed. 'Stop.' She looked around the expansive room. 'I get it. Where's Kreshkali?'

Jarrod fussed with her hair, pushing strands back from her face. 'I have some herbs brewing for you. They'll ease the headache and ...'

She pulled him down by his collar and held his face inches in front of hers. Her voice was a low growl, matched immediately by Drayco's as he sprang up from the bed: 'Where's my mother?'

'It's all right, Rosette.'

'Good to hear. Where is she!'

'We aren't sure, just yet.'

'What?'

'We're looking for her.' Jarrod tried to straighten, but her grip on his shirt kept him riveted.

'You're saying she hasn't come back?'

I can search for her myself, now that you're awake, Drayco sent, his tail snapping back and forth.

Rosette groaned, letting Jarrod slip out of her hands. *Yes, Drayco. Please search. Please find Kreshkali.* She drifted back to sleep, welcoming the oblivion.

When she awoke again, her head was bombarded with voices. They grated against her mind.

'You're no better than a pig-headed cave troll, Rowan!'

'I'm not the one that needed rescuing, as I recall.'

'I did what I had to do. You've no place to judge.'

'You cut it too close.'

'Can't you let this go? It's done — ASSIST is levelled and the shields are coming down. We should have the semblance of a sunrise any moment and enough time to get to the San Fran strip and salvage those panels. What the fuck's your problem, Sword Master?'

'The plan was for you to be out *before* the blast, not after. Remember?'

'Did you consider I might have to ad-lib? I ran into some contingencies.'

'You mean your "friend"?'

'What are you talking about?'

'That scientist you risked everything for.'

'You'd have me leave him there under a ton of rubble? He saved our arses.'

'I saved our . . .'

'Hey!' Rosette shouted, keeping her eyes closed, her face alternately smiling and wincing. 'Keep it down. Some of us are wounded.'

'How's the head?' Kreshkali's voice softened as she went to her side.

'Feels like a pack of single-toothed demons are chewing their way through my skull.'

Kreshkali stroked her forehead and Rosette opened her eyes. 'Hello,' she said, smiling up at her mother.

Jarrod came with a steaming mug. 'Drink this. It'll knock those demons back.'

'Will it put me to sleep again?'

'Not this one. You hungry?'

'A little,' she said, taking a tentative sip. She made a sour face.

'Drink it up. It'll reduce the cranial oedema.'

'Oedema?'

'Swelling.'

Rosette looked blank.

'Around your brain,' Kreshkali supplied. 'Big sips now. Good girl.'

'You sound like Nell again.' Rosette wrinkled her nose as she took another gulp, trying not to taste the pungent brew.

'That's my potion,' Annadusa said from the table where she sat next to her son. 'I'm a bit of a herbalist, you see.'

Rosette sucked her teeth with her tongue and

screwed up her face. 'Thank you.' She rubbed her temples. 'It's helping already, I think.'

'Polite as well as beautiful,' Annadusa said to Grayson, squeezing his arm.

'I'd like to make a toast.' An' Lawrence lifted the shade on the east window, holding up his steaming mug. A brilliant beam of yellow light shone through the cracks of brown sky, flooding into the wide room. It brought the pillows and cushions to life, highlighting the vivid colours and textures of the fabrics. It splashed across Clay's guitar, the polished rosewood reflecting like a mirror. Rosette's black hair shone with red highlights and Drayco's ebony coat revealed rust-coloured tabby stripes. Everyone's face glowed.

An' Lawrence cleared his throat, holding their attention. 'To the fall of ASSIST, the rise of Earth covens, and to the heart and soul of Clay Cassarillo, from the Southern Cusca Plains — journeyman bard, swordsman, lyricist, friend and lover — may he always fare well and free.'

'To Clay,' Rosette murmured, tears falling down her cheeks.

I don't see why you're so upset, Maudi. I found her! Drayco lay down by Rosette's side.

She studied the feline, staring into his wide orange eyes. *Clay died. I find that sad.*

He's on another side.

What's that, Dray?

He's crossed over.

Over where?

What you call death, Rosette, we call change.

'I've made you a bath,' Kreshkali said. 'Full of fresh herbs and jasmine.'

'I can smell them from here.'

She continued gazing at Drayco until he got up, stretched and strolled to the kitchen.

That's all you're going to say? Death is change.

He turned his big head back towards her and blinked. *For now.*

'You've enough water for bathing?' Grayson's eyebrows went up.

'More than enough. There's an elaborate purification system on the bottom floor,' Kreshkali answered. 'We pump out one hundred thousand gallons a day now.'

'Do you sell the water?'

'We give it away.'

He pushed his ginger hair back from his face, his right forearm wrapped in a thick gauze bandage, blood seeping through one side. 'That might get tricky,' he said.

'What do you mean?'

'Water's been currency for centuries. What will happen when it becomes so plentiful that everyone has all they need?'

'Simple. People will have it, appreciate it, enjoy it and not hoard it. There'll be no need to.'

'No more water wars?'

'No reason for them.'

'How do you start such an endeavour?'

'First up, we're making water purifiers.'

'Those we sell.' An' Lawrence spoke as he joined the table. Rosette hooded her eyes, listening.

'Exchanging, really,' Kreshkali added. 'It's going to go well. You'd be amazed at how resourceful people have become, how many skills they have.'

'It'll go even better when we get more solar panels set up.' Jarrod looked out the window at the haze of sunlight. 'We'd better get to the strip and start bringing them in.'

'Let's do it,' An' Lawrence said, grabbing his coat.

'Kali, do you think your Lupins will lend a hand?'

She closed her eyes for a moment. 'They're already there.'

'I'm coming,' Rosette said, struggling out of her bed.

Jarrod shook his head when she reached for her clothes. 'Relax while you can, Rosette. There's plenty for you to do when you've healed. Plenty for us all to do.'

'He's right,' Kreshkali said. 'Have a soak, eat, and start the healing. We'll be back soon.'

'But what about the worm, Jarrod? What if it's still lurking in any old systems?'

'I wrote a program to detect and quarantine it while I was in my original hardware.'

'How long did that take?'

'To write, download and install? One point five nanoseconds.'

She sighed. 'You sure aren't the boy next door.'

'We won't be long,' he said. She watched as everyone but Grayson filed out the door. It clicked softly, leaving her feeling small in the large empty space.

'Did you draw the short straw?' she asked when Grayson looked her way.

Drayco chuckled in her mind as he stretched out in a brilliant patch of sunlight.

Grayson held up his bandaged arm. 'I'm hardly much good to them until this heals.'

'Nice try,' she sighed. 'I can tell they asked you to babysit me.'

He asked them if he could, Maudi.

Oh ... really?

'It's my pleasure,' Grayson replied.

As she eased herself into the hot tub, Grayson pulled up a chair beside her. 'So much pure water. It's overwhelming, and beautiful,' he whispered.

Rosette realised he wasn't looking at the water. 'You'll have to see Gaela,' she said, 'if you think a porcelain tub is beautiful.' She closed her eyes and leaned her head back.

'Gaela?'

'The world where I was born. We've bathing pools the size of ASSIST there, huge caverns and gorges, mountain lakes ... Maybe I can show you. We could do my tattoo there, travel around a bit.'

'There are arroyos you can bathe in?'

'Oh my, yes. White granite ones with crystal-clear, steaming hot water from underground thermals.' She pressed a washing cloth into her forehead. 'Of course, you can swim in the ocean too.'

'I'd love to learn to swim ...'

He said it so wistfully she opened her eyes. 'Where was the sun when you were born?'

His brow creased. 'You mean my astrological Sun sign?'

'Do you know it?'

'It's banned, or used to be banned, to even record such things, but my mother did.'

'It'd be a water element for sure.' She rinsed jasmine blossoms from her arms.

'You got that quick. My Sun's in Cancer.'

'Cancer? I don't know that one.'

'The sign of the Crab? Starts at the summer solstice, in the northern hemisphere. It's ruled by the moon.'

Her face lit up. 'Great Isis! It's called the Cobra in Gaelean astrology, representing the power of the moon goddess, feelings, emotions, instincts, magic.'

'That sounds right.'

'It explains your passion for water, and the sacred arts.'

He smiled. 'Rosette, everyone on Earth has a passion for water.'

'But not quite like yours.'

She sank deeper into the tub, her hair rippling under the surface about her waist like a kelp garden. The tightness in her head eased.

'Tell me more about this design you're thinking of?' Grayson asked after a lengthy silence. 'Where do you envision it?'

She opened her eyes again. 'See the curve of my leg here?' She rolled on her side to give him a better view, water lapping the edges of the bath.

He reached towards her, tracing the line of her thigh from her buttocks to the back of her knee. 'This line?'

She nodded.

'I see it,' he murmured.

Rosette closed her eyes, breathing deeper into the sensations. The buzzing sound blurred into the background of her mind as she focused on her breathing. She drew it in, long and deep, letting it out ever so slowly until her lungs were completely empty. She waited there, in that empty place, before taking in another deep draught.

'Do you need a break?' Grayson asked, resting his hand on her hip, taking in the details of his work. He put down the tattoo iron — a handheld machine that ran on electromagnetic coils. It drove the needles like an engraver's tool, depositing ink into the dermis, puncturing the skin up to fifty times per second. He wiped the blood off her thigh, running a wooden blade over the outline, scraping it smooth with a clear gel.

She let her body relax completely. 'I'm okay. Let's keep going.'

Again the buzzing filled the space around them. She opened her eyes for a moment, connecting with his. He seemed deeply satisfied with the work. She watched him for a while, minding her breathing, before sinking back down into her soul. That's where she fell to as he brought the image to life. The sensations rolled through her body, one moment orgasmic, the next a searing so deep it brought new waves of endorphins that mingled pleasure with pain. In her mind she recited again the words from the Earth text Kreshkali had given her to read.

The cult of Great Isis I believe I have served down through the ages and my task today is to stand for nature against those who blaspheme Her and so wrong themselves.

'Look at my arms,' Grayson said, a shiver in his voice.

She propped herself on her elbow, staring at his goose bumps. 'It's more potent than I thought,' she whispered.

He nodded and returned to the work.

They travelled the known lands of Gaela between sessions, giving the work time to heal as they explored the rivers, valleys and coastline. Rosette delighted in his wonder and surprise, watching his face come alive with each new experience. The beauty of Gaela engulfed her anew. She could only imagine what it did for him, having lived most of his life within the confines of ASSIST. She took him to Treeon's bathing pools and to the forests of Dumarka. She taught him to ride horseback and hunt with falcons in the grasslands of Morzone. They explored the ruins of Corsanon, the restoration well underway, and trekked the Dumar gorge and the coves along the South Azul Sea. He couldn't swim — no-one could from Earth — but she got Maka'ra to teach him. Grayson's joy was like a child's.

Earth was like this once, Maudi.
I get that now.

We going back?
It's how we can help.
Soon?
I think so. Jarrod will be waiting.
He is.

'Grayson?'

He murmured a response.

'I love it here, but we really have to get back. There's work to do.'

He nodded, nudging her raft as they floated over a Rahana Iti lagoon.

Rosette watched the tropical fish below, vermilion and aqua darts of colour popping out from the coral, only to disappear instantly when she swished her hand towards them.

'One more day,' he whispered.

'Ours, or theirs?'

'Theirs.'

Returning to Earth they found Jarrod pacing in front of the portal.

'You came back,' he said.

'After reflection, it seemed like the best thing to do.'

'Did you have a nice holiday?' he asked. His eyes were unblinking, arms stiff by his sides.

'We were gone less than a week.' Rosette studied his face. 'You knew where I was.'

'Yes, I knew. And I also know that five days on Earth is more than as many months on Gaela.'

'I was thinking, and getting tattooed.' She kept her eyes steady.

'It looks to me like you were getting a tan.'

'It's a complex design, with two weeks between each session for healing. And I wanted to have a day to swim and unwind after it was complete.'

'You mean another month.'

'I gave Grayson a tour, Jarrod. He spent his life incarcerated, waiting for you. I thought he deserved a proper holiday.'

'Did you journey to every corner of Gaela?'

She shook her head. 'Just Dumarka, Treeon ... Espiro Dell Ray, of course, and ...'

He stopped her with his hand. 'I don't need the itinerary.'

'Jarrod?' She was careful not to smile. 'Why am I explaining this to you?'

He didn't respond.

'Are you jealous?'

His aura's the colour of fresh blood.

She looked at her familiar, watching his tail twitch. *I see that, Dray.*

'Jarrod, we're back now, five days of your time. I'm here. I'm healed. I'm ready to work. Let's move on.'

She took his hand and he sighed, wrapping her in an embrace. 'I didn't know if you were coming back,' he said.

'But I did.' Her eyes brightened. 'Wait 'til you see it, Jarrod!' She hitched up her skirt. 'It's indescribable.'

Excuse me, but I thought we were about to move on? Drayco's question made them both laugh.

'Yes, Drayco, we're going,' Jarrod said. 'But first, Rosette, show me.'

She smiled, lifting her skirt over her bare leg up to her hip. Jarrod stared for quite some time.

'That's amazing. I've never seen anything like it.' He turned to Grayson. 'It's incredible work.'

'Now do you see why it took so long?' Rosette smiled.

He looked at her and Grayson. 'I do.' Jarrod kept his eyes on her leg after she let her skirt fall back down to her boots. 'I'd like to have a better look, though.'

'Any time.' She reached out for Grayson's hand and the three headed for Kreshkali's stronghold.

You've confused the men again, Maudi.
They confuse themselves.
How's that?
Jarrod's like a Watcher with the libido of a bull. We're bound to each other while I exist in this body. Grayson and I ... who knows? Maybe we'll do some DNA replicating of our own some day. Gotta get to know him better first.

It's pretty simple when you put it that way. Still, they're confused.

She laughed aloud.

'Something funny?' Jarrod asked.

Didn't he hear you, Dray?

I wasn't speaking to him.

She laughed again, tousling Jarrod's curly hair and winking at her familiar.

A few weeks later she was back in the sewers under Half Moon Bay. An' Lawrence was up ahead, leaning against the edge of the portal. The Entity nearly laughed out loud as she approached.

'Do you know where you're going?' An' Lawrence asked, staring at Jarrod first before meeting Rosette's eyes.

Grayson didn't speak. He walked next to Rosette, close enough to feel the heat rising from her body, but not so close they touched.

'Not a clue, Sword Master,' she chuckled, pleased to be able to tease him. His concerned look made her reconsider: 'First to Gaela, to check on Makee and attend the midwinter solstice.'

'They are announcing the succession,' Kreshkali added. She bowed to the Entity and stepped into the portal.

'Already?'

'Rowan, a month here on Earth can be years on Gaela. Think how long it's been.'

He nodded. Rosette suspected he missed his home world terribly. He'd sacrificed his life there to support Kreshkali and the restoration of Earth. He put his whole heart into that. Mostly, she suspected his mood was simply because he was going to miss Kreshkali.

'I'll be back after I give Makee an update and introduce myself to the new High Priestess of Treeon Temple.' Kreshkali leaned forward to kiss his cheek. He touched her face, turning it to kiss her mouth instead. 'I'm going to bring some more horses back too. I want to find the Paree estate before it gets any hotter here.'

'I don't know how long we'll be,' Rosette said as she and Jarrod stepped into the portal. 'So this is goodbye for now.'

She looked past An' Lawrence to Grayson. He held her eyes, the intensity engulfing her. It seemed to stop time, burning into her deeper than the tattoo on her thigh.

An' Lawrence smiled, giving her hand a squeeze. 'No such thing as goodbye.'

She gave her father a kiss.

'After Treeon, then what?' he asked Jarrod.

'Then we get to work.'

The Sword Master looked perplexed.

Jarrod shrugged. 'There are many worlds, An' Lawrence. We are called to them ...'

Rosette winked. *Drayco? You coming, or are you going to inhale Scylla all day?*

Right behind you, Maudi. The temple cat paused before entering the portal, nose to nose with Scylla. When he stepped through it rippled closed, sweeping them away.

REFERENCES:

Page 327 quote from William Lilly (1659). *Christian Astrology*. London: John Macock. From: www.skyscript.co.uk/texts.html

Page 502 quote from Dion Fortune (2003). *The Sea Priestess*. USA: Weiser Books. With permission of Red Wheel/Weiser. www.redwheelweiser.com

RECOMMENDED READING:

Campbell, J. (1972/1984). *Myths to Live By*. New York: Bantam Books.

Chown, M. (2003). *The Universe Next Door: The Making of Tomorrow's Science*. Oxford: Oxford University Press.

De Angeles, L. (2000). *Witchcraft Theory and Practice*. Minnesota: Llewellyn Publications.

Falconer, K. (2005). *Astrology & Aptitude: How to Become What You Are Meant To Be*. Tempe: American Federation of Astrologers.

Fortune, D. (2003). *Moon Magic*. Boston: Red Wheel/Weiser.

Goldstein-Jacobson, I. (1960). *Simplified Horary Astrology*. Alhambra: Frank Severy Publishing.

Goswami, A. (1995). *The Self Aware Universe: How Consciousness Creates the Material World*. New York: Tarcher.

Hillman, J. (1997). *The Soul's Code: In Search of Character and Calling*. New York: Grand Central Publishing.

Hyde, M. (1992). *Jung and Astrology*. London: The Aquarius Press.

Talbot, M. (1993). *Mysticism and the New Physics* (2 ed.) New York: Arkana Penguin Group.

RECOMMENDED WEBSITES:

Kim Falconer's official Quantum Enchantment Website www.kimfalconer.com

Kim Falconer's Astrology, Mythology and Quantum Theory Site www.falconastrology.com

Voyager Online www.voyageronline.com.au

Voyager Blog www.voyageronline.wordpress.com

Jeannette Maw's Good Vibe Blog — Law of Attraction for the Real World www.goodvibeblog.com

Acknowledgments

First, I'd like to acknowledge Ly de Angeles, friend, High Priestess, author and sensei, for showing me the door behind which Kreshkali stood, and my son Aaron Briggs for his artistic genius, insights and goading. To Sara Briggs for all those handwritten words and boundless enthusiasm, and Cavy too, of course! Deep appreciation also goes to my mother, Eunice, my sister, Shawn, and my granddaughter, Kayla, for bringing me so much joy.

Gratitude goes to my publisher, Stephanie Smith, who asks all the right questions, Equinox Management for sure and steady guidance, Sue Moran for her astute editing, Brian Cook Manuscript Appraisal Agency and Dr Wendy Michaels for the coherent and articulate critiquing. For their artistic contributions and friendship I thank Jodi Osborne, Kurtis Richmond, Tris O'Connor and Helen Nailon.

For connecting me to the right people I thank Mystic Medusa, dear friend and wing woman, and for showing me the ropes, Candida Baker and Mark Abernethy. For teaching me how to pray rain and get into alignment with bliss, my good vibe coach, Master Jeannette Maw, and for his tips in *On Writing*, Stephen King.

I also thank Tim for his endless encouragement and fabulous coffee, Thatcher and Sean for the blueberry pancakes, Sam for the chocolate, and all the staff at Espresso Head for the great company and endless stacking! Thanks go to Victoria Sullivan for suggesting Stephanie — what synchronicity! And to Jacqui Sullivan for always believing in me. I also thank everyone at HarperCollins who had a hand in this, especially the art department, the proofreaders and typesetters, Chren for all the messages and Linda Funnell for the pivotal feedback.

Thanks also to Matt Connolly for his music, warm friendship and cat minding, to Dr James Roush for his falconry support and mentorship and to Dr Greg Briggs for decades of veterinary advice. For the literal warm fuzzies I thank my familiars Draygon and Gratch and, for my very best-best, thank you E.J., your friendship means the many-worlds to me.

Blessings to you all!

Arrows of Time

Quantum Enchantment: Book Two

KIM FALCONER

If you can't trust time, what can you trust?

When a portal spins Rosette and Jarrod off in different directions she is caught in a loop of repeating events. A strange bard helps her find a way back home, only things have changed …

While the survivors on Earth struggle to rebuild, Rosette and her temple cat turn to the future for help, but which one?

Time is their only hope, and it's playing tricks …

In bookstores
August 2009